DAVID NELMES

Billy Windmill

Self-published by KDP

Here's what people say about David Nelmes's lead character Billy Windmill

'Endearing and engaging, Billy's story draws you in. A character full depiction of working-class life in a small village. Billy's unsquashable hope propels him on a tumultuous journey and takes you with him.'
Kim Chapman, Freelance Editor

'An everyday tale of simple country folk, this isn't. Not in the sleepy Cotswold village of Abbotts Lovell where nothing much happens…unless your Billy Windmill. Half angel, half devil, all boy.'
Pam Pattison, Bardstown Writers

'The twists and turns of Billy's life engage you from beginning to end. Poetically written with vivid and believable characters and emotive storylines.'
Tracey Pengilly, Dutiful daughter!

****

'Beautifully written through descriptive dialog and strong and authentic characters'

'Billy Windmill is a boy on a mission, passionate, imaginative but troubled and misguided. Very authentic'

'A moving tale full of characterisation'

'Billy as a character is very strong and you empathise deeply with his chaotic journey through young life and misunderstood good intentions – and how wishful he is about his future'

'Billy, his mum, dad, Mr Barnes, the policeman, Mr Collins, are all very well painted and believable. This is the real strength of the book'

In memory of Bill Stanton, my mentor

CONTENTS

PROLOGUE - 1970

At first, I thought it the product of a tired body and mind, a trick of the fading moonlight, perhaps, but the fox kept on coming – definitely a fox – padding past the entrance to Cooper's Farm. Apparently without a care in the world, it raised its head and snapped at what appeared to be no more than thin air. A few yards more and it dug in the verge. Then, paw lifted, it paused – and was away.

It appeared again out in the open, downwind of the poultry sheds, where it turned and faced the way it had come, fixing me for one long calculating moment with the brilliance of its eyes. Having checked me out, it put its nose to the ground and, in its own time and at its own pace, went on its way, ahead of me, down into the shadows.

For the most part, nothing stirred, the only signs of life being the smoke rising from the chimney of Old Forge Cottage and Miss Pringle's broom left propped against the telephone box. The lights of her shop flickered and burst into life, the illumination striking the box, sending an elongated shadow out into the road.

"Over there!" it seemed to be saying, "he's over there!" prompting me to back-track and take temporary cover in the lychgate. There, shielded by its ancient timbers, it felt more like home than home itself, a reminder of childhood and childhood games. Kick-the-can, the twisting and turnings of Tig, the laughter… it all came flooding back, borne on a breeze playing through the upper reaches of the yews.

Seeking somewhere more secure to hide, though my legs burned from their efforts, I pressed on. A pitted handrail followed the curve of stone steps, past the bell chamber, upward and onwards in what seemed an ever-tightening spiral. It ended abruptly, at a door. Dried, ill-fitting and smaller than any normal door, it opened to reveal yet more steps, an almost vertical flight that led directly out onto the tower roof.

Shielded by a pinnacle, I peeped out at all I had previously taken so much for granted: the Cotswold village, appearing minuscule and neat, some sixty feet below; while above, beyond the line of The Ridgeway, the skulking dawn, poised as though about to spread its light over an empty stage. And it all began to make sense, even more so when the air about me stirred.

Mine "to fill with whoever and whatever" – eh, Ma?
Mine to fill …

Exhausted, alone, the injustice burning deep inside, I brushed my cheek against the pinnacle, put my lips to a nipple of stone, and waited for the images to form.

A boy sat waiting at a door; a familiar door, painted a garish yellow and bearing a number.
Number nine …

PART ONE – THE GIVEN CHILD - 1961

CHAPTER ONE

The boy fingered his sheet of paper, there, still in his pocket, and waited.

Waited and waited …

A sudden thought brought a strange feeling to his chest, but, panic over, there they still were, his six chosen names – seven, if he included the one his mother had made him cross out.

At the top of the village, Trisha Collins crossed the road and came running towards him, all limbs and hair. Virtually ignoring him, she made straight for her cousin Jenny's door and lifted its knocker. Even so, before letting it fall, she looked back and said, 'Billy? Billy, Daddy's got me a rabbit! Hutch and everything.'

'So?'

Up a fraction went the knocker – and came down. Almost at once, the door was opened by Mrs Duggan, her ample form filling the doorway, clutching the folds of her dressing gown to her chest and, at this hour of the morning, viewing her world with evident displeasure.

'Oh, it's you, is it, our Trisha? Madam's barely up. But then, what business is that of mine? I'm only her mother.'

Trish picked up three bottles of milk from the doorstep and followed Mrs Duggan indoors. 'I've got a rabbit, Auntie.'

The door closed behind her, shutting out the chance of any reply being overheard. Not that it mattered. Not when there was dust to be scuffed from the gutter; a nuclear cloud driven by jet-propelled heels, fatal even to boys who could hold their breath for at least one minute and four seconds.

With the dust still active, the emergency supply of air stored in his armpit gave out. Luckily, there was an antidote, a tuft of grass marking the boundary between the Duggan's cottage and the school playground. Grass did not grow on Mars. Grass which, according to Miss Wheatcroft, contained chlorophyll, deadlier than dead to alien dust.

Torn root by root from the gutter, the tuft resembled a hedgehog, a flying hedgehog that carried a cargo of fleas, three trillion fleas, which had a deadly disease and were to be dropped on Mrs... The hedgehog stalled and flew back to base unaided.

'M-Mrs Duggan!' he said, wiping his hands down his shirt. 'Nice colour, en't it? Your door, I mean. Sort of yellow, it is. Same as Mr Duggan's car.'

The glint in Mrs Duggan's eye hardened. She turned sideways on, cigarette raised, enabling Trish to squeeze past and pass beneath its crooked ash-stack. Behind her came the toddler, Allan, standing with his arms raised at the top of the entrance step. With him lifted off the step and seated on Trisha's hip no-one stepped forward to fill the empty space.

No-one.

'Mrs Duggan?' he said, tempted to pat the woman's arm. 'Mrs Duggan, en't Jenny comin'… Mrs Duggan?'

The woman appeared to have eyes only for her son and niece, however. Fixing the pair, she shaped her lips and blew smoke up towards the lintel, where it curled and unfurled along the grain of the wood. 'And, Trisha! I want him back in one piece, mind! You watch this rabbit of yours don't nip. Catch all sorts, you can!'

'Mixy!' he said. 'That's what you get! Sends yer round and around in circles, it does!'

Mrs Duggan looked sideways and then down, eyeing him in a peculiar, open-mouthed sort of way. Then, compressing her lips, she stepped back inside her cottage and gave its door a hefty push, the draught ruffling his hair and settling it across his eyes.

Stony face, he thought. Tough it out. And he confronted the door, broader and taller than himself, made of solid wood.

Shut.

'Trish? Trish! I wanna see yer rabbit! Wait, Trish. Wa-it!'

An old-fashioned clothes peg secured the door of the rabbit's sleeping quarters. Easily dislodged and tossed onto the roof of the hutch, it enabled Trish to lift out a young all-white rabbit and settle herself and Allan down with it.

'Trish? Trish, didn't Jenny wanna come? Can't be coz of me, can it? I mean, I weren't even comin', were I? Not at first, anyway. An'-an'-an' everybody likes rabbits, don't they? Go on, Trish. Tell us, why don't yer? I'd tell you if it were me.'

The girl scowled and strengthened her hold on the rabbit, cradling it to her chest as though it were a baby. 'There's nothing to tell.'

Further down the path, clearly intended as feed for the rabbit, lay a cabbage leaf. The system worked well. He tore strips from the leaf waiting for Trish to reach behind her and waggle her fingers. She never had to wait. But then, just when he had worked out the best way of tearing cabbage leaves, she looked over her shoulder and gave a thin smile.

'That's enough, thanks. For now, anyway.'

He shrugged and threw what remained of the leaf into a pile of logs. Stuck into one of them was a chopper. By working it from side to side it loosened in the log, eventually freeing its blade. 'This is real sharp. Don't you get havin' a go!'

'Me? Ooh, no. Not me! That's men's work, that is.'

Chuffed at her having recognised the fact, he selected a log, shuffled his feet to a more balanced position, and took aim. 'Probably be a lumberjack when I gets older. In Canada. 'Course, nobody'll want me t' go. Me mum'n that. Probably cry, she will. But I got the knack, see. It's all in the weight of the head. See how I brings it down.'

A chunk of bark flew from the log. The rest came away using his fingers, leaving the wood naked. It stood no chance, his chopper making short work of it, hacking off slivers that would serve as kindling. He could imagine what Mr Collins would say. "Impossible! No boy could have done all this! I mean, no ordinary boy, that is!"

Inspired by Mr Collins' words, he spat on his palms and gripped the chopper. This, he thought, would be a good one. Hold me chopper up real high. Open me shoulders and...

'Watch, Trish. Wa-atch!'

'I've watched,' she said. 'Very good!'

In truth, her look amounted to little more than a cursory glance, her hair already falling back into place, brushing across her shoulders as the curtain brushes the boards of the school stage, closing on him, shutting him out. Settled, its long strands lay either side of her neck, leaving it exposed, the nape, the nodules of her spine.

8

He relaxed his shoulders and brought the chopper down, sticking it back in a log. 'Trish? Trish, did you hear the one about the man who wore a rabbit on his head? Because, from a long way off, it looked like a hare! Get it? A hair! Blimey, Trish. I thought everybody knew that one.'

She made room for him, collecting Allan and shuffling with him and her rabbit further along the path. Organised once more, she ran her fingers down the length of one of the rabbit's ears. 'I think you missed a bit out. Why did the bald man wear a rabbit on his head? You forgot to say he was bald.'

'Never did!'

He landed a length of straw in her hair. He aimed another, only to stop short of actually throwing it, gripped by a sudden thought. 'I know! We could call him Wiggy!'

The pressure to explain the connection nearly burst his brain – but she was already laughing. Holding the rabbit up before her, she touched noses. 'Oh, go on, then. Yes! We like it, don't we, Allan? Wiggy it is. We christen you, Mr Wiggy!'

'Me an' the gang knows all about rabbits! Makes loops, we does. With wire. Pegs it in the ground and –'.

'Sounds cruel to me,' she said. 'And I don't like anything that sounds cruel.'

'No! It en't! Not really. Not the way we does it. An' – an' if you like, we could catch you one. To go with Wiggy, I mean.'

'Oh yes, be a great help that would. And end up having a load of little Wiggies, I suppose?'

He sniffed and squared his shoulders.

'Called tuppin', it is. Everybody does it. Even your mum and dad.'

She flushed and looked towards the house. Smoothing down a lock of Allan's hair, she said, 'Don't use that word. It's not nice. And, anyway, it's not the right one.'

'Oh? What is it, then, clever-clogs?'

'I … I don't know.'

'No! But I does, see! And it's tuppin'. Clem sez.'

She pushed Wiggy back into his sleeping quarters and groped on top of the hutch. Twice, she came within touching distance of the peg. Then, she found it and rammed it home, leaving him in no doubt as to what she thought of him.

Not until after Allan had been handed back to Mrs Duggan, did she speak to him again – and then only to sound like an adult.

'Use a handkerchief. And play with boys nearer your own age in future, why don't you? Like Tim. Or Kenny.'

'Kenny? Don't make me laugh! Clem sez –'

She swung round and stamped her foot. 'Clem sez! Clem sez! That's all we ever get from you these days, Billy Hughes. And this thing about, well, making babies. We've got years before we have to go worrying about things like that. Years and years!'

'That's just it, though! We en't. We en't got years and years. Clem sez there's a girl at his school and she's, you know. Up the spout!'

'So I've heard. But that's Hollersham. You name me one girl from around here who's had a baby at thirteen. You can't.'

At the school gate he stopped and stuck out his chin. In his experience, boys knew so much more than girls. Boys formed themselves into gangs where such matters could be discussed. Whereas girls …

She pushed open the gate and ran. He tried to grab her by the hair but was too late; she was away, racing across the playground to touch the main door before he could. Having done so, she stopped laughing. Her expression changed. 'You don't want to go believing everything you hear,' she said. 'Especially from the likes of Clem Cooper.'

'I don't! Well, not all on it, I don't. I mean, the Queen. She wouldn't, would she. Not how Clem sez, anyway.'

She paused, the hair that had fallen across her cheek collected between her finger and thumb. Slowly and deliberately she tucked it behind her ear.

11

'N-no. No, I'm sure that's right, Billy. I, er, I expect they find another way for the Queen.'

She leaned against the door, earning for herself that all important click, but no further. Neither in nor out, she made him wait, fixing him with those penetrating blue eyes of hers. Finally, having emptied out the contents of his head, she narrowed her shoulders and backed through the gap, into school, and out of sight.

CHAPTER TWO

He placed his list of names in front of Jenny and smoothed out the creases. 'It's me party list. I'll be ten.'

She kept on writing.

'I'm – I'm only allowed six.'

Still she kept on writing.

'You're on it. First name!'

She sighed and pressed her pen down alongside her work. 'You don't say. Underlined, is it? Got a full stop?'

'Sally's comin'! You won't be the only girl.'

'Oh?' she said. 'And there was me thinking I was first to be asked.'

'You are!'

'Can't be. Not if Sally Hicks already said she's coming.'

'She hasn't! I mean, she will. They all will. When I asks 'em, that is.'

She took up her pen once more and dipped it in her ink well. With her little finger sticking out, she first shed the surplus ink from the nib and then pressed it to her paper, hard. 'Better get askin', then, hadn't you?'

At the morning break he ran out into the playground brandishing his list. This was official, the fact highlighted by a lick of his pencil. Having done so, he picked out the name Sally Hicks. 'You'm comin', en't yer? Me mum never said you couldn't.'

'Then your mum's saft in the yud,' she said, gripping the high bar, hooked one leg over, then her other, and let go with both hands. As she unfurled, her dress followed her down, catching at her hips and then again at her chest, where it turned inside-out and fell as a skirt.

'Mind you, I might come. If Trish is, that is. But not if Jennifer Duggan is. And she won't let Trish go, not if she isn't. So, work that one out.'

Her hands dangled as unshod feet, while from the top of the inside-out skirt stretched a rib-cage and stomach divided by a natural line that led the eye upward, past her belly button, to an embroidered rosebud and lace.

With a somewhat lazy action, she began to swing, taking the rosebud away, bringing the rosebud back, pendulum precision, pendulum pace, opening his mind, making him aware.

'Piss off, Hughes,' she said. 'Before you go blind.'

Someone laughed, probably Cynthia 'Piggy' Perkins by the sound of it. Whoever it was, the laugh seemed to mark the start of something. Suddenly, there was energy about the playground, an extra buzz

… and then it began, ragged at first, but growing stronger and louder by the second.

> *'Billy Hughes loves Sally Hi-icks.*
> *Caught her swinging in her kni-icks.*
> *Billy Hughes loves –'*

'I don't! It en't true!'

> *'swinging in her kni-icks.*
> *Billy Hughes loves –'*

'Don't listen to 'em, Jen! I don't! Honest I don't!'

> *'Billy Hughes loves …'*

The chanting faltered and fell away, one voice only carrying it on. It, too, fell silent and Miss Wheatcroft walked among them, a wisp of hair hanging loose from her bun. 'Prefects! Follow me!'

Kenny and Susan Chambers followed Miss Wheatcroft into school. For a time, no-one in the playground moved. Then Sally turned a somersault over the high bar and everything returned to normal. A line of first and second-year juniors led by Tim's sister Carol and her mate Dawn Adams snaked across the playground, bright-eyed and giggling.

Aloof from it all, Ozzie Cutter wiped his nose on the back of his sleeve and jumped aboard a rope. 'Party. Ha!'

Overhearing Ozzie, there seemed no option but to slump back against the railings and slide to the ground. Clearly, there would be no party, reason enough to gather loose gravel into a pile and throw it a piece at a time, marrying each throw to the creak of rope fixings.

Trisha Collins stood before him and stuck out her hand. 'List.'

He pulled it from his pocket and tossed it in the air, but she grabbed it, stopping it from becoming fully airborne and subjected him to a glare. Taking longer over it than she surely needed, twice as long in fact, if not longer, she finally folded his piece of paper, giving it a crisp new edge, and handed it back without comment.

With Tim and Ozzie watching from the ropes, she said nothing.

Not a word …

After the dinner break Miss Wheatcroft ordered the floor to be cleared in readiness for Music and Movement. The man on the radio said they were to walk through the forest on the tips of their toes. However, what he failed to say was that the forest was mined. One false step and ...

'Wil-liam! It's the branches that are swaying, William. Not your arms.'

During the next exercise using one's arms proved vital. At first, he whirled both arms, then, stiff and unblinking, he tried using just one, taking it slowly past his nose, round and round and round. Miss Wheatcroft came and stood next to him.

'Very good, William. Look, everybody! Doesn't William make a lovely windmill?'

The class chorused its reply, including Jenny, her lips clearly shaping the words.

Although virtually hidden behind Trisha Collins, she appeared well placed to witness Miss Wheatcroft peel his reward from the roll and stick it on his forehead. A star. Not any old star, but a gold star. The personal identity mark of a fighter pilot that only the Queen knew was a boy.

After school, in disguise, he kicked away the chocks and opened the throttle. Mach 1 was reached within seconds. Then Mach 2, his twin engines screaming out a warning. Jenny squealed and jumped onto her doorstep while Trish added to the fun by shouting into his slipstream. At the telephone box his plane banked and lined itself up for home. Wings swept back, it dived all the way, breaking the sound barrier and over-shooting the runway.

A shout, clearly aimed at him, interrupted his play. 'Yes! You, boy!'

The man came marching down the other side of the front hedge, arm raised, finger pointing. At the gate, he swept back his few strands of hair and started some strange form of dance, one step back, one step forward. 'I've a good mind to see your father. Yes! You might well grin. Running out like that. Want to end up under the wheels of a car, do we?'

A tic created havoc, repeatedly pulling the man's cheek towards his ear. An aristocrat, he decided, one to be faced square-on, cowboys about to fight a duel. As suspected, rather than draw, the coward chose to talk.

'Utterly, totally, mad. Stark staring … I will have that word. In fact, I think I'll have it right now!'

'Nobody's in, Mister.'

The aristocrat raised a wagging finger, and made as if to go, only to pause, clearly having heard the fall of his opponent's hammer on a spent gun chamber.

'*Aut regem aut fatuum nasci oportet*, as friend Seneca is reported to have said. *Aut regem aut fatuum nasci oportet*, little man! And there, as you can now appreciate, you have the better of me. For I, unlike you, am born neither king nor fool. Not that I begrudge you that. No, no, no. Dear me no! For, *dulce est desipere in loco*, as they say. *Dulce est desipere in loco*!'

Having gibberished his way into the land of the smug, the aristocrat again made as if to go, only to pause yet again, this time to scrutinise the front gate and posts. 'Mm, yes, well, never mind. What need have we of a number, for we shall remember this day, you and I. Especially you, presumably one of Miss Wheatcroft's little brood, and soon to fly the nest judging by the size of you. Oh yes, we shall surely remember. But, *hora fugit*, little man. I must away. *Hora fugit*!'

In brisk military fashion he strode away, a spider of a man, complete with leather patches on the elbows of his jacket, handlebar moustache and an Adam's apple as prominent as a battery hen's breastbone. From behind the Perkins's Buddleia a door clunked, an engine turned, and a car, long in the bonnet and the deepest of blues, purred on towards the Rose & Crown.

His mother was in her place at the sink, potato knife in hand. 'Oh, was it now? An E-type? Well I never! Come looking for his Cinders, had he?'

'Nah. Dazzled by me star, he were. Nearly run me over, he did. Missed me by this much!' he said, his parted finger and thumb indicating a gap equivalent to the width of his school ruler.

'I sincerely hope not!' his mother said. 'Whatever would Mummy do if you got knocked down? Tell me! Whatever would she do?'

'Huh! Couldn't kill me,' he said, pressing his finger to the floor of the sugar bowl. 'Wanted to beat me up, he did. He did, Mum. Honest! But he chickened out. Got in his E-type – was an E-type! Tim's got this picture. Covers his whole wall, it does!'

His mother dried her hands. 'Well, work hard at school and you never know. One day, you could end up with one of your own, couldn't you?'

Later, when his mother had finished at the sink, he enacted for her the awarding of his star, starting with a wild clawing away of branches. Then, with all the dignity he could muster, he took his arm round as before, topping his display by mimicking Miss Wheatcroft.

His mother applauded, her laughter altering the shape of her face, making it appear rounded, more like her old self. A bad sign, he thought and, resigned to his fate, offered up his cheek.

'Now,' she said, opening her purse, only to put it down again and reach for her pot. 'This party of yours. You have sorted it, I take it? I mean, we do know who's coming?'

'Yeah, well,' he said. 'Trisha Collins is seein' to it, en't she? Give 'er the job, I did. Told 'er! Lists, I said, is women's work.'

'Mm. I'm sure,' his mother said, tipping out the contents of the pot. 'Sounds too much like you-know-who talking, to me. And, while we're on the subject. Not a word, remember. You're not a little boy anymore. You know the score. I mean it, Billy. Or you can wave goodbye to any party.'

At lightning speed, she scraped the spilled coins from the table and into her palm: a solitary shilling, a few quietly counted sixpences, an assortment of pennies and halfpennies and just two threepenny bits.

'Right!' she said, with a finality matched by the closing click of her purse. 'You be good while I'm over the road and you never know, there might be a little extra for tomorrow. But remember. Leave your father to me. Tell him about your star. He can hardly find fault with that, can he now?'

The instant the door closed behind her he laid his hand flat against his cheek and rubbed. Suitably purged, he positioned his stool at the table and sat hands in lap in best Miss Wheatcroft fashion, ears pricked for the rub of brake blocks and the scrape of a handlebar on the outside wall.

CHAPTER THREE

His father sorted through the scraps of his dinner, selected a bone and sucked on it. 'Badgerin' a man the minute he gets in! En't you learned nothin', boy?'

'Yes, Daddy. Thirty minutes of peace and quiet. Half an hour to unwind. That's all you ask.'

His father dropped the bone back onto his plate and grunted. 'Good,' he said, and pointed his fork in the direction of the clock. 'Then in a couple minutes more you can spit it out, can't yer, lad?'

At the sink his mother lifted a cup and held it under the tap, tilting and turning it in running water. Then, with a care normally reserved for the figurine left her by his grandmother, she placed the cup on the draining board making no sound. Almost as quietly, she turned off the tap, opened the oven door and took out his father's pudding.

'Sago, Charlie! To help celebrate your son's good news.'

'Oh? Joined the army, 'as he? Got himself a paper round, help pay fer 'is keep?'

For the first time since entering the house that evening his father appeared to focus on his star.

'M-miss Wheatcroft give it me. A gold star, Dad. For good work! Not had one before, I en't. Not never.'

'Not never, eh?' his father said. 'Ah well, that's the way it goes. Me, I got barra' loads on 'em. Stars fer this. Stars fer that. History. Sports. Pictures of me bin put up in the village hall, there 'as. Me as a goalie, lad! Newly framed. Part of this 'ere refurbishin' malarkey. You want to get yer ma t' tek you along and show 'em yer. Yours fer sport, were it, son, this star? Ten out of ten in yer spellin', summat like that?'

With his father poised, waiting for an answer, he wished the moment gone; as it might have been if not for the stupidity of his spoon-polishing mother. 'Drama, Charlie! You know. Acting. All the children do it these days. Learn a lot from it they can! All …all sorts.'

She turned away, abandoning him to his father: a man stunned, a man struck dumb – until the pigeon landed, and up came his fork, rising at a slow rate of knots, prongs to the fore. 'Drama my arse! Sprinklin' fairy dust, that's what you bin doin'!'

'We 'ave to! We all do. It en't our fault.'

His mother nudged his father's pudding into place, the handle of his spoon within reach of his fingers. 'Just you, Charlie. Billy's already had his. At school, I mean. Jam roly-poly, I expect. Your

23

favourite, I seem to remember you saying. I do. I – I remember.'

'Eh? Oh,' his father said, relinquishing his fork in favour of his spoon, momentarily confused, it seemed, before pushing and prodding at his pudding's covering layer of skin. 'Readin'. An' writin',' he said, speaking between each loading. 'Aye. Readin' an' writin'. That's what we want. Not. Bloody. Nancyin'!'

Having devoured the last spoonful, he scraped out his dish collecting what skin still clung to its inside and sucked it from his spoon. With nothing left to scrape, he pushed his dish towards the middle of the table and belched. Rid of the wind, he slumped back, his chair taking the full force of his weight with a creak. Settled, he made use of a fingernail and picked between his teeth. 'There's a bird in the passage needs bringin' in. D'yer hear, 'oman?'

His mother rolled her dishcloth over in her hands, tumbling it in slow motion from one to the other. Then, switching on the brightest of smiles, she wiped as never before, bringing a shine to the Formica that the rest of the table barely merited. 'Yes! Another bird. That's good, Charlie. Try and do something different, I will. A stew. Eh, Charlie? For a change?'

His father landed his pudding spoon in front of her.

'Turkey,' he said, and rose from the table. 'That hen of yourn is a turkey.'

Cloth in hand, his mother scurried after his father and emptied out the sink. Her immediate duty done, she turned on the tap and stood nursing the towel. 'Turkey in June? Well, something to thank Cyril Cooper for, I suppose. Him and his fancy ideas. Empty my pot, though, that's for sure. A right gobbler of gas is Mr Turkey.'

His father took the towel. 'So?'

'So, I'll … you know what I'm saying.'

'Oh? Know what you'm sayin', do I? Know what you'm sayin', 'omen? Well, let's see now. Turkeys need extra cookin' time. Time. Summat you en't got. That it?'

'No, that's not what I'm saying. You know it isn't. Please, Charlie.'

'Not what you'm sayin', en't it? Not what you'm sayin'? Well, I sez it is. I sez it's exactly what you'm sayin'. You en't got the time, is what you'm sayin', because you'm off seein' to other blokes. D'yer hear? Other blokes!'

'Barney's eighty if he's a day, Charlie. An hour a day. Money! And if only you let me, I could earn more. I could! You're not fair, Charlie. You're just not fair!'

His father sniffed and dumped the towel back in her hands. 'I've told yer. Your place is here, with the boy,' he said, pulling his tie from its peg. He studied himself in the mirror. Chin up and in full view of his mother, he tied a Windsor knot. Having achieved this, he bared his teeth and slicked down his hair.

His mother dug her fingers into the towel and faced the wall. With her back to his father she missed seeing him don his new hat, his trilby, already adorned for its maiden outing with a fishing fly. At the door, he looked back, and smirked. 'Frit by a fox, if anyone sez anythin', lad. And you, 'oman. By a fox … pluck!'

His mother made no reply. She did not move, even when the door closed after him; even when the front gate was heard to drop its latch. She just stared at a fixed point on the other side of the wall, the towel held to her chest, screwed into a ball.

CHAPTER FOUR

With his nose flattened against a pane, making faces, the Snug appeared empty. Then Billy noticed Mr Barnes, dozing in the inglenook. The landlord came through from the Lounge Bar, peered for some considerable time towards the old man, then reached up, and lifted a mug from its hook. In typical Reggie Loach style, before returning to his customers on the other side of the connecting door, he paused to fix his dickey-bow and his smile.

With no sign of his father, and Mr Loach out of the way in the Lounge Bar, he gripped the handles of his carrier bags and pushed open the door.

Mr Barnes raised an eyelid, drained his tankard and joined him at the bar.

'Come celebratin' has we, Master Hughes?'

'Er – no. Don't think so, Mr Barnes.'

'Oh? And there be I thinkin' maybe you had. Why might that be, d' you suppose?'

Showing no sign of either wanting or expecting a reply, Mr Barnes tapped the base of his tankard on the bar. Once again, Mr Loach came through from the lounge, the opened connecting door letting in the humour and warmth of human voices:

the tail-end of a joke, a burst of laughter, suddenly muffled and made distant.

Mr Loach opened a tap allowing a trickle of cider into Mr Barnes' tankard. Leaving the tap to run, the publican took time out to peer over the bar and grimace. 'You kids must think me just stepped off the banana boat!'

'Mum sent me, Mr Loach. It's for shillings. For the gas, Mr Loach.'

'Ah, I know. And how many've come out the ditch, tell Mr Loach.'

With Mr Barnes' filled tankard unclaimed on the bar, Mr Loach stood in attendance a while longer, sighed, and took charge of his carrier bags. One by one, he lifted the bottles, sniffing each one in turn. The majority, he transferred to a crate. The four that remained, he pushed to the front of the bar and, face set, propped open the connecting door with his foot. 'Charlie! I got your lad here. Can't be doin' with any more of this!'

A familiar face appeared, quickly joined by Clem Cooper's two older brothers Cyril and Walter and a purple-lipped Mrs Hicks. Four faces, ready framed as though for the benefit of a photographer.

'M-m-ma boy!' his father said. 'My – my clever little lad! See 'is star, Hilda? There, see. On 'is conk. Fer arithmetic, that. Aye, that were it. Arithmetic!'

Mrs Hicks blew a stream of cigarette smoke out over the rim of her glass. 'Mm,' she said, downing the best part of her drink. 'I like clever boys.'

Cyril gripped his lapels and made as though to speak. But he was beaten to it.

'Tup-tup, our Cyril,' Walter said. 'You hold them hormones. We know you's got a certificate. Hangs on the cowshed wall, don't it, now? But when it comes to, what one might call, matters of education, a bit of, er … dang me! What's them Latin words I be after, our Cyril?'

'Extra curricula, Walter?'

'Ah! Them be the ones. Sorter rolls of the tongue, it does. Extra curric-

'Now-now, lads!' his father said. 'Not in front of the boy. Friendship, remember. One fer all and all fer one, eh?'

Smirking, his father twisted and turned, toasting each of his companions in turn. And they drank, none more heartily than Walter. Ahead of the others, he held up his empty glass, monitoring a sliding globule of froth. Cyril did the same, following his older brother in what appeared a form of ritual. Mrs Hicks, on the other hand, with no froth to eye, parted his father's fingers and wedged the stem of her glass between them.

'Yes!' his father said, digging in his pocket. 'Aye. M-my round! 'Reg! Where are yer? Set – set 'em up. And one fer yerself while yer at it. Doubles! Make it doubles!'

The connecting door swung to; the Lounge Bar now visually disconnected. Its closure did little to soften the pitch of Mrs Hicks' laughter, suddenly raised to new heights at the explosive smash of a glass.

Mr Barnes touched him on the arm and, together, taking the rejected bottles with them, they left.

Mr Barnes walked as far as the duck pond bench, disturbing a rat rummaging by the litter-bin. 'Ah!' the old man said, gazing out across the Community Field and the darkening outline of the school. 'Gemini, Master Hughes. Born under the sign of the Heavenly Twins, you and me both.'

'Is that good, Mr Barnes?'

'Good? No, can't say as it is, lad. No, not always.'

'I - I'd better be going now, Mr Barnes.'

The old man swivelled his good eye and glared. 'Going, you say? Going! Tsk! Bring 'em here!' he said, leaving him in no doubt as to where he wanted the rejected bottles placing, up on the bench, at his side.

Exhaling Scrumpy fumes over the opened carrier bag, he rambled on, picking up from where he had left off. 'No, not always, lad. Not always, her being born under the sign of The Crab. Left me a bachelor man, her did. A bachelor man with nothing but his cricket.'

'Cricket?'

The old man stiffened. 'Official scorer for more years than I cares to remember, I'll have you know. An honorary position, Master Hughes! Mine to hold. And mine to pass on to whomsoever I chooses, wouldn't you say?'

'Yeah, well, 'spose so, Mr Barnes. Er … can I go now?'

In reply, the old man tightened his grip on the carrier bag and brought its handles together. 'Ten bob for 'em. Can't say fairer!'

'Ten shillings! A whole ten-shilling note!'

'Ha!' his benefactor said, showing his tongue and the few remaining stumps that served as teeth. 'You be one step ahead of me, you being a man of numbers, so to speak. A ten-bob note … and an extra tanner apiece for the gas! The gas, mind! For your ma, my little Mo. And you,' he added, placing a gnarled hand over his, 'from this day forth have my permission to call me Barney.'

The sixpences, he assured his new friend, would definitely go to his mother and dutifully slipped the coins into his trousers pocket adding to the three shillings paid him by Mr Loach. The ten-shilling note he folded and pushed deep into his breast pocket.

'Aye,' Barney said, gazing out once more. 'The noble and glorious game of cricket.'

Caught up in a world of his own, Barney smiled, no doubt recalling some well-timed stroke or the taking of a wicket. His smile faded, however, and when he spoke again it was of none of these things.

'Oh, it were me who pulled her pig-tails, right enough. But it were Jimmy Bassett her chose to meet down the aisle. Aye … Jimmy Bassett'

'Granddad Bassett? You on about me gran and granddad? The ones in South Morton churchyard?'

Barney slapped his hands to his knees, his stance suddenly that of a much younger and more aggressive man, 'Gawd luvva-duck!' he said. 'Who else we be on about? And there be I thinkin' you was something of a scholar! Mine, young Hughes, don't you go forgettin'! Mine to pass on to whomsoever I chooses!'

As suddenly as it had flared, the fire within the old man flickered and died. 'Knowd you all, I 'as. Seen you born. And seen you grow. Rag dolly and a shoe box, that were your ma. Happy little soul her were. Aways a-hummin' and a-tuckin'. Apple of yer gramp's eye! Apple of his goddamn eye ...'

He twitched and looked up. 'Be turnin' in his grave, if I knows Jimmy. Goings on! No good'll come of it, as sure as God made little apples, Master

Hughes! A wicked man is his own hell, I tell ye. His own hell!'

'Yeah – 'night now, Mr Barnes. Mum'll be worryin' – 'night! Thanks for the money.'

At the telephone box, he turned and waved. 'Thanks, Barney. Goodnight!'

In return, the old man raised the carrier bag and held it suspended for a moment, before slamming it down, bottles and all.

'I warn ye, Master Hughes! His own hell!'

CHAPTER FIVE

His mother spread a tablecloth on the front lawn and attempted to press it flat. Thwarted, she turned to his guests greeting them by name and passing pleasantries. Until, that was, it came to Sally Hicks, when her voice petered out and she busied herself elsewhere.

From a nearby cardboard box she lifted out beakers and cups followed by two bottles of pop, lemonade and his favourite cherryade. Last of all, she lifted out a dinner plate piled with sandwiches.

He clasped his hand to his forehead. 'Oh, no! Not turkey. Anythin' but turkey!'

Sensing laughter, he writhed on the ground, ending with a two-footed death thrash and, to cap it all, a state of rigor mortis.

A large lightweight ball bounced off his head, a brand new Frido given by Kenny and Susan Chambers. Tim presented him with his prized record-breaking Dutch arrow. Cynthia from next door gave him a jigsaw puzzle and Sally a pack of crayons. Trish waited in the background with her present balanced on the flat of her palm, the shape and size of it a give-away: a giant tube of Smarties, probably the largest tube in the world.

That left just one more present. But, rather than hand it directly to him, Jenny Duggan handed it to Trisha to give him, a box, too thin to be anything as ordinary as chocolates.

'Hankies!' he said, clawing away the cellophane.

In one corner of each of three pristinely clean handkerchiefs was embroidered a letter. The letter D. For "Darling?"

Trish bit into a sandwich. 'Hmm, you want to think yourself lucky, Billy Hughes. We only ever get turkey at Christmas.'

'Yes! Us, too,' Susan said. 'Thank you, Mrs Hughes. Thank you for inviting Kenny and me to the party.'

Later, when everyone had had their fill of sandwiches, his mother brought out what she announced was a sultana cake. 'Taken from my mother's recipe book!'

She lit the candles, ten in all, that he started to blow out before the count had been completed. Even so, she still served him first and led the way in the singing of *Happy Birthday*, after which everyone clapped and cheered.

Inspired, he dug out two sultanas from his slice of cake and held them up for all to see. 'Look, Jen. Trisha's chests!'

Kenny coughed, leaving the best reaction to his mother who compressed her lips and turned an ever-deepening shade of pink.

He could not help but giggle, his glee brought to a temporary halt by a slap. Landing on his wrist, it sent one of the sultanas flying.

'I don't know where he gets such talk! I really don't!' his mother said, wringing her hands in her apron. 'Perhaps it would be better if you all played a game. I mean, you could see to it for me, couldn't you, girls? Please? While I go and see to Miss Pringle's poor old dad.'

Susan and Trish formed a front line. They would see to everything, they assured her. 'Double promise!' Susan said. 'And everything away by seven. Not a minute over!'

With Sally hovering within striking distance, Kenny pulled bricks from the rubble piled next to the front path. The others searched in the tufts of grass, stubbing toes, going over and over the same ground. Tim broke into a run and joined Kenny and Sally. Ignoring the rubble, he raised the discarded corrugated iron sheet that once formed the roof of an outside toilet, peered under it, wrinkled his nose – and let it drop.

As though blown by a draught, Trish made for the front garden tree.

Jenny followed her as though linked by elastic, the greater the stretch the snappier the reunion. Holding on to Trish by the sleeve of her blouse, she searched wherever her cousin searched; around the base of the tree, up in its branches – then, puckering her lips, she glanced in the direction of the tablecloth.

And him …

'Warm!'

Led by Trish, the two girls raced towards him and stopped with their toes within inches of the cloth.

'Roastin'! Hotter'n Hell!' he said, and barely able to contain himself mimed to Jenny the gobbling of a sandwich. But she only put out her tongue and stared back – then away, towards the front hedge and a voice parroting his words.

'It's cold! Very, very cold!'

Susan tossed her head and faced the other way. 'Ignore them. We know exactly who they are.'

First Ozzie and then Clem appeared, both puffing on a cigarette.

'Give us a drag,' Sally said, her manner suddenly that of an older and more experienced girl.

Clem held his cigarette to her lips. 'That's it. You'm comin' along, gal. You stick wiv yer Uncle Clem and you'll soon get the 'ang of it. Wun't her, Oz?'

'Ar, Clem. That. Or summat else!' Ozzie said, upon which they wheeled away wheezing with laughter.

Then Clem stopped. Holding everyone's attention, he took one long hard drag on his cigarette then threw it, landing it on the tablecloth. 'So, what 'appened t' gang loyalty, then, Billy-boy?'

'You were on me list, w-weren't he, Trish? She knows! Only—'

'Only,' Trish said, flicking away the cigarette stub, 'he had to cross you off. What with the party starting at four and you being on the school bus and everything.'

'And he was only allowed six his mum said,' Tim added.

Clem took Ozzie's cigarette from him, pinched it out, and tucked it behind his own ear. 'Mm … yeah. Yeah, I can see yer problem, pal. Never let it be said yer Uncle Clem en't a fair man. Thing is, we'm here now. So, which one of you is goin' t' mek way? Along wiv Lady Chamberpots, that is.'

For the second time within a minute, Ozzie wheeled away bent almost double. 'Chamberpots! Ha, Chamberpots!'

Ignoring Ozzie, Clem pushed his way through the hedge and headed straight for the tablecloth. Using one finger, he flipped open a sandwich. 'Tut-tut, Billy-boy. Turkey. Now, I wonder where that come from.'

'A fox! It were frit by a fox. Me dad said!'

Clem lowered the meat into his waiting mouth, chewed, cocked his head, and gave a knowing nod. 'Frit by a fox, Oz. Can always tell.'

Susan stepped forward and stood before Clem in the manner of someone of importance. 'Mrs Hughes asked us girls to take charge of the party – didn't she, Patricia? And so, I think it is you and Ozzie who ought to leave.'

'Oh ar?' Clem said, flipping the open sandwich aside, exposing the hidden pack of crayons.

Looking peeved after failing to discover anything of interest hidden amongst the crayons, he skimmed the pack at Susan, hitting her in the midriff, and sniffed the air. 'Grammar school,' he said, and again, sniffed the air. 'Same stink as what comes from the front of the bus. Sweet as piss, it is.'

Susan pushed the pack of crayons into Tim's hands and aimed her nose at the sky. 'Don't strain your tiny little brain any further, Cooper. Us girls are going. Aren't we, girls?'

Clem rounded his eyes. 'Oh! Us girls is going, is we? Did you hear that, lads? Us girls is going. Well, speak fer yerself, Chamberpots. You can go. But Sal's stayin', en't yer, gal? You en't gone and passed no egghead exam, has yer now? And Billy-boy wants yer t' stay, don't yer, pal?'

'And Jenny! She can stay as well, she can,' he said, but Jenny was already at the gate.

Clem placed a hand on his shoulder and stayed with him as Jenny crossed the road. 'Knows how yer feels, pal. But then, perhaps it's fer the best. Considerin'.'

'Eh?'

Clem clicked his fingers, dispatching Ozzie to a gap in the hedge. From it, he extracted a rope, long and thick enough to tow a car.

However, Clem soon dispelled that theory. 'An 'angin', Billy-boy. En't that right, Oz?'

Ozzie stood with the rope coiled, clearly aiming to throw it up into the tree. His effort proved a flop, the rope snagging on a side branch.

'Clem …' Trish said. 'Clem, I hope you're not planning on doing anything silly.'

Undaunted, Ozzie tried again, this time managing to throw more of the rope and successfully loop it over a main branch. 'Yeah!' he said, freckles glowing. 'An 'angin'!'

CHAPTER SIX

Clem threw himself down on to the lawn, pole-axed, he would have the world believe, by laughter.

Ozzie joined him, buckling at the knees, slapping them hysterically with the flat of his hand. 'And w-when that, that brick —. His face! Did yer see? When the brick went from under 'im... Laugh!'

Clem nodded and sniggered on. Then, propped on one elbow, his mood changed. 'Summat up, Timothy? I mean, we en't gone and lost our sense of humour or nuffin', 'as we?'

Tim glanced in the direction of the commotion, at a tree and Kenny clawing at a rope. Tight-lipped, he turned back and faced Clem, his evident fury threatening to break free of his puny chest. 'You could've killed him! If that branch hadn't broke, then ... I mean! Kenny was panicking, you could see he was! And his colour. It —'

He broke off, chewing on the inside of his cheek as Clem idly plucked a stalk from the grass and laid it on his tongue.

Making great play of the art, Clem turned the stalk top to bottom and spat. 'Okay. So, on the face of it, Timmy-boy 'ere has a point. But, answer me this, pal. Answer me this! When the brick went from under 'im, how far did he drop?'

'His toes!' Billy said. 'Draggin' on the ground, they were! Didn't drop. Well, not proper, like, did he?'

Clem licked the tip of his finger, reached up, and made an imaginary mark. 'A man after me own heart, Comrades. Observant, see. Didn't drop, he sez. No drop – not one that mattered, anyways. But, what else? What else weren't there? Tell 'em, Billy-boy.'

'No knot! There weren't no proper knot!'

Ozzie sniffed and tore up a handful of grass, which he threw in the air leaving it to scatter over and behind his head. 'Yeah, well. Any fool could see that.'

'Exactly!' Clem said. 'A test, see! That's all it were. And you said it, Timmy-boy. Panic! When it come down to it, Chamberpots shit 'is pants. No use to a fightin' unit is that!'

Tim frowned, anything further he might have said stubbed, word by word, into an innocent tuft of Community Field turf, an act not lost on Clem.

'Bollocks to Chamberpots!' he said, scooped up the Birthday Frido, and, jaw set, sent it swerving into the air. Away it went, bouncing off the railings bordering the village pond and heading straight for the open Quarry Lane gate.

Like a Collie, never happier than when serving its master, Ozzie took hold of the tails of his raincoat and scampered off in pursuit. 'Yeah! Bollocks to all Grammar school wankers, eh, Clem? It were me who did the rope, weren't it? I knew there weren't no proper knot, I did. Must 'ave. Mustn't I?'

With Ozzie back and seated on the ball, Clem took a mass of knotted string from his pocket, unravelled it, pulled it taut, and laid it down in as straight a line as he was ever likely to get. 'Comrade Oswald.'

Ozzie looked up and about him, from face to face, and scrambled to his feet. Stood to attention at one end of the knotted string, he licked his lip, and paused. 'I. I er...'

'Propose,' Clem prompted.

'Oh ah! I propose that William Hughes be promoted from hauxiliary to … to professional rank. Yeah, that's it. And made a Comrade!'

After a period of silence reminiscent of school assembly, Clem began. 'William Hughes, now being of proper age, does you swear to serve the sacred knots, the regiment and its leader? Keep the names of all Comrades secret, even under torture? Share all ciggies? And defend the legally set borders of the Abbots Lovell military zone to the last man?'

'I swear!'

Clem bowed, first to Ozzie and then to Tim who stepped forward and took up a position at the unattended end of the sacred string.

With everything in place, Clem stood tall and puffed out his chest. 'Then let the knot be tied.'

Ozzie and Tim picked up their respective ends and brought them together. They bowed and handed the string to Clem. Like a magician, he held it up for his audience's inspection. Having demonstrated that it was just an ordinary length of string, obtainable from any village shop, he added yet another elaborate and somewhat lop-sided knot. 'What the Brotherhood have tied together, let no man loosen. Except on dishonourable discharge.'

'Or for bein' a titty-babbie!' Ozzie blurted

Clem raised his chin, adding to his air of dignity and cuffed Ozzie round the ear. 'Quite right, Comrade. The birthday boy in! Chamberpots out! Any other business?'

'Yeah!' Billy said. 'Baggies bein' in goal! Gordon Banks! No – me dad! I wanna be a goalie like me dad! An'-an' you can't say he weren't! Coz he were! I can prove it. Prove it, I can!'

Clem picked up the ball, bounced it – once – twice – and rammed it into the pit of his stomach. 'Better 'ad then, hadn't yer – Comrade.'

As leader, Clem marched at the head of the column, holding up the Community Hall key before him as though bent on doing the Lord's work.

The key turned freely in the lock and the door opened inwards aided by a kick from Ozzie. He then ventured in as far as a fire bucket where he stood trickling sand through his fingers.

Dust hung in the air, mingling with a fragrance Tim identified as cedar. 'I helped with the rubbing down. You want to try it some time, it was fun.'

Ozzie put his head round the door of the Gents' toilet, sniffed, and let the door close. 'Yeah, about as much fun as bein' a poxy Cub.'

Clem led the way into the Ladies' toilet, opened a cubicle door, closed it again, and found interest in a dispenser of something called sanitary towels. He thumped its button. Having gained nothing, he thumped it again and pushed his fingers up the dispensing chute. Still having gained nothing, he expanded his chest and took his belt in an extra notch. 'Remind me to try the Johnny machine on the way out. Always useful, a few spares.'

Back in the Lobby, Clem tapped the glass covering the photograph of the oldest recorded Abbots Lovell cricket team, dated 1897. 'A C Cooper, mateys. Coopers dominate, they does! Great-Granddad, Uncle Alf, even our Walter. And I'll be the next, you see if I en't.'

The first of the football team photographs covered Season 1923/24 and, like its cricket counterparts, listed each member of the team. The same goalkeeper, sporting a centre parting and moustache, appeared on the next four photographs enabling Clem to state the obvious.

'Nope.'

They moved on from photograph to photograph, some faces set as though in stone, others wax. Tim and Ozzie crowded him from behind, while Clem delivered the verdict, always the same.

'Nope.'

So regularly came the word, so expected the verdict, the faces began to lose clarity and became one, the same face staring back at him repeatedly. At last, familiar faces and names began to appear, but no matter how much he willed it, never a Hughes.

'Nope.'

Then, there he was. With only three photographs to go, on the first two, covering Seasons 1954/55 to 1956/57, staring back at them, the unmistakable face of his goalkeeper father.

Saying nothing, he pressed his finger to a covering glass.

Clem lifted the first of the two photographs from its hook and tilted it, as though to inspect it in a better light. After a while, he handed it to Ozzie and put his face close to the second of the two. 'Mmm, looks a bit like him, I suppose. But, well, I dunno. What say you, Oz?'

Ozzie held the pictured team of Season 1954/55 at arm's length and screwed up his face.

46

'Nah, Clem. Nah! It's easy to see why Hughesie was fooled. It fooled me for a bit but –'

'It's me dad, you know it is! Read the writin'!' He made a grab for the photograph, only to fail, Ozzie managing to turn his back on him hugging the photograph to his chest.

Clem gave a withering look and raised his photograph a symbolic few inches higher. Having made him wait, he lowered it again and began jabbing his forefinger at it. 'C Hugles! You remember him, Oz. Used to knock around wiv your old man, he did.'

'Did he? Oh! Yeah! Can make it out now, I can. Hugles. Looks a bit like Hughes, don't it?'

Tim attempted to say something, only to receive an elbow in the ribs. Having silenced him, Clem led Ozzie into recalling the days and deeds of Christopher Hugles, a man who bred Cocker Spaniels, a man who had once won a thousand pounds on the last race of the last day at Cheltenham.

'And then migrated to Ireland!' Ozzie said.

'Give it me! Give it —! You know it's me dad. You know it is!'

Clem widened his eyes and allowed his jaw to sag. 'Your dad, Billy-boy? Your –? We apologise! I mean. We never knew, did we, lads? Chris Hugles, the randy old … Phew! I shouldn't let your old man find out, Billy-boy. No way! No siree!'

Bouncing the ball off the double doors that led into the functions room, then off the notice board and,

47

finally, the entrance steps handrail, Clem and Ozzie passed out of sight, leaving in their wake nothing but whoops of laughter.

Tim puckered his lips and sighed. 'Come on. Let's go and take the key back to Sam.'

CHAPTER SEVEN

Mr Green appeared to be expecting them, waiting at his door with his hand held out. Tim dropped the Community Hall key into his palm and thanked him.

'A pleasure, young Tim. School project all done now, is it?'

'Well,' Tim said, and swallowed. Well we've seen one or two relatives. Billy's dad an' that … you know.'

'He were a goalie, weren't he, Mr Green? Me dad. A real proper goalie!'

Mr Green scrutinised him, clearly impressed by his height, and twisted his mouth into something resembling a smile. Suddenly, without warning, he brought his hand from his pocket and sent something looping towards him; a whole set of fobbed keys that he sent flying by the belated swing of his hand.

'Mmm,' Mr Green said, peering at him as though over spectacles worn low on his nose. 'As you say. A goalie.'

After a while, having asked about the health of Miss Wheatcroft, their school in general and other boring matters, Mr Green turned to something of far greater interest; the reincarnation, as the little man put it, of Abbots Lovell FC. 'When you're all two or three years older, that is. You know, one or two friendlies at first. Then see how we go. The main problem, as far as I can see, is numbers. I only ever see five or six of you kicking a ball about on the playing field. Not nearly enough, not by a long chalk. But, never mind, we can work on that nearer the time. As for now, keep practising, lads. Keep practising. Especially seeing as you've got a new ball!'

'Yeah!' he said, giving it a bounce. 'Kenny and Susan give it me for me birthday. Double figures now, Mr Green. Nearly a man!'

After leaving Mr Green, the conversation centred on the prospect of playing in a team, a real team, with a leather ball, an all-gold kit and, most important of all, nets.

'And if we're short of players,' he said, 'Me dad'll help out and play in goal – I know he will!'

'Yeah, well,' Tim said, lapsing into one of his silent frowning moods.

'You know summat, Tim Robinson!'

'Don't.'

'Do!' he said and inflicted a headlock on his pal. 'So, tell us. You've got to, it's me birthday.'

'Yeah, some birthday,' Tim said, working his neck and shoulders. 'Your party ruined. Susan hysterical and Kenny hanged. Great, that was. No wonder they both went home crying.'

'Huh! You wouldn't catch me blubbin' like that. 'Specially in front of me mates.'

'No, I know,' Tim said, stifling a giggle. 'Nobody'd ever catch you doin' that. Or,' he added, and made ready to run, 'see you catch a bunch of keys.'

The chase took them to within a stone's-throw of the Chambers' "residence", as Mrs Chambers invariably referred to it. Once the property of the now derelict Abbots Lovell Mill, it stood alone, ugly and intimidating.

'You ring,' Tim said.

Having recently been fitted with a modern multi-paned front door, the approaching image of a human figure could not only be seen, but also identified.

'Not today, thank you,' Mrs Chambers said, making ready to close the door on them.

'It wasn't Billy's fault, Mrs Chambers,' Tim said, 'Clem and Ozzie gate-crashed the party and, well, they're bigger and stronger than us. We couldn't do anything about it. Could we, Billy?'

Mrs Chambers paused, took a breath, and stated in the most civilised of tones that she was well aware of that. 'No. What I object to, knowing the likelihood of such a "gate-crash", as you term it, was the absence of adult supervision. A point I shall be taking up with your mother, William. Now, if you don't mind, I have two traumatised children to console. Thank you for calling.'

With the door well and truly shut, and with no sign of a face showing at any window, upstairs or down, there seemed no point in staying.

'Even the birds don't sing round 'ere,' he said, which was true, his cocked ear failing to pick up as much as a tweet.

'Too traumatised,' Tim said, which sent them on their way in a silly, irreverent mood involving Major Craig's moustache flying down the wing and Jenny's mum with her big belly playing in goal, an image that produced much thrusting to the left and to the right of the stomach.

A warning tug of his sleeve brought him to a halt.

'Oh, shit,' he said, for there, propped earlier than normal beneath the kitchen window, was his father's bicycle.

The bicycle ... the front garden tree... its main branch hanging for all the world to see, bent as awkwardly as the broken wing of a crow.

Tim joined him, the two of them propped, like the bicycle, within earshot of voices: his father's unerringly factual with no trace of confusion or slur: his mother's voice tired and submissive, agreeing to his every word. 'I know. I know, I know!'

There seemed no end to his father's accusations, swamping replies that grew ever hoarser.

So hoarse, in fact, that at one point they could barely be heard.

Yet still his father probed. 'Well, 'oman? Cat got yer tongue, 'as it? Eh? Cat got yer tongue? Look at me, damn you! Why, for two —'

'No, Charlie – please! Not again. It was your son's birthday, Charlie. His birthday! Oh god! God, no. No!'

Tim sprang away from the house, looking with darting eyes towards the window. He worked his mouth, but made no sound, until managing a dramatic whisper. 'She's dead. I know she is. What'll we do? What'll we –?'

He grabbed his pal by his shirt and yanked him around the corner of the house. 'You've heard nothin', Robinson. D'yer hear? Nothin'!'

Interior doors banged. The front door banged, followed by the clang of the iron gate, slammed so hard it failed to engage the catch. The heavy tread of work boots provided a clue to his father's progress further and further away from the house.

Finger by finger, he relaxed his grip on Tim – and slammed him back against the wall. 'Nothin'! Got it?'

Tim nodded, urgent and sharp. Once freed, however, his face told a different story and he sidled away, edging his way towards the open gate. Once there, he turned and ran back home, crying to his "Mummy".

CHAPTER EIGHT

Piece by piece, Billy's mother dismantled the stove and put the parts to soak in the sink. Other parts, she went down on her knees to and scoured.

A yawn overcame him. His breath misted a pane, the effect creating a sketch pad ready-framed in metal. He drew a figure, added extra curls and drew a second figure holding hands with the first. Next, came a pram and then railings, thick and strong and topped with spikes. No-one else was in the park, just him and Jenny and their baby who was hidden under his blanket and was named Roger.

Outside, in the real world, the Robinson family passed by closely followed by a puffing Mrs Dodds. None of them glanced his way being too engrossed in tittle-tattle, it seemed. Even Tim.

The group passed behind and beyond the Perkins' buddleia, the bush threatening more than ever to block his view of number nine. One day, he vowed. One day … and pressed the start button on his imagined chainsaw.

At the stove, his mother ran her Brillo pad over yet another rail of oven racking, rubbing with a vehemence that for the most part kept her face hidden. Rail after rail. The Brillo pad disintegrated into pieces, so small she was left working with little more than bare fingers. Finally, with the last scrap of pad of no workable use, she rummaged in her box of bits and bobs, raking and pushing aside soiled rags and old polish tins.

Without even bothering to look up, she said, 'I should go out to play instead of moping, if I were you. What's done is done.'

'Still hungry.'

His mother rested her forearm on the rim of the sink and levered herself upright, a stick of a woman fitted with the hair and fingers of a witch. Nevertheless, witch's fingers or no, they still managed to lift from the high cupboard a near empty bag of broken biscuits.

She went back to the stove.

A section of Ginger Nut broke between his teeth with a snap. The sound appeared to spark something in her. Different in some way, squarer shouldered, more erect, she lifted her head and pushed back her hair. 'Whoever it is you end up with,' she said. 'A Patricia. A Jenny. A Sally, even. Whoever! You do anything like this – you lay so much as a finger on her – one! – and I promise you, as God's my witness, I'll wash my hands of you for good. Understand?'

Something fierce rose from deep within him. Him, a boy of ten – of course he understood. And if his mother had bothered to look inside his head, she'd have seen all the lions and tigers he'd fought, and the daring rescues he'd made. Then she'd know exactly who it was he was going to end up with. But then, nobody could see inside his head, he realised. Not even his mother.

'Do! You! Understand!'

'Yes!'

'Make sure you do,' she said. 'Because from what I hear there's far too much bullying going on in the village – far too much! And you seem to be at the heart of some of it. Take a good look,' she said, pointing to her discoloured cheek and swollen eyebrow. 'Go on – look at it! And – and get out of my sight! Go on! Just …'

Tim's Dutch arrow came readily to hand, to be snatched from the kitchen table and taken into the back field. There, out in the open, he spread his arms and whirled around, washed from his mother's hands into the sink, the spinning waters taking him ever nearer to the eye of the whirlpool.

Flushed from a pipe, he landed in the centre of a gladiatorial arena, the assembled crowd hushed, knowing what was at stake.

The balance and weight of his arrow felt good; its bulbous nose and shaped point deadly.

'El Windmill! El Windmill!' the crowd chanted as he marked out his run up. Twenty-one paces, he counted, the required distance to enable him to pick up speed and launch his secret weapon.

It flew straight, but low, a victim of poor technique. Less power, he told himself, less power and better timing.

Undeterred, he saluted the crowd for having insisted on him taking the throw again, his first effort sabotaged by the release of a lion.

For the rest of the evening, until dusk began to settle, he ran and threw, again and again until, after an uncertain start, his style was perfected. Never had such adoration been earned by a mere boy.

Elated, he held his arrow upright, pressed it to his nose, and to deafening applause, left the arena. El Windmill would be back however, on demand, at the weekend.

Saturday, Sunday, hour after hour, he threw his arrow. He slew lions. He slew gladiators. 'Olé' the crowd shouted, as each one fell. 'Olé Olé!', until, bored by his self-imposed exile, there came the moment of his greatest triumph.

Concentrating as never before, El Windmill laid the blood-stained string in the groove over its knot and pulled it taut down the length of the shaft. With the surplus string wound tight round his wrist, he awaited the Queen's final nod of the tournament.

From the moment the arrow flew from the string, it soared and soared again. It rode the wind. It lowered its nose - and plummeted back to earth to land way beyond the existing record.

Witnesses – he had to have witnesses. However, apart from the distant laughter and squeals of younger children playing in the ruins of the old mill there was no one.

Not a soul.

He re-played in his head his arrow's final few seconds of flight, the memory leading him to the brambles that formed part of the Robinson's back garden hedge.

The bush presented him with a daunting prospect, its vigorous outer shoots arching as high as his chest. They yielded nothing, no glimpse of red or peacock blue so fluorescent either would surely have shown from even the densest of thickets.

Nearer the centre of the bush the shoots proved harder to part and too awkward to trample. Thorns as sharp as cat's claws persisted in attaching themselves to his clothing and hands. A shoot whipped back at him. Fearing more of the same, he held his breath, not daring to move – and saw her: Jenny, wide-eyed and open mouthed.

Only when the Collins's axe cart-wheeled from her grasp to land head-first perilously close to her toes did she come to her full senses. 'W-what you looking at, Billy Hughes? Who said you could look into my uncle's garden?'

He tore himself free of the brambles and made for the Collins's back gate. 'What you done? What you gone and done!'

'You can't come in! You can't – Trish said! Anyway – it was the gippos. I saw them!'

Wiggy recognised him. He could swear to it. 'He en't dead!' he said, not knowing what to do with his arms. 'You en't finished him off!'

Jenny stood before him, no more than a breath length away. 'You'll do it for me – you will, won't you, Billy?' she said, resting the tips of her fingers on his arm. 'I mean, you know all about rabbits. I know you do. So…'

'Eh?'

'For me?' she said. 'I mean, you would if you loved me. Really, really loved me and not just had my name scratched on your ruler. We could be, you know … sweethearts. Not now, but when we're older. It would be our secret. Our extra special secret. You'd like that, wouldn't you? Darling.'

Wiggy's eyes appeared fixed on him, dilated and glazed.

Pleading …

A straw came to grief against his hutch, trapped by the fibres of the wood. An insignificant piece of straw that flapped as though it wanted to break free.

Flapped, and flapped …

He turned the chopper over, blade up, and paused, distracted by a leaf that skidded along the path. But it was soon gone, blown by a wind that lifted Jenny's skirt, forcing her to clamp it to her thighs.

'Go on! Do it!' she ordered.

When he looked again, she had gone, leaving him with nothing but the wind and the ruffle of fur.

CHAPTER NINE

The knock had about it the rap of authority, one that demanded attention and respect. His mother brought more hair down over her face and, obeying his father's nod, went through to the back of the house.

His father rose from the table and went fork in hand to the door. 'Albert! What you got there? Want 'im skinnin', does yer? Make a muff fer this 'ere lass of yourn?'

Knowing his father and what was to come, he slid from his stool.

'Billy! Out 'ere!'

Wiggy lay across Mr Collins' palms, his head unsupported and left to dangle. At his side, Trish stood with her head bowed, biting on her lip.

Mr Collins lowered Wiggy and held him out for inspection. 'Nobody's going to hurt you, William. We just want to know. That's all.'

'Hurt 'im!' his father said. 'I'll bloody give 'im hurt! Spit it out, damn you! What you know about this young girl's pet?'

'It – it weren't me! I don't know nothin'!'

His father grabbed him by his hair and walked him round in an arc. 'Weren't you, weren't it? Weren't you! Then how d'yer know, eh? How d'yer know it weren't you? Seein' as you don't know nothin'!'

'I was lookin' for me arra, that's all!'

'Liar!'

And, with the word, came the pain. He tried to reach for his buttocks. He could picture his father's next jab, see his hairy fingers press on the shoulder of his fork and draw back its prongs.

Sensing the moment, he thrust his hips forward and rode the jab. But the third and fourth had no pattern to them. They came out of sequence. Round and round his father jabbed him. Round and round, held upright by the pull on his scalp.

'Dance, yer bugger you. Dance!'

Past Mrs Dodds stood with the tips of her fingers pressed to her lips, past Carol Robinson and Dawn Adams. Every circle brought another face. Major Craig running his finger over his moustache. Clem stood with his head thrown back, clearly thinking it funny – they probably all did.

But it wasn't …

The instant the door closed behind him, he moaned. Sucking air in through his teeth, he reached behind him, into his trousers, and peeled his underpants from his flesh.

Two faces rose up at the window and peered in. Ozzie twitched his nose and bared his two front teeth. Clem used his fingers to make ears. Then, as suddenly as they had appeared, they ducked out of sight.

His father entered the kitchen and made straight for the sink. 'You blubbin', boy?'

'No!'

A blood vessel bulged in the white of his father's eye, sharp and angry and surely fit to burst. 'No, what?'

'No, Daddy.'

His father softened his look, almost to the point of a smirk, and faced the mirror. 'Good. But I warn you, boy. If Albert Collins starts billin' me for me bits of weldin'… Then, by Christ, your life won't be worth livin'! In fact, if I were you, I'd get down on me knees and make me peace. Tomorra, lad. First thing!'

'To Mr Collins?'

'Mr –? The girl, yer numbskull! You sweet-talk the girl! Get 'er a chocolate bar or summat. Bleedin' rabbits!'

His father's anger proved short-lived, soothed by the tightening of a tie and meticulous settling and resettling of his trilby.

Ready at last, he flicked the brim of the hat and yanked open the front door — only to pause and look back.

A coin spun towards him through the air. 'Knees, boy. First thing!'

Jenny arrived during the first hymn, pushed into school by an unseen force. She tried to go back, grappling with a door that never allowed her a proper grip. Always that one step ahead, it closed on her, leaving her wild-eyed and heaving.

In class, Miss Wheatcroft ordered them all to stop what they were doing and stand. 'Time-keeping! It would appear those who have the shortest distance to travel also have the greatest difficulty in arriving before the bell. Lateness leads to disruption. And disruption, as witnessed this morning, tends to distract a childish mind. A boy who allows his concentration to wander from the stirring words of *He Who Would Valiant Be* is clearly a fool.'

She wiped the board, clearing it of Friday's English lesson and drew in its place what looked like a man about to kick a large ball. When she had finished, she faced the class. 'The British Isles!'

She started with Dawn Adams, the youngest pupil in the class, and worked her way towards the eldest. London, Birmingham, Glasgow, Newcastle, Sheffield, Liverpool, Cardiff and Manchester were all correctly marked on the map by the time it came to his turn.

'William. The City of Plymouth.'

Cynthia Perkins handed him the chalk. At the bottom of the map, just off-shore, Miss Wheatcroft had drawn a tiny island. He positioned the end of the chalk above it, on the mainland.

Instead of the expected praise, Miss Wheatcroft invited him to try again. Further along the coast, due south of London, seemed a fair bet.

Miss Wheatcroft remained silent.

He moved the chalk to a spot high on the east coast, then the west coast and, finally, the middle of the Irish Sea.

Miss Wheatcroft's eyes appeared sightless, made of glass. She drew breath. 'Patricia, kindly show William the port from which the Pilgrim Fathers sailed, would you please?'

Using his ruler, Tim prodded Trish from behind. At this, she looked sharply up, towards Miss Wheatcroft, and then, after a whisper from Tim, the map.

Miss Wheatcroft raised an eyebrow. 'Are you feeling unwell, Patricia?'

'Her rabbit's been murdered, Miss!' Carol Robinson announced.

'I see,' Miss Wheatcroft said. 'I see … in that case, perhaps you can take Patricia's turn, Kenneth. Afterwards, perhaps it might be beneficial to adjourn and take an extended break.

In the playground, Trish stood with Sally Hicks and Susan Chambers, her face the colour of the morning milk.

'I – I've bin told to tell yer,' he said. 'It weren't me.'

His lines delivered, the thought of chocolate sprang to mind; the forgotten sweetener that no amount of pocket patting could conjure.

He resorted to a sniff and waited.

So did the three girls. They also waited.

'I told yer! I were lookin' for me arra weren't I? The one Tim give me for me birthday. But I en't got it now, you ask me mum!'

'Oh?' Sally said. 'She knows, does she? Your "mum".'

The heat rose in his cheeks and spread. It reached his ear lobes. A dead give-away, he thought, and stuck out his chin.

In the end, it fell to Trish to look elsewhere, towards the other side of the playground. 'So,' she said, slowly bringing her eyes back to meet his. 'This arrow of yours is still in the hedge, I take it?'

'Yeah! Must be! I looked real hard, I did. But – well –. Anyway, I wouldn't. I mean, I couldn't. Not … you know.'

'No,' Trish said. 'Thinking about it, I don't believe you could.'

'Not on his own,' Sally added.

The two stood together, similar in height and hair colour, while Susan looked on, ominously quiet.

'Matchsticks!' he said, in a sudden fit of anger. 'That's what your dad made you from. An'- an'- an' your mum couldn't do nothin' about it. Matchsticks!' he repeated, with a sneer, and stubbed the toe of his shoe into a patch of loose playground sending a splatter of dust and grit towards the girl's appropriately coloured red sandals.

'Couldn't do *anything* about it,' she said, and turned to Susan, muttered something, and reached into her pocket. From it, she brought out a Kit Kat, removed its outer wrapper and ran her thumbnail down the length of the bar. Leaving it in its silver paper, she snapped it in half and held out one of the fingers. 'Come on – take it. Or I'll eat it myself.'

'I…'

He crammed the finger of chocolate into his mouth and made his escape. As if by magic, a path opened up before him, an empty space that brought him suddenly and unexpectedly, face to face with Jenny.

Making exaggerated use of his jaws, he pointed to his cheek and tried his best to laugh. 'Nearly choked!'

She attempted to hold him at arm's length, head turned as though to imply that his breath stank. Still pushing, he attempted to run her back along the railings. He blocked her way. 'I never told 'em nothin' – 'onest! Nor my old man. Did yer see what he did? Did yer, Jen? Did yer? I mean! The whole village were there!'

'Go away, you idiot! Anyway, who'd want to see a stupid boy being stabbed with a dinner fork? Not me!' she said and pushed herself free of him.

He followed. He dogged her every step, determined to be heard. 'It's all right for you. You wanna see me bruises? Real blood, there was. Bucket loads!'

She halted and looked wildly about her, towards Ozzie sat astride the parallel bars and Dawn Adams and her cronies who all giggled and ran off.

The second they had gone, sweetly, and in a voice only he was likely to hear, she said, 'Oh yes, darling. You're so brave, darling. Now leave me alone. Or I'll tell Miss Wheatcroft!'

She scurried away, glanced back, and slowed to a walk.

This time, he chose not to follow, but stood his ground, ready to acknowledge anyone who should come near or so much as look in his direction. Nobody did. It was as though he were invisible, a notion that, for a moment, served to placate him. But the moment, like all such moments, proved fleeting, and he came to see his self for what he was: an isolated figure stood on his own personal patch of deserted tarmac, while the rest of the playground went on without him: a mix of shouts and squeals, held together by the clip, clip, clip of a skipping rope.

Yeah, isolated, Ma. Just like I am now, up this bleedin' tower. And I'm bloody thirsty. I want to come an' beg for your help, my chance to prove I were wronged, but I daren't, it's the first place they'd

68

come and check out. And, let's face it, you chose to believe her over me? "On any of them", you said. "You lay so much as a finger on any of them, and I'll wash my hands of you for good." Your little boy, Ma! Getting' on fer three years – and not so much as a letter. Two years, eight months and not a bloody word.

CHAPTER TEN

Scanned through the meanest of narrowed eyes the street appeared deserted, home to nothing but tumbleweed and dust.

Satisfied, he patted the flanks of his tethered horse and pushed open the swing doors of the town's General Stores.

Even his Deputy failed to look him in the eye. Blushing, as only Tim Robinson knew how, his one-time friend immersed himself in studying a shelf lined with tins of peas, baked beans and tomatoes.

At the counter, Miss Pringle took charge of his chosen sticks of dynamite. 'Your mother knows about this money, does she? It is yours to spend, I take it?'

'Me dad give it me – for treats. You ask 'im!'

'Mm, yes. Well, that's all right, then,' she said, and popped the liquorice into a paper bag.

Outside, with the bag discarded, Miss Pringle's words, and the way they had been spoken, sank in. It was as though by whipping away the bag from his liquorice he had also exposed the absence of her usually twinkling eyes and the enthusiasm reserved for all she served. In fact, thinking about it, her whole manner had come over as distinctly matter-of-fact and cold – the silly old coot.

'Coo-ee! Mr Wabbit-killer!'

The taunt came from behind the churchyard wall.

'I can see yer, Ozzie Cutter!'

The second taunt sounded even more infantile. It mimicked the first and came from the vicinity of his school.

Only the first-year juniors' gang were in the playground, a line of four conga-dancing girls who screamed on seeing him and scattered.

Among them, shadowing Dawn Adams, zig-zagged Tim's sister, Carol.

Confronted, Tim narrowed his shoulders and, clutching his Sherbet Dab to his chest, did a sideways stumble back onto the shop doorstep. 'I en't scared of you.'

'En't meant t' be – crab!'

'Fool!'

'Pink, titty-babby crab. An' that sister of yourn! She can watch it, an' all!'

Tim dipped the ball of his lollipop into his sherbet and sucked on it. 'Carol?'

'Yeah, you know what I mean. Just tell her from me. If I hears 'er say anythin' about me and Jen, I'll 'ave her. Marmalize her, I will. And that Dawn Adams – I'll 'ave her an' all!'

Tim withdrew his lollipop, sucked as clean as Susan Chambers' face and eyed him. 'Jennifer Duggan? Why should they say —?

'Oh … oh, nothin', it en't. Sort of, you know. Big kids' stuff. Tell yer some other time.'

'Don't want to know,' Tim said. 'Don't want to know anything. Not even why Trish gave you her Kit Kat.'

'Half.'

'Half, then. Which probably means she only half —'

'Yeah? Go on, then. Half, what?

His ex-best pal answered with a characteristic twitch of his brows and dabbed once more in his sherbet.

Not to be out done, he eased himself up onto the shop's litter bin and tugged a length of liquorice from its stick with his teeth.

Tim heaved a sigh, grimaced, and joined him, sharing with him the bin's narrow rim of rolled metal. They sat in silence. Not a word passed between them, even when Mrs Dodds came waddling towards them decked out in a hair net and pink slippers.

Not so much as a quack.

Tim screwed the top of his sherbet bag around the stick and cast him a sideways look. 'Must've … you know. Hurt. What your dad did.'

'Had worse.'

'Yeah, I know. All the same ...'

Tim's words invited normality, the prospect of a game of Nudge. A game he would sort of 'lose' and thereby quite happily land his buttocks down into the interior of the bin and its welcome cushion of discarded cartons and wrappers. But an inner voice ordered 'no'. It made him lock his elbows and push himself off the bin and away without breaking stride.

Look, everybody! Everybody look! Look at William's hell! A wagging finger – the aristocrat! The gibberish spouting man with the E-Type suddenly swept up and over – laughing at him. No, snarling at him, with rabbit's teeth and giant whiskers. Everyone was riding the sails of his of his windmill: Mrs Hicks, with her lips and lashes looming in on him, even Dawn Adams, sitting on Old Barney's shoulders, all of them in one way or another mocking him. But not Jenny – they had gone without Jenneeeeeeeeeeeeeeeeey! He tried shouting her name, but his teeth – He couldn't … couldn't part his …

'Shushh! Billy, shush. Shush, now. It's all right. Mummy's here. Mummy's got you.'

'I didn't. Didn't tell daddy about. About me Kit Kat. Trish give me. She give —'

'Yes, we know, we know. But shush. Wake up now. That's it. That's better. We don't want to wake your father, do we? Eh? Not Daddy. And certainly not at this time of night, heaven forbid.'

'But I want to. I want —'

'Billy, please! For pity's sake, child. What, with you and…'

"Him", he wanted to fill in for her. "Him", the goalkeeper featured in the two Community Hall photographs. Even so, the word was left to hang over them, a physical thing, larger than life itself.

In stony silence, his mother ran the flat of her palm slowly and deliberately up over her bruised face and into her tangle of hair.

'Mum?'

She moistened her lips and eyed him. More her normal self, she took hold of his pyjama cord and picked at its knots. Picked and picked until the weight went from his hips.

In one movement, she hoisted him out of bed and stood him on his mat. 'Now. Don't move – or else!'

With his bottom sheet and pyjama trousers bundled together, she picked her way across his floorboards: a short step, two long steps, and out onto the landing, clear of the shark-infested waters.

The monsters were everywhere. Teeth bared, they closed in on the castaway left by the wicked witch as bait. But he had a plan. With Mr Jock ticking his way round the headland locked in the belly of the largest shark in the world, he pulled the stake he was tied to out of the ground and ran with it carried on his bent back. 'Can't catch me, Mr Shark. Can't catch —'

He halted, alarmed by the creak of a floorboard. But it was only his mother. She made as though to speak, only to obviously think better of it. Instead, she merely motioned with the flannel draped over her hand for him to make ready.

'Ah dear, I don't know,' she said, and brought the flannel up from between his legs. 'Mr Windmill. That's what we'll have to be calling you – eh? I bet he doesn't wet his bed, though. Not Billy Windmill.'

She turned the flannel over and picked at non-existent crumbs. 'I think we'd better give school a miss. Just for a day or two. A bad tummy – eh? That's what you had, I expect. A bad tummy, shall we tell Miss Wheatcroft? Like before.'

He hung his head and stared blank-minded into his mat.

'What a pair we are,' his mother said, towel in hand. 'Just look at us. You stood there with your willy hanging out. And me looking like something the cat's dragged in. But there it is, as your granddad used to say. There it is …'

All too soon, she was standing with her finger hovering over the light switch. But even after she had pressed it, she was still visible, the light now coming from behind her, from the landing; a softer, less penetrating light that cast elongated shadows on the stairwell wall and lurked in his doorway, drawn to every tuck and fold of her nightdress.

CHAPTER ELEVEN

With no sheet to pull up next to his skin the coarseness of his blanket irritated him. He discarded it. Uncovered and unable to sleep, he stared up at his ceiling, the only boy of his age likely to be awake at such a late hour; able, if he concentrated hard enough, to leave his own body and float about his room.

Music carried on the air, thin, tinny sounds, not coming from a record player or transistor radio held on someone's shoulder next to the Community Hall lamp-post. No, it was nothing like that. It was though it came from outer space, the melody serving to lull him note by note towards sleep.

The scrape of a chair leg roused him, the sound of wood on stone. Nothing came of it, however. There was no further sound, nothing, other than that of padded feet passing across his inner ear.

Something brushed along the other side of his wall. His door tilted and swayed towards him. He could swear that its knob had turned. 'Daddy?'

A moth beat against the window. It tried again and again, working itself to a frenzy. Then, for some inexplicable reason, it fell silent. Even the darkness, it too, fell silent, leaving him with the comfort of his thumb and the point of a star, lifted now and starting to curl.

His father tilted his cup and scowled. 'You bin swiggin' the milk?'

'No! I mean. No, Daddy. I haven't. Honest!'

Still scowling, his father bit away the greater part of the last piece of toast. 'Then why,' he said, and paused to suck the dripping from his fingers, 'has yer ma had t' go t' the shop?'

'I en't drunk it! I en't!'

'That weren't what I asked yer.' Was it, sunshine? Why, is what I said. Why, lad! Because if you en't drunk it. And I en't drunk it. And it wuz there last thing last night -- a good half inch of it – then who's 'ad it? Father Christmas?'

'I dunno!'

His father glanced towards the clock, slowly turned his head back to face him, and narrowed his eyes. Peeping through the malice, however, appeared the glimmer of a self-congratulatory smirk. 'Grey matter,' he said, tapping his skull. 'Some on us 'as it. And some on us don't. Sherlock Holmes has nothin' on me, lad. I don't need no Watson t' help work it out. Washin' on the line. You bumpin' round all night. Yer ma missin' from me bed. Be the death of her – d'yer hear? Put her back in 'ospical, yer will! And what'll yer do then, eh? Me, I can get another 'oman just like that!' he said and clicked his fingers.

'But you, yer bed-peein' little – get that star orff. Go on! Orff with it. Damn the woman! What's her up to?'

Like the genie summoned from the lamp, his mother entered the room, her countenance over-bright, her cheeks blown as though having sprinted to the Morton crossroads and back. 'Phew! Dear me! A newspaper, Charlie! The Craigs' have gone away and hadn't cancelled. And look. A pork pie and a few tins — beans and that – for free! Had to give Miss Pringle a hand, I did. Fifteen minutes, that was all. Worth it though, eh?'

His father sniffed. 'And milk?'

'Yes. A tin of evap. Had to pay for that, though. But it does mean a fresh pot. You've got time.'

Again, his father glanced at the clock and picked up the Craigs' newspaper, a *Sunday Times,* already two days old.

'Good, is it, Charlie? The paper, I mean. Lots of reading in that – keep you going all week!'

His father looked thoughtfully up from a sports page. 'What you got t' be so chipper about so sudden?' he said, eyes narrowed to the point of a squint.

His mother pierced the tin of evaporated milk and set it before him. 'Well. I was wondering … just a thought. What with the pork pie and the weather being what it is? We could, you know. Go for a picnic

78

by the river this evening. The three of us – as a family,' she said, and rose from the table to stand with her back to his father, waiting, it would appear, for the kettle to come back to the boil. 'And there's apples!' she added. 'Past their best, of course. But, tidied up – you know. What do you think?'

'Think?' his father said, and slowly brought the pages of the Craigs' newspaper together. 'Well, let's see now. When things get back t' normal, is what I think. When things is normal, that's when I'll consider playin' 'appy families. Good enough for yer?'

His mother turned back and faced his father, the colour re-arranging itself in her cheeks. Quietly, with a detectable edge to her voice, she said, 'It was no small matter, Charlie. My op.'

'Aye. Aye, I know. But what am I supposed t' do in the meantime? Eh? And all this depression stuff. There's worse off than you, yer know. At least you got a kiddie.'

'We, Charlie.'

'Yeah, yeah,' his father said, waving aside the correction. 'Whatever. Me and the lad is sound – en't we, son? Had a good chat while yer wuz at the shop we did. En't fair on yer ma, I told 'im. Could put 'er back in 'ospical, I said. All this bed wettin'.'

'A nightmare, Charlie. He couldn't help it. A nasty nightmare, that was all. And he – well, he wanted to tell you something. About a Kit Kat! You

79

did, didn't you, Billy? Go on, tell Daddy, why don't you? Before he has to go to work.'

The way ahead could not have been more clearly signposted. With his mother staring into her empty cup and his father mindful of the time, he followed a plan that unravelled even as he spoke. 'Yeah! Did what you said. It were your idea, weren't it, Dad? Shared a Kit Kat with Trish, I did. An' – an' it's all right now, it is. Her dad thinks you're a good bloke. An'-an' – an' he's sorry for any trouble he caused.'

'Yes, well,' his father said, and tapped his skull. 'Told yer, didn't I? Strategy. It's what wins wars, lad. Wars!'

Only after his father had passed by the window and had been seen to mount his bicycle, did his mother stir. "Well done", her twitched smile seemed to imply, aided in no small part by words more shaped than sounded. But words all the same; praise he would remember for ever, he thought.

For ever and ever and ever …

CHAPTER TWELVE

Not until the summer holiday did anyone bother to call for him.

His mother edged his curtains further apart. 'Yes, I was right. It's Tim. And that ridiculous Cutter boy.'

What she failed to mention was the peak of Clem's flat cap, hung on the end of a stick of some sort, peeping out from behind the corner of the house. After having moved the cap up and down, he showed his face. 'Red alert, Billy-boy! Bring yer weapon!'

'What … me? Ah! Brill!'

In a matter of minutes, fully armed with a broom-stale and toast, he was out on patrol. 'Bet they'm townies, eh, Clem? Tryin' a dawn raid!'

Clem cocked his head and noisily sucked in air. 'Townies? Now, there's a thought. And a dawn raid, yer reckon. All fits, don't it, men?'

'Yeah, Hughesie!' Ozzie said, herding him as a dog would a sheep. 'Top field – better get up there we 'ad!'

Clem shouldered his walking stick and led the way, over the gate and into the meadow. Ozzie threw his sawn-off line prop over and followed, the tail of his Secret Service raincoat catching on a post. Tim unhooked it and went next carrying his Bill Cody rifle.

A kid's toy, Billy thought, and climbed the gate backwards, protecting their rear with his declared telescopically sighted bazooka. No! A twelve bore. Same as Clem's!

Their leader put his arm round his shoulders and walked him across the meadow, up front, at the head of the patrol. They had been worried about him, Clem said, him having been off school.

'Me belly. Real bad, it were. Me mum had to write a note to Miss Wheatcroft.'

Clem gave his shoulders a brotherly squeeze. 'Well, not to worry, pal. You'm here, now. And we'm impressed – en't we, men? I mean. When them townies of yours comes at us on them Bonnevilles, armed wiv chains and knuckle-dusters... You'll be waitin' for 'em, wun't yer, pal? Sweep 'em back into the sea, yer will!'

'Blimey!' he said. 'They en't Vikings, yer know!'

'En't Vikings!' Clem said. 'Did' yer hear that, lads? En't Vikings. Likes it, I does. You'm a hoot, pal. En't he, lads? A real hoot!'

'Huh!' Ozzie said, only to brighten and add in a rush. 'Oh ah! A hoot. And what a weapon. Eh, Clem? Bleedin' nuclear, it is.'

'Yeah!' Tim said. 'Goes broom-broom!'

At the stile, Clem ordered all weaponry to be checked and loaded. One at a time, on the count of five, he's over and into the war zone. 'Go, Billy-boy. Go-go-go!'

Crouched and running, they fired volley after volley into the quarry and reached the rat-hole unscathed. Once through, they regrouped and ran in single file up the blind side of the top field hedge, heading for the summit and almost certain death.

The bracken provided perfect cover. A belly-wriggle away, the top field stretched before them, a swathe leading the eye forever downhill to where a line of hawthorn and the occasional oak marked the boundary between earth and sky.

Clem crawled forward and lay alongside him. 'Any sign of 'em, Comrade? I mean, don't want no damage doin', does we, pal? Not wiv our Walter havin' booked the contractors.'

The corn barely stirred. It revealed nothing, no track or any other sign of human interference. In fact, the only relief came in the form of a poorly seeded patch largely taken over by twitch and the occasional poppy or thistle.

Ozzie groaned. 'This is borin'. I thought we…'

Leaving his sentence unfinished, their Corporal sighed and rolled onto his back, arms flung wide. A few moments later, he rolled back again and buried his nose in a cushion of grass and dead bracken, until moved to arch his neck and look skyward, gifted by some sixth sense to pick out the flight of a kestrel.

The bird dipped and turned until backed by the sun. Then, there it was, almost upon them, legs to the fore. A puff of corn dust, a twist and with three flaps it landed on a fence post.

Evil showed in its eyes. An undeniable anger aimed towards the rubbish patch. An anger suddenly and without warning transferred to where they supposedly all lay hidden in the bracken.

Its talons empty, the kestrel went sleek and made ready to fly, exposing the down on its chest and its feathery plus fours. An easy target, one none of them could have failed to hit. But the bird seemed to know they were mere boys and, furthermore, that mere boys did not carry guns. Not real guns that could scatter its giblets and provide easy pickings for the crows.

With no wind to lift it from its perch, it launched itself, to glide low over the ripened barley. Away it flew, a speck heading for the square crown and over-sized eye of the church tower.

Clem rose to his knees, twelve-bore levelled, only to lower it again and wave a midge away from his nose. Almost immediately, he aimed again, and this time fired. 'Got 'im!'

Ozzie also fired, then Tim, and the pair scrambled to their feet. Ordered into battle, they charged forwards, firing at will. Then Tim retreated and crashed back into the bracken.

Ozzie, on the other hand, delayed his retreat. Giving the game away with a typical Ozzie Cutter look of gleeful malice, he put his head down, and charged.

CHAPTER THIRTEEN

'De-bag 'im!' Clem ordered. 'Come on, Robinson. You an' all! De-bag the bastard!'

'Geroff! Geroff of —!'

'Hands, Oz! Get his —. Right, yer little bugger. Fight yer Uncle Clem, would yer? Eh? Fight yer Uncle Clem, would yer, Billy-boy?'

'Ha!' Ozzie said. 'Bollock-naked under 'ere, he is. Bollock-naked!'

'Tut-tut, Billy-boy. Pissed our pants, 'ad we? Mummy run out of nappies?'

'I en't! I en't pissed me pants – geroff!'

'Oh? En't what your old man told our Cyril – wuz it, Oz? "Cyril", he sez. "Cyril, that there lad of mine's gone and pissed 'is pants again. Pisses 'is pants. And pisses 'is bed. Just like a babbie".'

'Chest-taps!' Ozzie demanded. 'I votes —'

'And I vote you stop!' Tim said. 'This isn't what we said. Come on, Clem. That's enough.'

'Enough?' Clem said. 'Nah, you don't want us t' stop, does yer' Billy-boy? You wanna show us if you'm a babbie …or a man. Don't yer, pal?'

Clem held a crooked finger over him … and brought it down. 'See, Timmy-boy. He don't want us t' stop. Not until he sez rabbit. I killed six. Ozzie

86

killed – phew! Dozens, I reckon. While our Timothy, our lickle Tim-de-Tim. Well! Did yer see 'im, Oz? Wiv his Bill Cody? A right hunter of rabbits is our Tim. But you, Billy-boy. We en't so sure about you. So, you'd better tell us. Hadn't yer, pal?'

'Piss off!'

'Now-now! No need fer that – is there, lads? Killed a rabbit, did we? Eh? Killed a rabbit?' he said, and brought his crooked finger down, on his chest, right on the bone. On and on it went, regular and hard. On and on, Clem's voice soft and persuasive, telling him what he did not wish to hear. 'Better own up, pal. Can keep this up all day, I can. I mean, don't want yer t' puke does we now? Or cough up blood. Be bad that. Coughin' up a load've – what's that? Did I hear summat?'

'Air …' he managed to say, 'I, I can't...'

He went limp and stayed limp, even when prodded. The final humiliation, it seemed, his wrists freed, the weight taken from his ankles.

From behind, close by, the bracken rustled. 'Come on,' Tim said. 'They've gone now.'

On impulse, he sat up and threw whatever came to hand at his friend's face, his stupid, stupid face. Things felt better after that. They did. They bloody, bloody – did!

'You!' Tim said, his bottom lip curled, making it appear fleshy and pink. 'I wouldn't throw at you like that. I was on your side. I tried to help.'

'That's just it, en't it? You didn't, did yer? Like with Kenny and that prattin' sister of his! "Oow, don't you hurt my brother. If you hang my brother I'm going to tell the pol-eece". Like her, you are. A cissy!'

'What was I supposed to do! Nothing?'

'No!' he said, grabbed his pal, and put him to a headlock. 'You don't do nothin'. You does what they does – got it? Have yer, Robinson? Got it, 'as yer?'

'Yes! I've got it. I've got it! Let me –!'

Ruddy-faced and rubbing at his neck, Tim stumbled away towards an attempted hooting of an owl. He had not gone far, however, before he stopped and looked back. 'I will! In future, I'll do what they do. Even if – even if you're tied to a tree and being kissed by Cynthia Perkins!'

Ahead of Tim, Ozzie and Clem stepped out from the back entrance to the newly erected farm shop. Each held up and waggled a pint bottle of milk.

'Get stuffed – the lot of yer!' he shouted, and retraced his steps through the bracken, securing, as he pushed through the fronds, the top button on his flies.

Once through the rat-hole he slackened his pace. Out of view, if not earshot, the gang's voices gave their position away, but they made no attempt to catch up with him: or so it seemed. With one leg cocked over the stile, and the richer grass of the meadow beckoning him, a mix of whistles and whoops announced they were already through the rat-hole.

'Coo-ee! Mr Wabbit-killer! Coo-ee!'

'What's up, Doc? Got mixy?'

The swish of grass took him ever closer to the gate and Quarry Lane. Nettles eyed him from the ditch. Cow parsley, buttercups – it made no difference. It was all the same. All, that was, except for a lone ox-eye. One swipe, that's all it took. Just one swipe and it buckled at the knees.

The Community Field gate clanged shut behind him, the distinctive ring of metal on metal a dead give-away. Through the gate, inevitably exposed once more to catcalls and whistles, he kept his eyes fixed on the way ahead, a goalpost aligned to a climbing rope, until losing focus and, with it, concentration.

Appearing the size of thumbs, the gang waved and cheered as though with one voice. Ozzie and Tim squatted and performed bunny-hops. Clem levelled his twelve-bore, took aim, and discharged both barrels. The rabbits stood erect, clutched their chests, and tumbled. Over and over they went, down the slope and into the open mouth of the old stone quarry.

Clem shouldered the gun and followed, leaving in his wake the eerie spectre of an empty stage.

And yet ...

He walked on, plagued by images: Wiggy, lying bloodied and panting, the heel of a palm pressed to an eye, a whole line of eyes, lit by the giggles of four conga-dancing little girls. So vivid was the image, so mocking their laughter, that he levelled his weapon and with the face of Dawn Adams fixed in his sight, saw his bullet strip the flesh from her skull: all of it, leaving until last, the horror written in her eyes.

The rooks left the trees. The villagers opened their doors to jabber and point. And yet the overriding factor was one of silence, so oppressive, that he flung his broom stale aside – and fled.

CHAPTER FOURTEEN

His mother practically ignored him. Without even bothering to look up from the kitchen table, all she did was mumble something about him being back early. She never asked why. No, what interested her more was the working out of stupid shillings and pence sums on a piece of cardboard.

Tired of waiting, he started to whine. 'Mu-um, Tim and Ozzie did bunny-hops an' pretended to be shot. An' I 'adn't done nothin', I 'adn't.'

His mother tightened her lips and sat back, the joints in her chair giving out their customary squeak. Gently, in a tone that in no way matched her mood, she said, 'Mummy's busy, can't you see? So, if I were you, I'd go back out to play while you've got the chance. It's supposed to rain later.'

'But Mu-um,' he said, intent on more whining, only to stop short, made to think better of it by the slapping down of her pencil.

'Outside! That or your room.'

His bedroom held a sudden appeal; a face at a window, a boy clearly suffering from cruelty and neglect. A skeleton is all they'd find, nothing but bones.

On the verge of tears, he stomped stair by stair to his room. 'Bones! Bones! Bones!'

According to Mr Jock, it was over two hours before his mother relented and tapped on his door. She entered and stood with him at his window seeming content to remain as silent as he was and face the air that wafted in through his open window.

From the other side of the road, Mrs Dodds beamed a mass of wrinkly smiles and repeatedly waved.

'Oh!' his mother said, and shot up her hand, offering a belated finger wave at the retreating back of his Godmother. Away she waddled, past Jenny's house and on past the school gate, the distinctive Community Hall key levelled some thirty yards or more before it was required.

'Daft, en't she?' he said, only for his mother to correct him with a sudden sharpness of both eye and tongue.

'She's a treasure!' she said. 'Just look how she took care of you while Mummy was in hospital. There's not many who'd have done what she did, I can tell you!'

'Yeah, well, I know,' he said, and breathed in the memory of freshly baked scones and fairy cakes.

'Mm … well, just as long as you do,' his mother said, her splurge of hostility giving way to a more reflective and somewhat philosophical mood.

'My world…' she said, as though dreamily addressing her own reflection. 'That's what your granddad had me believe. Mine to fill with whoever and whatever. And I did. Children – I always imagined children. In my arms. In my pram. That, and a smiley-faced husband, home after a day's work. Meet me at the gate, he would. Take me by the hips and raise me to the sky.'

The picture she painted hung before him full of action and panache, only for it to be immediately scowled at and treated to the indignity of a snort.

'Me! The "late gift from The Lord". The "surprise package", a baby girl, who grew up thinking all men were like her daddy. All men!' she repeated – and snapped a loose thread from his curtain.

Breathing hard, she wound the thread around her finger; wound, and pulled, as though to set a top spinning.

Leaving the top to hum, she thrust the thread deep into her apron pocket. From the same pocket, she produced first one apple, and then another, and arranged them on his windowsill like ornaments. 'There,' she said. 'They should keep you going. Dinner will be on the table at seven.'

'Seven!'

She lifted Mr Jock from his shelf and wound him, each twist of her wrist tightening, not only the main spring, but also her lips.

She returned Mr Jock to his shelf – and smiled. 'Take it. Or leave it.'

The only sad thing about his dinner was that, once eaten, it was gone. No more bubble and squeak.

'Worth coming down for, I take it?' his mother said.

He gave less than a shrug and eyed his father's meal, set opposite him, sandwiched between two plates. His mother lifted them from under his nose, opened the oven and slid the dinner inside.

Later, after many glances in the direction of the kitchen clock, she re-lit the oven and altered the setting of the regulator. 'Always has to have the last word one way or another, does your father.'

Nearing eight o'clock, she turned the oven off. One by one, her fingers slid from the knob and reached, as might a blind person, for the kettle. 'Well, that's it!' she said, her grip tightening on its handle. 'That is –. I just can't take ...' She shook her head and wrenched the cold water tap on. The water gushed. Over the draining board and down her apron it went. She thrust in the kettle spout. Almost immediately, she moderated the flow and, with the calming of the water, also appeared to have calmed herself. She placed the kettle on an unlit gas ring and raked in the Swan Vesta box.

Nothing but black-ended stumps, it seemed. Yet, still she raked, spilling spent match after spent match to the floor.

'Mum? Mum – I'll go next door!'

Recognition of him came, but slowly. She nodded, the spilled matches and the kettle incident put aside in favour of her mother's teapot. Used as an ornament, she stood with it clutched to her chest as though it was something of value, which as far as he knew, it was not.

'Matches,' he said. 'Wun't be a sec!'

To his relief, she was much as he had left her. Rooted to the same spot with the teapot clutched to her chest, she appeared to be making a mental note of everything, even the sink, which she reached for, and touched.

Her fingers closed, withdrawn as though burned by the fires of Hell. But it was not for the Devil that she searched. It was not at him that she voiced her agony; it was God.

Stared at, the rain had the same mesmerising effect on him as The Reverend Chatterton's renowned polishing of a spectacle lens. A fellow sufferer, reportedly having been tortured in a jungle, he would identify with a face at a window and preach on his behalf. 'Let no man,' he would say, working his false jaw like a ventriloquist's doll. 'Let no man be the one to throw the first stone. Mm – Amen.' The voices of the mob drown out the Vicar. Holy or not, it makes no difference to them. As one, they tumble out of church with the man. They tumble … and disappear, wiped from his imagination by a familiar tap and tentative opening of his door.

This time, his mother did not join him at his window. She sat on his bed nursing a large cardboard box. Staring into it as though it was something other than empty, she said, 'We haven't got long. By the time I get back I want you to have taken your clothes from your drawers and put them in here with your toys.'

'Me –? I en't goin' to Mrs Dodds! Not her, I en't! Wash yer hands an'-an' – an' comb yer hair. That's all she sez!'

His mother ran the flat of her thumbs over and over the rim of her box. 'Please, I beg you. Don't make this any harder for me than it is already. I was born in this house – d' you understand? Born!' she emphasised, the bags under her eyes matching more than ever the yellowed bruises still evident on her cheek.

She stood up, abruptly, and pushed the box into his midriff. 'Ten minutes. No ifs or buts. I'll expect you to be ready.'

Leaving him with the box, she made her way downstairs. Within seconds, she appeared beneath his window, her apron discarded, her bloodless legs scuttling across the roadforty, a solitary figure, bent into the rain.

CHAPTER FIFTEEN

Mr Barnes leaned on his walking stick and pointed to where their luggage was to go. Her carrier bag to be placed over there, her battered suitcase here, his cardboard box upstairs to a room already designated as his.

His mother led the way up bare-boarded stairs to an equally bare-boarded landing. From it, one door opened onto a fair-sized back bedroom, while the other opened on to what she proudly announced was his.

'Just look at the view!' she said and with her little finger held aside a fly-ridden net curtain. 'There! You'll be able to see when your friends are out playing. I don't know! Aren't you the lucky one?'

It was as she said, the window overlooked the village pond and the Community Field, beyond which lay the school playground. Of more interest, on the far side of that, was a side view of number nine. Even better, set near the apex of its roof was a window. Stared at, however, the further away it seemed to get. It appeared worse than minuscule, as good as useless.

'I en't got no friends,' he said.

His mother seemed to agree. 'Yes, well, it can sometimes feel like that but... Give it time, that's all it needs. Look on this as a fresh start – a sort of holiday. A whole new chapter in your life.'

'Yeah, in a smelly old book. Stinks, it does. Of – of old rags!'

His mother put her arm round his shoulders and drew him to her. Not content with just a hug, she planted a kiss on the top of his head. 'Don't worry, I'll get it sorted. Open this window for a start and let in some air. As for the netting… Well, we'll see. What I can do though, is give those shoes of yours a birthday. Mr Barnes is bound to have a tin of black polish. Then you could go, let's see … to Sunday School! Tim goes most Sundays. So does Kenny. Now, he's a sensible boy, and you haven't played with him for a while, have you? Not since your birthday. Perhaps the two of you could go fishing together. In fact, I'm sure I saw him with his rods only the other day. I know! I could get you a net. I'm sure Miss Pringle's got some old stock tucked away somewhere. Bright orange, they are. Quite fetching!'

He knitted his brows and said nothing, even when her attempts at opening the window proved futile.

Free of her arm, the back wall offered a place to slump and adopt an attitude of just … attitude.

Muttering to herself, she said, 'If only I could be sure of where your father is. Monday now, I suppose. The rest of our stuff will have to wait 'til then, when he's at work.'

'If he goes,' he said.

Directly above him, within reach, hung a dingy, sombre-framed piece of embroidery, better suited to a chapel or church than a bedroom. Elaborately stitched and incredibly ancient, the work still retained a degree of colour. What at one time had probably been red was now a faded brown, and what had been yellow, a dull beige. Around the margins, loops and swirls bonded together to form a complex array of flower-heads and foliage, the whole affair more likely as not the work of an earlier Mrs Dodds.

A picture of his godmother waving to them from the other side of the road unexpectedly appeared in his head; an intrusion that reminded him that all that was familiar was now lost. No longer would he be able to spy on the comings and goings of the shop, nor on those on their way to the Rose & Crown, Church or Community Hall. Then there were the three facing windows of number nine now reduced to just one, and that the size of one of Miss Pringle's postage stamps. It was, as his gran would have forcibly put it – "the last straw!".

He scrambled to his feet. 'I was born there as well, I was! You shouldn't 'ave done it. He'll come and get us. Bash both our brains in, he will!'

His mother let the curtain fall back in place, her manner peculiarly calm and self-assured. 'No. Don't worry. It won't come to that. Behind closed doors – oh yes. But, here? In front of a witness? No,' she repeated. 'No more bruises. No more scratching around for matches. Peace of mind, Billy Windmill! Normality – smell it seeping up from beneath your feet. Beef and dumplings, together with vegetables from Mr Barnes' back garden.'

'Don't like vegetables.'

'Then push them to the side of your plate,' his mother said, and turned her back on him.

However, she sighed and turned back. 'I'm sorry. It's been an emotional day – and look at the time! Come on! Shift yourself. Go to the toilet, why don't you? While it's still light. And if you need to go in the night make sure you know where the torch is.'

'Yeah – don't worry. Already sin it, I 'as. Danglin' from the 'ook screwed into the back door.'

His mother shook her head. 'Go on – I haven't the energy. But quietly, please. We can't afford to go disturbing Mr Barnes. And wash your face and hands while you're down there. Makeshift beds for tonight, I'm afraid. But I shouldn't think that will trouble you too much. You look done in. And so am I,' she admitted, the corners of her mouth raised in a pathetic attempt at a smile. 'A good night's sleep then, eh? And tomorrow? Yes, well. Heaven only knows what that might bring.

Only Heaven...'

CHAPTER SIXTEEN

Left to sleep, the day proved to be half gone by the time he joined Mr Barnes downstairs.

'Had to go to the loo in me bare feet,' he informed him. 'B-but it weren't no trouble.'

The old man nodded and went on to extol the virtues of blue bricks. 'I remembers settin' 'em,' he said, his smile and reflective snort implying that it had all been a long, long time ago. In fact, so reflective was he, stood there with the poker poised some way short of the fire, that to rouse him required a second, more forceful question on his part, about the old embroidery hanging in his bedroom.

'Oh – the sampler. Yes, well, no test piece, that,' he informed him. 'The real M'Coy, I'll have you know, young shaver. Stitched by Ethel when we wuz both kiddies. About your age, her were – no older! Aye, that were it. About your age ...'

Swaying slightly, the old man stood poised before his fire once more. Although permanently lit, no flame ever seemed present, only a glow whenever the crust of the fire fell in on itself and sent slack-laden smoke out into the generously crotched fabric of his trousers. He seemed unaware of this. In the main, he tended to react only to things alien to the normal workings of his home. A footfall and he was all ears. The click of a door opening, and he was all eyes. 'Little Mo! Come in! Come on. Sit yourself down. Perfect timing! Just right.'

Making use of his cloth, Mr Barnes lifted a large pot from his oven and set it down on the hearth. 'There! A Barney special. Early tatties. A nice bit o' stewing steak. And lashings of onions! Put hairs on that chest of yourn, young Hughes. And flesh back on them bones of yourn, Maureen Bassett. Seen more meat on a twig, I 'as.'

His mother placed her hand across her throat and brought the lapels of her frock together. Both pale and flushed and with eyes that never seemed to rest, she said, primly, 'Given time.'

'As much time as you needs, Mo,' Mr Barnes said. 'As much as you needs – you knows that. Now! Afore we has our vittles, a few words to the provider without whose order the rivers would surely run dry and the soil of this earth turn to dust. Thank ye, Lord. Thank ye for the rain. And thank ye for the sunshine, without which our crops would surely perish. Amen.'

'Amen,' his mother said, and nudged him with her knee.

'Amen!' he said. 'And thank you for our daily bread.'

'Oh ah!' Mr Barnes said. 'A slice each for moppin' up. Waste not, want not. Thank you, lad!'

With his ladle overloaded, Mr Barnes piled an extra helping onto his plate, including a second perfectly swollen dumpling.

'Ethel's speciality,' enthused the old man. '"Dumplin's to nourish the body", her would say. And "stitchin' to nourish the soul." A God fearin' woman, if ever there wuz one. And that be her room you be in, Master Hughes. Empty now for nigh on fifteen years. Winter of forty-six, it were. Just afore the snows came. That there bomb them Yankies dropped – that were the cause of it! Never knowd snows like it. Piled higher'n the hedgerows, it were. Aye. Higher than the hedgerows ...'

After taking what could only have been a few mouthfuls, his mother arranged her knife and fork quietly and neatly on her plate and, averting her eyes, rose from the table. 'I'm – I'm sorry. Please, you'll have to forgive me. I – I'll finish it later. I'm sorry.'

Without a word, Mr Barnes scraped the best part of his own meal from his plate and back into the pot. Finished scraping, he looked to the ceiling, rubbed his hand across his chin, roughing up his stubble, and concentrated his one serviceable eye on him. 'You be the man o' the house now, young Hughes. Always remember that. So enough of that,' he said, gesturing him to leave his meal. 'You go and see to yer ma. A-snifflin' and a-snufflin' up there, her'll be. Well? Go on. Start as you mean to go on – away with yer!'

Neither 'a-snifflin' nor 'a-snuffling', his mother was where he had expected her to be. She could just as well have been a statue, so much so that he stood with her and adopted the same pose – but there was no response. Nothing …. until she unexpectedly handed him control of the curtain.

Given prime position, he concentrated on the gap created by the Community Hall roof on the one side and the side wall of number nine on the other.

The upstairs of what already felt like alien territory was for the most part visible. But not its downstairs, and especially not that part of the wall used by his father to park his bicycle.

His mother spoke. 'I'll just be glad when it's all over,' she said, toying with her wedding ring. 'I will. I'll be glad,' she repeated, and let out a self-deprecating laugh. 'I left him a note.'

'Note …?' he heard himself say.

'Well I had to, didn't I? If only to let him know there was a dinner left over from yesterday in the oven – you know what he's like. Billy? W-w-where are you going?'

'Where's the key? I want the key. Please, Mum. Or I'll 'ave t' break a winder or summat.'

'You'll do no such thing!' his mother said. 'You leave that note where it is! Your father has a right to know where we are. Especially you, his son.'

'Mum! It 'ent nothin' t' do with that. It's me own note – the ten bob Mr Barnes give me for me birthday. An'-an'- an' Mr Jock. It were too quiet and spooky last night, an' I couldn't get t' sleep. For ages, I couldn't – honest!'

His mother composed herself and said, calmly, 'Your birthday money from Mr Barnes. And your clock. Right. I'll lend you my key. But on one condition. Promise me you won't go in if there's any sign your father's there. It wouldn't be safe, Billy. It just wouldn't.'

'Yeah – I promise! But I ent daft. I'll see if he's in the pub first, wunt I?'

His mother sighed and gave him a long, drawn-out nod. 'Yes, well. You make sure you do. And don't hang about. You get what you want and come straight out again.'

'You bet I will. Thanks, Mum!' he said, and, as the man of the house, gave her a peck on the cheek.

CHAPTER SEVENTEEN

There was no need to go any further than the entrance lobby. The bursts of laughter, the chink of glasses, the goading – it all came from The Lounge Bar – voices egging on the man at the centre of it all: his father, oblivious to the fact he was being encouraged to make a fool of himself.

'Well good on yer, Charlie. What a man!'

'Yesh,' his father managed to slur out – and belched. 'Oomph, shcuse me. Yesh, it were me ... a man.'

Plied with alcohol and answering seemingly innocent questions, his father ploughed on, applying admirable concentration and ponderous forethought to every word he uttered. He was, it had to be admitted, in his element, not only fuelling Mrs Hicks' shriek of a laugh, but also spinning a yarn that apparently even he had come to believe.

'Never mind, Charlie,' came the voice of Cyril Cooper. 'We get it – don't we, Hilda? Spread yer legs or "gesh" out, you said. But, when her obliged you wuzn't up to it – so her went!'

The laughter followed him out the door, as did the likelihood of his father being thrown out by Reggie

Loach and dumped on the doorstep by his giggling mates.

Me money, me flippin' money. The fear of losing it drove him on to the telephone box, across the road and over the front hedge, his mother's house key gripped at the ready.

The silent coolness of the house came as relief, a place of calm in which to regain his breath and gather his wits about him.

Pressed for time, he took the stairs three at a time and pushed open his bedroom door. Going down on all fours, he searched the floor. His heart raced. His stomach tightened. Then, there it was, wedged between the next two floorboards, his beautiful, beautiful, ten-shilling note.

Holding it up to the light, glorying in the intricacy of its artwork, he paused, ears pricked. But it was nothing, only the tick, tick, tick and familiar face of Mr Jock.

'Straight in, straight out,' he told Tortoise and Hare, took the tail of his shirt to the clock's covering glass – and froze.

At the foot of the stairs, pointing an unsteady finger, swayed the smirking figure of his father. 'No par-par - ies,' the drunken old sod said, and frowned. Clinging to the newel post, he tried again. 'Parshies,' he said, and belched. It proved his undoing. As though having had a knife plunged into his back, his eyes bulged, he looked uncomprehendingly up at him, giggled, and slumped forward, face down in his own spew.

'Daddy ...?'

His bedroom window sprang to mind, the drop calculated, the waiting rubble-strewn ground brought into focus. There was only one other way. Without thinking any more about it, he unhooked his snake belt and pushed Mr Jock into his trousers. With both hands free, the banisters and drop to the hall floor proved easy. The front door stood open, as did the front gate. He closed it behind him and sauntered away, a boy going nowhere in particular and with no obvious purpose in mind.

Folded in half, his ten-shilling note fitted into a discarded cigarette packet. Working quickly, he propped Mr Jock against a tuft of grass, lay flat and wriggled his way under the Community Hall.

A broken piece of roofing tile came readily to hand, a tool for scraping away a mixture of rubble, soil and what felt like damp coal slack. Within seconds, his hole was deep enough, even with the cigarette packet stood on end. Less like a grave that way, he thought, and marked the spot with a lump of concrete.

Sunlight blasted his eyes. Shielding them, he rolled into a sitting position. Just in time, because from out of the glare, linked at the elbow like lovers, emerged Trisha Collins and, not Jenny as one might have expected, but Sally Hicks.

'Look, Trish! A mole!'

'Mm, so I see. A smudgy-faced mole, by the look of it. Billy! Your mum'll go berserk. Look at you – it's all down your shirt!'

He shrugged and treated the pair to a sniff. 'So? Buy another, I can. W-when I wants to, that is.'

Trish gave a knowing nod. 'I see. Got plans, have we?'

'No!'

'Ah, well. We have,' Sally announced. 'Clem said we could help stack the bales this year. And don't say we're not strong enough – because we are!'

To prove the point, she took a deep breath and bent her elbow raising a lump no one could argue was anything other than a knot of muscle.

Laughing, the two squirmed together, cheeks flushed and shiny-eyed. The stuff of Dawn Adams and Carol Robinson, it struck him. a fact that the two appeared to recognise, and correct.

'Jenny en't gonna like it,' he said, pointing to each of them in turn. 'You an' 'er.'

They confronted him, suddenly less dependent on one another.

'What's that to you – mole? Sally retorted.

'No, Sal. Be fair.' Trish said. 'He's no mole. Not really. And he's right. Jenny probably won't like me having another friend. So, Billy, if you see her, tell her she's welcome to join us. I mean, we're not stopping her, are we, Sal?'

'Us? No, Trisha's right. Instead of just hanging round the Duggans' door, try knocking it for a change. That's if you got the guts.'

'Course he has,' Trish said. 'Haven't you, Billy? And it's just what Jenny needs. Someone to look after her. Someone big and strong.'

'Yeah,' Sally added. 'And handy with a chopper.'

Aiming for his best sneer ever, he pointed to the obvious difference between the two girls, showing crisp and pink under Sally's blouse. 'Don't know what you're wearin' one of them for.'

For a moment, Sally appeared almost likable, an embarrassed girl, round-shouldered and hollow-chested. But then, re-igniting the spark that was the real Sally Hicks, she filled out and grew. 'No – don't suppose you do. Seeing as your old lady en't got none. A right pancake chest she is!'

'And everybody sez yours is a bike! W-with wheels from out the ditch!' he said, his clever added words landing as good as any punch.

Sally advanced on him, arm raised, fingers closed in what he took to be a girl's idea of a fist.

With a whoop, he skipped out of arm's reach. 'All purple an' pink – that's all she is. 'Orrible, it is!' he said, the image of lipstick and lashes peering in at him from the Lounge Bar of the Rose & Crown.

111

Sally's own momentum as much as anything sent her tumbling up and over his thigh, a mere featherweight, nothing but a sack of straw.

However, unlike any of the gang, when he threw her, she neither rolled nor sprang back to her feet. She stayed put, as splay-legged as his drunken father and showing more of herself than Miss Wheatcroft would ever have allowed, even during games.

'Winded,' he said. 'That's all she is. Winded.'

Ignored, he stood as a bystander, the incessant tick-tock, ticking of Mr Jock marking the passage of time. It grew louder.

At last, Sally spread her fingers and tested the ground on either side of her. Still testing, she nodded in response to something muttered to her at close quarters and, with Trisha's help, struggled to her feet.

Away they went, back the way they had presumably come. But before passing out of sight around the corner of the Community Hall, they paused, and looked back. The nice guy, and the not-so-tough guy. Only, in this case, they were both girls, a double-act that should have known better than to mess with a boy.

'And she can stay away from my dad! D' yer hear, Hicks? Buy her own drinks, she can!'

Sally paused with a handkerchief poised ready for use. No doubt prompted by some comment from

Trish, she attempted a laugh. It proved short-lived, the pretence ruined by a tell-tale shiver.

'Why?' it seemed to say.

'Why?'

Minute by minute, Hare closed the gap on Tortoise. Tick, tick, tick, went their little legs. Tick, tick, tick. Tortoise focused on the way ahead: Hare with his brows arched and tombstone teeth bared, thinking himself untouchable behind that covering layer of glass.

Tick, tick, tick, tick...

CHAPTER EIGHTEEN

Mr Barnes vented his anger on his fire, jabbing and ranting in equal measure.

'… what with sputniks and rockets punchin' holes in the sky. And now this! Enjoyed my England, I 'as, mister. But something tells me you'll not enjoy yours. Fisticuffin' with girls. Never heard the like, I bain't. Never!'

Having exhausted himself, the old fool abandoned his poker and turned on him, the glare of two eyes concentrated in one. 'Suppin' with the Devil, that's what you be doin'. And that's where you'll end up if you don't mend your ways. The Devil's parlour, mister – his parlour!'

His rant finally over, Mr Barnes took up his walking stick and made his way to his sideboard. From it, he lifted out a pudding bowl, straightened with obvious difficulty and made his way back to the hearth.

For a second time that day, the instant the lid was lifted from the pot the aroma of hot stew wafted into the room. Muttering and grumbling, the old man ladled out two helpings, filling the bowl with slices of carrot, potatoes the size of eggs and chunks of meat soaked in onion-rich gravy … but no dumpling. 'Eat.

Go on. You've already thanked the Lord. Now get on with it.'

A spoon landed on the table and slid towards him. He clamped his hand over it. He had a spoon. A bowl of stew sat begging to be stirred and eaten. Yet there was something in Mr Barnes' manner that held him back – and more, much more, brought into focus by the sound of a poker being skewered deep into the heart of hot slack.

'It were her who attacked me! It were an accident, Mr Barnes. An accident!'

In place of fork prongs came a poker, the pointed end, levelled at his head. 'Eat, I said. Your ma wants you upstairs afore her gets back. Man o' the house. That's what I told yer. So, start actin' like one. Up t' me neck in muck and bullets for the likes of you, mister. Three years of it. Nothin' but muck and bullets! So, away with yer – go on! Finish that. Then to yer room!'

A picture rail encircled his bedroom, linking the door frame to the chimney breast, the chimney breast to the window and, from there, back to the door frame. It also served to divide the wall into two sections, an upper and a lower, separating distemper from something that came across as a solid colour. However, on edging the sampler aside, it pointed to the fact that it was a dense pattern of millions upon millions of pale green flower heads.

After a more detailed inspection, variations in the degree of fading could be detected, revealing barely discernible furniture shapes.

Faded, faded, faded – the whole lot faded except for that one tea-tray sized patch protected by Ethel's sampler.

"Thou Lord Seest Me" read the text; similar, it struck him, to that sometimes read out on Friday mornings by Miss Wheatcroft or Old Chatters, who was better at it than Miss Wheatcroft. Unlike her, he never shirked or gave the impression there was anything wrong when having to read out a naughty word, such as "pisseth".

Mimicking the Vicar, he mechanically opened and closed his jaws while forming words towards the back of his mouth. 'Thou Lord seest me. Thou Lord seest –'

His heart thumped. Thinking the moment had come, he moved to his bed and sat hands in lap. Yet still he had to wait, listening to the sound of voices and movement from below. A good sign, perhaps, his mother not coming to him straight away. But, then again, perhaps not. Once more, he eyed the sampler, slightly askew and in need of correction.

His mother closed his door behind her and leaned against it like a child with its back to the school railings. 'Key,' she said, and held out an open palm.

His mouth dried. Images flashed across his mind: his prostrate father, the drop from the banisters, the front door, hearing once more its closing click. The key, he could not recall – but there it was, tucked deep into his pocket.

With it safely tucked in his mother's hand, her attitude changed, though not necessarily for the better. Letting out a shriek, she grabbed the front of his shirt and pulled it from his trousers. 'What's this! And on your school shirt. I'll never get this out. It's tar! And where am I going to get…? I can't afford...'

Shaking, and evidently on the verge of a breakdown, she swung her hand round, key, fob and all, and connected with his cheek and ear. 'Oh … oh,' she said, and sucked on her knuckles.

Still sucking, she sought refuge at the window, her breathing irregular, until clamped down on, and held. Held and held, until out it came, the release fuelling the smack of her palm on the window frame. 'Can you imagine it? Can you! What it took to go kowtowing to that Hicks creature? Her, of all people! And I warned you. You lay so much as a finger on any of them,' she said, positioning one of her own to the tip of his nose. 'One!'

He ran the back of his hand across his nostrils as though to brush away pain or, even better, blood.

But she would have none of it, being too busy bemoaning her lot to the walls, the ceiling, or some unknown creature living in her head. And on their first day, she went on. On what was supposed to be a fresh start. 'Well! Some start, I must say. I mean! What must Mr Barnes be thinking? Tell me. Whatever must he think?'

She fell silent, blessedly silent; Sally's pancake chest, decked out in a frock that offered no cleavage or motherly flesh, just the outline of bones.

'I hate yer! Hate yer. Hate yer. Hate yer!'

Slowly, she brought her face into line with his. 'No doubt you do. But if we're not careful... If I don't get some stability into our lives... Then it will be PC Timms we'll be dealing with, or worse. There's people who could take you from me. Is that what you want? To be taken away and put in a home for naughty boys?'

'Yes!'

'Well, that's all right then. Because you're certainly going about it the right way. It's a small village, Billy. Things you do now can stay with you all your life. I should think about that, if I were you. In fact, I'd think about it very, very hard.'

CHAPTER NINETEEN

He woke, roused by something warm and pleasurable – until reality struck. Panicking, he leapt out of bed – but too late. 'No...' he pleaded and released a long hapless groan. There seemed no end to it and nowhere to direct it other than onto his mat.

Like before, his window refused to open, its frame twisting when thumped. Fearing he might crack a pane, he tried again. One solid thump on the sticking point and it eased a little. Thumped again on the same spot and it swung open, juddering at the manner of its release.

Still dark. Hours yet. Strip off me sheets and —

The room came alive, flooded by artificial light. 'Billy? What on earth are you –?'

His mother took the sheets from him and gathered them into a ball.

'Mum, I don't feel –'

'In the morning,'

'But...'

'No buts. The morning. Or we'll wake Mr Barnes,' she said, and paused, as though listening for the old man. Evidently having heard nothing, she made ready to go, leaving him smelly and with nothing but a rubber sheet covering his mattress.

'It weren't my fault – it weren't!' he said. 'There en't no bathroom. An' you said –'

'A bucket – yes. I'm sorry. Tomorrow – I promise. I'll see to everything then. But now, I need my sleep. Just take everything off and make do for tonight. Here!' she said, tucking his spoilt sheets under her armpit and, before he could stop her, reached with her free hand for his blanket.

'I'll get it!' he said.

But she had already lifted it from his box. Lifted it – and froze. 'How … how did that happen?'

Keeping hold of both blanket and sheets, she bent and struggled for a moment to get a proper hold on what he knew only too well would be Mr Jock.

'Did Sally do this?' she said, straightening. 'Is this what the fight was about? Tell me, Billy. I need to know.'

The splintered glass front of Mr Jock stared back at him, as did Hare, brows arched as if to say, 'Come on, then. Tell her what you did'.

'Was it, Billy? Because, if it was, then –'

'No!' he said and snatched at the only plausible answer he thought he could get away with. 'No, it weren't Sally. He fell out me winder. Down onto the rubble pile.'

Silence.

'It did! You never believe me, yer don't! About nothin'!'

From below, the sound of ashes being cleared from the grate resonated in the chimney-breast.

His mother cursed under her breath and sighed. 'I might have known.'

She would go downstairs and that would be that, he thought. But she stayed put, mesmerised it seemed by the scraping of the old man's hand shovel.

The spell broke and it became clear that her mind had been elsewhere. 'Your father. You've seen him, haven't you? And don't lie. I can always tell.'

He hung his head. 'Yeah, well. Sort of.'

'And my note? Did you see that? I mean. Had it been opened? And what do you mean, "Sort of"?'

'He was asleep.'

His mother gave a knowing nod and drew breath, words at the ready. But whatever had prompted them died. 'Asleep,' she settled for. 'Yes, well, we all know what that means. Too "asleep" to have read letters painted a foot high on the road, let alone a hand-written note.'

Still clutching his sheets, she dropped his blanket onto his bed, and sat on it. 'Well,' she said. 'Let's hope for your sake he's "asleep" the next time you see him. Because if Hilda Hicks has her way, and that daughter of hers has cracked a rib… Then as sure as eggs is eggs we all know who she'll get to do her dirty work for her — don't we now?'

121

CHAPTER TWENTY

In an atmosphere of frosty silence, his mother placed his breakfast before him. Miss Wheatcroft's face materialised on the surface of the porridge, a horror to be exterminated by a vigorous stirring. Nothing said, either during or after the obliteration. The tea was poured. The tea was drunk.

Mr Barnes was the first to finish. Having blown on his tea prior to every sip and, before that, done the same to every spoonful of porridge, he sat back and rubbed his stomach; but even though he had clearly enjoyed his breakfast, he still had it in him to grumble. 'A whole bottle of turps, mister. It weren't tar. It were oil. Good for nothin', that shirt. A whole bottle! And it'll be a tin of boot polish next, I shouldn't wonder.'

His mother reached across the table and patted the old grouse's hand. 'Go on, you old softy.' she said. 'Stop frightening the child and tell him about the cards. Cabbage, or whatever the game's called. While I go … you know.'

'It's called Cribbage,' Mr Barnes said. 'Cribbage!'

'Yes. Of course. Crib. Same thing, I suppose. It's what Charlie … Anyway, I'll try not to be too long. Just go and tidy myself up a bit. Then I'll leave you to it.'

She hesitated, as though intent on clearing the table, but Mr Barnes waved her aside, making her blush with the strength of his one-eyed glare. There seemed no trace of malice in it, however. On the contrary, the instant his mother had closed the scullery door behind her, the old rogue's look softened, aided in no small part by a mischievous rubbing together of his palms. 'Cards!' he said, pointing to the top right-hand drawer of his sideboard.

He spied the pack of playing cards attached by a rubber band to a narrow board drilled with four rows of holes and placed them in front of Mr Barnes. In a matter of seconds, the cards were out their packet and, with the aid of a licked thumb, being dealt face down on the table and counted. 'Now! Matches, lad. Four, mind. You'll find 'em on the settle,' came the order as the breakfast dishes and jug of what was left of the milk was pushed towards him.

As instructed, he placed the dirty crocks and cutlery in the trough that served as a sink and stood the jug of milk in a bucket of water housed under what he assumed was the settle. On the top of it, staring him in the face, was a box of Swan Vesta.

'What you doin' out there? Whittling down trees? On the settle, I said. On the settle, lad!'

'I'm comin'! Wun't be a minute!'

Movement sounded overhead. 'What's with all the shouting?' his mother said, appearing on the last tread. 'I could hear the two of you from upstairs.'

He held up his four matches. 'Couldn't find the box. That were all.'

'Mm – well – just as long as that's all it was. I need you to be good for Mr Barnes while I pop out. You will won't you, Billy? For Mummy?' she said, her hair brushed, the blues and mauves of her Sunday frock at odds with the drabness of the scullery.

And it was not only her hair that had been brushed. It was also her shoes. They matched the yard … blue-black bricks, blue-black shoes, both noticeably scuffed and worn.

Away she went, picking her way towards the gap that separated the coal hole from the only serviceable toilet, one of the original block of three, all housing creepy-crawlies and laced with rat poison.

'Cut!'

He did as Mr Barnes ordered, the cards having come from the lower portion of the pack being used to deal out what the old man called dummy hands. Many dummy hands, as it turned out. 'Numbers, lad! As you can see. All to do with numbers and runs and pairs.'

'And threes! An'-an' – makin' fifteen when you're puttin' them down.'

'You've got it. And fours. Any set of four up to and including four sevens – which don't mean the next player can't top that with a three and make … what?'

'Thirty-one! The top number.'

'That's right – good! Now. Hows about a proper game? You agree to keep score and I'll let you have first box.'

'Box?'

For the first time since starting to teach him, Mr Barnes held his breath in obvious irritation. 'The two cards we both chucks in,' he said, only to immediately soften. 'Don't worry, there be a lot to take in. Just concentrate on the numbers and when it's your box, you can drop in two cards that adds up to fifteen, like a six and a nine or an eight and a seven. Numbers, see. It's all to do with numbers.'

But there was more to it than that, he soon discovered. Much, much more …

Later that morning, the letterbox gave out a squeak and a solitary letter dropped onto the floor. Mr Barnes ignored it, the current game clearly of more importance to him. A game, that for the first time that morning, he was in danger of losing.

His mother came in the same way that she had left, via the back door. 'Only me!' she called, and, looking uncommonly pleased with herself, eventually came through to them.

'Mum – I won a game! I did, didn't I, Barney?'

Mr Barnes gave his mother the solemnest of nods. 'Fair and square, Mo. Fair and square.'

'Mmm,' his mother said. 'Very good. But what's with the "Barney"? Mr Barnes, to you, if you don't mind.'

'No,' he said. 'No, Mr Barnes said I could call him Barney ages and ages ago – you did, didn't you, Mr Barnes. Only, sometimes, I forget.'

'That's right,' Mr Barnes said. 'Now, watch him play, Mo. See how much he's learned.'

To his dismay, his mother stood behind him, making unhelpful comments and pointing. Even more infuriating, she messed with his hair.

'Don't!' he said and threw down his cards to sit with folded arms.

'Oh dear,' Mr Barnes said, placing his own hand down. 'Perhaps we've gone on a mite too long.'

'It en't that – it's her!' he said – and demanded to know where she had been. 'Bin gone ages, you 'ave – ages and ages!'

She picked up the letter that had dropped from the letterbox earlier and handed it to him in stony silence.

Sat on the throne, in the privacy and stillness of the toilet, he chose his moment. There it was, as he had first glimpsed it; his name, written in uneven lettering across the centre of the envelope. Carefully, avoiding any tearing, he eased open its flap.

Inside the envelope, lay his first ever letter. Written on a page torn from an exercise book and in the same exaggerated lettering used to spell out his name, was a straightforward message.

> Abbots Lovell is boring
> COme back Out sOon.
> X
>
> D

D; its significance struck home. D – exactly as it had been stitched into his birthday handkerchiefs. He had insisted that it stood for Darling. And Duggan. Brill, he thought. Nobody but me'll ever guess who it's from. I just need a hiding place. Somewhere no-one will ever think of looking.

No-one.

His mother was waiting for him in the scullery. 'Now wash your hands,' she said, handing him a fresh bar of soap, one of the posh sort, oval and smelly.

Of more interest, coming from the settle, was the competing smells of pickled onions and cheese.

She popped an onion into her mouth and spoke while crunching. 'From Tim, was it?'

'What?'

'Your letter!'

'Oh – dunno. It didn't say. Probably Ozzie muckin' about.'

'Ah well, never mind,' she said. 'Get your teeth into this. A drink. Then to my room. You can wait for me there.'

He groaned. 'Do I 'ave to?'

His mother replied with the most peculiar of slow nods. 'Mm,' she said. 'Afraid so.'

CHAPTER TWENTY-ONE

It was like stepping into a different world, a castle, or a place where a Pope would live. For now, though, it was King William's palace. King William, known to his servants, who all loved him, as Billy Windmill.

But the carpet, there was something about the carpet. Underfoot it felt the same as the ones in Tim's house. But there was a difference. There were no wooden or linoleum surrounds. It covered the whole floor, from skirting board to skirting board, cut to size from an even larger carpet, the pattern having been interrupted on reaching the outside wall.

Like it, he thought, clever – and eyed the furniture, all matching and as shiny and hard as a conker: single bed, dressing table and padded stool, wardrobe, and a chest of drawers with not two, but three drawers.

His mother entered the room like a teacher, a bundle of books and papers clutched to her side. 'Right!' she said, dumping the pile down on the chest of drawers.

'You bin t' see Miss Wheatcroft?' he said, getting in before she could go any further. 'You 'ave, ent yer? You bin an' sin 'er!'

She placed a hand on each of his shoulders and brought her face in close to his. 'The simple truth, Billy, is no. I've not "bin" nor "sin" anything,' she said, and sat down onto the dressing table stool. 'Do you know who you sound like – do you! I mean, it doesn't take much working out – does it now?' Especially after this morning's little episode. Demanding to know where I've been, like that. Well? Want to grow up a bully and a wife beater, do we? Sally a foretaste of what's to come, is she?'

'It weren't like that. You ask Trish! An'-an' – anyway, you can't talk. You hit me, didn't yer?'

'Yes,' his mother said, 'I did. And I shouldn't have, I'm sorry. But it's now or never. Billy. You either knuckle down and mend your ways — let me and Mr Barnes' help you before it's too late – or you go.'

'Go? Go where?'

His mother straightened, raised her brows, and gave him one of her unsettling weak smiles. 'That's for me to know and you to worry about. And, thinking about it,' she added, 'I might well have a word with Trish. Unless you've had second thoughts on that one, of course. After all, I wouldn't have thought that she, of all girls, owed you any favours.'

He restricted himself to a twitch of his shoulders and cast an evil eye over the pile of what was undoubtedly school work.

'I've had it some time,' she said, simply. 'From when I collected your end of year report. To be honest, I'd intended making a start on it straight away. But – and it's a big "but" – you may recall that neither of us were in any frame of mind to tackle it. Now, though, now, things are different,' she said, and took both his hands into hers. 'What did I tell you when we first came here? What did mummy say? You were to think of this as a ...?'

'Holiday.'

'Yes. Good. A holiday. But that wasn't all, was it? There was something else. Something beginning with the letter F, she said, and waited, mouth open, putting pressure on him, making it hard for him to think.

'I dunno!'

'Never mind,' she said, showing no sign of disapproval or annoyance. 'Don't worry. A holiday, yes. And that's the important one. If anyone should ask, you don't say anything else. Just that. We're here for a holiday. But, also, a fresh – any nearer now?'

'Start,' he said. 'A fresh start.'

'That's right. A fresh start like I promised. And, well, let's just say, what with one thing and another, the future looks bright. Just imagine! No more living off bread and scrape. And no more chicken fit for a cat. Self-respect!' she said, giving his hands a sharp tug. 'That's what it means. And I'm prepared to go the whole hog to keep it. A fresh start.

131

It wasn't easy believe you me, leaving the family home and a husband – far from easy. It took guts, Billy – guts! And now, it's your turn. You're a bright boy. If only you'd think before you act and cut out the silliness, then – well! It's up to you.'

'I en't goin' t' no Grammar, if that's what you think.'

His mother took a deep breath – and sighed. 'Well, there's progress. You don't like fresh vegetables and you "en't goin' to no Grammar School". Well, well, well …'

In the left-hand corner of a new exercise book, using ink and a pen fitted with a new nib, he printed his name, the day, the month and lastly, the year. A year, his mother pointed out, that would read the same if turned upside-down.

'Why you're not allowed to use a Biro is beyond me,' she added, adjusting the position of the ink bottle. 'Blotting paper. Perhaps I should have asked for that as well – and don't press so hard!'

His first lesson was to list in alphabetical order a surname of anyone who either attended his school or lived in the village.

'For a start,' his mother said. 'I can think of an A straight away. You know, that pretty girl who plays with Tim's sister. And B shouldn't give you any trouble. As for C, well, there's so many to choose from we could invent a whole game just based on them.'

'And Duggan for the D!' he said.

'That's it. You've got it. According to Miss Wheatcroft, it's the middle of the alphabet where you go astray. Think 'lemon'. 'LMN', followed by 'Our pretty Queen' – and then you won't get confused.'

It took the best part of the afternoon. Only the letters 'U' and 'X' were left blank, twenty-four names, starting with Adams and ending with Yeomans and Zollman.

Writing exercises were like puzzles, he decided, almost fun. Until, that was, his mother presented him with a list.

'My ten commandments,' she said, placing the list on the dressing table, together with a pile of scrap paper. 'A behavioural guide, is what Miss Wheatcroft called it, not wanting you to think of it as a punishment. Neither of us wanted you to think that. But I do want two copies, please. In your best handwriting every day until … let me think. Until you can recite them off by heart.'

'That's not fair!'

'Fair?'

'No. You said it weren't a punishment. And it is!'

His mother stared like an idiot, mouth open and wide-eyed. 'And why would I want to do that?' she said. 'I mean. What possible reason would

Mummy have for handing out a punishment? Tell me. I'd like to know. Although, thinking about it, it's true. It wasn't "fair", was it? Me leaving you to play cards with Mr Barnes while I went to see, no, not Miss Wheatcroft. How could I, even if I'd wanted to? The school's shut ... or had you forgot? No,' she repeated, hardening her tone. 'For your information, Mr Clever-clogs, I went to see Miss Pringle. She's offered me more hours in the shop. And no one, but no one, can stop me.'

She rose and clearly having come to a decision, returned to her list; her precious behaviour list that she lifted from the dressing table and, by opening her fingers, let zig-zag down into his chest.

'There, I've done my bit. Now it's up to you,' she said, brushing her palms together as though clearing them of garden dirt, and left the room.

CHAPTER TWENTY-TWO

Sadly, when his knock was answered it was not by Jenny. On the other hand, nor was it Mrs Duggan standing in the doorway, but Mr Duggan.

As willowy as his wife was solid, the man used his height to play his usual trick of feigning ignorance of anyone's presence. Finally, after having scanned the village from top to bottom, he glanced down. 'Is that a bucket and sponge I see before me? And on a Sunday!'

'All I need is water, Mr Duggan. A shilling wash only. And sixpence extra for a polish – I'd do a brill job!'

Mr Duggan withdrew his finger from the pages of his newspaper and scratched his chin. 'Mm, well, I don't know about that. Apart from me already having taken a bath, we haven't exactly, what we might say, managed to endear ourselves to too many folks of late – have we, sunshine? My cuddly queen for one,' he pointed out, gently closing his door behind him. 'As for our Jenny. Well, what with one thing and another, my little princess seems scared to show her face. I mean! Anyone would think it were her who'd clobbered the poor rabbit. But, well – ha! We all know that's not the case – don't we, lad?'

With a cock of the head and decisive nod the man effectively answered his own question. Having earned for himself an air of self-justification, he inserted his key in his door.

'Please, Mr Duggan. Mum sez I've got to help people. And talk better – an' all sorts. An' I need to earn money for a new shirt. For school, Mr Duggan.'

His chance of success appeared to rest on that key, positioned in the lock, but, as yet, unturned. 'An' – an' I've got a message for Jenny, Mr Duggan! She can help stack the bales this year. We all can. Trish said.'

'Hmph!' Mr Duggan said, and turned his key. 'Don't you go mentioning that name round here, niece or no niece. Dumping my little angel for that Hicks horror. Our Mary must be mad letting – well! Can you make any sense of it?' he continued, appearing at a loss to know what to do with his newspaper, leave it tucked under his arm or hold it as one might a relay baton.

Clearly caught in two minds, the man finally stopped prancing and caught him completely off guard. 'Stay!' he said, mistaking him for a dog. 'Two minutes!'

Mr Duggan emerged from his side passage carrying a bucket full of soapy water. In it, bobbed a sponge similar in colour to his front door and car. 'Here.

Dump yours over there,' he said. 'Health hazard, that. What you been doing? Peeing in it?'

As instructed by Mr Duggan, he washed the front of Betsy first, from windscreen to bumper avoiding, again as instructed, rubbing too hard on the brown bits.

'Sprayed her myself!' Mr Dugan said, puffing out his chest. 'Same paint as used at work on the diggers.'

Later, with the bonnet rested on its bent support arm and a rag and tin of brake fluid perched ready for use, Mr Duggan sat himself down on his doorstep with his newspaper.

However, even when accompanied by a rustle and turn of a page, he would often peer in his direction, and probe. 'Off school a fair bit last term, I understand. Expelled, were we?'

On this occasion, his ruined shirt came to his rescue.

'Ah, yes,' Mr Duggan said. 'Of course. The shirt.'

'It's why I'm doin' jobs, Mr Duggan. To help pay for another, remember. Bin hackin' down weeds all week for Mr Barnes, I 'ave. And waterin'. Man of the house, see. Got responsibilities.'

Clearly impressed, Mr Duggan made a face. 'Man of the house, eh? Mmm, I suppose you are after what I've been hearing. Pay you the going rate, does he? The old skinflint?'

Having posed his question, Mr Duggan sank his head back behind the wide-open pages of his newspaper. There was no sense of any reading being done, however, the air surrounding him being detectably charged, held as one might a breath. "I'm waiting", it seemed to be saying.

I'm waiting …

'It's only a holiday, Mr Duggan! Mum sez we're only there for a holiday. An' I works for nothin', I does. That, an' loads of homework.'

'Mm, I see,' Mr Duggan said, mumbling into a column of print. 'And your father?' he added, bringing his face up from behind his screen. 'What about him? Be joining you in Abbots Lovell-on-Duckpond at some point, will he?'

Water trickled from a corner of his sponge and down onto his shoes, then crept away, threading its way in a few meandering rivulets towards a pitted depression in the road.

'I en't sin 'im,' he said, fixing on a pool of soap suds. 'Not since last Sunday, anyway.'

Mr Duggan sat clicking his tongue. 'No,' he said, at length. 'No, I don't suppose you have. Too busy getting his feet – never mind. Come on. We've got work to do. Can't do it without your help, Captain!'

A man of action suddenly, his employer launched himself up from his doorstep and, rag in hand, took hold of his tin of brake fluid.

Good intentions were not enough, however. Before he had barely started, he brought his head back out from under Betsy's bonnet, and gave him what he said was a tip. 'Don't stand between the dog and the lamppost, lad. Your mum and dad. Just leave them to it. Let them sort it out.'

He replied with a nod, anything further nullified by a recognisable group of good-humoured Churchgoers.

'You've missed a bit,' Tim said, pointing.

'Underneath the back tyre!' Kenny added, and they passed on by.

Mr Duggan watched them go, sank his head back under Betsy's bonnet, and tinkered.

Finally, at long last, with everything presumably set and ready, the real business began. 'Okay!' Mr Duggan shouted. 'Slowly, mind. Not too fast. And down!'

In between times, during the many lulls, he began checking on the car's other features and controls. The steering wheel proved cumbersome, far too sloppy and large, in his opinion. As for the handbrake, when worked at speed it made a satisfying sound, like that of a zip being closed. Worked slowly, tooth by tooth, the clicks could be counted, nine offering little or no resistance. The tenth, equivalent to his age and therefore of special interest, proved slightly more difficult … but only slightly. He pulled out the choke, an imagined fault demanding a more detailed inspection.

Something induced him to look up. And there they were: the lip-sucking, tongue-in-cheek faces of Carol Robinson and Dawn Adams.

Dawn, prompted by a nudge, poked her head in through the open car door window. 'What you doing, Billy?'

He pushed the choke home and gave an appraising sniff. 'Air lock. Soon got it sorted.'

Slowly, but surely, Dawn digested the information and widened her eyes. 'Do you know about cars? Do you, Billy? Really, really?' she said – and spun on her heel. 'Does he, Mr Duggan? Does Billy know about cars?'

Mr Duggan straightened, oily rag in hand, and blew air from his cheeks. 'Well now, just about everything, I'd say. Just about everything, girls.'

Carol joined Dawn at the window and the two heads pressed forward, uncomfortably close.

'Betsy's an A30,' he informed them with great authority. 'Different from an A35 because the A35 has a larger back window.' This, he knew to be true and worked the gear stick, up, sideways and whichever way it would go, before letting it be with an affectionate pat. 'Yep! That seems okay.'

The two girls watched his every move: his adjustment of the rear- view mirror, his turning of the

140

knob on top of the dashboard. Left or right made no difference. No light came on either way.

'My dad's car's got proper blinkers.' Carol said.

'Yes,' Dawn said. 'Will yours, Billy, when you have a car? Can we have a go in it? Can we? Please, Billy – please! And will it be one like this?'

'Nah,' he said, returning to the gear stick. 'Nah, probably be a Triumph Herald. You know, the one where the bonnet opens the wrong way. Summat like that.'

The two girls faced one another, mouths and eyes rounded. And out came an elongated 'Ooooh'

Off they skipped, hands held and singing.

> *Park the Herald angels sing*
> *Glory be to Billy's new thing.*
> *Sounds like a scooter pippin' its hooter*
> *Following yonder car, ha-ha, ha-ha.'*

Mr Duggan closed Betsy's bonnet. Wiping each of his fingers individually on his rag, he came to him, replacing Dawn and Carol at the open window. 'Well, seems you've got a couple of admirers there, Captain.'

'Nah. Just kids, en't they?'

'Just kids, eh? Pound to a penny you won't be saying that by the time you're eighteen. So, in the meantime. Keep your head down. And that,' he said, tapping his oil-smudged nose, 'clean.'

'I am! I mean. Could've said I was havin' an E-Type, couldn't I? That's what I really want. But that'd bin breakin' mum's new rules. Boastin', probably. Or too much imagination. One of 'em, anyway.'

'An E-Type, eh? An E-Type! Well, let's call that ambition. And I can assure you, there's nothing wrong with that. We must all pursue our ambitions. Mine?' his new-found friend said, stroking Betsy as though she was a family pet. 'Mine is to keep this old girl on the road. Twice round the clock and prone to embarrassing bouts of flatulence, but she's never let me down. Not in all the time I've had her.'

'What, never?'

'No, not once. Not that that'll count for anything when it comes to this new-fangled test they're on about. Stands no chance, do you, old girl? Another year, and more likely as not it'll be a one-way ticket down to Scrappy Watton's. I dunno! Anything to put the working man down, that's all it is! Anything to put the likes of me down.'

Having said his piece, Mr Duggan slapped his hand to Betsy's roof and brightened. 'Out you come!' he said, holding Betsy's door open for him. 'A polish. Perhaps that'll put her to rights. Dodgy rod-brakes, oil leaks, and all!'

'Yeah!' he said, willing to believe in the magic of what his mother always referred to as elbow grease. 'A polish!'

142

CHAPTER TWENTY-THREE

The back door stood open, propped to stop it from closing by Mr Barnes' shoehorn. Prompted to look down at the sodden state of his shoes, he paused and listened. What reached his ears meant little, his mother exasperating Mr Barnes over some legal matter.

'But I tells you, Mo! How many more times? It be your house. Your ma and pa left it in your name. Yourn and nobody elses! Jimmy were against the marriage right from the start. So were yer ma. Her gentle soul wouldn't allow her to speak up but her knew all right – her knew!'

'But I'm married, Barney. To honour and obey, remember.'

'Ah! And to forsake all others!' came the retort, punctuated by the stamp of wood on stone.

And that was that, it seemed. But he was wrong, the silence unexpectedly broken by a snort. 'Vintage Charlie,' his mother said. 'Change the lock and keep the bitch out.'

'I can get in!' Billy yelled, bursting in on the pair. 'I know a way!'

Mr Barnes growled, turned his back on them and poked at his fire, thrusting at it as though sticking a pig.

Left to confront him on her own, his mother merely tightened her lips and gestured for him to take off his shoes. 'And your socks. You'll have to put your pumps on.'

'Me school pumps?'

She snatched his sock from him. 'You have a choice?' And away went his other sock.

'It en't my fault I en't got no wellies,' he said, his voice threatening to crack – and down onto the table went the money paid him by Mr Duggan.

Stamp, stamp, stamp, went his bare feet on the stairs, the louder and more painful the better. And up it came, all his pent-up rage and sense of injustice poured out in an involuntary roar.

Ignored, he slammed his bedroom door and perched straight-backed, Miss Wheatcroft style, on the edge of his bed.

Not noticed at first, no more than a step and arm stretch away, sat a pair of squat, spray-legged binoculars.

Obviously left there by his mother, when she came to him, which she would, she always did, she would be expecting to see him using them, all excited and grateful. Well, tough toffee. They would still be on the windowsill, untouched. That'd show 'er. It would. It'd show 'er.

He ran the hem of his T-shirt across his eyelids. The binoculars made no comment – they daren't – but it was clear what they thought. The whole rotten room thought it, including Ethel's sampler, its text making it so bloody obvious.

Even when lying on his bed, face to the wall, he could still see it in his mind's eye: the loops and swirls sneering at him – until cleared from his head with a two-fisted attack on his pillow.

'Come on sleepy-head. Wakey-wakey. It's your mummy.'

'Go away. I en't asleep. An' – an' stop callin' yerself mummy. It's how you talk to babies.'

'Is that so?' she said, gently pulling his thumb away from his chest.

'Geroff! Go away, I said. Go on!'

She did not go away, her continued presence in the room sensed rather than heard. Not until the silence was broken by the distinctive chink and clunk of coins being placed on the windowsill did he weaken. And there she was, caught in the act of taking up the binoculars. More to the point, when she shifted her position, there, back behind glass, were the figures of Hare and Tortoise.

'Mr Jock!'

'Yes,' his mother said, handing him the clock. 'And you can thank Mr Barnes for that. Not that you deserve it. One step forward and – oh, I don't know!

No doubt you meant well. But Mr Barnes isn't used to that sort of thing. You bursting in like that. But, well, not to worry, I suppose. At least Mr Duggan seemed impressed with you. Gave me the thumbs up he —

'When! When did he? I never saw yer!'

'Oh, don't worry,' his mother said, looking through the binoculars. 'I wasn't going to embarrass you in front of Carol and Dawn.'

'Humph! Them.'

'Yes … "them",' she said, busy focusing and refocusing. It was as though by constantly altering her stance and angle of view, she could by some miracle be able to see what lay behind the Perkins's buddleia.

Put together like pieces in a jigsaw, his mother's muttering and mumbling began to make sense. Like a detective, he looked for other clues, one immediately springing to mind. The binoculars – they were not angled in the direction of their old home as he had supposed, but more to the right, towards the gap between the Hicks's end terrace and the vicarage. And, as Granny Basset would have said, "the pigeon landed".

'Daddy wouldn't go the back way,' he said without thinking. He should have kept his mouth shut, his mother probably not realising he knew all about 'fancy pieces' and 'bits on the side'. But she seemed unconcerned. 'No, not his style,' she mumbled, more to herself than in answer to him – and

146

suddenly eyed him. 'Hang on! Has your father given you a key? Is that it?'

'No!'

'Then how can you get in? With a new lock fitted.'

'The bathroom winder after he's had a bath or bin to the loo!' he said, illustrating the latter with pinched nostrils.

'Yes, well, enough of that,' she said. 'Anyway, it's only a top window. A cat would have a job getting in through that.'

Breath held, he slapped his hands to his thighs and told her that he had already done it. 'When you was in hospical! Climbed onto the outhouse roof, I did. Then up the drainpipe, higher'n the winder. Put a leg in still holdin' onto the drainpipe. Then me other leg, an' slid in. Easy, it is – easy-peasy!'

His mother appeared stunned. 'I doubt that,' she said. 'In fact, I doubt it very much. And it's dangerous. One slip and you could have broken your neck, you silly boy!'

'Mum, Mum it's only like climbing a tree – 'onest!'

'No, Billy. It's nothing like climbing a tree. For a start, you'd have been half the size you are now. And that outhouse roof has been threatening to fall in on itself for years. So, no, Billy. No! No! No!'

CHAPTER TWENTY-FOUR

His mother placed a small plate in front of him.

'What – a sandwich?'

'That's right. A sandwich. So, get on with it. And don't ask questions.'

He lifted the top slice of bread and grimaced. 'Don't like lettuce.'

'Put it to one side, then.'

Like the grab on a crane, his fingers picked out the offending strips of green. Next, went three slices of tomato. Nothing was said, leaving him to chew until his jaws ached on extra thick home boiled ham and the dryness of yesterday's bread.

Given the choice of tea or milk, he chose milk. It came with biscuits, plain and boring, but biscuits all the same, just begging to be dunked. With one delicately poised between milk and mouth, he met his mother's look. Sat elbows on table cradling a cup in both hands, she reminded him of his father. But there would be no trick question or levelling of a dinner fork from her. Clearly, there was something on her mind: something pre-empted by the run of her tongue across her lip. Even so, still she said nothing … not until her cup was settled back on its saucer. Choosing her words carefully, she said, 'It was …

unfortunate. You having done me proud all week, helping Mr Barnes in the garden and Mr Duggan with his car, only to go and spoil it all by bursting in like you did. Just bad timing, I suppose. And Mummy's sorry. I handled the whole thing rather badly. I was, well, the thing is, Mr Barnes took it upon himself to have words with your father in the pub this morning. A right to-do, apparently, enjoyed by the likes of the Cooper brothers. I knew nothing about it, of course. But then, when I came in and said about the lock … oh, I don't know. Barney is so black and white about things. While I,' she said, giving her head a hapless shake. 'I'm ...' And she was gone.

The flickering flames of a fire, the blankness of a wall, the other side of some non-existent window, they all amounted to the same thing: a refuge, a way through to some other world. But, not this time, it seemed. The beam that ran the width of the cottage was evidently too dense and dark for her mind to penetrate.

Easily distracted, she looked towards Mr Barnes' prized possession, then away, not waiting for the long-case clock's impending three chimes.

'Look,' she said, not fully focused on him. 'I think it best if you made yourself scarce. No school work. No washing cars. Just fresh air and play. Out there, mind. On the playing field, where I can keep an eye on you – got it?'

He screwed up his face, feigning reluctance. But his mother was having none of it.

'Go on!' she said. 'All work and no play isn't good for a growing lad. But be careful.'

'Watch what you say. I hope you did with Mr Duggan. And, as for the Carols and Dawns of this world... Little girls, they might be, but they're not stupid. They soon pick up on things. Especially that Dawn.'

'Mum! I never said nothin' to any of 'em, I didn't. Only about me shirt an' bein' on holiday. An'- an' – an' Mr Duggan made a joke of it. Abbots Lovell-on-Duckpond, he said. Oh, and he sends his regards.'

'Regards, is it?' his mother said, adding a cynical laugh. 'Oh yes, they'll all be lining up to give me their regards. A sitting duck, that'll be me, stood behind that counter all morning. And on my first day. Gawd!'

'Ah! You swore. Rule number five,' he said, and in his best Miss Wheatcroft voice pointed out that one could not both sit and stand at the same time.

'Yes – very clever,' his mother said, gripped his shoulders and faced him in the direction of the scullery. 'Now, get your ball – and go!'

Despite his mother's rush to get rid of him, she blocked his way at the foot of the stairs. 'Look,' she said. 'Forget what I said about Mr Duggan. He's a nice man, is Donald. Very generous and – and kind.

Kinder than me, I'm sorry to say. Especially when it comes to the likes of Sally.'

'Sally? Ha! Mr Duggan called her the Hicks horror!'

'Yes, well. Mr Duggan might. But then, perhaps he has good reason to. But it can't be easy for Sally, having to cope like she has with a whole string of, well – "Uncles". Far from easy.'

'No … ,' he said, bringing to mind the scene in the Rose & Crown: the opening and closings of the connecting door, the laughter at the smashing of a glass, and his father, shiny-faced and tee-heeing with the purple-lipped Mrs Hicks.

"Goings on", Mr Barnes had called it, which, added to what he already knew on the subject, could mean only one thing. A Clem word he shied away from using in front of his mother. Instead, having considered the matter, with an adopted air of innocence, asked the obvious child-like question. 'Is me dad…? Mum!' he said, having to repeat his self when she faced the sink and failed to answer. 'Is he? Is he Sally's uncle now? And, well, if he is, he'll still be me dad, won't he?'

'Oh yes,' his mother said. 'Oh yes, you can put your two shillings and fourpence on it. Whether he's Sally's latest uncle, or whether he isn't, your father will always be your father.'

CHAPTER TWENTY-FIVE

Wearing his plimsolls, he took his ball out onto a deserted Community Field. Deserted, that was, except for the stirring strains of *Climb Up Sunshine Mountain* coming with angelic innocence from the Community Hall.

He tagged on, quietly following the words of the song until lustily picking up on its closing line, foot at the ready. Up his Frido swirled, the first ball in the world to punch a hole in the sky.

Impressive, he thought. Especially to anyone lucky enough to have witnessed it from inside the hall … or from number nine, from that window set near its apex. But the window appeared as it always did, as blind and expressionless as Mr Barnes' glass eye.

Cynthia Perkins and the Granger twins were the first to appear. Susan Chambers and Trisha Collins came out next, guiding out the younger ones. But there was no sign of Tim or Kenny, not for ages. Then, there they were, stood facing him, along with a key-fumbling Mrs Dodds. 'Ah! William! Just the very boy. I understand you intend joining us at some point. Yes?'

'Well. I er, only got this,' he said, pulling the front of his T-shirt away from his chest.

He would be barred for sure, he thought. Wrong. Baggy-necked and holey T-shirt or not, Mrs Dodds tidied his hair and viewed him as though he was the sweetest of boys.

'A healthy mind and clean hands. That's all the good Lord asks of us, William. So, no excuses. See you next week!'

Kenny took her place, swerving into position on a new bicycle fitted with drop handlebars and twin drink bottles. For passing the Eleven Plus, he explained, adding that Susan had been bought one, too. 'But not like this. Not a racer.'

Tim joined them, all Sunday scrubbed and polished as usual, the only boy who could roll on muddy ground without dirtying his knees. But then, boys who sang in church choirs as well as attend Sunday School were often like that.

'Pity you couldn't come in last day,' he said. 'Went up the bell tower, we did. Right brill, it was. Could see everything for miles and miles, couldn't we, Kenny?'

'True,' Kenny said. 'You were nowhere to be seen though, Hughesie. Not that I blame you after what Ozzie and Clem did. A right pair, they are. But, well, at least you seemed to be enjoying yourself this morning.'

'Yeah – and earned nearly half a crown! And if you'd 'ave 'gone up the tower this week you'd 'ave sin me workin' away in Barney's back garden. Done loads, I 'ave. You know, all the heavy stuff.'

'Well, well done you,' Kenny said, idly circling them on his new bicycle. 'Won't be a sec,' he added, giving one determined push on a pedal. And away he sped.

Tim retrieved the ball. 'That right, is it? What Doddy said. About Sunday School.'

He mentally revisited the brush of his Godmother's hand across his hairline and spat out his contempt. 'They must think I'm thick. It's not me who wants t' go t' flippin' Sunday School. It's me mum. It's her who set that up!'

'Yeah, well,' Tim said. 'It wouldn't hurt, though, would it? I mean, if nothing else, it's something to do. And we get prizes, remember. I bet you'd be good at that. Answering questions.'

'Prizes?'

'When you've answered twenty – and it doesn't matter how long it takes. It's not a competition. I chose a train spotting book last time. London Midland locos. I spot, while Mum shops. I've got quite a few already. You could come as well if you want. But only if,' he said, edging away, 'you turn up next Sunday!' And off he darted, avoiding Kenny's free-wheeling return with a neat body swerve.

Unfazed, Kenny stood on his pedals and drifted to a halt holding out a carrier bag. 'Here. Tim's having my old bike. So –.'

In the bag were two ironed and folded school shirts. 'Ah! Ta! B-b-but how much? I mean, well, they 'ave bin worn, en't they? It en't as if they'm new.'

'Mmm, let me think,' Kenny said, furrowing his brow. 'I know! The same as Tim paid for the bike. That'd be fair,' he said, and forming a nought with his finger and thumb idly circled once more, effectively closing the matter.

With the score standing at seven goals to four in Kenny's favour, Charles Hughes of Abbots Lovell and England fame, almost having brought off a miraculous save, retrieved the ball and placed it in readiness for a kick back into play.

He paused.

'Uh-ho!' Kenny said, mounting his racer. 'Sorry, folks. But I'm off.' And, for a second time within the hour, he pushed hard on a pedal. However, once having picked up a modicum of speed, he coasted, his departure a leisurely affair and in no way influenced by the appearance at the Quarry Lane gate of Ozzie and Clem.

Through the gate they trudged, Clem in his rolled-down Wellingtons, Ozzie drawing importantly on the stub-end of a cigarette.

'To me, Billy-boy!' Clem called, setting himself up to receive the ball. It failed to reach him. No matter, a click of the fingers and Ozzie was dispatched tail-wagging on his way.

Tim sighed. 'Whatever they say. Don't take the bait.'

The ball skidded back into play followed in a graceful arc by a Wellington boot. Without bothering to summon Ozzie, Clem slipped his foot back into the wayward boot and settled it back into place with a vigorous stamping. 'There we are, Comrades. No hands!'

As though to mark the event, the church clock sounded the hour, its solemn strikes leaving in their wake an air of reverent stillness.

Clem selected a grass leaf and lay back, hands clasped behind his head. 'Look at that sky. Bootiful, it is. Just bootiful, mateys. Makes you feel good to be alive, don't it, Tim?'

Tim eyed Clem's manipulation of the leaf, its withdrawal into the confines of his mouth and subsequent re-appearance guided by the deftest use of the tongue. 'Er – yeah!' he said. 'Well – better than a kick in the pants any day.'

Clem wheezed out what passed as laughter. 'Like it,' he said, running a knuckle across his eye. 'Likes it, I does. Humour, mateys – humour! And a bumper harvest t' boot! Got t' be, if this weather lasts.

156

What say you, Billy-boy? A bumper harvest, d' yer reckon?'

'Yeah!' he agreed. 'And we're goin' t' help stack the bales. An' the girls! They'm helpin' this year!'

'Girls?' Clem said. 'Mm, well. A nice thought, me old son, but our Walter's said no to that. Not wiv machinery about, he sez. And, well – reckon he's right. Perhaps when they'm a bit older, pal. When they've got some tits on 'em – eh, Oz?'

A muddle of expressions flitted across Ozzie's features, a sure sign of his being none too sure of what was expected of him. But he got away with it.

'Yep!' Clem said, and spat out his leaf. 'No girls. And no trainee pen pushers. Not fair on 'em, see – that's all it is! Them bein' delicate, they could strain their little hearts. Known fact!'

Tim stepped forward, red-faced and decidedly agitated. 'It's just an excuse! Kenny's done nothing to you. He's a decent kid, is Kenny. And if—'

'Whoa! Whoa there, Timmy-boy. Take it easy,' Clem said, raising himself up on one elbow. 'Kenny's fine. Pity he had t' go. No, pal. It en't Chamberpots I'm on about. It's 'im!'

It was like staring into the barrel of a gun. But there seemed no reason for it. 'Me?' he said, taking in every detail of the accusing finger. 'Why me? I en't goin' to no egg-head school.'

157

Clem sat up and, shaking his head, sucked air in between his teeth. 'Out the 'orse's mouth Billy-boy. Well, not exactly the 'orse. Not yer actual 'orse, like. But the next best thing to it. The randy old goat who used to shoe 'em. Had a right go at your old man, he did. "Your son, back there studyin' his books", he sez. "A-readin' and a-spellin'. And all without a father!". Then he prattles on about summat else. Laugh! Protectin' the interests of his fancy piece, he were. So, if you wants t' come stackin' bales with the rest of the lads, you'd better fill us in on the facts – hadn't yer, pal? And none of the borin' stuff. Just the juicy bits. Come on, spit it out. I mean. We'm all ears, en't we, Oz?'

'Yeah! Just like yer corn, Cooper. I 'opes it pisses down!' he said and, eyes fixed on the Quarry Lane gate, made for Old Forge Cottage

CHAPTER TWENTY-SIX

The inevitable tap and easing open of his door only served to deepen his dark mood. But it was not his mother who peered in. It was Tim, with his ball.

With it placed in the box housing his clothes and the rest of his crap toys, his pal sat with him on the bed, suitably quiet.

From outside, the distant sounds of Clem and Ozzie's tomfoolery bore witness to their continued presence.

'Pathetic,' Tim said.

'Yeah,' he said, experiencing a sudden and unexpected uplift of his spirits. He nudged Tim. Tim returned it. Nudge and be nudged, turn and turn about as of old. However, with no litter bin to decide the winner, a draw was agreed.

The game over, they sat sandwiched between the starkness of a closed door and the musty antiquity of Ethel's sampler.

'There's me mat,' he pointed out. 'It en't all bare.'

Tim appeared not to have heard. Suddenly enthused, he leapt up and grabbed the binoculars. 'Cor! Can I have a go'

'S'pose – if you want,' he said, and took to swinging his legs, bored out of his brain by the prolonged changes of focus and angles carried out by his infuriating little shit of a friend. 'Well?'

'Well, what?' Tim said, unable to keep a straight face. 'Ears. Ears of corn! Pish!' he went – and fell back, spread-eagled on the bed. 'Pish! Pish! Pish!'

'Yeah – an' I meant it. I 'opes it pisses and pisses and pisses down with the harvester stuck in the mud.'

Tim frowned, one of his thoughtful, introspective frowns and slowly raised himself into a sitting position. 'I do understand,' he said, slipping an arm about his shoulders. 'I mean, I was there, wasn't I? Under the window when – you know.'

'Yeah, well,' he said, in response. 'You wouldn't like it if it were your mum and dad - and I en't daft! I know what Cooper was doin'. Tryin' t' say … you know. Which is more'n daft. I mean. For a start. Barney can't even get up the stairs! And, anyway, she wouldn't. Not me mum.'

'Not with a smelly, wrinkly old man – yuk!' Tim said. 'Yuk to all of it. Except, well – depends, doesn't it?'

'Rabbits do it all the time,' he said, sure of his ground, adding as an afterthought. 'But not the Queen. They find another way for her. Trish said.'

Tim made as though to speak, then seemed to think better of it, restricting his response to a barely perceptible twitch of his brows.

'You callin' me a liar, Tim Robinson?'

'No. I just don't think they do, that's all. I mean, why should they? It's only nuns and the Pope who don't do it. And, anyway, it's nothing special – just yuk.'

'Yeah, well,' he said. 'That's how I feel about Dawn Adams. Mum thinks she's pretty. And Mr Duggan told me to wait until I was eighteen. I'd think different then, he said! But then, he don't know about me secret.'

'What secret?'

'Can't say.'

'Don't, then,' Tim said, and fell silent, until, out the blue, he began babbling on about Dawn and his sister, stressing what great pals they were. 'You ought to see them climb. A right pair of monkeys, they are – and funny with it!'

Leaving Tim to recall and laugh at the memory of some antic played out by the two girls, a scenario of his own took shape. Not of an action already taken, but of one still to come.

He told Tim, describing in military terms the whole escapade.

'Oh - I dunno about that,' Tim said. 'What if Mum and Dad found out? And yours! I mean, your mum's already worried about you. Asked me what was up, she did.'

'You never said nothin'?' I mean. You didn't, did yer? Coz if you did...'

Glancing sideways at him, Tim edged nearer the door. 'If you're going to get rough, then I'm off. The trouble with you, Hughes, is that you take things out on the wrong people. Like smacking me up against a wall. And – and throwing stuff into my eye! Made it red and sore for days, it did. You know, you'll do something you'll be sorry for one day, you will – really, really sorry!'

He grabbed his pal by his sleeve and eased him back into place. 'Sit down! It weren't serious, none on it. Just friendly scraps – that were all. I mean, I have t' take it out on someone, don't I? And you're me mate. Who else is there? I can't thump meself, can I?'

Tim took a deep breath and composed himself. Having done so, he stared fixedly ahead, sharing with him the perfect round of a sun, and a sky still showing no prospect of rain let alone a corn-flattening storm.

'Yeah, well,' he said, eyeing the floor, 'it just gets to me, that's all. Coz it's my fault. All on it, us havin' t' live here an' everythin'. So, you goin' t' help, or not?'

'Help?' Tim said. 'Oh, that.'

162

'Yeah. "That". Might get into trouble might we, Tim-de-tim? Might get told off, might we?'

As he guessed he would, Tim licked his lip, and nodded. 'Go on, then. I'll help. But not my sister. Not Carol.'

'Fair enough. Dawn, then,' he said. 'It'll have t' be Dawn.'

CHAPTER TWENTY-SEVEN

Downstairs, there was still no sign of Mr Barnes.

'If you'd have listened instead of being paranoid about having lettuce in your sandwich,' his mother said, 'then you'd know that Major Craig's taken Barney to the cricket. It's just what he needed after the to-do with your father. Fresh air. And lots and lots of his beloved cricket.'

'Well, there it is!' Billy mimicked, adopting a knees-apart, round-shouldered stance, complete with walking stick and – most important of all – the voice. 'Official scorer I'll have you know, for nigh on a hundred years now, Mistress Mo. An honorary position. Mine to hold. And mine to give to whomsoever I chooses!'

'Mmm,' his mother said. 'At least Tim's put you in a better mood. But you be careful. You've a lot to gain and a lot to lose where that man's concerned. Getting your shoes dried and polished for one. There, look. Over by the clock.'

'Ah, great. Can go slidin' now, I can.'

His mother gave a half-hearted shake of the head and gazed haplessly about her. 'Sunday. You'd have thought by now…'

'Not if he's changed the lock,' he said.

She shot him a look, only to then accept the fact and let go a long- held sigh. 'No, I suppose not. No. Not now he's changed the lock.'

Mr Barnes entered his cottage full of muttering and growls and was still at it half an hour later while carving slices from the hock joint.

'I don't know,' his mother said. 'First Billy, storming in and going straight to his room without so much as a by your leave. And now you with a face like thunder. If this is what fresh air does for the pair of you, then your time would be better spent in the coal hole!'

Mr Barnes slapped a freshly cut chunk of ham down in barely contained rage. If possible, he would have surely danced on the spot like a frustrated infant. As it was, restricted by the infirmities of old age, he made dramatic use of his carving knife. 'Coal hole!' he said, banging the base of its handle on the table. 'I'll give you coal hole, Maureen Bassett. Because that's where you'll be livin' if I has to suffer any more of it. Sniggers and – well – never you mind. And all from out the mouths of filthy-minded toe-rags not long out of short trousers! Had it afore, I 'as. And I bain't havin' it again. Up t' me neck in muck and bullets for the likes of them, I were. And what for, I ask meself. What for?'

165

His mother laid a hand on the old man's and gently guided it and the knife it held down. 'There,' she said, squeezing. 'All done now.'

'Clem and Ozzie!' Billy said. 'I bet it were Clem and Ozzie.'

Neither his mother nor Mr Barnes spoke, leaving only the draw of the fire to break the silence.

Clearly, without intending to, he had spoken out of turn. Even so, his only punishment came in the form of a request, politely put by his mother to take a strip wash and then wait in his room. 'Go on, there's a good boy. Then we can try on those shirts.'

The rumble and occasional rise of muffled voices sounded in the chimney breast and seeped through the cracks between his floorboards. By holding his breath, individual words and phrases could be made out. With a finger poked into one ear and his hand cupped round his other, his hearing became even more acute. But nothing new entered his head, just more of the same.

Bored, he took to studying the lines in his hand, a remarkably clean hand, car-washing pink and fragrant – unlike his armpits. One sniff at each told its own story … as did the shuffle of feet on the landing.

'Billy? What on -?'

His mother pulled his licked fingers out from under his T-shirt, pulled him up off the floor and pointed him in the direction of the door. 'Jug and basin. Go on. As if I haven't got enough to worry about!'

Disembodied words followed him into her room, predictable grumbles, easily mimicked.

The water from the jug barely covered the floor of the basin. Ethel, he thought. Ethel's Royal Devon jug. Ethel's matching Royal Devon basin: a magic basin, able to reflect the pictures stored in his head. Like the changing patterns of a kaleidoscope they fell one after another into place; a series of traumas experienced since … since his tenth birthday party.

He came to with a jolt. A face, not his own, as he might have expected to see reflected in the dressing table mirror, but his mother's. Sure enough, there she was, in the flesh, although not altogether with him, stood as she was, frozen in time.

'Mum?'

Blink by blink, she brought her eyes round to meet his. Not quite managing a smile, she stared down at the shirt, evidently wondering what it was doing in her hands. 'Yes! Yes, it's fine,' she said, pulling out the whole of the shirt, quietly adding, 'Absolutely fine.'

'Mmm,' she said, back in her body and his room again. 'You'll just not have to grow. But, never mind. I can always borrow material from the tail. Nobody'll ever know.'

167

'But what about games? When I 'ave to get changed? They'll know then!'

'Not the way I do it,' she said, playfully pulling his new shirt up and out from his trousers, her buoyant mood introducing a shine to a face that only minutes before had shown no trace of colour, let alone life.

It did not last, however. Happiness had always been something to be clamped down on in his mother's world; glimpsed only on occasion, like now, with her fingers dug into the shirt. She tilted her head back and closed her eyes. 'My sewing basket,' she said. If only she could get her hands on her sewing basket. 'It was Mummy's. The last thing she … And I want it. That, and a bath. That's all. Mummy's sewing basket. And a bath …'

Away she drifted, though not for long, returning perhaps a little too soon.

'He expected me to use the tin bath,' she said. 'In that scullery of his. Me. With not so much as a curtain at the window.'

To his mind, the solution appeared simple. He could stand on guard. 'I could, Mum! Outside the back door when Barney goes to the pub. We could do it tonight!'

No reply. Nothing … not so much as a sniff. Away with the fairies, his father would have said. But his father would have been wrong – so wrong. Fairies were gently creatures, with kindly eyes. Whereas his mother's eyes were something quite different.

Ethel's sampler provided no answer, nor did Mr Jock. His mother appeared as good as dead. But, then again, not dead. Inanimate and staring, yes ... but not dead. He realised where he had seen it all before. In Tim's house. In his sister's room. A real live German doll just blankly sitting there in the corner of his room.

CHAPTER TWENTY-EIGHT

The instant Mrs Dodds had passed out of earshot, his mother turned on him. 'You silly boy! Whatever made you think that? But then – we know, don't we? Eh? We know only too well.'

'Too much imagination?'

'Exactly!' his mother said, fuelling the fire in her cheeks. 'Number one on my list, copied out – how many times?'

He shrugged. Then, sensing the injustice of it all, fought back. 'You were ill! Mrs Dodds said so as well. "It were no wonder", she said. She'd bin expectin' it all week. And, anyway, it's got you a bath, en't it? It's what you said you wanted.'

'Yes,' his mother said, relenting. 'But not this way. Never again – please! A doll, indeed. And no ordinary doll. Oh no, not according to my ten-year-old son. But one of those creepy German things. And it was only Mrs Dodds, I hope? I mean, you haven't blurted it out to anyone else, I take it? Ye Gods! You haven't, have you? Please tell me you haven't.'

He drew breath and went through it all again. How he had knocked on Mrs Dodds' door and how she had invited him in. "Ooh – whatever's the matter, William?" she said. And so, I told her you were ill.

An' that I didn't know what t' do. That were all. Nobody else heard – 'onest! Oh, an' I said I'd go to her crummy Sunday school.'

His mother took in air…and nodded. 'Yes,' she said. 'Yes, all right. I forgive you – well done.'

And that, it seemed, appeared to be that. Saved by the Sunday School bell.

After dinner, taken late in an atmosphere of strained politeness, his mother suggested that he went upstairs and read another chapter of *Treasure Island.* 'While I go and see … you know. I shan't be long. Half an hour or so – okay?'

Clearly, the situation called for a nod and tactical retreat. 'Night, Mr Barnes,' he said, thinking that even at this late stage the old man might suggest a game of cards.

No such offer came, only a barely audible comment, something muttered about "apple barrels and time" virtually drowned by the scraping of the remains of his meal onto his fire.

Before straightening, the old grump took up his poker as though intent on plunging it into the heart of the chimney breast, or his eternally smouldering pile of slack. He did neither. 'Curtains!' he said, turning as though set on conducting an orchestra. 'You'm right, Mo! I can see that now. What's more, the wire's still there – no need for no fancy rail. You could measure up – and – and catch the bus into

171

Hollersham market. Only the best, mind! No expense spared. Well, what d' you say?'

His mother opened her mouth, only to hesitate, and start again. 'It's very generous of you, Barney. It really is. But I couldn't let you. Not when we're only here on a temporary basis.'

'Temporary? You don't mean that, do you, Mo? Say you don't. I mean, this is your home now. Yours, Mo. Yours and the lad's. I'm an old man. On me last legs, Mo.' he said, ageing five years in as many seconds and, thumping his chest, wheezed into every nook and cranny of his inglenook.

He awoke to the feel of his book being drawn from his hands. 'Come on, sleepy-head. Mummy'll make us both a hot drink. Then we can settle down for the night. Old wheeze-a-lot's already snoring his head off.'

'You're late!' he said, glaring at Mr Jock. For a moment, it appeared that Tortoise and Hare both winced, but apart from his mother's tightened lips, it seemed he had got away with it.

'Well,' she said, 'longer than expected, yes. But, oh, just to lie there and soak away the stink of bleach and disinfectant. You can't imagine – you just can't! And all thanks to my clever little boy.'

'Huh!' he said, although, noting the transformation in her, lifted her arm and snuggled up.

172

'A doll, indeed,' his mother said. 'I don't know. Whatever next?'

As though in reply, a knock came at the front door. His mother's arm instantly went from him and with one bound she was at the window. But she could not force it open and began to panic.

'Let me!' he said, and with one thump at the window's sticking point, it juddered open as before.

From below, staring up at him, stood Mrs Hicks, the light cast by the Rose & Crown highlighting the brashness of her beehive hair-do: also, and perhaps of more significance, the pappy flesh of an upper arm elevated in the manner of a rocket launcher. 'You!' she said. 'I've still got a bone to pick with you. So, don't you go thinking you've got away with it. Because you haven't! Where's your mother?'

Hands guided him gently aside. 'Oh?' his mother said. 'Hilda. How lovely to see you again? A bit late for callers. But – well – never mind. I mean, it must be important, you missing out on valuable after-hours drinking time.'

'Ha-ha, Maureen Bassett. Gawd! No wonder Charlie kicked you out – you and yer six School Certificates. Well, with any luck, one of 'em's for washin' an' ironin'. Here!'

As triumphantly as if having produced John the Baptist's head, Mrs Hicks raised a pear-shaped potato sack. His father's overalls, she informed, plus

173

his rotting vests and one or two other bits and bobs. 'I don't mind cooking him the odd bird, tough as they are. But I'll be damned if I'll do any more of yer dirty work. I'll leave it on the doorstep. Night, Maureen. God bless!' she said, and click-clacked away, suddenly plunged into semi-darkness by the turning out of the Rose & Crown lights.

Even though the woman had gone, his mother stayed at the window, the traces of a smile tugging at the corners of her mouth. 'And God bless to you, too, Hilda. God bless, and good riddance,' she murmured into the night air: and shut the window, first time, no messing.

CHAPTER TWENTY-NINE

His mother delved into Mrs Hicks' potato sack and holding everything else back, pulled out his father's overalls. 'The tin bath comes into its own!' she declared.

'The man's a tyrant, Maureen Bassett. A tyrant, I say! And you bain't no better. Too saft by half. That be your trouble. Always is – and always was!'

The rattle and clatter of the poker being inflicted upon the slack and surrounding ironwork interrupted his mother's reply. But, evidently not to be outdone, she took a deep breath and bided her time.

'Barney. I know where you're coming from,' she said once the poker had been laid to rest. But it wouldn't do any of us any good, Charlie getting on the wrong side of the Cooper brothers. Or their father, come to that. Dirty overalls could mean no work, especially where that Cyril's concerned. And then where would we be?'

'Oh?' Mr Barnes said. 'So, Charlie Hughes is pushing his coins into the gas meter all of a sudden, as well as keepin' another woman, is he? And what about this 'ere lad of yourn? I bain't noticed—'

'Barney!' his mother said. 'Not now. Let's face it, anything could happen. And, well, no matter what you think … Charlie's not entirely stupid.'

'Oh, Mo. Mo, Mo, Mo!' Mr Barnes said, and sat slumped on his stool, eyes closed, and drained of all facial colour.

'Barney? Barney, have you had your tablets?' his mother demanded, and responded immediately to the old man's shake of the head.

For his part, he filled a cup with water and stood in attendance, moved by his mother's fondness of the man.

Not until later, in his bedroom, meant to be reading another chapter of *Treasure Island*, did he feel the urge to lay the book aside and put his ear to the most favourable crack in the floorboards.

Much of what he could pick out meant little. Only when his mother became audibly agitated did it become interesting.

'Look, Barney. I know what you're thinking. What you've always thought, if the truth be known. It's no secret. Daddy was of the same mind. Quite blunt about it, in fact. I'd let him down. Him, Mummy and, most of all, myself. But what was done was done, he said, and that I wasn't to worry. That he and Mummy would take care of me. Me, and the

176

baby. And that I didn't have to marry Charlie, not if I didn't want to. But I did. I wanted my baby. And I wanted my baby to have a father – can't you see that?'

'Oh ah – I sees it, right enough,' Mr Barnes said, struck by what sounded like, well – grief. 'Poor little mite. Tragic, it were – tragic! Didn't stand a chance, you didn't. A lost babbie – and a husband who bain't no proper husband, nor a father to that lad of yourn. And there be you about to wash the man's overalls. Well, Maureen Bassett, I tells you now. It won't be no dirty overalls that'll lose him his chicken-shit shovellin' job. Nor his pilferin'. Oh no! The flame that'll ignite the firing of Charlie Hughes will come from the thwarted ardour of another – you mark my words!'

'No doubt it will,' his mother said, and grunted, presumably with the effort of lifting yet another loaded kettle from the hearth.

The distinctive sound of the kettle having been lowered to the stone floor came before it was due. Put down, not for his mother to ease her back or regain her breath, but, as it turned out, for her to have the last word. 'Yes, Barney. 'Far too saft, she said. 'But not anymore. As far as Charlie's concerned, I've turned the corner. The road ahead has opened up before me. And, believe you me, for the first time in a long time, I know where I'm heading.'

The whole of Old Forge Cottage seemed to hold its breath. Then, somewhat wistfully, Mr Barnes said, 'Do you. Mo? Do you really?'

CHAPTER THIRTY

Almost inevitably, his early morning knock was answered by a sour-faced Mrs Duggan. 'Yes – what is it? Come on. I haven't got all day.'

'It's for me mum, Mrs Duggan,' he said, and straightened. 'It – well – it'd be better if I could see Mr Duggan. Oh, and – and I'm sorry, Mrs Duggan but girls en't allowed to help stack the bales this year.'

Mrs Duggan curled her top lip and eyed him with her usual show of disdain. 'I wasn't intending to,' she said. 'Anything else?'

'Just that you're looking well, Mrs Duggan. And can I speak to Mr Duggan, please?'

The verdict seemed a long time in coming but then, when he was virtually resigned to failure, the woman summoned her husband.

Stood there on the pavement, on his own, the wait seemed endless. Endless: nothing coming from within the cottage but the irritating drone of a wireless.

'Hello?'

Caught day-dreaming and disorientated, the source of the call took a head-spinning moment to locate. But there he was, Mr Duggan, busily towelling his hair at an upstairs window.

'Mum sends her regards, Mr Duggan! She sez you're a nice man – kind, she said. And I was wonderin –

'Well – wonder on. Betsy doesn't need another wash. Not yet awhile, anyway. Blimey! What d' you think I am? Made of money?'

'No! You don't understand, Mr Duggan. For free! Next Sunday, Mr Duggan. That's if me and Tim can borrer yer ladder. Just for a day to help clean our winders. For mum, Mr Duggan! She's worried about 'em, see, an'— an' it's making her ill.'

Mr Duggan ran a finger and thumb in a pincer movement down his chin and mused. 'Mmm, ill, you say. Yes, well, so I heard. A women's thing, I expect. But then, a splash of make-up and she'll be fine. Works wonders does a touch of dolling up.' He laughed but stopped abruptly. 'No. No! I'm sorry. That's not funny. Not funny at all. Of course, you can borrow the ladder. Give me a few minutes. Shan't be long. Not as long as the ladder, anyway.'

Once the window had been closed on him, and the significance of Mr Duggan's idea of a joke sank in, it began to play on his mind, and fester.

The long-awaited drag of wood on stone arrived. Mr Duggan stepped out from his side passage to pull up with a start.

'Who told yer? Me mum'll kill me. Kill me, she will! An' I didn't say she were a doll – I didn't! All I said – it were Mrs Dodds, weren't it? Well I en't goin' to her poxy Sunday School. Not now, I en't. She can stick it up 'er arse!'

Duggan opened and closed his mouth, as vocally inept as his hold on his ladder, wrenched from him and dragged across the road in defiance of a car and screech of tyres.

CHAPTER THIRTY-ONE

Tim trailed on behind him, silent for much of the way. Then, evidently exasperated, demanded to know where they were going.

'Obvious, en't it?' he retorted, and trudged on.

Tim sighed. 'What you gone and done? Come on! There must be something. I can tell.'

'It en't what I've done!' he said. 'It's Doddy! Gone blabbin', she 'as. About me mum. An' because of 'er I've gone and, well, sort of fallen out with Jenny's dad.'

'Ah ...' Tim said, not saying more until they were pulling the ladder out from behind the stinging nettles fronting the back hedge of the churchyard. 'It might not have been Doddy,' he said, pausing with the pull. 'I mean, could've been anybody, couldn't it? Not that I know anything. I'm just – you know – saying.'

Having said his piece, his best mate averted his eyes, the rising colour in his cheeks giving him away.

So, he thought. If it wasn't Doddy, then ... 'Barney! It were 'im, weren't it? I'll kill 'im. Kick 'is

182

stick away, I will. Kick it away – an' crack 'is 'ead open!'

'No, you won't. You know you won't,' Tim said – and yanked up his end of the ladder. 'And this better be worth it. I must be mad!'

Once in place, Tim eyed the ladder as though visually climbing every rung. Having done so, he then eyed the bathroom window. 'I can't see how anyone could climb in through that.'

'Hang on, Robinson! It were you who said Dawn could climb. Like a monkey, you said. Anyway, I've already told me mum I'd done it. When she were in 'ospical, I said.'

'Yeah, but you – well – you didn't. Did you?'

'No,' he said. 'But she believed I did. And she still believes it, because she don't want me climbin' on the out-house roof.'

'But it still –

'Look!' he said, stifling the urge to thump his pal. 'It's simple. If me mum believed I could climb in through there when I was about eight – an' big – then it must be easy-peasy for a skinny seven-year-old girl. Right?'

'It was your mum,' Tim said.

'Me mum? What about me mum?'

'Shush! Not now.'

'But –?'

'Later!'

The intrusion of childish chatter and giggling faltered at the back gate. Like two miscreants caught red-handed by Miss Wheatcroft, Carol and Dawn stood as a matching pair, eyes like owls, taking everything in.

Instructed by Tim, Carol stood on guard at the gate. Dawn plonked her bucket down between Tim and himself then looked to each of them in turn, not once, but twice. 'What's wrong?'

'Nothing,' Tim said. 'There's nothing wrong, is there, Billy?'

'Er … no,' he said.

Dawn tapped his arm. 'Just climb the ladder? Is that all?'

'No' he snapped. That en't all. Wouldn't need the likes of you if that were all, would we, stupid.'

Dawn stared, just stared, leaving her fingers to work as though with a mind of their own, locking and unlocking.

Tim slid an arm about her, cast him a contemptuous scowl, and guided her to one side, speaking to her in low tones.

Copying how Mr Robinson would mollycoddle Carol, it struck him. As different as pop and piss to his own father.

"You blubbin', boy?"

A boy: that was the difference. A boy trained not to cry, no matter how severe the punishment. A

184

hard-knock. That was him. Made to jut his chin out at the world — and sneer.

But for now, a boy left with little option but to sit on a ladder rung and wait.

'Ready?' Dawn said, nervously flipping up the loose sides of her skirt.

'Er, yeah – course!' he said and cleared his throat. 'Yeah. I'll come up behind you. Make sure you don't fall. Unless – well – unless you'd rather let Tim.'

'No. You. I want you,' she said, taking on a superior air. 'As long as you promise not to look at my knickers.'

A cupped palm aimed to land on her buttocks did the trick. Immediately picking up on the pretence, the girl let out a squeal and scrambled up the first few rungs. As Tim had said, a right monkey.

After the first attempt proved difficult, Dawn turned her head sideways and manoeuvred both it and the upper part of her body through the opening light. Half in, half out, she protested, professing to be stuck. 'The sticky-up thingies. Oowah!'

'Put yer skirt through first,' he said. 'Go on!'

'I can't.'

'Come back a bit, then. Then do it.'

For what seemed an age, the distorted view of Dawn's upper body hung upside-down, her breath adding to the obscuring nature of the window. Then,

185

after taking a deep breath, she pushed and wriggled her way back enough to rest the soft flesh of her stomach on the window bar.

'That's it! Now shuffle to the side.'

Breathing hard, she did as he urged. Furthermore, without complaint, she pulled up the full length of her skirt and threaded it through into the bathroom, where it hung, reminiscent of Sally Hicks and her knee-hanging from the playground high bar.

Rather than it being a lesson in the thinly disguised front of the female form, on this occasion, it was of the rear, full on, in his face.

Positioned with just one peg-stay to hinder Dawn's progress, all seemed set.

With her ankles brought up to the back of her knees and held level with her hips, it only needed a minor adjustment. 'Push yer bum up!'

With as much meat on her back end as a skinned rabbit, her spirited effort brought little or no reward. But it was now or never. Rammed over the troublesome peg stay and down, she plunged head-first into the bathroom.

'Brill!' he said, marvelling at the way in which she pulled off a back-arching roll over the rim of the sink not only to land on her feet but also to perform what looked like a celebratory jig.

But this proved no celebration. 'Me Nellie – ooh! Ooh me Nellie, me Nellie!' she wailed, her dance necessitating much bending and facial contortion coupled with a one-handed clutching of her privates.

'Aah! Me Nellie ...!'

CHAPTER THIRTY-TWO

It wasted valuable time, cutting through Dawn's watery glare.

'Go on,' he said. 'Or it'll all be for nothin', wun't it? All your brill work. And brave! Nobody else could've done it. Go on, Dawn. Then we can have a look and see what you've done.'

On reflection, it was probably the best thing he could have said … or possibly the worst. On the one hand, having managed to bring a halt to the girl's tribal jig, while, on the other …

'Come on, Dawn. Go and unbolt the side door. I mean, you've got to, en't yer? I mean, you en't comin' back the same way, are yer now?'

Dawn shook her head. But still she just stood there, holding back the tears. 'I'll see for myself,' she managed to say, her look even more scathing. 'Just go away.'

'Then you'll come down?'

She looked away, chin-up and at long, long last, gave a short nod.

Tim was waiting for him at the foot of the ladder, his face a picture of concern, as was Carol's.

'It weren't my fault!' he said. 'I didn't mean it – honest!'

Tim signalled Carol to leave it to him. 'Mean what? What didn't you mean?'

'Yes!' Carol said, leaving her post at the gate. 'What you done to my bestest ever friend?' And before anyone could stop her, she was on the ladder. Up she shot to stand on the top rung, clinging by her fingertips to the opening light. 'Dawn? Dawn!' she shouted, only to descend a couple of rungs and look back. 'She's not there.'

Tim looked aghast. 'I knew I shouldn't have agreed to this. What do we do now? Isn't there another way in? We'll just have to go and see your dad.'

'No way! Anyway. Carol's wasting her time. I knew Dawn wouldn't be there.'

'No,' said a voice from behind, 'because I'm here.'

Tim's face said it all. 'Open! Open all the time!'

'Yeah, well,' he said. 'How was I t' know? The old man must've bin pissed. And – you know…'

Tim shook his head and slid that arm of his round Dawn's shoulders as before. 'Look. You've been great. You really have. But, why not go back to our house now? With Carol – eh? See Mum. She'll – well. She could give you something from out the first-aid box. You know – a plaster. Or cream. Vaseline – that's good.'

If anything, Tim's molly-coddling only seemed to remind Dawn of her predicament. Screwing up her face and making it obvious where the problem lay, she nevertheless declared in no uncertain terms that she was staying put. 'I can, can't I, Billy? Say I can.'

'Only if you fetch me the bucket.'

Off she went, walking like a duck on ice. She collected the spare bucket and, keeping her side of the bargain, placed it at his feet.

Tim unearthed a Chamois leather from under the kitchen sink, the skin dry and stiff, until soaked and worked into something usable, All right, Boss?'

'Tek it all into the hall,' he said. 'Then come back for a chair.'

Tim did as he was instructed, first the leather and part-filled bucket, then a kitchen chair, carried as though it weighed a ton.

Their alibi in place, the next step was to set about finding a spare front door key. But there was no sign of one, not on the windowsill, not in any of the cupboards or drawers – nowhere. The search proved fruitless.

'Ah well!' Tim said, continuing to gaze about the kitchen. 'At least we tried. Nobody can say we didn't. Make a start, shall I? On the back first, d' you reckon?'

'Yeah, whatever. I'll sort out me gran's sewing basket. At least I reckon I know where that is.'

Hardly ever used and never heated now, the best room still had about it an air of seclusion and comfort.

Mentally able to turn back the clock and rekindle one of his grandfather's infamous fires, it all came back to life: a shoe box for a garage, his Dinky toys arranged on roads marked out by toy bricks linked by cotton or string. Reliving it all, it was as though they were still alive, his gran, and his granddad.

Still alive …

Angered, but not knowing why, a measure of relief came with the yanking open of the sideboard door and seeing his grandmother's sewing basket, ready and waiting to be lifted out and tucked under his arm. But gently, its ancient wickerwork reminded him, its creak sounding at odds with the chilly atmosphere pervading the rest of the cottage. Coupled with the absence of Tim on the other side of the window, it could only mean one thing. And there he was, waiting for him on the other side of the door.

Shrewd-eyed and gleaming, his father angled his head to the side and noisily sucked in air. 'Oow. Catched you out. En't I, boy?'

'No, Daddy! No – we en't broke in or nothin'. The back door were already open. You ask Tim. It were, weren't it, Tim? An', well, we thought you were here. I mean, I en't sin yer, have I? Not for ages. And look! Look what we were goin' t' do. There's the bucket and rag and the chair for standin' on. An' – an' we've borrered Mr Duggan's ladder so's we can do the upstairs. For you, Dad. To help!'

Unable to contradict anything, his father wrinkled his nose and sniffed. Then, as though for the first time, he took note of Dawn – and turned on him. 'You bin messin', boy? Where you shouldn't have – eh? Bin messin', 'as we?'

'No! I mean. No, Daddy. I wouldn't.'

'No, Mr Hughes,' Tim said. 'No. Dawn asked if she could use your toilet. Desperate, she is. That's why –'

'Yeah-yeah. All right, lad. I get the message. No need to go overboard.'

Paused on the third stair, Dawn obeyed his father's jerk of the head and continued her climb. Up she went, hauling her way from one step to the next in the manner of a three-year-old. An amusing spectacle, judging by his father's smirk, who evidently thought the obvious; that for Dawn, using the toilet had come a mite too late.

With the last glimpse of ankle sock passing out of sight, his father's attention turned to the sewing basket, motioning at it with what appeared no more than a passing interest.

'Mum's washed yer overalls, Dad! An' – an' she noticed some stitchin' needed doin'. A button. Hangin' loose, it were. Nearly off!'

'Mm,' his father said. 'Decided t' toe the line, 'as 'er? Yes, well. Not before time. And Thursday, mind! Tell 'er I want 'em fer Thursday – savvy?'

In reply, he firmed up his mouth, and nodded.

'That's right, son … that's right. You look after your old dad. And he'll look after you,' his father said, eyeing for a moment the upper reaches of the stairs. 'A pretty little thing that,' he added, and took his leave of him with a friendly ruffle of his hair.

Not until after the side door had been heard to slam did Dawn re-appear, pausing at the turn on the stairs. 'I've put the window back as it was,' she said, and made her way awkwardly down to stand before him, her demeanour peculiarly adult. 'Do you like me now?'

Trapped, he gave an involuntary shrug, but no words. Those, he left for Tim. 'Yes – of course he does! There, see? You've made him blush. And his mum thinks you're pretty, too. Doesn't she, Billy?'

'Er. Yeah. An' - an' me dad. Ruffled me hair and said so, he did.'

193

Not that convincing, he had to admit, but enough to restore the dimples to the girl's cheeks. They proved short-lived. Panicking, she turned to Tim.

'Yes.' Tim said. 'Let's get you to your Mum.'

Carol made as if to follow them, only to pause, part-turned, and glare at him. 'Why did you tell her she could stay? She wasn't right, you could see she wasn't. Why do you think she had to go back up to the bathroom?'

'I dunno!' he said, not wishing to fall into the trap of stating the obvious.

'No,' the seven-year-old pain-in-the-arse said, hands on hips. 'I don't suppose you do. But whatever it was she did, didn't work. The blood still came through onto her skirt – you could see it! But you,' she said, arm raised. You …!'

He emitted a low rumbling growl and left it at that, silenced by the closing slam of the door.

CHAPTER THIRTY-THREE

On his return, Tim flopped down onto the kitchen chair. Once there, he gazed about the hall, towards the side door and finally the stairs, fixing on them as though expecting Dawn to miraculously re-appear. 'I just hope she's all right, that's all. if only for your sake. Come on!' he said, grabbing the handle of the bucket as he rose. 'Let's get this over with before he comes back.'

'Me dad? Nah, he wun't be back. Not yet, anyway. He's taken his dog for a walk.'

'Dog?'

'His trilby,' he said, for the benefit of his thicko mate. 'Walkies. To the pub – get it?'

'Oh,' Tim said, finally cottoning on. In brighter mood, he then put it to him with typical Tim optimism that, rather than the Rose & Crown, his father might have gone to see his mother: a suggestion that could only be answered with a shrug.

The arrangement worked well. One applied the water, leaving the other to rub over and dry. Turn and turnabout, that was the thing, as with their games of nudge: four windows on the back and four on the front.

'I wonder if your mum's seen us,' Tim said, descending the ladder for the last time. 'So, what do we do now? Go and see her? Give her the sewing basket … or what?'

'Could do,' he said, only to experience a flashback. 'Hang on, Robinson! I've just remembered. Earlier on, when Carol and Dawn came to the gate, you shushed me! "Your mum", you said. It were her, weren't it? It weren't Barney or Doddy who blabbed. It were me mum. Her! And you knew!'

'So?' Tim said, and thrust up his hand to bat away the chamois leather. 'Why take it out on me? It's not my fault. You didn't want everybody knowing, did you?'

'No,' he conceded and, with a drawn-out groan, collapsed back, arms spread onto his father's dumped sheet of corrugated iron. 'Me brain. It can't take any more. It'll burst.'

'If it does, I baggies the sawdust,' Tim said, and spare bucket in hand, landed the drying cloth on him. 'Bye-bye! See you later!'

His mother barely afforded him a glance. Busy counting coins into Miss Pringle's till, she blew air up over her face, not for a moment appearing to lose concentration. Coin after coin, all dropped into their appropriate sections until, at last, she was able to close the till drawer.

And yet, still she failed to look up.

'Impressive,' she said, scribbling something on a pad. 'But I thought I told you not to go on that out-house roof.'

Eyed by tins and packets, display racks and boxes, he snatched up his gran's sewing basket and slammed it down on the counter. 'The side door were open!' he said, already on the turn.

'Billy!'

The nature and tone of his mother's voice spun him back round. 'You blabbed. You bloody – bloody well blabbed! After all you said. And there were me blamin' … blamin'…'

Unable to get his words out, a sticky bun came to hand, just begging to be rammed between his teeth and torn in two. Away it flew, powered by rage and the undeniable urge to maim.

Only when the crash of wood upon wood seemed to shake the fabric of the whole street did the mist clear, leaving him with nothing but an empty pavement and the prolonged tinkling of shop doorbells.

Back spread-eagled on the roof, acting as his corrugate iron bed, the image of his being nailed to a cross came to mind: a martyr, stoned by the mob and wept over by angels.

To his delight, given time to assemble, they came. There they were; a host of angels borne on wings disguised as wispy clouds. But slowly – they came slowly, Heaven being such a long way away. Probably a million miles or more, further than Ethel's binoculars could reach, anyway – much further.

Only with his eyes closed did the blondness of their curls and purity of their smiles form. How fragile they all seemed, appearing as delicate as butterflies and yet, at the same time, reassuringly comforting.

Dozens upon dozens of angels …

'Eh? What?'

'Sorry,' said a disembodied voice – not of a Heavenly Angel, but Patricia Collins. 'I tried not to make you jump,' she said, trailing her fingers off and away from his arm. 'But I've been asked to give you a message.'

'Message?'

'Yes – a message. From Tim. He's been kept in. So has Carol.'

'Huh! Might've guessed.'

'Guessed, Billy? That's very clever of you. What else have you guessed? Let me see. What about my mother having to take Dawn to hospital? Did you guess that?'

'Hospical?'

'That's right. You've got it. Only there's no 'pical' about it. The only pickle is the one you're in – again!'

'Sez who?'

'Sez me, Billy. Mum was horrified when she saw what you'd done to Dawn. And she agreed with Mrs Robinson. Hospital, straight away, no messing. And that set Dawn off crying. Not because of the pain she was in. Oh no. But because her daddy would be angry. Not with her. But with you!'

'Me?'

'Yes. You, Billy. Who else?'

'But it were an accident! And, well, she shouldn't 'ave blabbed. Should be more like me, she should. An'-an' - an' kept 'er trap shut! That's all kids do these days. Blab. And me mum – she's as bad! Well, I en't livin' with her anymore. I'm stayin' here. With me dad. Mates, we are now. Ruffled me 'air, he did. Never done that before.'

'No,' she said. 'Just grabbed it and spun you around in circles, jabbing your – backside. But – yes. You do that. Live here with your dad. It'll be handy – for Dawn's father, I mean. Finding the two of you together.'

'Ha! And then what? A Commando, is he?'

'Something like that,' she said, and rather than say anymore shuffled to the edge of his makeshift bed. However, instead of making ready to go, she began stubbing the heel of her sandal into the rubble

199

pile, freeing what turned out to be a jaggcd piece of roofing tile.

'Billy?' she said, taking hold of the tile. 'If I brought this up between your legs, would it hurt?'

'Might.'

'Might? There's no "might" about it,' she said, elbowing him in the ribs. 'So, don't tempt me.'

'You wouldn't dare,' he said, knowing with every cell in his brain that she had not got it in her to do it.

'No,' she conceded. 'Because, unlike you, I think before I act. Girls have soft parts as well, you know. And you've hurt Dawn. Really, really hurt her.'

'I told yer! It were an accident!'

She tossed her piece of tiling back onto the rubble pile and stood up. 'What gets me. What really, really gets me. Is that you don't seem to care. And, for your information, Dawn didn't "blab", as you put it. She did it on the fallen tree, she said. She slipped, she told them. It was Carol, under pressure from her mum, who "blabbed". So there!'

As though calling time at the end of a boxing round, the church clock sounded the hour. One o'clock. Just that one solitary strike, delivered into an atmosphere of ominous silence.

'I do care.' he said and waited for a reply that seemed destined never to come. 'Trish?'

200

Even then, she did not speak, leaving him to stare up at a darkening sky. Gone was the pastel blue. Gone were the trails of wispy cloud. And, from beyond The Ridgeway, there came a distant low rumble of thunder.

CHAPTER THIRTY-FOUR

Trish pulled out a key from her skirt pocket and inserted it in the lock. 'Don't look so worried,' she said, opening the door to reveal a run of carpeting flanked by the same wood block flooring as in Kenny's house.

'Toilet,' she said, indicating a door to his left.

'Nah. I'm all right, ta,' he said, more interested in the stairways that led up from either side of the hall to form a galleried landing. 'Cor! I've only ever bin in yer kitchen!'

'Yes. And that's where we're going. When you've washed those hands of yours, that is. Go on!'

The room smelled of lavender. It housed a toilet and, almost laughable, what must have been the smallest sink in the world. But it served its purpose, as did his pad of three toilet-paper squares used to wipe it clean afterwards.

Trish, in his absence, had presumably made her way to the kitchen at the far end of the hall where she was ready and waiting with pen and paper. 'Right. Number one! A *Get Well* card to send to Dawn. If we hurry, we can – what's the matter?' she said. 'It's only thunder.'

'Ha! I en't scared of that. The louder the better if you asks me. An' I 'opes it pisses and –'

'Er, excuse me?'

A deep breath, forcibly exhaled, answered that one. Although, perhaps not entirely. 'I h-h-hopes it pisses and pisses down.'

'Better,' she said. 'Only you don't need an S on the end of hope. Now, do you want me to help you, or not?'

'Yeah – go on then. But you'll 'ave to go into the shop for us. It en't the money - I've got that! A bit, anyway. It's just… well,' he said, and poured out the whole saga, including his slamming of the shop door. 'Fanny Pringle weren't in the shop. But she must've felt it. Probably thought it were an earthquake!'

'Well, seeing as you think it so funny, there's no reason for you not to go in then – is there?' she said, ears cocked to another rumble. 'Going around us.'

'Huh', was all he could muster, that and a contemptuous sniff.

'Oh, this is hopeless,' Trish said, slapping down her pen. 'I mean, apart from Dawn and her father, your mum and most probably Miss Pringle, who else is there?'

'Jenny's dad.'

'Uncle Donald?'

'Yeah – and he don't like you, neither. "Don't mention that name round here", is what he said. Meanin' you.'

She made a sad face and nodded. 'Yes, well. Even more reason for me to help take his ladder back, then,' she said, and screwed up her piece of paper.

'Mm. Yeah,' he said, distracted by a bowl of fruit at the far end of the table and, in particular, a rather large, slightly over-ripe, orange.

'Have it if you want,' she said, obviously having been fitted with wing mirrors, and down clanged the lid on the waste bin, a natty affair worked by means of a foot pedal.

'One bite out of an iced bun isn't enough to keep you going,' she said, and, as well as the orange, she set before him a bowl of Cornflakes and a jug of milk.

'Tea? Or pop?'

'Pop! Er – please. Ta, Trish. I'm real thirsty.'

'It's no wonder,' she said. 'Lying out in that muggy heat on that sheet of old roofing. Really, you ought to be drinking water.'

Even so, despite what she said, she still poured him a full-to-the-brim glass of lemonade.

Ignoring him, Miss Pringle greeted Trish with enthusiasm and warmth that made him want to puke.

204

'Billy's come to say he's sorry, Miss Pringle. He's told me all about it. How things had all gone wrong and how upset –'

'Wrong?' Miss Pringle said, removing her spectacles. 'Well. "Wrong" is his middle name, is it not? "Wrong" to nearly take my door off its hinges. "Wrong" to take a bun. And "wrong" to throw at his mother – the poor soul! And I tell you now, young man. One more "wrong" where she's concerned, and it might be the last thing that either you or that father of yours ever does. So, think on!'

'Yes, Miss Pringle. Sorry, Miss Pringle.'

'I should jolly-well think so!' the silly old bat said – and held out a cupped palm. 'Sixpence, if you please.'

'Eh?'

'For the bun, William. The bun.'

The contents of his pocket amounted to one shilling and five pence, a paltry pile that with Miss Pringle's raiding gained more coins, but less value.

Trish brought a soppy-looking card complete with envelope to the counter. 'It's for Billy to send to Dawn, Miss Pringle. Oh, and a stamp, please.'

Miss Pringle separated a First-Class postage stamp from the rest of the sheet and laid it before him. 'There. The sooner that card reaches its destination the better, going by what Mrs Perkins told me,' she said, and with the use of a single finger slid coin after coin from his little pile into her waiting palm.'

Trish clicked open her purse. 'If Billy hasn't –

'No-no, Patricia. Seeing as William is so adept at cleaning cars and windows, he can work his debt off. Two hours should do it. Breaking rocks, if I had my way, William. Breaking rocks!'

As though having seen their reflections in Mr Barnes' smouldering slack, his mother turned her face towards them, suddenly more animated. 'Oh. Oh – Trish! Come in, poppet. Come in! As for you! It's a wonder you dare show your face!'

Trish nudged him.

'Sorry, Mum. Sorry. I didn't mean it – none on it.'

It was as though she had not heard a single word. 'How could you? How? And on my very first day!'

Mr Barnes appeared in the doorway. 'The strap, Maureen Bassett! The strap. That's the only remedy that boy understands.'

'Yes. Well,' his mother said. 'He's experienced more than his fair share of that, thank you.'

Trish stirred at his side. 'Perhaps I ought to be going now, Mrs Hughes. I've done my bit, carrying the sewing basket. He thought it was too sissy to be seen with it.'

'Mm,' his mother said, more her usual self. 'Afraid to face me on his own, more like. But thank

206

you anyway. It's lovely to see you. And, yes – yes, perhaps that would be for the best in the circumstances. You shouldn't be dragged into this. But, before you do, I'd be grateful – more than grateful – if we could have a word in private. Just the two of us. Woman to woman, as it were.'

Trish licked her lip, and with eyes only for his mother, raised her chin, and nodded. 'Yes. Of course, Mrs Hughes.'

Led by his mother, the two entered the scullery and shut the door behind them, the rest of their journey being marked by the tread of feet on the stairs.

CHAPTER THIRTY-FIVE

Mr Barnes listened long after the footsteps had finished sounding on the stairs, lost in thought, it seemed. Finally, he eyed him. 'An old head on young shoulders that one. You could do worse.'

'Gerroff! I en't even out the juniors yet! Anyway, she's too bossy.'

'Mm, well,' the old man said, gazing up at the ceiling again. 'Happen you'm right. Happen you'm wrong. But the Collins's, along with the Chambers and the Robinsons of this world is where your opportunities lie. Juniors today … the jobs trail before you realises it.'

'I'm goin' in the army,' he said, the idea only that second having come to him. To his surprise there was no response, Barney's thoughts clearly having returned to the ceiling; pleasant thoughts, or so it seemed because the old man grunted, and smiled. 'Yes …' he reflected. 'It were Albert Collins who had the foresight to buy me out and move the forge, lock stock and barrel, to the old airfield. 'And she,' he said, jabbing his finger skyward, 'she be cut from the same cloth.' He frowned and moved to his table, hooked his stick over the back of a chair – and caught him completely off guard. 'Cards, lad! No pegs or board. Just the cards.'

He focused the full probing force of that one eye of his on him. 'The Army, you say? Well, then. We must pave the way.'

Mr Barnes emptied the pack out onto the table, spread the cards face up and selected somewhere in the region of a dozen or so, certainly enough for a hand each of cribbage.

But that notion was soon dispelled. 'A clock,' the old man said, laying down the queen of hearts, representing, as he put it, 'Young Janice Robinson.'

'Mrs Robinson? Tim's mum?'

'The same. Came a-knockin', her did. And mightily peeved, her were. Seems as you'm blacklisted, mister. A bad influence, you is. A menace her sez. So. And there sits them two kiddies of hers,' he continued, placing the ten of hearts after the queen, at two o'clock, followed by the seven of hearts at three o'clock. 'Never bin in trouble afore, they bain't. Now look at 'em. Tainted!'

On he went, placing down card after card, until only three spaces were left unfilled. There remained four more cards to be found a home, however: the seven of diamonds, the queen of clubs, a joker, and a card that from the start had been left face down.

'Right, lad. Now you've got the drift on it. Who does you think this seven of diamonds represents? And this joker? Can crop up when you least expects it can a joker. Well? Spit it out!'

'The seven is Dawn, because she's seven, like Carol. And the joker … I dunno.'

'Oh, but I think you does, mister. In fact, I'm positive you does. Because he's no Phyllis Pringle or Duckie Duggan, or any of the Chambers clan. We knows what to expect from the likes of them, as with the Hilda Hickses of this world. Whereas this chap,' the old bastard went on, thrusting out the joker and waving it under his nose, 'he's — '

'Dawn's dad,' he said. 'But it weren't how you make it all sound. It en't fair!'

No emotion was reflected in the old man's one focusing eye, no malice, no warmth … nothing. It was like his other, as unseeing as a marble.

'No. You'm right, lad, it bain't fair. We agrees on that. For a start, it baint fair on this lady,' Barney said, slotting the queen of clubs into position at the top of his clock. 'Look to her left. Look to her right. And what does her see? Tell me, lad. What will her see? And what will her hear? And, if not hear, then sense. Carries on the wind, it does. It be in the air, like them there radio waves. Now, an old fool, I might be. But I knows what I knows. And so did my sister. As pure as driven snow, Ethel were. But it didn't stop 'em. Oh no! And why? Because they had the power and the mind to do it. That's why! And there be nothing juicier to pass from mouth to mouth than malicious gossip. And all to get at me. So. Looking at our little clock, who'll be your mother's Ethel, I wonder. Who?' the old man said, flipping over the unused card.

There it lay, face up at the centre of the clock. The ten of clubs, stared at by every card that encircled it.

'The queen's one and only son, lad. Recognise him? The one her went through Heaven and Hell to hold on to. Heaven and Hell! And her paid for it. Clear, they tells her. You'm clear! But anymore of your shenanigans and that there trouble of hers could well —'

'Enough!' His mother stood in the scullery doorway, wringing her hands. 'That's enough!'

If the old fellow's stick had been within reach it would have undoubtedly been stamped down.

'No, Maureen Bassett. No! The boy needs to be made aware. Look! This Jack of spades. The Chambers lad. Young Kenny. Even now you can hear what they'll be a-saying. Touch and go, it were. What'd give first, the branch – or his neck. And the Hicks girl. Busted her ribs, he did. And you, I'm sorry to say, young lady – you'm here!' Mr Barnes emphasized, jabbing his finger down onto a card. 'Butchered it were, the poor critter. Or 'as you forgot?'

'Stop it! Stop it, now!' his mother demanded, her hand going to her temple.

For a moment, it seemed she would faint. But no, a lick of the lip and she looked about her, eventually settling on the arm linked with hers; an arm that guided her outside, from where muttering filtered in through the many gaps in and around the door.

'It were for your own good. Your own good, lad,' Mr Barnes said, and sat back in his chair, hands clasped on the round of his belly

CHAPTER THIRTY-SIX

Trisha's appearance at the top of the village coincided with the first of the church clock's expected six chimes. Once across the road, she broke into a sprint – and almost made it.

'You'm late!'

'Only by one chime,' she said, leaning against the telephone box, although on the opposite side to him, back to back.

'Trish, what's cancer?'

'Well … a disease, I suppose. Like any other. Why? Who's used that word?'

'Dunno. It's just … sort've hidin' in me head.'

Before he knew it, she was at his side, forcing him to make room and, as she had done with his mother, link arms. 'Look. If you're worried, then talk to your mum. That would be the sensible thing.'

'Yeah, well. Thing is, I en't very good at sensible.'

'You can be when you want to be. Talk!'

'Yeah, well … perhaps.'

She tugged his arm. Come on. Last job!'

Side by side, they crossed the road and made for the front garden tree and her uncle's ladder.

'The infamous tree,' she said, holding up its broken branch. She let it fall, inevitably shedding more of its few remaining leaves.

Tight-lipped, she snatched at a few more and threw them angrily aside. 'Your mum just doesn't deserve it. She doesn't! It's been one thing after another for her. And this garden. Just look at it. I can remember when it was a real picture.'

'Yeah, well. An' I suppose that's my fault an all.'

She shook her head and scowled. 'Of course, it isn't. It's just – oh, I don't know,' she said, lifting an end of the ladder out from the grass and, despite her spindly arms and legs, managed to twist it over onto its side. Having done so, she sat astride it.

'Crikey! It en't an 'orse, yer know!' he said, to which she clicked her tongue and whipped the beast into action.

However, as suddenly as the pretence had begun, it ended. 'Sometimes,' she said, aiming a sigh skyward. 'Just sometimes, I feel like bursting out of who I am and doing something completely mad. Something – I don't know. Naughty.'

'You could show us yer belly-button.'

'Mm, I could, couldn't I? But I'm made out of matchsticks. And girls made out of matchsticks aren't fitted with belly buttons. Pity that,' she said, posing Miss Wheatcroft style, finger angled towards the other end of the ladder and, presumably, his desk. 'It

214

helps keep it steady,' she said, as though he couldn't have worked that out for himself.

'Yeah – and,' he said, wobbling the ladder. 'What else? What's me mum said? This is what this is all about, en't it? And you can't say it en't!'

'I can,' she said. 'And I will. But, before I do, I'd have thought by now you might have asked about Dawn.'

'Dawn?'

'Yes! Dawn. You know. The little girl you pushed through that slit of a bathroom window?'

'Yeah, well. If there'd bin anythin' to tell, you'd've said it by now.'

Silence.

'Well you would! Wouldn't yer, ladder-rungs?'

She looked down, over the length of her body, and adjusted her skirt. 'Doesn't anything we did this afternoon count for anything with you?'

'Yeah. Course. Lots. Especially the pop!'

'Then don't call me names. It's bad enough being a Skinny Lizzie without you making fun of it. It's not nice.'

'No! And it weren't nice me mum tekin' you upstairs so she could talk to you about me behind me back,' he said – and wobbled the ladder, almost unseating her.

Not so much as a blink. 'Why d' you do that?' she said.

What? Try and knock yer off yer 'orse?'

'No. Stick your chin out. You're always doing it.'

'Don't!'

'Yes you do. And for your information, Dawn is still at the hospital – thanks for asking.'

'That's all right,' he said, defiantly jutting out his jaw, willing it to reach the other end of the ladder. Not that it would.

'You're hopeless,' she said. 'No wonder your mum worries about you. And – yes! Surprise, surprise, we did talk about you. But, don't worry. Not just you, but about lots of things. About Dawn. About me. And about her – your mum. And about how much we have in common.'

'Yeah,' he said, stifling a laugh. 'Yer both bony. Dem bones, dem bones, dem...'

It was as though she was made of stone, her face set, her unwavering look as straight and true as any arrow.

'Only teasin',' he said, compelled to break the silence. 'It don't mean nothin' – 'onest. Me an' the lads do it all the time.'

'Yes, well. I'm not one of "the lads". So, stop it. It's not funny. And it's not clever. Grow up! Then perhaps your mum might talk to you like she did me.'

'Oh yeah? About what?'

As though having been set a tricky question by Miss Wheatcroft, she deliberated for a while,

216

frowned, and raised her chin. 'She thinks you're going the same way as your father,' she said, and, blink by blink, softened her look. 'And, well, Barney's card clock sort've – you know. That's why I took her away from it. Out into the fresh air where she could …'

'Yeah, well. The old bastard wants to watch it. Upsettin' her like that. And what's he know, anyway?'

'You,' she said, simply. 'You, Billy. He knows you.'

Under his guidance, the two of them laid the ladder on top of the front hedge, collected it from the other side and carried it across the road to the Duggan's cottage, Trish faltered. 'Uh-oh. I think we'd better just leave it round the back.'

Angry exchanges from inside the Duggan household accompanied their every step. Gently, making no sound, they placed the ladder against the back wall and tip-toed away. For him, it came as something of an anti-climax to be back at their six o'clock start point. 'All done! And in less than half an hour! What now?'

Leaning splay-footed against the box and gazing into the distance, Trish expressed the opinion that the village was a horrible place. 'Horrible. Horrible. Horrible,' she emphasised. 'I'm glad we're going away!'

217

'Away?'

She jerked her head his way. 'Oh, don't sound so alarmed. Not until Sunday afternoon, now. And only for a few days. Why?'

'No reason,' he said, suddenly aware of what his chin was doing.

'Better,' she said, and, smoothing down her skirt, stood away from the box.

'Trish?'

'I've got to go,' she said, glancing towards the church clock. 'What?'

The words were there, all that needed unburdening, only for it all to be swallowed away.

'You'll be all right,' she said. 'Just keep your head down. And make yourself useful. In Barney's garden, perhaps, like you've done before. And at Miss Pringle's. Pay your debt off. Be polite and open the door for people, especially the oldies. And go to Sunday school. I won't be there, but Tim and Kenny probably will. You never know, perhaps the three of you could have a kick about or something afterwards. How about that?'

'Yeah – yeah, I will. And Betsy? I promised Mr Duggan I'd clean Betsy for free on Sunday. What about that, after – you know?'

'Definitely. But not too early, mind. Don't knock the door. Just do it. Uncle Donald's bound to come out to you. And that's everything sorted. Voilà!'

'What?'

'French', she said. 'Only we're not going to France this year. Daddy can't afford the time. But I'll still have fun. Sally's coming with us. It's the best thing I ever did, getting together with Sal. We have a right laugh.'

'Yer jokin'! I wouldn't let 'er in the 'ouse!'

She paused and turned to face him. 'Why not? I let you in, didn't I?' she said, and with a discreet finger wave, made for home.

CHAPTER THIRTY-SEVEN

With a little coaxing, Ethel's sampler relinquished its grip on his secret letter.

AbbOts lOvell is bOring

cOme back Out sOon

X

D

The six over-large "O"s not only intrigued him but also introduced an element of gnawing doubt. Then, it all fell into place. It was a code, an ingenious code. When all the capital letters were added together, they amounted to nine – nine, nine, nine! Knock the door and what d' yer get? Mrs Duggan, probably.

Scary …

Ethel's binoculars, on the other hand, instantly hit the target, but, as on all other evenings, time passed without so much as a glimpse of an arm, let alone a face, at that tantalising apex window.

A tap and subsequent opening of his door interrupted his vigil.

'Any luck?' his mother said, lowering her bottom onto his bed.

'Nah,' he said, an answer that to his inner glee fell well short of telling any lie.

'Well,' his mother said. 'If you stay there a few minutes more you may well spot a much larger creature scurrying across the playing field … unless, of course, you'd like to come with me.'

'Where?'

'Well, to face the music and find out how Dawn is, for one. And then to –'

'What? At the 'ospical?'

The tightening of his mother's lips warned him to pause and think. 'Hospi - tal.'

She gave a solemn nod. 'Yes, well, not before time. Get it wrong again and I'll make you write it out a thousand times.'

'A thousand!'

'That's right. But, in answer to your question. No. Not the hospital. The Collins's. And – and I've changed my mind. No ifs or buts, you're coming with me whether you want to or not. I mean, you did meet Trish outside Miss Pringle's as arranged, I take it? The two of you haven't fallen out or anything?'

He shook his head. 'No!' he said, somewhat hurt and mystified at the suggestion.

'Good.' his mother said. 'That's something, at least. It's building bridges time. You've made a start. Now's the time to consolidate.'

'Cons what –? What's –?'

'Oh, don't look so peeved,' his mother said. 'Just hand over a small present for Trish to share with

Sally – that's all! Now, no messing. Go and brush your shoes.'

'One of em's wet.'

His mother opened and closed her mouth, and finally came up with the only option open to her. 'Then put it to dry and make do with your pumps.'

After an initial show of faltering surprise, Mrs Collins welcomed his mother by her Christian name. Finally, noticeably cooler, she acknowledged him as well

'William.'

She stood to one side in open invitation for them to step into what for him was now a familiar hallway.

'Oh, I say!' was all his mother could muster. Still appearing to be taking everything in, she followed Mrs Collins into what the woman referred to as a lounge where Mr Collins sat one of two well-padded armchairs.

'Visitors, Albert! Come out that paper. And put out that smelly pipe, there's a love.'

Having issued her instructions, Mrs Collins closed the bowed doors on a radiogram while at the same time, as though by magic. bringing down a matching lid.

Chuckling, and apparently in no hurry, Mr Collins folded his newspaper and laid it down. His pipe, he seemed less inclined to relinquish. 'Mm,' he said, eyeing it with an air of regret, 'it's the one thing

222

we disagree on. Smelly, she calls it. And so does my daughter.'

'Outnumbered, then,' his mother said, affecting a laugh.

'Constantly,' Mr Collins said – and with one athletic bound left this armchair to plump up the cushions on its twin, angled to match his own to the side of a large inglenook. 'There!' he said, finished plumping. 'That's better. Whatever was I thinking of? Make yourself at home, Mo. That's what we used to call you at school, I seem to recall. A few years back, now, eh? And what do they call you, young man? Billy, I expect.'

He nodded, intending to commit himself no further, but there was something about the man that led him to impart more. 'Girls call me Billy. But me mates call me Hughesie. B-but the one I like best is what Mum calls me. Billy Windmill.'

'On about two occasions,' his mother said, unable to refrain from smoothing down a lock of his hair.

His time clearly at an end, the attention switched to that other annoying habit peculiar to adults: small talk. On and on it went, eventually culminating in an apology from his mother for having intruded for longer than intended.

To his dismay, this immediately dismissed quite forcibly by Mr Collins. 'Nonsense! You stay as long as you like, Mo.'

'Yes,' Mrs Collins said, backing up her husband. 'You make yourself comfortable. No doubt you've earned it. Now! What would you prefer Coffee? Or tea?'

'Or a G and T, perhaps?' Mr Collins chipped in with.

Sandwiched between Mr Collins' joviality and the need to answer Mrs Collins, his mother attempted to satisfy both – and broke down. 'Oh dear,' she said, entangled in a web of snuffle and watery laughter. 'I don't know where that came from. I really don't.'

'Something had to give, Mo,' Mr Collins said, taking up his pipe and settling himself deeper into his armchair. 'Leave me with Mr Windmill, here, why don't you? And show Mary how to make a decent pot of tea. Little milk, mind. And no sugar. There's a good girl.'

With his mother and Mrs Collins gone from the room, Mr Collins eyed his unlit pipe, and laid it back down. 'Perhaps they're right,' he said, arching his brows and sighing. 'Perhaps they're right. They usually are, you know. But,' he added, tapping his nose. 'Never let 'em know it. Diversionary tactics, see. While they're concentrating on the pipe, they're missing something else. Like you, making out all you and young Tim were doing was cleaning windows. Clever, that. Only, a good General assesses all the risks before going into action. Cool-headed, he is. Thinks of the safety of his men.'

'Yeah,' he said, looking down and fixing is gaze on a silky swirl of moss green.

'Turkish,' Mr Collins said, his voice penetratingly soft, like the greyish-blue of the man's eyes. 'One thousand, five hundred double knots to the square inch,' he informed him in the same level tone. 'And all stitched by hand – or so they say. But then, one never knows, does one? Not really.'

'I never meant to hurt Dawn, Mr Collins. I just wanted t' get a key for me mum. An' – an' her sewing basket. It were me gran's. An' she en't bin well. Me mum, I mean. Not me gran. Me gran's dead. So's Granddad. They'm both dead.'

'Hmm,' Mr Collins said, frowning. 'And, Old Barney? How's he been treating you?'

'Okay,' he said. 'Only …'

He shrugged and left it at that, the gripes too muddled and complex to be aired any other way.

'And Patricia? What about her?'

'She's fun,' he said, the words tripping off his tongue with no effort on his part. 'Just bossy. A bit anyway,' he added, thinking it wise. 'But not too bad.'

Mr Collins gave an amused "humph" and, as though puffing on his pipe, hardened his look against the effect of the smoke. 'Mm. Yes. Bossy. Doles out advice and support in equal measure, I'm told. Not to mention the occasional orange. Quite remarkable really, don't you think? Considering.'

'Yes, sir.'

'Yes … my serious-minded, loving daughter. So strong and capable on the outside. But hurt, deeply, deeply hurt on the inside, William. And I never want to see her hurt like that again – d' you follow?'

'Yes, sir.'

'Mm. Well. "Yes, sir", it had better be,' the man said, striking a match.

The instant its flame touched the bowl of his reclaimed pipe, he paused however, ears cocked to the animated chatter of girls. A door closed and seconds later the knob turned on the lounge door.

'Oh!' Trish said, her abrupt halt suggesting more than surprise.

'Sally set off all right?' Mr Collins said.

'Yes, thank you, Pops. And, well, she's ever so grateful. You wouldn't believe how grateful she is. Me, too. I am – really!'

'Yes, Petal. I know you are. But it's early days. Early days, my love. The thing is, did you make sure to thank your mother? That was some spread she laid on for us this morning.'

'Yes! Brilliant. All a bit much for poor Sal to take in at first, I think. It wasn't what she'd expected, not from Mum. And not just the breakfast. But you know — everything. And we did make for the kitchen when we came down, only, well, Sal thought it best if she didn't interrupt and came back later.'

'Ah …' Mr Collins said, a simple enough expression, was it not for the manner of its delivery. His "Ah …" said everything.

'William? Come to, lad. Best left to it, I say. The two ladies, I mean – d'you reckon?'

'Eh? I mean. Y-yeah.'

It was written in their faces. Especially in "Pop's" goody-goody daughter's supposed absorption in the spinning round of a global atlas.

Tea making, my arse …

Yes – 'Mummy'. Trish knew, alright. She knew exactly what was taking place in that kitchen. She couldn't help but know, along with the whole ruddy house. I could sense it. Sense it, I could. And I couldn't do nothin' about it. Surrounded, I was. Me, on me tod. A big lad for me age. But small. So very, very small, stood there on the bloke's precious ruddy carpet in me tatty school pumps.

Just - just stood there

CHAPTER THIRTY-EIGHT

A goalpost served as a backrest, the pencil-thin spire of the distant South Morton church a landmark on which to concentrate his stare.

Stare and stare and stare …

'Get up!' his mother's voice demanded. 'Come on!'

'Ow! Me arm!'

'Arm? I'll give you arm – and it'll be spelt with an aitch. What on earth do you think you're playing at? Eh? Disappearing like you did? Answer me! Or have you lost your tongue as well as your senses?'

'I'm a Red Indian.'

'A -? Oh, so Red Indians suddenly up and go without a word to anyone, do they? I see.'

'No, you don't. You don't see nothin'!'

'Oh. Don't I, now? Well, we'll see about that. Move!' his mother said, pushing and prodding him towards the Quarry Lane gate and her precious Barney.

'A Red Indian banished from the tribe!' he said – and dug his heels in.

Leaving him where he stood, his mother opened the gate and passed through into the lane. Only then did she turn and face him, the fury reflected in her eyes verging on hatred.

When she spoke, though, it was with a measured calmness. 'Is it any wonder? Well? Is it? What with Dawn in hospital with – well – having to – having to empty her bladder by means of a tube. Not to mention Mr Collins having had to scrub his back path clean of that poor little rabbit's blood. In fact, on the whole, I think people have behaved surprisingly civilised about it all. Don't you?'

A shrug saw to that, not caring one way or the other.

She bent towards the gate, bringing her face to within an inch of its top bar, and rewarded the shrug with the thinnest of smiles. 'I'll take that as a yes, then.'

From up near the quarry field sounded the prolonged squeal of some rodent or other careless enough to get caught out in the open.

His mother immediately latched onto it, adopting a psychology that would not have fooled a five-year-old. 'Right!' she said, finally losing patience. 'Fine. Have it your own way. You go back to waiting for your Red Indian ancestors to whisk you away to the happy hunting ground. Because – yes — that's what the old women of the tribe used to do when there was no-one willing to take them in. Being frail and elderly I don't suppose it took long. A few days or so at the very most, I should imagine. But, well, a young lad like yourself? Oh, I wouldn't like to say. But you get on with it. I'm not pandering to you.'

'En't askin' yer to.'

Out came the air from her puffed-up cheeks. 'Well, that's a relief. Otherwise I'd have it on my conscience, leaving you out here without food or water. Especially as there'll be no Trish to bail you out. Unless she plans on running back from Guernsey every day, of course. But I can't imagine that. Can you?'

'Huh. Her!'

'Ah. Now we're getting somewhere,' his mother said, altering her attitude. 'You upped and went because this Good Samaritan who'd rescued you from the rubble pile and spent the best part of the afternoon with you was with somebody else. Someone who'd taken your place, as it were. And it hurt. Mummy can understand that.'

'Geroff! It's not Trish. It en't her I like.'

Stupid … stupid, stupid, stupid.

The expected probing never materialised, however. It never came, nor the telling off. Pre-empted by a kindly smile, his mother stressed that his having a girl as a friend was nothing to be embarrassed about. 'Patricia's a nice girl. A friend for life if you —'

230

She broke off, startled by the closing slap of the Rose & Crown outer door.

'Don't worry,' he said, rewarding her with a scowl. 'It weren't me dad.'

'No ...' she said, staring chin-up as the loping figure of Cyril Cooper left the lane, gave a furtive glance back, and vaulted the churchyard wall. 'No ... not your father.'

Finished staring, she turned her head slowly back, and eyed him. She had a letter to write, she said. Only, she did not say write. She said compose. She had a letter to "compose". 'An important letter, that Mummy has to give a lot of thought to. So, if you don't mind, I'll take my leave. Unless there's something you need to tell me, that is. I mean, you're not being bullied or teased, for instance? About Trish, I --'

He stamped his foot. 'Shut it! It en't nothin' like that – it en't! It were them gigglin' and laughin' at me from the hall. Her'n Hicksie. An'-an' when Trish come into the best room, she give me a look.'

'A look?' his mother said. 'You mean to say. That what this is all about. A "look"?'

'You weren't there, you didn't see it! An' – an' they got everythin', they 'ave. Everythin', Mum! An' we en't got nothin', we en't. Not even a telly.'

'Heaven help me,' his mother said, aiming her words skyward.

'Well, we en't!' he said. 'And you can't say we 'ave.'

'No.' she said. 'I can't. And how do you think that makes me feel? Mm? Seeing that lovely hall and kitchen? And that lounge of theirs – eh? How do you think it makes me feel! As for that "look"! For your information, all I saw were two excited young girls falter and change course because they've got something way beyond the reach of you or your father – manners! They know better than to burst in on adults obviously engaged in a private conversation.'

'Yeah! About me. They heard yer goin' on about me!'

'Heaven forbid! I mean, whatever would there be to talk about?'

'Funny,' he said.

His mother straightened and stood tall. 'I think,' she said, her tone matching her look, 'that it's time we had a little chat about the facts of life. And I don't mean the birds and the bees, but the duties of a parent. So, open your ears, and pay attention.'

She paused. 'Good,' she said, having inflicted on him the demanded silence. 'Unbeknown to you, Mrs Collins saw fit to give her daughter a bit of a ticking off about inviting boys into the house when no adult was pres –'

'Me, you mean! Not Kenny or Tim. Just me!'

232

'Maybe. Maybe not. But that's not the point. The thing is, Trish took it all a bit too much to heart. Having –'

'Huh! Couldn't 'ave bin much of a tellin' off or she wouldn't 'ave bin gigglin' an' —

'Now, you "shut it",' his mother said. 'And, while we're on the subject. Don't you ever speak to me like that again. Do you hear? Ever!'

'Yeah, well.'

'Yeah well, nothing. Pay attention. And then you might learn something. So, if you don't mind, I'll start again. Good parenting is making a point, seeing that it's been taken on board, and then moving on. In Mrs Collins' case, that meant allowing Trish to invite a friend to a sleep-over. So, it wasn't two girls laughing at your expense, but having something called fun. And for your further information, neither Trish nor Sally were at the kitchen door long enough to have made sense of anything. So, you're wrong – on all accounts. So, just stop and think. After what her mother had put her through, imagine what it must have been like for the girl to open the lounge door and come face-to-face with, no other … but you. Can you? I wonder.'

'Huh! The sun shines out 'er arse, don't it? Well you wouldn't think that if you knew what she'd said she wuz goin' to hit me in the gooly-gongs with. An'-an' – an' she showed me her belly-button.'

'Really? All praise to Mrs Collins for stepping in when she did. Otherwise, who knows what you might have been shown next. Nipping things in the bud, Billy. Something, I must confess, I've failed miserably at. Though I've tried. God only knows how I've tried!'

She shook her head and broke off, but it was no hand-wringing mother of old who stood before him. Nor for that matter was it an escapee to the land of the fairies, but a woman with a letter to compose; a mother full of sweetness, topped by an unnerving smile.

'So,' she said. 'It's over to you. It's your turn.'

'What d'yer mean?' he said, stumbling towards the gate, only to hear a familiar metal on metal chink.

'No you don't,' she said. 'You go back to where I found you. And, while you're there, decide on what sort of man you aim to be. One who throws away every advantage handed him on a plate. A man who drinks and gambles away the best part of his wage packet every week. Or a man who started with next to nothing. Who had a vision and a work ethic? Who ignored the scoffers when he bought two derelict barns off the Coopers? Yes. Not one. But two. Now renovated and linked by that beautiful hall and galleried landing.'

'Well!' he said. 'You should've married him then, shouldn't yer?'

'Yes!' she said, landing her clenched fists on the gate. 'I should!' And she strode away, leaving the gate off the latch and juddering.

CHAPTER THIRTY-NINE

Mr Barnes cackled to such an extent that no amount of walking stick stamping helped hold back his tears. 'Ah dear! Ah dear! And there be you, a country lad born and bred!'

Pale-faced and drawn, his mother finally intervened. 'Enough now, Barney. I thought something similar when I was his age. And, well. At dusk. And no doubt starving.'

Dabbing his eyes and nodding, Mr Barnes gained control of his self. It proved no more than a temporary respite, however. 'A woman bein' murdered,' the old bugger said, succumbing once more to a mix of cackle and stick stamping.

'Shut it! It en't funny, it en't!'

His mother raised a warning finger. 'Billy …'

'Ah dear,' Mr Barnes said clearly oblivious to anything going on about him. 'Come – come in 'ere, he did. Come in – ah dear. With his butt on fire!' And off the old man went again, rocking and cackling until overcome by a fit of wheezing.

His mother whipped away the old sod's breakfast bowl. 'Serves you right. Both of you!'

Without being asked, he took the tea-towel from its peg and began drying the items already stacked in the rack. Even so, as far as his mother was concerned, he was as good as invisible.

'Mum, it really were like a woman screamin' – it really were! An' – an' if it had've bin, it would've bin me who could've saved 'er life. Couldn't it – Mum?'

She raised her brows and gave in with a sigh. 'Yes, well, whatever. And you'd have been a hero,' she said, and tipped out the washing-up water, staring at it as though monitoring its swirl and gurgling disappearance. Then, while picking out the debris from the P-trap, she reminded him of the two derelict barns Mr Collins had bought and what people said and did at the time. And how they re-acted.

'Well, they didn't laugh,' he said.

'Sometimes,' his mother said with yet another sigh. 'I wonder. I really do. Scoff, was the term I used. They scoffed, which is as good as saying laughed. Scoffed, sneered, derided – get the message?'

He cleared his mouth of saliva and nodded.

Yes, well,' she said. 'Take it on board and do the same as Mr and Mrs Collins. Ignore it. He who laughs last, laughs longest, as they say. And it tends to be true. Ask the sulking high and mighty Coopers.'

'The Coopers?'

'For letting those two barns go. Unlike Albert, they hadn't done their homework. But then, that's another story,' she said, made breathless by the whole affair. That, or the rushed drying of her hands.

'Mum?'

'What?' she said. 'I'm late enough as it is. What is it? What now?'

Such a declaration as he was about to deliver was not one to be rushed however. 'I've decided,' he said, and paused for effect. 'I'm gonna be a Mr Collins.'

'Glad to hear it,' she said, busy ridding herself of her apron, before giving her hair a last few seconds' of finger-tidying.

All done, she lifted the latch on the back door, only to pause and issue him with a last-minute instruction, repeated, as though he was an infant and likely to forget.

Mr Barnes' inspection of the base of his walking stick provoked a fair deal of muttering and grumbles. Rubber ferules, it seemed, were not what they used to be. 'And what were it yer ma wanted?' he demanded rather than asked.

'Oh, nothin' much,' he replied. 'Just that she'll be back at one o'clock. Oh, an' if anyone comes for me dad's overalls, be sure to give 'em the letter.'

'Oh – that!' the old grouse said. 'No point in no letter. Wastin' 'er time, her is. Women don't 'ave rights, they don't. Not in this world. Be better off puttin' arsenic in 'is tea, her would. Fly-paper, that be the thing!'

Finished picking and peeling, Mr Barnes threw his pieces of rubber ferule onto his fire. 'Going to me greenhouse,' he said, tip-tapping his hollow-sounding way to the back door, across the yard and beyond, out of sight.

Millstones, every last man jack of us, eh, Ma? Me, me dad and, if that weren't enough, Barney. Nothin' but millstones …

CHAPTER FORTY

There seemed only one thing on his mother's mind after her morning stint at Miss Pringle's. 'Mm ... I take it no-one's been, then?'

He raised *Treasure Island*. 'An' I've bin in all mornin' like a good boy. While he,' he said, nodding in the direction of Mr Barnes' three-legged stool, 'while he's bin sulkin' in the greenhouse.'

His mother pulled a chair out from the table and slumped down. Sat spray-legged, she let go a yawn so strong and prolonged it left her having to blink away the water from her eyes. 'Oh well,' she said, and sniffed. 'Best left where he is, then. Best left …'

And she slept, exhaling via a sagged mouth, her posture so finely balanced it could be called precarious.

It was some twelve minutes before she stirred, not roused by the occasional mini-collapse of the fire or the chimes of Mr Barnes' long-case clock, but the returning tip-tapping of the bare end of the old man's walking stick.

'Oh, back then is we, Maureen Bassett? Back, is it?' he said, positioning his stool nearer his fire as though it were the middle of winter.

As when his father had entered a room, his mother rose and busied herself elsewhere. Billy followed her, into the scullery, where she began slicing bread.

'It's coz of me, en't it?' he said.

His mother faltered in her slicing, only to pick up the rhythm once more and take the knife at speed through to the board. 'Let's just say you don't help. Cheese or jam?'

'Jam,' he said, and pointed out that he had dried the breakfast crocks that morning. 'An' I am gonna be a Mr Collins – you'll see! Already started savin' me money, I 'ave. Loads on it!'

'Of it,' his mother corrected, and paused to apply her strength to a successful twist of the Branston Pickle jar lid. 'There! Apply that, and that's him seen to. Can you take it through to him, please? Then come upstairs.'

'Upstairs?'

'You've got it,' she said. 'To the top floor restaurant where it's private.'

'What!'

His mother swallowed the last of her sandwich, licked the margarine from her thumb and eyed him.

'It's nothing for you to worry about,' she said. 'Just something for another day. Yes. Another day, when Mummy's got some money put aside. Money, you see. It's all down to money and ways of making it grow. What they call interest. And I work in the very place to help that money you mentioned grow.'

'What? You mean, give me money to Miss Pringle!'

His mother laughed and wobbled his knee. 'No, silly. Not Miss Pringle. The Post Office. They're the ones who give you the extra money. And I can see to it for you. Tomorrow, perhaps. What d'you say?'

'Yeah, well. I …I dunno.'

His mother seemed unconcerned. 'Well, you think about it,' she said. 'Oh, and by the way. Talking about it, I'd almost forgot. We did have a television. Daddy had it installed for the Queen's coronation. I'm surprised you don't remember watching Sooty and Sweep and – what was it? Ah yes – Andy Pandy! Surely, you must remember Andy Pandy.'

'Sort of,' he said. 'And that soppy girl puppet.'

'Looby Loo!' his mother said. 'See, you do remember.'

'Yeah,' he said, the memories piling in one after another, not only of hand puppets and the Flowerpot Men, but also of a much larger man, a real man, who came and argued with his father.

'Yes,' his mother conceded. 'You'd have been about five, pushing on six, perhaps. Not long after my Daddy died.'

She twitched him the thinnest of smiles, her earlier enthusiasm having evaporated. 'Money,' she said. 'Your father hadn't kept up the payments. But you could. When you're older, that is. In fact, you could afford to buy a television outright. That's if you opened a savings account, of course. Start small and think big. I know you've got it in you. But for now,' she said, pointing to the jug and bowl, 'hair wash.'

Towelled and able to open his eyes once more, his mother caught him off-guard. 'The ten-shilling note Mr Barnes gave you for your birthday. Where is it?'

The forthright nature of her question threw him, leaving him with a memory blank. Then, in a rush, it came back. 'Hidden.'

'I see,' she said. 'Good, that's very sensible of you. At least it's not lost or spent. But, if you want to grow up and be a Mr Collins as you've said you do, then you need to have a plan – agreed?'

'Yeah. Well … sort of.'

Making him blink, she brought her hands together in the manner of an ecstatic child.

'Excellent!' she said. 'I always knew you had it in you. To be clever, that is. And it doesn't have to be a Mr Collins. It could be, say, a Mr Duggan. He's a lovely man with a nice little cottage and steady job. A car, even. Not an E-Type, I know. But that could come later.'

'Hang on!' he said. 'I en't daft. I know what yer doin' – an' it's my money!'

She began combing his hair. 'Of course, it is, I'm not questioning that. But you would be daft if you left it hidden away where it would only lose its value. On the other hand, you do what I suggest, and Mummy will add a little extra to it. From little acorns, as the saying goes … there! All done!'

CHAPTER FORTY-ONE

Squeaky-clean and cold about his ears, he entered Miss Pringle's not a minute early nor a minute late.

Miss Pringle eyed him over the rim of her spectacles. 'This is William Hughes, I take it? I mean the real William Hughes and not some cousin of his?'

'Sorry, but Billy couldn't make it, Miss Pringle. I'm Henry, his twin brother.'

'Ah, yes … I see,' Miss Pringle said. 'Well, a marked improvement on William, I have to admit. Fit for duty, I would say – wouldn't you?'

'Yes, Miss Pringle.'

Given a damp cloth and an old towel, his first duty, one that would surely take up his whole hour, was to clear, wipe clean, dry, and reload the shelves holding all the tinned foods and a host of miscellaneous items ranging from shoe polish to tooth brushes.

Being a Saturday there were numerous interruptions, some more troublesome than others; like Mr Bevin, ignoring the tins on the shelf to point his cane at the ones stacked on the floor, invariably near the base of the tower.

'There we are, Mr Bevin!' he said, cheerfully enough for a third time. 'One large tin of Pineapple Chunks.'

'Ah … no. I'm not too sure, now. Perhaps it was peach slices. Or pear halves in syrup. No, no – peaches! It was definitely peaches. We always have peaches on a Sunday. Couldn't get them in the war, you know. Not peaches.'

After half an hour, the top shelf was not only wiped clean, but also dried and re-stocked. The shelf full, with all labels facing to the front, his chest swelled at the sight of his handiwork.

Mr Barnes tip-tapped his way into the shop and asked for rubber ferules.

'No, I'm sorry, Barney,' Miss Pringle said. 'As much as I'd like to, I'm afraid I can't stock everything.'

'Ah,' Mr Barnes said. 'Ah, 'appen you're right Phyllis Pringle – 'appen you're right. Us old uns don't count for much these days. Up t' me neck in muck and bullets and can't get a ferule t' stop me stick from slidin' from under me – tsk!'

Away he went, still mumbling and grumbling, only to return almost immediately for a packet of mints.

When all three shelves had been cleared, cleaned and fully stocked, Miss Pringle clasped her hands before her and pronounced herself more than satisfied. 'And a packet of crisps to compensate for the extra ten minutes. Pick from the rack – your choice! And I'll' see you tomorrow morning if that suits. Sort that stockroom out, perhaps? But early, mind! I shut at half ten. As for now, well done William's brother. Top marks!'

At the door, still playing the part of his brother, he almost came to grief, forced to take evasive action as it burst open.

'Good heavens!' Miss Pringle said. 'Mrs Craig! Whatever's the matter?'

'Matter!' the woman said, bustling past. 'You might well ask, Phyllis – you might well ask! Not that you should need to, knowing the day and date!'

'Ah …' Miss Pringle said, removing her spectacles. 'Same old trouble, I take it?'

'Same" is definitely the word! The very word, Phyllis!' Mrs Craig said, taking tin after tin from his tidied shelf and thrusting them into what appeared more of a rucksack than a shopping bag. 'Years of service, the Major and I have given. Discipline and experience of church matters second to none! Yet, will that awful man be told? Not on – well! Best left unsaid. Be it on his head, though, I say. Insisting on the church being left unlocked. Night and day, Phyllis – I ask you. Night and day!'

'Old Chatters?' he said. 'He's brill! Tells us all about the jungle, he does.'

If it were true that looks could kill, then Mrs Craig's glare would have turned him into a pillar of salt. 'That,' she said. 'is where both he and thee belong – the jungle!'

Back home, no-one had called for his father's overalls and accompanying letter. Furthermore, Mr Barnes was still bemoaning the lack of a ferule.

'Tim's mum!' he said. 'She goes to Hollersham this afternoon. I could go with her and train-spot with Tim while she goes an' gets you one.'

Mr Barnes turned his one proper eye on him. 'You'm banned, remember. A bad influence, you is. Or 'as you forgot?'

He gave the old man a slow, reluctant shake of the head, his euphoria at having attracted Miss Pringle's praise suddenly of no consequence. However, as though to compensate, his mother's hands were placed supportively upon his shoulders.

'Good idea,' she said, squeezing. 'I'll see Mrs Robinson and ask. No doubt she'll oblige – especially when I tell her it's for a grumpy old man.'

Mr Barnes merely growled.

The knocking was not with the door-rattling force that could possibly mean his father, nor for that matter the crisp knuckle rapping of a woman, but more the tentative tap of a child.

'Sally!' his mother said, upon opening the door. 'Yes, well. You'd better come in.'

'Better not, Mrs Hughes. I mean, I was told to just – you know.'

'Yes. Don't worry, pet. I understand. I'll be right back.'

His mother gathered up the carrier bag containing his father's overalls and paused to check on the whereabouts of her supposedly all-important letter. Satisfied, she them stepped outside.

With the door not fully closed, much of what was being said could still be heard. As she stepped back inside Mr Barnes could barely contain himself. 'What copy, Maureen Bassett? And with what solicitor? You bain't got no solicitor!'

His mother planted a noisy kiss on the old man's forehead. 'Yes, I have,' she said, giving the old man the first of four pats on the cheek. 'Messrs Barney, Barney, and Barney.

CHAPTER FORTY-TWO

The second bout of knocking caught his mother completely unprepared, flustered, bordering on panic. 'Oh, what now? Who could that be? Not Charlie. I mean, he hasn't had time to…'

'I'll go! he said, already on his way to the door.

On the other side of it, blocking out the light, stood the uniformed figure of a policeman. 'Mum! Mum, it – it's for you!'

'Mm …' the policeman said, reaching in his breast pocket. 'Chief suspect attempts to flee.'

'No!' he said. 'No – I'm, I'm just makin' room for me mum!'

'Inside,' his mother ordered, ushering him away from the door. 'Yes? Can I help, Constable?'

'Sergeant, actually, Mrs Hughes. Sergeant Adams, off duty, I might add. Made a little detour on my way home. May I come in?'

'Yes. Yes, of course. Dawn – how is she? I mean, any better? Less – you know.'

'Unhurried, in silence, Sergeant Adams appeared to take everything in; the room, Mr Barnes's smouldering fire, his long-case clock, the sideboard

… everything. 'Barney,' he said, giving Mr Barnes a nod. 'Long time no see.'

'Aye, a good while, Stewart – a good while. Not since I catched you and that brother of yourn up my plum tree. Come t' take the lad away, 'as we? Lock 'im up and throw away the key.'

Sergeant Adams placed his helmet on the table and worked the muscles at the corners of his mouth into something approaching a smile. 'If only it were that simple,' he said. 'A pot of tea might help matters, though. Keep things nice and civilised. Wouldn't you say, Mrs Hughes?'

'Er … yes. Yes, of course! A pot of tea.'

Sergeant Adams eyed him over his cup and sipped. 'The *Get Well* card. Your idea, was it, William?'

'Billy paid for it!' his mother said, butting in. 'Well, some of it. The rest he's working off by tidying shelves in the shop. J-just an hour at a time. Two hours in total, nothing more.'

'Mm. I see,' the sergeant said, taking his time in settling his cup back on its saucer. 'And you, Mrs Hughes. A regular thing, I believe,' he added, resorting to a thoughtful clicking of the tongue. 'You er … how can I put it? Having had to play the part of proverbial door mat?'

She answered with a short, almost imperceptible nod. Then, as though having had second thoughts, raised her chin and looked the

251

sergeant fully in the face. 'It's not all my husband's fault. There – there were frustrations.'

Mr Barnes gasped, held his breath – and stamped his stick down. 'I'll be outside! Make of it what you will, Stewart. You bain't daft.'

'There en't no ferule on Mr Barnes' stick,' he said, rising from the table. 'I'd better go with 'im. I mean, he might slip in the yard!'

'No doubt,' the sergeant said. 'Nice try, lad. But first things first. As I was about to say. Your card went down rather well. Occupies pride of place on my daughter's bedside locker, it does. However, putting that to one side… Having listened to her account of events, I'd now like to hear yours. If the two stories match, then maybe – just maybe, you can make yourself scarce. Sound reasonable?'

Reasonable? Too damn right, it were. And I were doing okay. I were winnin'. But then, you had to step in. Didn't yer – "Mummy".

"The thing is, Sergeant Adams, you see, we're locked out of our own home. And it's my house – not Charlie's. My parents left it to me. The deeds are in my name – mine!"

Yeah ma, that pricked up our Stewart's ears. Oh yeah, don't think I hadn't cottoned on. "Yes, Stewart. No, Stewart. And signed off by the doctor on

252

Tuesday with any luck, you say? Just in time for the new school term, Stewart."

Called for a top-up of tea, it did. Yeah, all that and more before I were sent to check on Mr Barnes. Made me want to puke, it did, the thought of the two of you being left on yer own. Mind you, I did get a proper haircut out of it. A right wizard with the scissors was our Stewart.

'There we are, young man. How's that? A right pukka crew-cut, that!'

'Yeah! Cor! Thanks, Mr Adams. The first in our gang t' get one. You wait 'til they see it!'

The Sergeant merely nodded. 'Yes, well, that done, I'll be on my way. Thanks once again for the card. And not prompted by your mother, I understand. In future, though, a bit more of this,' he said, tapping his skull. 'Goes a long way, William. Especially in my job. Yes … as my dear wife failed to appreciate' he added, and paused, as though for the sole purpose of giving his inner thoughts a sad and somewhat reflective smile.

A police sergeant once more, he abruptly pointed out that the yard needed a sweep. 'Or we'll bring the wrath of Barney down on us, Heaven forbid!'

He wiped the blades of his mother's scissors on his thigh and took a deep breath. 'I'll leave you to it, then,' he said, handing him the scissors. 'Just

253

collect my helmet and tell your mother I'm more than satisfied. We'll say no more about it. Case closed!'

CHAPTER FORTY-THREE

The morning could not come soon enough.

'So.' Miss Pringle said. 'It's to be Henry from now on, is it?'

'Yeah, well. You can't keep on calling me William's brother, can you, Miss Pringle?'

'No … no, that's right. I can't. So, Henry, it is! And, I must say, such a fine name, well suited to a young man noble enough to have already stepped in to pay off his brother's debt. He's, er – he's well, I take it? Your "brother"?'

'Oh yes, Miss Pringle. Only he's a bit jealous of me crew-cut. None of the other lads in the village 've got one, see – only me!'

'Yes, well. I do see,' Miss Pringle said. 'And it's no wonder. It's very … American. Or, do all British policemen have their hair cut like that now?'

The matter required serious thought. All a game, he knew, Miss Pringle playing her part surprisingly well. But he foresaw difficulties. For a start, where would he get something resembling a wig from when he had to change back to being William?

Luckily, his mother came to his rescue. 'Yes. William's quite well, considering,' she said, pulling a long face at Miss Pringle. 'Reading another chapter of

Treasure Island, I expect. That or getting his hair cut like his brother's. You know what boys are like. What one has, the other one has to have the same. The thing is, I'll never be able to tell them apart!'

The shop doorbell tinkled and in marched Mrs Craig. On seeing him, she brought herself to an abrupt halt. 'Suits you,' she said. 'All you need now is a ball and chain.'

Inspired and accompanied by geriatric female tittering, he dragged one foot behind him and with a cannonball of a cabbage tucked under his arm, made his way to the stockroom.

At what turned out to be almost nine o'clock. he re-entered the main body of the shop, an accepted member of society, smiled at when placing his cabbage back on the vegetable rack and thanked by Miss Pringle for, in her words, "Infusing the shop with a welcome ray of sunshine".

King William was long gone, it seemed, killed in battle. Long live Prince Henry!

Rather than accept a packet of crisps as before, he pocketed the promised two shillings and requested the ownership of a flattened cardboard box earmarked for burning.

'You're welcome to both, Dear!' Miss Pringle said. 'But, cardboard?'

'It's so I won't get me clothes dirty, Miss Pringle. I'm gonna be a success, see. I'm gonna open a savings account an'-an' - an' go t' Sunday school. An', before then, I'm gonna clean Mr Duggan's car. For free, Miss Pringle!'

'Well! That's admirable, Henry. All highly commendable. But, promise me one thing, dear. Let's have less of the "gonna". It does grate on one. I mean, it's such an ugly word. Whereas "going to" is gentler, so much easier on the ear.'

'Ho! Right,' he said, edging towards the door. 'Hi'm going to go now, then, hi ham. Cheery-bye!'

Miss Pringle had not finished with him, however. Overseen by his mother, she said: 'Before you go, dear. In my experience, seeing as Henry's birth probably hasn't been registered yet, it would save a lot of time and trouble if you opened a savings account in your brother William's name … just a thought.'

'Yeah – s'pose,' he said, his main thought already having drifted towards the mind-boggling flaunting of his prestigious crew-cut in full view of number nine.

No matter how many times having been rinsed and washed in washing powder, his bucket still carried with it a whiff of stale urine.

Undeterred, feigning deep concentration, he rubbed at imaginary stains on Betsy's roof. At no time did sight or sound of life come from within the Duggan household. Surely, it was late enough, the

257

scurrying figure of Ozzie's dad attempting to get to the shop before it closed establishing that. In fact, as Mr Cutter admitted when he came out again clutching his Sunday Mirror and Sports Argos, he had thought that Miss Pringle closed at ten o'clock. 'I normally send Oswald,' he said. 'But he's gone fruit picking'. He laughed. 'Probably eat more than he picks!'

The fact it was another way of earning money registered with him. To car wash, or pick strawberries, that was the question – or do both. He slopped more water over Betsy then sat himself down on the kerb, hidden from much of the anticipated drift of the usual folk making their way to Church. But not sufficiently hidden from the eagle-eyed Mrs Dodds who caught him daydreaming.

'Well, I must say!' she said, 'You could put some beef into it, William. And, oh dear me! Dear, dear me, I don't know. Wait there!'

Within minutes, his Godmother returned with her familiar yellow bucket and matching sponge, the latter floating in a sea of generously soaped water. 'There! Now you've no excuse. Regards to your mother. See you this afternoon. And don't be late – you, or your haircut!'

With only Betsy's hubcaps to buff up, there came from within number nine the rising wail of a child, presumably Allan, his cry suggesting both pain and surprise.

It triggered a full-blown family rift. Allan screamed out his distress. Jenny protested her innocence. While, throughout it all, Mrs Duggan repeatedly demanded the presence of Mr Duggan. 'Now, Donald! Before I do something I might regret!'

Mr Duggan, although the man of the house, did not and reportedly never had, possessed a strong voice. The most that could be said of him was that when angry his vocal cords produced octaves readily attributable to a hysterical cat, the greater the crime the higher the pitch. This morning, the man's words rang out as clear as the church's treble bell.

As though summoned, Mr Duggan emerged from his side passage beady-eyed and dishevelled. 'What the -?'

'It's your free car wash, Mr Duggan! Remember?'

'Oh,' Mr Duggan said, sweeping back his hair. 'Yes. Yes, but not now. I've too much on. N-n-not now.'

'I could help! I could press the pedals down like before!'

Mr Duggan sucked in a chest-expanding lungful of air … and held it. Then, like a punctured Frido, the air seeped out of him. Deflated and seemingly beyond repair, he raised his palms in abject surrender. But that was as far as it went, whatever he might have wanted to say being denied him by a renewed bout of infantile wailing.

Mr Duggan cast him an unreadable look. 'Right,' he said, rolling up his sleeve. 'Right!'

Left to his own devices, he went through the covering motions of sponging yet more water over Betsy's roof, while from inside number nine the octaves rose. 'No! You're not coming with us! To your room, I said! Go on! And leave,' – "slap" – 'Allan alone!'

The silence told its own story. Even before Jenny retaliated, he could picture the intensity of the venom concentrated in her eyes, the withheld breath, while the words … the words did not have to be imagined. 'Go, then! And don't come back!' Never!'

Well, who'd 'ave thought it? Your nice Mr Duggan losing his rag with his "little princess". Hard to imagine, eh, Ma? Take her side eh, Ma? Hmph! Imagination – too much of it in my case, you always reckoned. But, then again, perhaps not enough. I never imagined what was to come next, did I now?

No, I never imagined that …

CHAPTER FORTY-FOUR

Mrs Dodds ended Sunday school by having them sing *Onward Christian Soldiers* followed by a short prayer asking for their safe return home.

'Well?' Tim said, afterwards.

'Yeah, 's'pose,' he said, and launched himself, nose pinched, from off the top step. 'Is it a bird? Is it a plane? No! It's—!'

'You're barmy,' Kenny said. 'And dead jammy with it, Doddy thinking you'd got your question right.'

'Well I did, didn't I?'

'Only if Jesus was riding into battle on a horse. Calvary, you twit. But, never mind, you got your point.'

'Yeah, right. Another ninety-nine an' I might be able t' choose some junior goals.' he said, a quip which seemed to sway the choice of what to do in favour of going home and changing for a kick-about rather than make their way to the South Morton Summer Fete.

'Let's face it,' Kenny said. 'By the time we got there, it'd be time to come back. Unless you're going to borrow your dad's bike, Hughesie.'

'Oh yeah – an' get me block knocked off, I suppose?'

In the end, a kick-about was agreed, the trio joined within the hour by a lonesome Ozzie Cutter.

Ozzie was the first to realise that something had happened. 'He's mad!' he said, as Clem bounced and roared a tractor down the blind side of the long field hedge. Not until he had slewed the tractor and its trailer fully into view did his gestures and shouts hit home. 'Crash! Come on! You an' all, Chamberpots! Crash!'

He met them at the stile, the trailer bed within jumping distance. All aboard, and they were away, jerked forward by a poor selection of gears. Then, up they went, the tractor making short work of the climb. 'Hang on t' yer hats, Comrades!' Clem shouted over his shoulder – and took them round in an arc, the waiting lip of the old sand quarry temporarily out of sight beneath the trailer over-hang.

No one spoke. No one jumped ship. Everyone, himself included, just laughed … and regained colour.

The tractor tyres threw up rubble clattering it against the underside of the trailer, then gripped, and climbed once more. Up they went, heading for The Ridgeway, forever onward, through open gateways and on into the farm yard.

262

A series of gear changes slowed the tractor. It allowed Clem to stand, presumably for a better view. 'Nobody can get through! But yer Uncle Clem can!' he said, and choosing his moment, pulled out on to the road. He followed it to their first closed gate. 'Open it, for Pete's sake. Quick! Before one of them coppers sees me.'

Through the gateway, with Ozzie back on board, Clem drove on. 'Be there in a jiffy, Comrades. Be there in a jiffy!'

The knot of people gathered at the milestone seemed undecided whether to go or stay, some leaving for no apparent reason, others joining for no better reason. The majority stayed with their vehicles, those with a mind to glean information questioning those sauntering back.

No one sounded a horn. No one so much as coughed.

Two ambulances waited, engines cut.

A police inspector waited, slapping his gloves into the palm of his hand.

Then, spoken softly, with no sense of urgency, someone gave an order. And the awful truth of the matter began to unfold.

From beneath the jacked-up cabin and front axle of a Smith and Sons grit lorry, winched out inch by inch, emerged a barely recognisable, garish yellow Austin A30.

'Jenny weren't with 'em!' he blurted. 'I – I mean… She weren't. I know she weren't.'

It was as though he had not spoken.

Inch, by inch … A man, clearly the driver of the lorry, drew on a cigarette as though it was all part of a normal day. Cut by cut, the back end of Betsy was opened up.

'Yeah,' Tim said. 'But Allan was.'

'Poor bugger,' Clem said. Just "poor bugger" – and gave the order to leave.

Back in Abbots Lovell, news of the crash had reached the village ahead of them. Shouted instructions followed by the slam of car doors sounded from all sides. In the event, only two cars pulled away, leaving in their wake a practically deserted street. Apart from themselves, only Miss Pringle remained, the woman staring hand-over-mouth in the direction of the crossroads.

Prompted by Kenny, they went to her.

'Oh, the poor, poor woman,' she said. 'Both of them … both.'

'We've bin up there!' Ozzie said. 'Saw everythin', we did!'

Bypassing Ozzie, Miss Pringle looked to Clem, her expression conveying all too clearly what she wanted to know.

Clem gave an appraising sniff and shook his head. 'Sorry, Miss Pringle, I can't say as there's much hope for either of 'em. Pretty gruesome, it were. No place for these young uns, that's for sure.'

Miss Pringle gave what passed as a nod, an act which seemed to trigger the release of a solitary tear. Letting it run, she turned and bid them follow. 'Treat yourselves,' she said, her face, devoid of spectacles, appearing ancient, almost as old as her geriatric father's.

They chose modestly. Clem selected a packet of crisps: Ozzie, Kenny, Tim and himself, liquorice sticks.

Either chewing or crunching, they stared down at Betsy's empty parking slot.

'Well,' Clem said, and followed Miss Pringle in looking towards the crossroads. 'It's one way of curing an oil leak.'

Ozzie pressed the toe of his baseball boot to a solidified black patch, an island set in a sea of islands, most of them going back months, possibly even years. Others, thinner and tinged with swirls of purple, green and an insipid red, told a different story.

'Do you remember its bonnet and boot?' Tim said. 'Faded, they were. Made it look, well, sort've two-tone.'

'Yeah,' Ozzie said. 'An' the dragon flag. D' yer remember that? Welsh, it were.'

Clem burst his empty bag of crisps. 'Welsh my arse! Duckie got it from that new Eye-tie garage up at Middle Morton. Anyway, what the hell? Flag or no bleedin' flag, the rusty old crate shouldn't 'ave bin on the road.'

'No,' Kenny said, restoring a sombre air to their staring. 'It shouldn't.'

Yeah, staring, staring, staring, each and every one of us stood there with his own personal thoughts and memories. Or were that just me Ma – eh? Just me, after what I'd overheard coming from inside number nine that morning?

Yeah, me. Had to be, didn't it, "Mummy"? Always me ...

CHAPTER FORTY-FIVE

'The question is…' Kenny said, breaking the silence, '…and I think I know the answer… The question is — when Mr Duggan got to the crossroads and more than likely found he'd only got his handbrake and, well, possibly gears to bring him to a halt, why did he choose to turn the way he did?'

'Yeah!' Ozzie blurted. 'And slap-bang into that dirty great big grit lorry?'

Clem gave Ozzie a withering look. 'Shut it,' he said, and took his belt in a notch. 'Yep! Wiv yer all the way there, Kenny-me-old-son. In fact, I were thinkin' along them very same lines meself, I was. But you carry on, pal. Don't want t' steal yer thunder, as it were. Then I can see if you'm on the right track, like.'

Kenny eyed Clem, appeared to think for a moment, and said, 'Yes, well. There's nothing to say I'm right, of course. But it'll set the ball rolling, as it were. Then, well, see what we come up with,' he said before being brought to a halt by a panic-stricken shout and chasing figure of Mrs Collins. 'Stop her, somebody! Somebody stop her! No, Jenny! Stop!'

'Oh shit – come on!' Clem said, only to stand, powerless, at the roadside, the blockage at the crossroads evidently having been cleared.

A Morris Minor responded to their frantic waving: but too late. At full pelt Jenny swerved and weaved her way past the outspread arms of Major Craig to reach and pass through the lych-gate.

The churchyard wall presented no obstacle, but still they could not make up for lost ground. In a cluster, they burst into church, clattered into from behind by an open-mouthed chest-heaving Mrs Collins.

She sank onto a pew, no more than a witness, as they all were, to the scene being played out at the pulpit: Jenny, down on her knees, tugging and clawing at the Vicar's cassock.

'Tell him! Tell him I didn't mean it. You tell him. Tell him!'

But the Vicar's concern appeared to be reserved solely for the safety of his Bible, held aloft, out of harm's way.

Jenny cast aside the cassock and scrambled to her feet. She twisted. She turned. Wild-eyed and searching, she did not seem to recognise Major Craig or Mrs Perkins until they had taken hold of her.

'No!' she said. 'No!'

She slumped, a dead weight, feet pressed flat on the flagstones. She clung to a pew, lost her grip and grabbed at another. She kicked. She spat. She

268

broke free and ran between the pews. There seemed no means of escape … nor was there. Boxed in, overseen by the stained-glass figures of St. Francis of Assisi and St. Anne, she flopped to the floor, and rocked.

CHAPTER FORTY-SIX

At ten o'clock, on the first day of the new school term, St. Nicholas C of E Juniors assembled as instructed, orderly and silent in the front playground.

Miss Wheatcroft addressed them. 'Attention! Pair up, please, youngest with the eldest!'

Dawn Adams grabbed his hand. 'I'll go with you, Billy.'

'Yeah, s'pose, if you 'ave to.'

'I do,' she said. 'And you've got to be nice to me after what you did. It still hurts,' she added, and leaned back, face screwed as though scrutinising some hat he was wearing.

He ran his fingers through his hair, still a crew-cut of sorts, and sighed. 'Sent yer a card, didn't I?'

She gave a slow somewhat distracted nod and frowned. 'Was it really bad?' she said. 'I mean, really, really.'

'Yeah,' he said, the police inspector and driver of the lorry vividly recalled, the one with his gloves, the other with his cigarette. 'Yeah …it was.'

Miss Wheatcroft clapped her hands, just once, but loud. It demanded silence, duly granted and received with a slight raise of their headmistress's chin. 'You are aware,' she began, chin raised a notch higher. 'of the tragedy that has befallen the village. As you will have noted, Jennifer Duggan is not with us this morning. Neither is Patricia Collins. The two of them will be with their respective families and return to school when appropriate. Unfortunately, it is possible that Allan Duggan – a likely future pupil of the school – may never return. In our prayers, prompted by the Vicar, we will concentrate our thoughts on Allan. We will ask that the skill of the doctors and nurses treating him prevails. We will also pray for Mrs Duggan, that she may recover from the loss of her husband and gain strength for the battle being waged to save the life of her son. In the meantime, I wish to enlist your co-operation in keeping all noise to a minimum, both in the playground and on your way to and from school.'

Having delivered her message, Miss Wheatcroft narrowed her eyes and looked along the line passing from pupil to pupil, until pausing. 'William Hughes,' she said. 'Do I make myself clear?'

He opened his mouth to speak but could only stare. Miss Wheatcroft showed no intention of moving on, however. Not until he had moistened his lips and said, 'Yes, Miss Wheatcroft.'

She took her eyes from him and moved on, pupil to pupil as before. At the end of the line, she pronounced herself satisfied. 'Right! Good,' she said, not having spoken to anyone other than him, no-one, not even Phillip Granger.

Once through the lych-gate, they assembled once more, strictly to the left of the path and still in pairs. 'And remember,' Miss Wheatcroft said. 'The Service is not only held in memory of Jennifer's father, but also in celebration of his life. Therefore, sound all responses clearly, and sing heartily. Your pew will be pointed out to you and an Order of Service will be provided, one for each pairing. Share sensibly. You are not only representing the school, but also yourselves. Proceed!'

Their pew could not have been situated further from his lovely Jenny if those who had allocated it had tried. Sandwiched between Mrs Duggan and Trish in the front pew, she appeared as docile as she had previously been wild. At no point did she do anything other than face the front. When spoken to, her response amounted to no more than a short, barely detectable, nod.

Drugged, he supposed: probably injected by Dr Murdoch. The same Dr Murdoch who, witnessed by St. Francis of Assisi and St. Anne, had spoken softly to her, opened his arms, closed them again as she fell against him, and held her tight.

A tug of his sleeve broke the spell. "Shush", Dawn's finger-pressed lips urged. Flustered, he took hold of his share of the proffered Order of Service.

'Let us pray.'

'Our Father which art in Heaven,
Hallowed be Thy name…'

Recited by villagers and strangers alike, the familiar phrases washed over him. No word escaped his lips. Not so much as an "Amen". Not one. All about him were evidently oblivious to his silence, a particular silence, concentrated on a particularly easy picked out bun of greying hair.

The boards beneath his feet vibrated, awakening him as though out of a dream.

'The day Thou gavest, Lord is ended,
The darkness falls at Thy behest,
To Thee our morning hymns ascended…'

And Miss Wheatcroft's warbling certainly did ascend. Decidedly "hearty", it joined the combined efforts of the organ and choir to soar higher than any fluted column and enter the cavernous emptiness lying overhead.

Transfixed by the pattern woven by laths and beams, he likened it to stairways; many stairways placed side-by-side like ladders, there to be climbed, rung by rung, leading to who-knows-where … probably his godmother's. "They'll not be letting you in, William, that's for sure. Not with hands like that."

273

At his side, Dawn let go her hold of the shared Order of Service, sniffed, and licked away the remnants of a tear. She looked up, sharply, the long curl of her lashes revealing eyes he had always assumed to be black but were in fact the darkest of browns.

In a husky, part-whisper, she said, 'He was your friend.'

He reached for her hand and, on reflection, nodded … 'Yeah.'

To his mind, it was not the hand of Dawn Adams that lay cradled in his. No, not hers, but another's, hidden from him for the most part by a line of shoulder-to-shoulder outsiders; townies judging by the cut of their suits.

Not until Mr Duggan's coffin, borne steadily out down the aisle on shoulders, could he see his Princess. On she came, holding hands with Trish, second in line behind Mrs Duggan and Mrs Collins, her eyes expressionless and fixed. Behind the foursome, the pews emptied in orderly fashion, from one side, then the other, until all had passed by: Miss Pringle, Mr and Mrs Dodds, his mother and Mr Barnes, the Coopers – so many known and unknown faces. But not, he noted, his father's; neither his, nor that of the bee-hived and purple-lipped Mrs Hicks.

Last of all, bringing up the rear, came the lone figure of the Reverend C. T. Chatterton, his steps in time with those of the coffin bearers, never faltering, never a look to either left or right, not even to acknowledge the on-guard Miss Wheatcroft.

Not until Tim emerged from the vestry did she step into the aisle and by implication release them from their pew. In pairs, in silence, they followed on, out via the south door and down the main path, only pausing to allow Tim to break ranks and open the lych-gate.

She scrutinised each pairing as it passed through, missing little, if anything: an untied shoelace, a crooked tie … 'Oh dear,' she said, when it came to Dawn. 'Had a little cry, did we? Yes, well, quite understandable. Fully recovered now, though, I trust?'

Dawn raised her chin and nodded. 'Yes, Miss Wheatcroft.'

'Good,' Miss Wheatcroft said, and twitched one of her headmistress smiles. 'Then perhaps William can safely let go of your hand now. Wouldn't you say …mmm?'

A robot, he looked through and beyond Miss Wheatcroft and sprang open his fingers, the hand that had wormed its way so compliantly into his now gone, a thing of the past, along with Mr Duggan. And Betsy.

'I'm not stayin',' he said, once back in the school playground. 'You can tell the old bag what you like – anythin'.'

275

'But' – Dawn clearly intended to say more. If only he had given her the chance.

She ran and caught up with him. 'Billy?' she said, from the other side of the school railings. 'Please, Billy – for me?'

Realising that she had run out of railing, he relented. 'Just say I 'ad to go 'ome, okay?'

'Miss Wheatcroft probably won't even know you've gone!' she said, a whole new expression suddenly lighting up her face. 'She won't! What with extended playtime and everything. I mean, you will be back for dinner, won't you? Then it's craftwork. And you're good at that!'

'Yeah, well, perhaps …I dunno,' he said.

'I'll get my dad to give you another crew-cut!' she shouted after him.

He walked on.

He waited until last before choosing from the materials table. He worked alone, only looking up at the sound of Miss Wheatcroft's voice. 'That's a splendid looking spire, William. St Mary's is it?'

After she had gone, he lifted his model from his board and balanced it on the palm of his hand, studied it, closed his fingers around it, and squeezed.

CHAPTER FORTY-SEVEN

A tight-lipped Tim came across him sitting in the Community Field.

'Comfy are we?'

'Might be.'

For a moment, it appeared his friend would give up on him and go. But no, he squatted beside him, silent and reflective, until giving a meaningful nod in the direction of the neighbouring village. 'It's where Miss Wheatcroft lives, across the road from that spire you destroyed. Made her neck go all red, it did, you doing that.'

'Good! I 'ope it gives 'er spots. An' before you go on, you can shut it. I've already 'ad it all from Ozzie. It were nothin' t' do with me. It were Dawn the old bag 'ad a go at. Ignored me, 'er did. Never even looked at – what's so funny? Come on, Robinson! Before I bash yer one.'

It made no difference. Tim, trying to lighten the mood, started writhing around as though on broken bottles rather than parched grass. 'Oh! Ouch! All those dropped aitches, so prickly for you. Ouch! Oowah!'

His party-piece discarded, an entirely different Tim lay with his arms spread as though shot, though very much alive, and frowning. 'I wonder if there is anything like a Heaven up there,' he said, took in a lungful of air, and directed it skyward as though gently blowing away an obscuring cloud.

For a while, neither of them spoke. Then, still gazing upward, Tim said, 'Aren't you hungry?'

'No. Why should I be?'

His friend paused, caught in two minds, it seemed; whether to keep his mouth shut and say nothing, or open it and risk a smack in the teeth.

After much chewing on the inside of his cheek, he chose the latter. 'I know Dawn can be a pain. Like my sister. She's as bad! But Dawn can be, you know, quite grown up at times. And, well . . . perceptive.'

'Per-what?'

'Perceptive. You know – canny. Reads into things – can suss things out. '"Billy never cries", is what she said. But you were, she insisted. You were crying on the inside, where it wouldn't show.'

'Load of bollocks.'

Tim turned towards him, eyeball to eyeball. 'Then why hold of her hand? It's no disgrace, you know, to be upset. I mean, we all were in one way or another.'

'Piss off!'

Heaving a sigh, Tim lay back as before. 'Sometimes,' he said. 'Just – oh, I don't know.'

278

'Look! It were titty-babbie Dawn doin' the snivellin', not me – right?'

Tim firmed up his chin and stared as though sightless into the distance.

'Right, Robinson!'

Still gazing, Tim said. '..."Strange'', that's what Dawn said you were. "Billy was strange. He held my hand and kept on holding it even though he doesn't like me. I know he doesn't".'

Suddenly, without warning, Tim turned on him, his evident anger colouring the whites of his eyes. 'She's seven, Billy. You frightened her. And she didn't know what to do!'

'Aah … does Timmy-wimmy love lickle Dawny-warny?'

Breathing hard, Tim stated in no uncertain terms that. no, "Timmy-wimmy" didn't love "Dawny-warny". 'And don't think for a minute that she was fooled by you saying you were going home,' he added. 'Neither of us were. Could have got us all into trouble, you could – especially me.'

'You?' he retorted. 'You! Goody-goody Robinson? Don't make me laugh.'

On his feet, fists clenched at his side, "Tim-de-Tim", as Clem called him, finally exploded. 'Yes, me! I didn't report you for bunking off without permission. I didn't report Dawn for climbing onto the old air-raid shelter. And I lied to Miss Wheatcroft when she asked where you were – the kid who's always up for seconds. Thirds, if he can cram them in. Lied! And on my first day as a prefect. Thanks, Billy – thanks a lot!'

Having said his piece, Tim sat back, fiercely silent and evidently determined to remain so.

In response, he treated his friend to a half-hearted snort, rested the back of his head against his goalpost, and closed his eyes.

The church clock marked a quarter.

It sounded the hour.

The Hollersham school bus belched its way towards the top of the village, where it would turn and with a joyous whine make its way back down, leaving in its wake the usual stink of diesel fumes.

'We'll be on that this time next year,' Tim said.

'Yep,' he said.

He wished to have said more, and opened his eyes, his look concentrated, fixed as though with a mind of its own on that spike of a spire. A spire that suddenly and inexplicably divided and blurred.

'It's the only time I've ever bin 'appy. Proper 'appy,' he said, barely able to recognise his own voice. 'Th-th' only-'

'What?' Tim said. 'Yes – sorry. Of course. I – I didn't think. The car washing and, well, the pressing down of pedals and that. But, if you think about it. Well, it wasn't for long, not really – was it? And I know Mr Duggan lent us his ladder. But, well, there's others worse off than you, you know. Think of them. From little Allan all the way down to poor Sal. Real excited she was. Never been on a holiday in her life, she hadn't. And there she was, sitting with Trish all packed and ready to go, only for it all to blow up in their faces. Five minutes more and they'd have been away.'

'So what?' he said. 'She en't the only one! Abbots Lovell-on-Duckpond – that's me. And it en't nothin' t' do with bleedin' car washin' or ladders – none on it! You know bugger-all, Robinson. So, stick it up yer arse, why don't yer? Just –'

Tim glared at him, red about the gills. Whatever he was about to say dried on him, however. Then, as though having followed his line of sight, his friend finally arrived at somewhere near the truth. Shame-faced and mumbling, he said, 'St. Mary's. Your gran and granddad. I should've realised. I – I'd forgot. I'm sorry.'

'Why should you be? What's it to you?'

Tim cleared his throat. 'Yeah, well … nothing, I suppose. But you and your mum – especially your mum. It must've brought it all back, seeing the coffin and everything. And, let's face it. It wasn't that long ago, was it? Not really. And, well, look how everything's gone to pot since then. And I don't just mean the garden. Your mum's health for a start, and-and – and having to live with Barney. But sitting out here, just staring at that spire. What's the good of that?'

'They'm me ancestors,' he said. 'Married there. And buried there.'

'Yes, well – look! Tell you what. Hows about me and you going over there and visiting their graves? After Sunday school, say. What d'you reckon?'

He shrugged.

Tim waited, chewing on the inside of that cheek of his, shook his head, and sighed. 'I don't know why I bother. In fact, I think I'll go and see how Kenny and Susan got on. Don't bother getting up.'

'Weren't goin' to.'

As tight-lipped as when he had arrived, his so-called friend gave him a wide berth and went on his way. On reaching the other goalpost, he paused, part-turned and said, 'You don't deserve friends. You're just like your dad – d'you know that? Nothing but a bully. All self!'

'No I en't! You come back 'ere and say that t' me face, Robinson – I dare yer!'

Tim walked on. He did not pause. He did not look back. Never, it seemed, having intended to.

Not once.

CHAPTER FORTY-EIGHT

Back home, his mother greeted him with little more than a cursory glance. ''You're late,' was all she said. Busy spreading margarine on a slice of crusty bread, she paused as though about to say more, only to continue and pick up from where she had left off at a faster and more determined pace.

He waited.

The spreading done, she laid down her knife, wiped her hands between the folds of her apron, and said, 'I want a word with you, young man. But later – look!'

Slowly, as though about to perform a magic trick, she pulled a length of string up from her apron pocket. Out it came, some ten inches long, at the end of which dangled a key. 'Voila! Took his time, mind. But he got there in the end.'

'He's bin, then? Me dad, I mean?'

'Don't be silly. When did your father ever do his own dirty work? No, that fell to Sally, decked out in her new school uniform. Well, her second-hand new uniform, I would say, judging by the look of it, bless her.'

She lowered the key onto her waiting palm. Next came the string, lowered and wound until it encircled the key in a neat coil.

A wreath, he thought, one that appeared to mesmerise his mother.

'Put it somewhere safe,' he said. 'Mum …?'

Either away with the fairies as of old or so preoccupied with her thoughts, she appeared not to have heard.

'Mum!'

She frowned, slowly turned her head, and faced him.

'I said, you need to put it somewhere safe, Mum – the key.'

'Yes – yes, of course. As if I didn't know that,' she said. 'But there's no need to shout. It's been an upsetting day. Now, wash your hands and face – go on!'

Full of bustle and efficiency, she pocketed the key, changed the water in the washing-up bowl and handed him the soap. Then, gesturing him to get on with it, she stood watching, monitoring his every splash, every spread of soap, every rub, every swill and repeat, until pronouncing herself satisfied.

'Now,' she said, face set.

'What?'

Clearly not in a proper state of mind, she plucked the soap out from where he had left it and held it to within an inch of his mouth. 'If I get any

284

more reports of you using foul language in public – or anywhere else, come to that — I'll use this to scrub out the inside of your mouth – d'you hear me!'

Held by something evil registered in her eyes, he pressed his lips together, and nodded.

'Right,' she said, although even then she had not finished with him. On and on she went, on and on and on, salvation coming in the form of a knock on the front door.

'Stewart!' sounded the voice of Mr Barnes. 'Come in, lad. Mo!'

Attempting to tidy herself as she went, his mother disappeared into the lounge. 'Sergeant?'

'Oh, don't look so worried, Mrs Hughes. 'There's nothing amiss. Nothing that I'm aware of, anyway,' he said, giving him an interrogating look – and smiled. Dawn had missed her bus, he explained. 'But, before I whisk her away from the Robinson's, I'm told by said daughter that I have a duty to perform. A hair trim,' he said, and poked his helmet, not on his own head, but on his, gave it a pat firm enough to send it down over his eyes, and carried on talking. 'But first, if possible, a private word in your shell-like, Mrs Hughes.'

'Oh! Well, yes – yes, of course, Sergeant. Come on through.'

By the time he had lifted the helmet off his head the pair had entered the scullery. By sound alone he could picture his mother's fluster and blush – and

285

strained to hear more. The privilege was denied him however, cut short by a closing clunk and drop of the back-door latch.

"Sergeant" … "Mrs Hughes" – a dead give-away, it struck him. A cover for what was really taking place: hugs and kisses in Mr Barnes's greenhouse more than likely. Worst of all, overlooked up until that point, came the horror of gaining Dawn Adams as a sister.

He looked to Mr Barnes. 'Why've they gone out there? I mean, what for? What they doin'?'

Mr Barnes raised an eyebrow. 'Doing? Well,' he said, poking at his fire. 'Knowing Stewart, pinchin' more o' my plums. Why, lad? Got a guilty conscience, 'as we?'

'No.'

The old man gave his poker a final thrust. 'Then it won't be before time, will it, mister? So, keep it that way. For those with sense enough to realise it, to greet the first cuckoo and marvel at the song of the thrush be a good life. Something now denied the likes of Duckie Duggan. God rest his soul.'

'There!' Mr Adams said. 'Not that there was that much to take off. First in the school, according to my daughter. Must keep in with the ladies, eh, William?'

A few more tidying up snips and the job was pronounced done. 'And now I must make tracks,' his barber said. 'Before I do, though. A question for you – under oath, mind!' he said, no longer the barber, but very much the Police Sergeant. 'A new hair style … a new identity. Not unknown in my trade, especially by those seeking to escape from something …or someone. Ring a bell?'

'William,' he said, the name escaping his lips without conscious input or forethought on his part.

'Hm …' the sergeant said, 'interesting. And I suppose people take to this other character, this new Henry, do they? Better, perhaps, than they do to William. That must be very annoying. I mean, the two of you virtually being brothers – twins, in effect.

'Yeah,' he accepted, with a nod. 'And it en't fair, Mr Adams – it en't!'

'No …' the sergeant said, as though pondering. 'No, it isn't. The thing is, as far as I can see, friend Henry's fairly new on the scene, is he not? As such, he hasn't had to experience all the upheaval that William has. In fact, William has borne the brunt of it all. Henry should be grateful – more than grateful. And, perhaps he is. Perhaps – and it's just a theory -- perhaps he's trying to pay you back. You know, provide you with a break, a form of escape. Don't you think?'

He shrugged. 'I – I dunno,' he said, the memory of the leap from the top of the Community Hall steps still fresh in his mind. Also, seeping in, a replay of Henry's time spent working in Miss

287

Pringle's shop, making people laugh, and laughing himself, out of sight, in the storeroom.

'I wanna be William,' he said. 'But I'm Billy, Mr Adams. The one who's always gettin' laughed at. Even when gettin' the shit stabbed out of 'im.'

The sergeant sat on his haunches and placed a hand on each of his shoulders. 'I'm not too sure I wanted to know that, William.'

'It-it – it weren't a proper dagger!' he blurted, alarmed at the severity of the sergeant's frown and slow thoughtful run of the tip of the man's tongue. 'J-just a dinner fork.'

The sergeant stood to his full height, and looked down at him, clicking his tongue.

The clicking stopped.

'Dawn tells me you took care of her this morning. Took hold of her hand when she got upset, she said. Well, thank you for that. It's not been easy for her, losing her mum like she did. On the surface she's a live wire, over the top at times, no doubt a pest to a lad of your age. On the other hand, she's sensitive and caring with a heart of gold. So, let's strike a bargain. A gentleman's agreement, if you like. Keep up the good work and it's worth a regular hair trim. On the other hand, any more pushing through windows or anything else that might do her harm and understand this — I promise you, I'll be down on you like a ton of bricks. Do I make myself clear —

'William?'

'A ton of bricks …'

CHAPTER FORTY-NINE

Kenny's bat, ball and stumps lay abandoned by the time he escaped from Sergeant Adams and managed to make it outside. Sat in a circle, the gang cut short what had sounded a serious discussion and eyed his approach.

Ignoring everyone else, he made straight for Tim. 'I'm sorry,' he said. 'Real sorry.'

His friend's eyelids flickered. 'Yeah, well … okay,' he said, and made room for him.

Kenny looked to Clem. 'You going to put him in the picture, seeing as we more or less agree?'

Clem gave his customary self-important sniff and cock of the head. 'If you like, Kenny-me-old-son. As you say, we'm as one on most of it. Well, almost, anyway. So, Billy-boy. I'll keep it brief. The thing is, we reckon it's all your fault fer havin' messed wiv Duggan's handbrake.'

'Eh?'

Tim laid a restraining hand on him. 'He's having you on. There was something Carol mentioned, though –'

'Yeah!' Ozzie butted in. 'Summat about you messin' wiv Duggan's handbrake. And we wuz-'

Clem's reprimanding cuff silenced him. 'Who's conductin' this enquiry? You – or me?'

'You, Clem.'

'Right. Then listen and you might learn summat. The missin' piece in yer Uncle Clem's jigsaw, Comrades. The handbrake! How far could you pull it up, Billy-boy? Think, pal. How many notch –?

'Ten!' he said, only too eager to share his knowledge – and accurate knowledge at that. 'It were ten. Ten clicks, same as me age. Workin' well, it were!'

The reaction was not what he had envisaged.

'Yes, well,' Kenny said, breaking the silence. 'There we have it. Enquiry over, I reckon.'

'Not quite,' Clem said. 'And it were our Walter who put me on to it,' he added, with uncharacteristic modesty. 'The lorry, Comrades – the lorry!'

Silence …

Then, everyone spoke at once.

'Exactly!' Clem said, when they had evidently come up with the right answer; that the Smith and Sons lorry had collided with Betsy while straddling the white line.

'Yes, well,' Kenny said, slightly flushed. 'it wasn't as if I'd overlooked that. The thing was, the police had already picked up on it, making chalk marks and measuring.'

291

'Huh!' Ozzie said. 'You can't measure skid marks when there en't none – you needs brakes fer that!'

Clem widened his eyes and sucked in air. 'You don't say, Oz. Well I never! Takes a genius to work that one out – don't it, lads?'

'Yes, well,' Tim said. 'That's the problem. It doesn't.'

'No …' Clem said. 'It don't. So, let's hope Duggan's old crate was so smashed up no one could say one way or the other what condition anythin' was in. But it don't look good.'

'Insurance pay out …' Kenny said, simply.

Clem gave an accepting nod – and scowled across to where Tim and he were sitting. 'Yeah. So, Billy-boy. If yer know what's good for yer, you'll keep yer trap shut. Not a dicky-bird about you helping old Duggan with his car, pal. Nor you, Oz – got it?'

Ozzie looked sheepishly about him – and grinned.

Whatever might have been said next had to wait, put aside by the familiar voice of Mrs Dodds, hailing them from the railings. 'Boys!' she repeated, hands-clasped and beaming. 'Boys, I just wanted you to know that Allan's been taken off his life support machine and the signs are favourable. Only,' she added, lowering her voice to no better than a full-lipped mime. 'Likely to be paralysed from the waist down.'

'But alive,' Tim added.

'Yes!' Mrs Dodds said, full voiced once more. 'Thanks to the Almighty, boys … thanks to the Almighty. Never underestimate the power of prayer. So, keep praying, boys.' she said, already on her way. 'Keep praying!'

Not until she was out of sight did they make a move and drift back to their sitting positions.

'I'd rather be dead,' Ozzie announced, at length.

'Can be arranged, Oz,' Clem said, and made as though to go on, only to frown, clearly having thought better of it.

In the end, it fell to Tim to fill the gap. Furrowing his brow, he said, 'I think Ozzie's right. At least where Mr Duggan's concerned. I mean, if he'd lived, imagine him being reminded every hour of every day what he'd done to Allan.'

Clem gave a slow, thoughtful nod. 'Yeah … Allan,' he said – and sprang to life, their undisputed leader, positive and full of drive. 'I can see that bastard lorry in me head, I can. Roars up to the crossroads, it does. Sees there's nothin' comin' the other way – an' so moves to the centre of the road. Our Walter's sin 'em do it! Not just straddlin' the white line, but well over, some of 'em. And why? So's they can swing in onto The Ridgeway and thunder along the strait, past our place like there's no termorra! It's our only hope, Comrades. Get our

293

Walter t' speak up and prove there's shared blame. Agreed?'

'Agreed!'

At the pinnacle of his triumph, even as their chorused support must have been ringing in his ears, their leader's verve and self-belief visibly ebbed away. Chime by chime, it was as though the marking of time had stepped in to bring him back down to earth.

'Who're we kiddin'?' he said. 'Obvious, en't it? Duggan's as guilty as hell. We en't got a pigeon's chance in a cattery. What a berk! I mean, the bloke even worked at a bleedin' digger factory. It weren't as if he weren't some sort of engineer!'

Kenny eyed Clem, biding his time, it seemed, before tentatively agreeing. 'Yes …what he did was unforgivable. But I couldn't help but like the bloke. And, to be honest, I'd have still liked to have gone to his funeral. Relatives only, though – our school rules.'

'Huh!' Ozzie said. 'Yer didn't miss much. Jeez! Didn't old Chatters go on!'

'Just a bit,' Tim admitted. 'In fact, I don't suppose as many as half the congregation knew what he was on about – eh, Billy?'

'God's will,' he said. 'All part of a divine plan.'

Clem aimed a kick at him. 'Don't come that crap with me, Billy-boy. Divine plan, my arse! You don't know what that means any more than I does,' he said, and held his foot at the ready, only to lower it again, the threat of a second kick no more than an empty threat.

'Hughesie probably does know,' Ozzie said. 'He's bin visited.'

'Oh ah?' Clem said. 'What by? Carter's ice-cream van?'

'Nah, Clem. Should've sin 'im, yer should. Gawpin', he were. Holy Ghost, weren't it, Hughesie? Filled yer with a sudden light, he did. Look!' Ozzie continued, motivated to shuffle close enough to reach out and yank up the front of his shirt. 'See? Glows, he does!'

Clem sniggered. 'That right, Billy-boy? Goin' out into the wilderness, is we? Well. If yer spreads the word as thick as you spreads the drippin' on yer toast, pal. Then you'll mek us all sick – sicker than you already does, that is. Gawd almighty! Pity the bit o' skirt that ends up wiv you, sunshine.'

He sprang to his feet. 'I en't scared of you, Cooper! I know what I knows – and you lot en't in on it. I got an understandin', see. It's all fixed for when we'm older. You just wait. You wait!' he said, and strode away, ignoring as best he could Ozzie Cutter's hoots of derision.

Rising above Ozzie's taunts, came another, however. Clem's words, crystal clear and full of mocking echo. 'We can't wait, Billy-boy. We can't

295

wait! Here's till when we're older, sunshine. Till we're older…!'

PART TWO – ADOLESCENCE 1964-67

CHAPTER FIFTY

In many respects it felt like any other start to a new school year: a freshly ironed shirt, the whiff of shoe polish, his cap – yes, even a cap, perched precariously towards the back of his Beatles' haircut, a symbol of non-conformity and Billy Windmill rebelliousness. Never though, had he been decked out in long trousers.

The arrival of the familiar ex-army bus evoked a communal groan. 'It's an elf risk!' Ozzie shouted, adopting the absent Clem's familiar quip, to which only one person responded.

Perpetually seeking the attention of a boy – any boy – Cynthia Perkins rang out the equally stale, 'Yes! An elf risk. Quick! We'd better go gnome!'

As usual, he sat with Tim, both suitably placed to observe those yet to climb the three boarding steps. Up they came; Tim's sister, Carol, Sally Hicks, Ozzie and a reluctant Jenny, scowling at Kenny who had grabbed the sleeve of Trisha's blazer.

'Good luck to him,' Tim mumbled, only to perceptibly brighten. Trish, despite Kenny's obvious intentions, and the fact that her transfer from Hollersham High to the Grammar School qualified her to sit with him, passed down the aisle and sat with Jenny.

By the time a grinning Dawn Adams had been collected from Hollersham Halt, the bus was practically full when it reached the first drop-off point. The six Grammar School pupils disembarked and trailed away, the distinctive colour and length of Trish's pony-tail rendering her an obvious target for a sniper.

'She deserves shooting,' Tim said. 'How Trish came to pass her Eleven-Plus I'll never know.'

'No …' he said, as though in thoughtful agreement. Better left that way, he thought – and saw his imagined bullet hit home.

On impulse, he seized his opportunity, leapt away from Tim, and sat in the now vacant seat beside Jenny.

'Just t' say. If anyone mucks you about now you en't got Trish, then Billy-boy, 'ere to sort 'em out for yer – okay? Bye!' he said, already on his way back to Tim, sufficiently satisfied by the success of his mission to punch the air.

As third year pupils, transferred from the New to the Old Block, the front five rows of the main assembly hall awaited them. Sat nose height to the stage in the first row, he had either a worm's eye view of footwear, or a crick in the neck. Worst of all, he was in the eye-line of someone who, up until now, he had managed to avoid.

"For we shall remember this day, you and I,"

And as Mrs Dodds might have said, it had come to pass.

Oh, he remembered right enough, even down to the leather patches on his bony elbows. And that Adam's apple of his. Like the breastbone on one of Cyril Cooper's plucked battery hens. Mr E-type 'imself.

The hall quietened and fell silent. Miss Smithers took her place at the piano. The deputy head, affectionately known as Old Grumpy, led the rest of the teaching staff to the chairs set out at back of the stage.

As one, the orderly line bent at the knees, and sat.

Seconds later, again as one, they stood, a signal for all to stand as the headmaster entered and mounted the stage, towering over him, exactly as he had remembered him with the aristocratic tic, his leather patches and ridiculous Adam's apple. It never rested – like the man's eyes. In the main, they appeared focused above and beyond the first row, even while pacing across the stage, thrusting up his palms in pursuit of an ever lustier rendition of *Jerusalem*.

The gangliest and most ungainly of men, he possessed, it had to be admitted, an instinctive eye. An eye that focused without warning, not on him, but on Tim.

'Me, sir?'

'Yes, you, sir,' he replied. 'What is the name of the boy to your right? Do you know?'

Tim licked his lip. 'It's William, sir – William Hughes.'

'Ah … William Hughes. Well, will you kindly see to it, that after streaming, you ensure that Mr Hughes waits outside my office until summoned. Is that understood?'

'Yes, Headmaster,' Tim said, a manner of reply that the headmaster seemed to appreciate, drawing from him a gentlemanly nod.

After assembly, with only the third-year pupils left on the floor of the hall, Old Grumpy licked his thumb and turned over a sheet of foolscap.

'Avon!', he announced without ceremony or introduction. 'Anderson, Andrews, Blake, Cox D, Edwards …

'Trust you,' he said, as Tim prepare to leave the hall. 'You in Avon. An' me probably in Wye.'

Tim shrugged. 'Not my doing.'

'Quiet!' Old Grumpy demanded, flicked over a second sheet of foolscap and laboriously went on barking out names until, after Severn and Thames,

300

with neither his nor Jenny's name having been called, it came to Trent.

'Argent, Bradley, Bunn, Cox S, Dukes …

He held his breath – no Duggan. Unless Old Grumpy had made a mistake, Jenny would more than likely be with him in Wye.

'...Hartwell, Hughes …

The name Hughes, with no letter attached to it. It was him. He was in Trent, together with a Perkins. Cynthia ruddy Perkins!

CHAPTER FIFTY-ONE

Tim was waiting for him on the other side of the exit doors.

'See! Not Wye after all.'

'Yeah wonderful, I don't think. Daft, it is! Bleedin' streaming'. Bugger off – go on! I'll find me own way, thanks. All twenty foot of it!'

No sound came from within the headmaster's study. No one went in. No one came out. He raised his knuckles to the door, only to think better of it, sigh, and lower them again.

The door swung inward. Miss Jenkins stood before him, the headmaster's fancy-piece it was rumoured, but weighed down by box-files, she appeared the epitome of respectability. Neither flustered nor dishevelled, her demeanour spoke of nothing other than cold efficiency.

She glided past, leaving the door open behind her.

'Enter.'

He entered and stood to attention.

The headmaster closed a file and relaxed back into his shell of a chair. 'Mm ... the boy who delights in swooping across roads in the face of on-coming traffic,' he said, gazing, hands-clasped, to the ceiling. 'And, if I remember correctly, something of a comedian in those days.'

'Yes, sir.'

'Indeed …' mused the headmaster, a state of mind which seemed to require the bringing together of the points of his two index fingers in support of his chin.

A decision evidently having been made, he lowered them again and opened the file he had previously closed. 'Allocated to Trent, I note, Hughes. Any comment?'

'I'd rather be in Wye, sir.'

The headmaster turned a page and nodded his way down it. 'No, Hughes,' he said with a finality which brooked no argument. 'No, you are correctly streamed. You'll never make an academic I think we can agree. Mathematics, History, Geography – when you pay attention, that is, — all passable. The Sciences? Well, the least said about those the better. As for English, both oral and written, this is what determines you to be in Trent. Your native tongue, Hughes. Despite Miss Watkins' efforts, it still leaves a lot to be desired. Do you read?'

Thrown by the bluntness of the headmaster's question, he was caught in two minds, whether to shake his head or own up to having read part of *Treasure Island*.

Of the two, he snatched at the latter, adding, 'an'-an' – and my friend's *Eagle* – every week, Headmaster, sir!'

As though in time to a lazy rhythm the headmaster swivelled his chair from side to side, his chin supported as before, clearly a vital aid to academic deliberation.

His swivelling done, he sat forward. 'What I recommend, Hughes,' he began, cautiously, as though not fully having made up his mind. 'What I recommend, is that you concentrate above all on your English and Maths, the production of the perfect dovetail joint, the disciplines of Technical Drawing … and our star athlete Benson.'

'Sir …?'

Round went the headmaster's chair, full circle to within an inch from where it had started. 'It's all in here, Hughes,' he said, repeatedly stabbing his finger on the open file. 'It's all in here!' he said again, as enthusiastic as any Carol or Dawn having been told they had won a trip to Disneyland. 'And I quote. "Charges round like a mad bull". "Undisciplined". "Competitive to the point of annoyance" – just the chap to take over the baton of cross-country and middle- distance running! In short, to become a hero, Hughes – another Benson! Think of it, m'boy. The roar of the crowd as you enter the arena. And all for you, Hughes. You! And the continued glory of the school.'

More his usual self, the headmaster patted his desk as though in search of a pair of spectacles. 'It er – it's important to me,' he said, eventually touching on his fountain pen. 'I – well – never mind … never mind. You qualify for a free school meal, I understand.'

'Yes, sir.'

The headmaster nodded, more to himself than anything. 'Yes, well,' he said, scribbling away on a pad. 'Suitable footwear will be provided courtesy of the school. Benson will guide you on those. But, first, you must decide. What's it to be – yes … or no? The decision is yours, Hughes. Entirely yours, m'boy. And now, if you'll excuse me,' he added, signalling with the back of his hand for him to go. 'Tempus edax rerum, I'm afraid. Tempus edax rerum!'

CHAPTER FIFTY-TWO

Benson sought him out at the morning milk-break. Sixteen, possibly even seventeen years of age, powerful, and rising to within a whisker of six foot, he filled him with dread. Seen from a distance, as something of a novelty, running around the perimeter of the playing field each Tuesday and Thursday was one thing, seen close up, in the flesh, another.

'I – I dunno about this,' he said. 'And it's Billy. I prefer Billy.'

Benson placed a hand on his shoulder. 'Just give it a try. After all, you've got nothing to lose – have you now? And,' he added, making an encouraging face, 'much to gain. Not least, the goodwill of war hero extraordinaire, Sir Sidney Craig.'

'Who?'

'The head, you numbskull, Major Craig. But never let on I said anything – about his war record, I mean. "All in the past, m'boy", is all he'll ever say. "Best forgotten". So, if you know what's good for you, never mention it. And remember, with him, it's not necessarily the winning that counts, but the fact you've tried. Give it all you've got, and he'll forgive you everything. Well, almost everything. So...?'

306

'Well,' he said, eyebrows raised Tim style.
'Yeah – go on, then.'

'Good man!' Benson said, took two bottles of milk from their crate, and proposed a toast. 'To Sir Sidney!'

At the afternoon break, Tim tried his utmost to get him to admit to what had taken place in the headmaster's study. 'Come on! You must've been in some sort of trouble, or why else would he have picked you out?'

'Cos of me angelic singin', he said, his friend's evident exasperation at this serving to fuel the nucleus of an idea; a master plan the effect of which he could already imagine.

With the last of the stragglers about to board the bus, the driver started the engine. On they came, puffing their way up the steps, none more welcome than the predictable, eaves-dropping blabbermouth, Piggy Perkins.

As anticipated, she played her part to perfection. 'Hi-ya, Billy! Guess what? Me and my friend Christine are going to be your cheerleaders! Pom-poms, sexy skirts and everything – like in America! Good, eh?'

'Mm – yeah,' he said, savouring the turn of more than the one head his way, the questioning eyes and Tim's nudge.

'What she … ah! Benson. You could've said. And I did ask.'

That let in Ozzie. 'Ask what? Sexy skirts? Yuk! I wouldn't want t' see your legs in anythin' sexy, Piggy Perkins. Scare the livin' daylights out of me, it would!'

Cynthia stretched a leg out into the aisle. 'I've got nice legs. Haven't I, Billy?' she said, running her hands up to her knee and beyond, exposing a thigh that, together with its twin, could crush any man, beast or boy stupid enough to lie between them.

'Yeah,' he said. 'Lovely.'

Thankfully, with the boarding of the Grammar School contingent, the focus returned to where it rightly belonged. With mainly countryside ahead, Kenny left his seat at the front of the bus and made his way to him. 'That right is it, Hughesie? Picked out by your headmaster? Well done, mate! But why keep it a secret?'

'Well,' he said, and shrugged. 'If I 'adn't, it would've bin, you know, sort of, like braggin'.'

'What? You? Never,' Kenny said, and gave him a friendly punch on the arm. 'But, seriously, you've always been the best runner in the gang, especially over rough ground. So, good on yer. Congratulations!'

'Yes, Billy.' Trish said, turned to face him over the back of her seat. 'From me as well. Congratulations.'

308

At her side, Jenny's head of black curls remained static. It never moved, not so much as an inch … not even to feign total disinterest by looking out the window when Kenny asked about his spanking brand new two pairs of running shoes.

'Oi!' Tim said. 'Trish is talking to you.'

'Eh? Oh, sorry. Yeah, thanks, Trish. B-but I mightn't be any good. I'll try, I'll try real hard, trainin' an' that. But, even then. An'-an', to be honest, I don't want to be letting anybody down. 'Specially not the headmaster after he's kitted me out with the proper gear. Cost a bomb, they did. Mega bucks!'

Studying him in that unsettling way of hers, Trish widened the corners of her mouth into something just short of a smile and, with the deftest of finger movements, beckoned him to hand over his bag of goodies.

'And me!' Piggy said. 'I want to take a look!'

She was joined by Dianna Cox. Jostling one another, each managed to pull a shoe out from his carrier bag. They commented on the spikes, the depth of a tread and on how posh and professional they looked.

On the periphery of it all, Carol and Dawn waited their turn.

'And socks!' Dawn announced, pressed them to her nose and, eyes closed, inhaled what could well have been the scent of some exotic flower.

309

Tim drew breath. 'Dawn!' he said. 'Your stop, Dawn!'

The girl stared open-mouthed, pushed the socks into Carol's hands and called for the driver to stop. To her obvious embarrassment and relief, he did, exercising all the caution one would have expected of him.

With Dawn safely deposited on the roadside verge, the bus pulled away. Dawn, a diminutive figure in comparison to the old crate, stood stock still. Stock still, that was, until he and Tim came alongside her, when she burst into life, her look gleeful, her wave ecstatic.

'The youngest girl in the school, apparently,' Tim said, and faced him, lips pressed in that prim disapproving way of his.

'What?'

'You could've waved back. You know, just a tinky-winky lickle waggle of the fingers? I mean, it wouldn't have hurt – would it?''

'Yeah, well. Whatever,' he said, and retreated into a cocoon of silence, his mind picturing Dawn, his eyes fixed on the back of Jenny's head.

At long, long, last, the bus turned into Mill Lane. 'I've got homework,' he said, a half-truth that Tim accepted without comment.

Ignoring Jenny, he accepted his carrier bag back from Trish, acknowledged Kenny and Susan, left Tim at his gate, and dawdled, distancing himself from the likes of Ozzie and Piggy. But not, as it turned out, Sally Hicks.

As cool as you like, she stepped out from behind the Community Hall water butt. 'Took yer time… modesty man.'

'Dunno what yer on about.'

'Ooh, I think you do,' she said. 'But, that's your business. No, I just thought you ought to know. It's yer dad. Mum's kicked him out. For good, tell your mum. She's welcome to him. That's all. Ta-ta!'

CHAPTER FIFTY-THREE

Benson called a halt to his warm up jog, 'Now you. Come on!' he ordered. 'To the goalpost and back. Nice and easy, mind. Just enough to loosen up and get the blood flowing in the calves.'

'Now,' he said, when the warm-ups were done. 'I've given this some thought. With my eight years of professional training, it's highly unlikely you'll be able to shadow me for long without knackering yourself. So, for today, and for some time to come, don't worry if you fall behind – which you undoubtedly will. Just get into a rhythm you're comfortable with and keep going. See how far you can get, make a mental note of it, and that's our start point. First things first, see? Stick with it and you'll gradually improve. You'll get faster and go further, I promise. Okay?'

He nodded. 'Yeah, think so.'

'Right. Off we go. After three.'

'Three!'

Off they went, Benson's stopwatch set, his long legs covering the ground with consummate ease. For his part, he did as advised and set his own pace taking at least five strides to his trainer's every four. Even so, the gap between the two of them inexorably widened – five, ten – by halfway round on the first lap, an alarming thirty yards or more. Higher and higher Benson's knees seemed to rise. Nevertheless, not to be outdone, he stuck with it, pounding his way round for a second time on a circuit that took in three sides of both the football and girl's hockey pitches, no flagging on Benson's part, hard breathing on his … when disaster struck. Bent double, gasping, his thighs turned to jelly.

Benson strode on, not for an instant altering his faultless rhythm, and when the prescribed moment arrived, kicked for home.

'Phew! Well done,' Benson said. 'No – really! Three laps are as good as a mile and three quarters. And you managed – what? At least, let's say, getting on for two thirds of it. Timewise? Well, that's for me to know, and you to improve upon. Set targets. A full three laps Thursday, for instance. Now, if you've got your breath back, one last half lap. Something of a warm-down jog. So, you set the pace, leaving yourself with enough in the tank for a twenty-yard sprint finish. Then a shower followed by fodder for the hungry horses.'

Only two tables were in use, the one fully occupied, the other, headed by Old Grumpy, boasting two empty seats. Benson guided him towards them.

'Well now,' Mr Jones said, addressing Benson in his broad Welsh accent. 'How did he do?'

313

It felt alien, eating in the company of teachers, a good half of them expressing views as though he was not present, as much a part of a prolonged analysis of his running performance as the salt cellar. Times were quoted and projections made, the speed of the calculations going over his head? Although, not the opinions of those with sufficient interest and knowledge to express them.

'Yes, well,' Mr Jones said, at length. 'Told you, didn't I, boyo? The boy's got something about him. Tame that and you've got yourself a winner.'

'Especially if he wore that cap of his the other way round,' Mr Charles said. 'You know, with its peak turned up, acting as a mainsail.'

Miss Smithers rested her spoon on the rim of her dish, dabbed her lips and said, in all innocence, 'Would that be allowed? I mean, wouldn't it amount to cheating?' 'Not at all, Mavis – no, far from it!' Mr Charles assured her. And so, it went on, serious discussion turned to farce in the space of three thoughtful stirs of his sago pudding.

The laughter seemed to mirror his life, a sobering thought to take with him into the afternoon lessons, and beyond, on to the bus for the tedious journey home.

As much as possible he kept himself to himself, even when pressed.

In the end, Tim shook his head. 'I don't know. You get a bit of recognition, the prospect of something good and anyone would think you'd been expelled.'

'Yeah, probably,' he said, with a sigh; closed his eyes, and brooded on matters mistakenly thought long dead and buried.

A high-pitched revving stirred him, a clutch slipped whether by accident or design, allowing the driver to free wheel the bus towards what remained of Hollersham Halt and its surrounding wasteland.

It was towards this that Dawn picked her way. She passed below them, head down, offering no grin, no wave, nothing — not so much as a glance.

'Happy now?' Tim said, and with a slow turn of the head, went back to his window gazing.

No words passed between them from then on, nor seemed likely to be, a state of play that finally got to him. With the Morton Crossroads almost upon them, he cleared his throat and broke the ice. 'Yeah, you're right. Yesterday, I – I should've waved. She's a nice kid.'

'Exactly,' Tim said, and left it at that.

For a second day running Sally Hicks stepped out from behind the water butt. 'How's yer mum?'

'She, er – she already knew,' he said, and grimaced. 'You know how it is. Someone in the shop. B-but she wanted me to thank you. An', well, sorry I 'aven't before now. I would've, but …I dunno.'

315

'No, I don't suppose you do,' she said, and leaned back against the Community Hall. 'She's okay, though? You see, the thing is, I like your mum,' she said, chin up as though in defiance. 'I wish she were mine.'

'What!' he said. 'Me and you? Brother and sister? Ha! We'd never stop scrappin'.'

'More than likely,' she said, idly poking at a stone with the toe of her sandal. 'After all, it's what you're good at. Isn't it, Billy? Making a girl cry.'

Having managed to dislodge the stone, she nudged it aside and looked up. 'Remember?'

'Hang on! It were you who attacked me!' he said, the day of her rush and tumble over his thigh etched on his memory. Also, helping to moderate his temper, her tears glistening back at him from the sanctuary of the lychgate.

'Anyway,' he added. 'How was I t' know it'd end up with you getting a busted rib?'

'Cracked,' she corrected. 'But it wasn't that – never think that, Billy Hughes. That's not what made me cry. For a start, I wouldn't give you the satisfaction. No, it was because of what you said about my mother. About her bleached hair and gaudy lipstick. I was ten! I didn't need it pointed out to me. I already knew what she was. And it hurt. It's always hurt. The truth, Billy. It never goes away – never!'

Having said her piece, she lapsed into silence; this girl of fourteen, hardened by life's experiences

316

and "well stacked" as Clem was fond of boasting, enough in itself to intimidate the likes of Tim and Ozzie.

But now?

He licked his lip. 'If it helps,' he said. 'Me mum likes you as well, I know she does. She said she doesn't know how you've coped with – you know. All your different uncles. I mean, th-that's what she calls 'em. Men like, you know, like me dad.'

Betraying no emotion, she stared down at her feet; perhaps in search of another stone to dislodge. But, no, presumably having been lost in thought, she lifted her brows as though in acceptance of something and, in stages, blink by blink, brought her eyes up level with his. 'Yes. Men like your dad. And worse,' she added. 'Far worse, believe you me. Except for one, who sat on his heels in front of me one day, rested his hands on my shoulders, and said, sorry, Bab. I'm so, so sorry. But I have to go. And, with that, told me he loved me and closed my fingers on what I later found out were two folded pound notes. I was six … just six.'

She paused and looked at him in a way she had never looked at him before, that chin of hers lifted once more, and she said, 'He was the nearest thing I've had to a real dad. In fact, for a time, I deceived myself into thinking that he was. Daft, really. I mean. How could he have been? I wasn't black.'

'Oh,' he said, vaguely remembering the gossip, but not the man. 'It – yeah – well. Is that why your mum … 'cos he were – you know?'

'Black?' she filled in for him and shook her head. 'Testicular cancer. My stupid cow of a mother thought it was catching. But,' she added, suddenly full of bounce and smiles. 'Just like the proverbial bus. Miss one. And, hey presto! Another one turns up. Couldn't keep his hands to himself, her white, Anglo-Saxon Rodney.'

'I, er, I don't know how she does it,' he admitted. 'I mean, she en't no Bridget Bardot.'

'No,' Sally said, and put her face close to his. 'But, unlike Bardot, she's available. And, what's more, good at it. And so am I,' she added, giving his cheek two farewell pats. 'Ask Clem.'

CHAPTER FIFTY-FOUR

Mr Green called the meeting to order. 'Thank you, gentlemen, thank you! First off, I'd like to say how encouraged I am by the turnout. A fair mix of locals and non-locals, who, I trust, will be made more than welcome. Without them, there can be no club. Fourteen is just about a workable number. So off we go. At this juncture, I'm going to hand you over to our financial benefactor, who not only dug out the old nets and other essentials but has also promised to fund the supply of a full kit, boots excluded. A big round of applause then for a talented wing half and former captain of Abbots Lovell FC!'

A beaming Mr Collins raised both palms and waited. 'Thank you,' he said, somewhat prematurely. 'Thank you, thank you, thank you. Now, hands out of pockets, William. No good is that to an aspiring goalkeeper.'

Having raised a laugh at his expense, Mr Collins then built on it. 'And I expect,' he went on, frowning over the rim of his spectacles. 'Nay demand, that as well as a safe pair of hands in goal, we'll get super-human displays from the young Kenny who had the audacity to come knocking on my door in pursuit of my one and only daughter.'

'Da dat de da,' immediately went up the chant. 'Speech!' someone shouted, at which, as though with one voice, the members of the reincarnated Abbots Lovell Football Club bonded.

With one notable exception. Tim, not even attempting a smile, stared fixedly ahead, as mute and immobile as his sister's gruesome German doll.

He took his friend by the elbow and guided him to one side, away from the worst of the din. 'Look. You could see that one comin' from a mile off. And it's yer own fault. I mean, if it bothers you that much, you should've got in there first. Shouldn't yer!'

Tim gave his trademark flick of his brows and accepted the fact. 'Yeah, well, I know. But, to be honest, I don't sort of, you know, feel ready for that sort of thing. Kenny's a year older, more athletic, better looking, cleverer and goes through the same school gates with her. While I'm...well, me. I'm just the kid from next door.'

'No,' he told his friend. 'Yer not. You'm the 'orrible kid from next door. So, cheer up!'

'...Tuesdays and Thursdays...' Mr Collins was saying. '...on the weather, of course. And soft footwear. Pumps, trainers, baseball boots, but not, if you please, rolled down wellington boots, Mr Cooper.'

Shielded by laughter, they slipped away. Even then, out in the fresh air, Tim still seemed determined to sulk.

'Look!' he said, resisting the urge to give his pal a thump. 'They're probably only goin' fer a bike ride or summat. You never know. it might rain!'

Tim snorted, gave him an apologetic grimace – then grabbed him by the elbow. And he saw him: his father, digging out what appeared to be a pond in the front garden of Jasmine Cottage.

In a whisper, Tim said, 'You could bury a body in that.'

'Yeah, yours if you don't watch it. 'Come on. We can go t' mine.'

They retraced their steps, back across the car park and past the open Community Hall door, taking with them as they made their way down the side of the hall the inescapable banter of familiar voices.

As they neared the water butt, he half expected, would have welcomed even — but no, nobody stepped out, nothing, not so much as a frog. He shook his head and thought little more of it. Not until later, when Tim had gone home leaving him with nothing but the empty stillness of his room.

At his mother's summons, he made his way downstairs, washed his hands, and sat at the table in his usual place opposite Mr Barnes.

To break the silence, he said, 'Me dad's diggin' a dirty great big 'ole in our front garden.'

'Is he now?' his mother said and placed his dinner in front of him. 'Well, miracle upon miracle. Perhaps after that he'll do something about the grass. Eat your dinner.'

Tim returned flushed with evident excitement. 'Hey! Guess what?'

'Er – you've challenged Kenny to a duel.'

His friend aimed a sigh at the ceiling. 'I've no problem with Kenny, he's a decent kid,' he said, and gave him a sideways glance.

'So, come on, Robinson. Spit it out!'

Tim raised his chin. 'I will,' he said, assertively. 'I'll tell you. Not that you deserve it. And only if you promise to stay calm and not risk being heard from downstairs.'

'Yeah-yeah, cross me heart and 'ope to die.'

'Mm,' Tim said. 'Well, the thing is, it's your dad. Him and Mr Perkins were busy shovelling that rubble pile into a wheel-'

'Agh! No, don't tell me!' he said, and sucked air in through his teeth. 'I bet they wheeled it t' the 'ole – and lit a fag!'

'Ha-ha, very funny, I don't think. Especially with them messing with petrol.'

'Petrol?'

'For Mr Perkins's mower.'

322

'I knew it!' he said, recalling his mother's miracle upon miracle quip. 'Bloody well knew it, I did. But, go on. Get on with it!'

'Well, I would, if only you'd let me. The thing is, I said hello to the two of them and kept on walking. Then I paused, tucked in behind that buddleia bush. And what I heard your dad say, was that your mum had begged him to take her back. Begged him, he said!'

'No way! Oh no! I en't 'avin' that,' he said, brushing Tim aside, and made for the stairs.

'Is it true!' he blurted. 'Is it? You going back to me dad. Because if it is, you're mad. Bloody mad!'

His mother glanced at Mr Barnes and moistened her lips. But that was as far as she got. No words came from her, but from behind him, from Tim.

'Sorry, Mrs Hughes. It's all my fault. I'm sorry.'

His mother rose. 'Wait there, Billy. Tim, if you please.'

Tim followed his mother, guided by her into the scullery and from there, by the sound of it, out into the backyard.

His mother returned. 'Tim will be waiting for you out the front when this has been sorted. Sit down, please.'

'You sure, Mo?'

323

'Yes, Barney,' his mother said. 'It's only fair and … and right. He's not a child anymore. Are you, Billy? If I explain what we're about, you'll see the sense of not breathing a word of it to a soul. So, do I have your solemn word on that? Do I, Billy? Because, if not then I'm not telling you anything. Not a solitary word. Is that clear? Not one!'

CHAPTER FIFTY-FIVE

Tim was where his mother said he would be, not patiently waiting, exactly, but dancing away the time by moving his head like a demented puppet to some tune he was humming.

'Boo!'

Evidently not caught by surprise, his pal came straight to the point. 'Well, what was that all about, or can't you say?'

'You got it,' he said. 'Shtum's the word. For now, anyway. Then the whole world can know, including you, my mate.'

'Fair enough,' Tim said. 'Now, here's one for you. Name me a seaside town that has a funfair and tower.'

'Er, I dunno. Oh! Yeah. Blackpool!'

'Phew! Well done, brainbox,' his piss-taking little shit of a friend said, the point being, as he later found out, was that the reborn Abbotts Lovel FC were to play in tangerine shirts and black shorts.

'Oh! And there'll be two green goalkeeper jerseys. One medium. And one small.'

'Oh yeah? You windin' me up, Robinson? What use is a small one t' me? I mean. I can see the point of an extra medium one fer when the other's in the-'

'Look, look, look!' Tim said, risking life and limb by butting in. 'Look, give us chance. According to Ozzie, training will include a seven-a-side match. Get it? Two teams. Two jerseys. Right?'

'Yeah-yeah. I get it. Anyway, who's this other – no! Don't tell me! It's either Dawn Adams or a midget from out the circus.'

'Phillip Granger,' Tim said, simply. 'He's very good, apparently.'

'Phillip Granger?'

'Yep!' Tim said. 'Phillip Granger. So, you'd better pull yer finger out and concentrate on the game instead of doing your usual dramatic stuff in the hope of impressing you-know-who.'

'Load of rot, Robinson. Don't know what or who yer on about. An'-an' - 'an anyway, I'll play a blinder no matter what. Nothin'll get past me, mate. Not s'much as a sausage!'

'Well, good for you,' Tim said. 'It'll entertain Allan. According to Mr Collins, Trish and Jenny are going to wheel him out to watch. How about that? Spectators! Never imagined that, did you, Sunshine?'

'No, Tim, you're wrong. I don't 'ave to imagine it. 'Specially not the sunshine. I can see that comin' out yer arse. So, what's made you so chipper all of a sudden? Come on, I wanna know! There's summat you en't tellin' me, so don't try an' kid me there en't.'

'Wait until we get to Kenny's,' was all Tim would say, and taunted him with his stupid hum and head bop.

All became clear the instant they set foot in Mill Lane. For there, prominently displayed, stood a boldly lettered For Sale sign.

In contrast to Tim's buoyant mood, when Kenny eventually showed it was as plain as Piggy Perkins that he was far from happy. 'I mean, now of all times. What with Trish, and the footer, not to mention the disruption Susan and I are going to have to go through with our education. And you guys, of course. After all, we've had a few laughs together over the years. But East Anglia? Jeez! It's miles away!'

'Mm,' Tim said. 'At least two hundred, I reckon, depending on which part, of course. Could be further! Probably too far to keep on nipping back, anyway. Er, have you had any offers? I mean it's a nice house after all the work your dad's put in on it. It could sell in no time. To a cash buyer, even. Hope not, though. I mean, I'd hate you to miss out on the friendly matches.'

'Finished, have we?' Kenny said. 'I'm not stupid, Tim. I know what you're about. And it won't work. You're not good enough at it for that. Anyway, what's all this about friendlies? I've not heard anything about any friendlies. What friendlies?'

'Oh,' Tim said, widening his eyes in what seemed genuine surprise. 'I'd have thought Trish would've said, seeing as you're, you know, sort of, "lovers".

Kenny blushed, squared his shoulders and stated somewhat huffily that Trish was not that sort of girl. 'And, anyway,' he went on. 'She probably didn't know herself. Why should she? Girls aren't interested in football – are they now?'

Tim wrinkled his nose. 'Oh, I don't know s'much. She's coming to watch us train this Tuesday.'

'Er, for Allan's sake!' he got in with. 'It's for Allan, poor sod. Jenny and Trish are going to wheel him out to watch us play a seven-a-side game. Should be —

'Yes, okay. Okay!' Kenny said. 'Thanks, Billy. I get the picture. And for your information, Robinson, I will be popping back from time to time. And, yes. I will be lodging with Trish's mum and dad. And Trish will be doing the same with mine. Okay? Do we have your permission? Or do you want to make an issue of it right here and now?'

Tim stayed tight-lipped and subdued. Then, having found something from somewhere, he stuck out his jaw and said, 'You can't choose who you have feelings for. You just have them. Ask Billy.'

And, having dragged him into it, Tim spun on his heel, stuck his nose in the air, and strode away.

CHAPTER FIFTY-SIX

Carol opened the door to him. 'Good, it's you,' she said, her agitated state telling him all he needed to know.

'Puppy love,' he said, in explanation, at which she arched her brows and grimaced. 'He's in his room,' she said, and led the way up to Tim's door, signalled to leave it to her, and knocked. 'It's Billy, Tim. Open up, there's a love.'

No sound came from inside the room. Carol remained calm, however. 'Tim?' she said and waited. Then, seeing the doorknob turn, she slipped away: a girl who had matured beyond all measure both physically and mentally without him having noticed.

'Well? You coming in or what?' Tim said, and leaving him to close the door made straight for his bed where he landed his behind down onto it with a 'humph'. And there he sat, hands in lap, gazing up at the ceiling.

After a while, he sighed. 'I suppose I've made a right ass of myself. Well, don't worry. I'll apologise to Kenny the next time I see him. Although ... Oh, I don't know. Cooper's right. Tim-de-Tim, that's me, a weed who probably couldn't punch his way out of a wet paper bag.'

'Tim, me old beauty,' he said, and put his arm round his friend. 'Don't do yerself down. You'm the best mate anyone could 'ave. And what you said about feelings. Well, that were real brave, that were. And true! We either 'ave 'em or we don't. An' if your Carol gets any leggier or boobier then, well! Unless, of course, the up-top bit is mostly cotton wool. I mean, you never know what yer getting' these days do yer?'

Tim gave him a rueful look. 'I can assure you, it's not,' he said. 'Like all girls around her age, it's hormones, their bodies getting ready to have babies. To be honest, I feel sorry for them.'

'What? The babies?' he said, and they succumbed to a fit of the giggles.

They ended as abruptly as they had begun, pushed aside by a sudden thought. 'Don't laugh,' he said. 'But in, say, two years' time, I could be with Carol and you with Dawn. A foursome; out for a laugh!'

Tim freed his self of both him and the bed. 'A laugh, is it? Well you don't have to wait two years for that! As far as I'm concerned, the comedy's already here. Or tragedy, more like. How's it go? "Oh, what a tangled web we weave" and all that stuff. Ha! Whoever wrote that wants to come to Abbots Lovell and see what the love-spiders have spun round here. And keep your eyes off my sister! Making personal comments. She's twelve – just twelve!'

331

'Yeah! And I were on about when she were fourteen! As fer the other, I were only pointin' out that she'd growd up, that's all!' he said, and he, too, got up. 'I'd better go.'

'No.' Tim said, at the first click of the door. 'No, stay. Please. I don't want you to go. I'm sorry. Sorry, sorry, sorry. It's just, oh I don't know. The weeks, the months… Years, even. Where've they all gone? it seems only yesterday me and Carol were being sat in the bath together. Now? Well, it would be unthinkable, a right no-no. She was my little sister, but not anymore. In fact, she's more grown up than I am. Ha! And there was me thinking a girl like Trish would be…'

He shook his head and looked haplessly about the room. Clearly having failed to locate whatever he was searching for, he rested his forehead against the wall. And there he stayed.

'Tim? Tim, I'll stay. Of course, I'll stay.' he said, and, with that, quietly closed the door.

Not speak for a time, eh, Ma? But, if ever there was a time when I needed to, it were then. I thought I'd recognised the symptoms. I thought Tim were going as doolally as you went. I was frightened. I didn't know what to do. Then, as calm as you like, he stood away from the wall, and said "I'm alright now. You can go if you want".

He looked so pale, though, Mum. Deathly white, as they say, and I weren't going to leave him. Not in that state. Not young Carol's "There's a love". No, not my mate ...

Tell you what though, Mummy-dear, what with Tim all cut up, and seeing Carol in a new light — that day changed me. I turned a corner, as it were. I grew up, an adult all of a sudden, with responsibilities. But what a week t' dump 'em on me, what with Benson, the footer trainin' and the end of year schoolhouse sports, dreading Dawn screamin' out me name and Piggy and her mate in them ridiculous American cheerleader costumes. Which, in a way, brings me back to Carol. Told 'er I were goin' t' win the cross-country race fer Tim, I did. Chuffed 'er t' bits. Even more so when I did it. The main thing, though. before that, on the Monday, after Tim's funny turn, she came and sat next to me on our smelly old bus journey home. It were a good job I was there, her said, and linked arms. Shyly, she said she loved her brother. And, I must confess, that at that particular moment, I felt I loved her.

CHAPTER FIFTY-SEVEN

Right from the off, Mr Green took him and Phillip Granger for some personal training. 'What I want to impress upon you is that the six-yard box is yours to boss. Be positive and, above all, make yourself heard. Communication, that's the key, especially between you and your centre half. Every man knowing his role and sticking to it! And that, gentlemen, is what we are going to work on this evening. So, you in goal, William, while Phillip sends some crosses into us. Then, after a quarter of an hour, the two of you will swap places. Any questions? no? Then, off we go.'

The nets were up, the flags on the four corner posts fluttering, the white lines pristine; If only the grass had been mown.

Sadly, there was no Tim and therefore no Carol standing on the touchline. Making up for it, though, sat Allan flanked on either side of his wheelchair by Trish and Jenny.

'Hi, Jen! Shouldn't be long now,' he muttered struggling to think of anything more meaningful to say and marched on. From behind came the tread of feet hurrying through the grass. 'Billy!' Trish called.

'Billy. can I have a word please? Later - if you're busy.'

'Er, yeah,' he said, playing it cool. 'Yeah, okay. Could be here another three-quarters of an 'our or more, though.'

'No problem,' she said. 'I'll wait all night if necessary. At the phone box, then? Eh? Like old times?'

'Times?' he said. 'I can only remember the once.'

She struggled for a reply, thrown it seemed by his unintentional curtness.

'Sorry,' he said. 'I didn't mean, you know …'

She studied him for a moment, not unkindly, but with a reflective sadness. 'So, Kenny and I are to blame? I'm not allowed a boyfriend, I take it. Is that it?'

Not knowing what to say, he pulled a face, and shrugged. 'Can we leave this 'til later? When I've got me head round it?'

'Please,' she said. 'I just want to know how Tim is.'

With one man short, Sam Green went in the opposition goal leaving Phillip to make up the six outfield players. Twenty minutes each way was declared, with Mr Collins acting as referee; a no-nonsense man, unlikely to stand for foul play from the likes of Clem Cooper who'd been giving him the evils since his recent chats with Sally.

As it turned out, there was none. Not until after the game; in the changing room.

Clem blocked his way. 'Hughes. You stay away from Sally or else!'

'Hey, hey hey! What's all this?' Mr Green demanded to know.

'Keep out of it,' Clem said. 'it's a private matter between me … and 'im.'

Sam, for all his lack of inches proved no pushover. In a flash, before Clem could land a punch, his saviour had the sod's head pulled back and his arm pushed up to his shoulder blades. 'Private grievances don't get aired in here, Mr Cooper. So, get your belongings and go – go on! Get out.'

He imagined Clem waiting for him, perhaps hidden behind the water butt. Pity, he thought, knowing he would be going the other way, towards the phone box, and Trish.

However, it transpired, to his unease and slight embarrassment, that Mr Collins had learned all about the planned meeting. 'No daughter of mine is going to hang around a telephone box on her own at this time of night' he declared. 'She's waiting for you at the house. Your mother knows, and why. So, why not come back with me and have a bite to eat? Then, business concluded, I'll run you back home – okay?'

'Er. Yes, Mr Collins. Thanks, Mr Collins. Might be safer, F-fer me, I mean. seein' as Clem's on the warpath.'

'Mm, the Coopers,' Mr Collins said. 'I know all about those gentlemen. Only too right, I do. But, there it is! A mug of whatever you fancy will help put things to rights no doubt, especially after all your heroics, Both in and out of goal. I was most impressed, even if Clem wasn't Mr Windmill. In fact, at one stage I thought it a personal duel between you and Kenny. It's a pity we're about to lose him. What with one thing… Between you and me, I'm beginning to wonder whether it's all worthwhile.'

CHAPTER FIFTY-EIGHT

Mr Collins immediately made him feel at home and ushered him into the kitchen where what he called a supper had already been prepared by Mrs Collins.

'Tea, coffee, or a soft drink?' she said, adding to the warmth of the welcome. 'And tuck in! I expect you're quite ravenous after this evening's exploits. Go on. Don't hang back!'

He tucked in to what turned out to be a beef and pickle sandwich. No mention was made of Tim. In fact, nothing was said of him during the whole meal, only after, when a glass of orange squash had been placed before him.

It came from Mrs Collins. 'So, what's all this I'm hearing about poor Tim?'

'Mum – please. It's private.' Said Trish

Three rapid taps on the table from Mr Collins ensured silence from both wife and daughter. 'Let us retire to the lounge, Mary, and leave these two to it. Your mother and I are here to help, Patricia, nothing more. What's private can remain private.'

Trish blushed, tightened her lips, and nodded. 'Yes. Sorry, Pops. I'll fill the two of you in later, when I know more myself.'

She then turned to him. 'What do you want to do? Stay here, or go to my room?'

The thought of choosing her room seemed improper, certainly questionable and … and embarrassing.

'It's all right, William.' Mrs Collins assured him. 'She won't eat you. Go on up, if you want. Then you can see that she's not as spoilt as you think she is.'

'It's just the stairs,' he said, and fearing there was no connection or, worse, it made no sense, quickly added, 'Posh, I meant. Spoilt havin' stairs like that. Knocked mum fer six, they did!'

Mr Collins chuckled as though to himself. 'Well, in that case, you must bring her back for a tour of the whole house.' Pausing at the kitchen door, he added, 'How is your mum, by the way? She certainly seemed well when we saw her last. Not completely one hundred percent, I didn't think.'

Many images of his mother flashed through his mind, the beatings, the humiliations … and the extra flesh now covering her bones. 'Sh-she's gettin' there. I mean, Dr Murdoch gives her these tablets, like the ones he'll probably give Tim.'

'And they've helped, have they?'

He sensed rather than remembered that Trish was still sat at the table, presumably paying attention, ears flapping.

'Well, to be 'onest, I think it were more gettin' away from me dad and movin' us in with Mr Barnes,' he settled on. 'Come on a bundle since doin' that, she has.'

'A bundle, eh?' Mr Collins said. 'A bundle, you say. Well, she's not the only one who's come on a bundle. Keep it up, lad. Keep it up! See you Thursday. And if the Club can help with Tim in any way just tip us the wink. And now, you'll probably be glad to hear, I'll leave you to it. Although, not too late, there's a good girl. I've promised William's mother I'll run him home after.'

With Trisha's dad gone, he helped himself to an apple. 'Better stay here,' he said. 'I mean. Wouldn't want Kenny getting the wrong idea, would we?'

'No, we wouldn't,' Trish said. 'And, well, thanks. Things are complicated enough as it is.'

'Yeah,' he said, noting that she appeared more than a little nervous, as in fact she had throughout the supper, constantly fiddling with her hair and saying precious little.

That changed, however. 'Tim,' she said, in the manner of a Miss Wheatcroft. 'I need to know how he is and what caused it. The truth, mind, no matter what. All I've had from Mrs Robinson was a snappy "He's fine, thank you!"'.

He told her. In great detail, he told her: from the moment Kenny had tugged on the sleeve of her

340

blazer, to Tim's humming and head-bopping. Lastly, he told her about Tim's goading of Kenny, resulting in Tim coming off worse. 'Yeah,' he said, taking a deep breath. 'That were the killer blow. But he went off with his head held high after saying summat about feelings, obviously meaning fer you. An' well I caught up with him later, when he 'ad his … whatever yer call it. Frightened me, though, I can tell yer.'

'It's the talk of the shop – you know that, don't you! You just wait until I see Kenny. In fact, I've a mind to go around there right now. I was supposed to see him after the training, anyway. How dare he say we were going to lodge with each other's parents at the weekends!'

'So, it en't true.'

'No!'

'Then perhaps you ought to tell Tim that. Or Carol might be better. She's okay, is Carol. But, well, Tim was goading him, remember.'

She pushed her hand up into her hair. 'What a mess! Poor Tim. Poor, poor, Tim.'

'Yeah, well! It en't no surprise, is it? You must've known he's got a crush on yer. An'-an' – and Clem labelling 'im Tim-de-Tim don't help. He's my mate. He's always looked out for me. Well, now it's my turn. An' I'm tellin' yer now, I don't care how you do it, but put things to rights – okay?'

She ran a knuckle under her nostrils and nodded.

CHAPTER FIFTY-NINE

At the bus stop Kenny acknowledged him with a nod. He did the same in return.

On the bus, with no Tim for a third day running and now no Trish or Carol either, not until the Morton Crossroads crew were on board did something nearing normality begin to take shape.

Piggy, now joined by her sidekick, Poxy Coxy, came into her own. 'Don't worry, Billy! We've got our costumes all ready for tomorrow.'

'Can't wait.'

'I bet!' Christine said. 'Especially as you're now our hero. Is it right that if it hadn't been for you Tim would've topped himself? Poor Tim. I mean, he's such a sweetie.'

He sprang out of his seat, calmed himself, and went to the pair. In a low voice, levelled inches from their faces, he said, 'I don't know what you've heard, but it's probably a load of bollocks. Tim's fine, just 'ad a bit of an upset, that's all.'

'Yes, Billy,' the pair chorused, the smugness of disbelief plastered across their faces like gaudy make-up.

He made his way back towards his seat. 'Caused by lies!' he said, ensuring that Kenny could not help but hear.

At Hollersham Halt, Dawn clambered aboard as usual. Presumably due to the fact there was no Carol, she plonked herself next to him: a girl who like Carol, although to a lesser degree, had also begun to blossom. In many ways, she reminded him of Jenny at that age, the colour of her eyes, the black curls and … hmm, perhaps not the face, distorted as it so often was by the cheekiest of grins.

'Don't start,' he said. 'I've already 'ad a belly-full from —' and finished his sentence with a jerk of his thumb in the appropriate direction.

'My lips are sealed,' she said, and did as Carol had done, linked arms.

At the Grammar School off-loading, Kenny took the trouble to gaze up at him and scowl. For his part, he responded with a finger wave and smile, evidently not unnoticed by Dawn. Apparently in approval, she rested her free hand on his arm. 'Carol needed to talk.,' she said. 'Last night, on the 'phone, that is. Her and Tim are so close. Always have been, it seems.'

'Yeah, well,' he said. 'Wouldn't you be if you'd bin sat in the same bath together?'

344

The effect on her was not as he had expected. Rather than giggle, she looked down into her lap and, toying with a loose thread, said that she wouldn't know, 'I've never had a brother.'

'And I've never had a sister,' he said, inclining his head towards her. 'Give us a kiss.'

Not until the boredom generated by Mrs Fisher's geography lesson did he give his thoughts free rein to wander – given a little help, that was. Otherwise, they settled of their own free will on his and Dawn's kiss. A bit wet, he thought. On the other hand, not nearly as wet as being plonked in a tin bath together. Splish-splash – laugh! Imagine the look on Barney's face on walking in and-'

'Hughes? Hughes! Pay attention, boy. Answer the question.'

'Er – sorry, Miss. I mean, Mrs Fisher. I don't know, Miss.'

'No. And you're not likely to, are you, Hughes? So, instead, perhaps you'd enlighten the Class on what it was you found so amusing.'

'Er, me, Miss. Sat in a tin bath with me plastic duck.'

The Class burst into open-mouthed laughter. Mrs Fisher did not laugh. Nor did she appear angry, a thinly disguised smirk putting paid to that.

Composing herself, she came and stood before him, placed her finger under his chin, and studied his eyes 'You don't look at all well, William. Nothing contagious, I hope?'

Trisha's words sprang to mind. 'It's private, Miss.'

'Yes!' Piggy burst in with. And he's a hero. Deserves a medal, he does!'

He gave Mrs Fisher a hapless smile. 'Just tired,' he said. 'An' I've promised t' win tomorra's cross-country fer someone.'

'I see …' Mrs Fisher said. 'In that case, seeing as it's virtually the end of term, I can see a way open for me to let you off on this occasion. But never again, Hughes. Is that clear?'

'Yes, Miss. Thank you, Mi-Mrs Fisher.'

The woman nodded. 'Good. It took a time, but you got there in the end. Mrs Fisher from now on, please. So, all that leaves me to do is wish you every success with your race tomorrow. And that goes to everyone who's participating, of course – good luck!'

Tomorrow, it was said, never comes. But it had – and at the sound of the whistle they were off, three teams battling it out over a course of roughly five and a half miles. One lap round the circuit pounded out on a Tuesday and Thursday for nigh on a year with Benson. Out through the back gate and out over open farmland, the early sprinters already puffing and blowing. Others were there to be picked off in ones and twos if he set his rhythm and stuck to it. As

346

Benson would say, "leave enough in the tank for a sprint finish". And it was thanks to Benson that it was an unfair contest. Barring accidents, a sprained ankle or bad fall, victory was there for the taking. How to make it look good, that was the thing. For now, just plod on, mile after mile, footfall after footfall after footfall, the rhythmic tread of his feet evoking thoughts of sex ... and Dawn. Recalling Tim's "youngest girl in the school" comment allied to a swift calculation of his and Dawn's respective ages – horror upon horror! What were I thinking of! Potter and Williams had broken free and sprinting to the gate. In desperation he went full pelt after them. Once through the gate and out onto the home straight only then could he gauge the distance to be made up: a sickening fifteen yards or more. But they were flagging, only a cacophony of shrieks and screams driving them on – driving all three of them on, none more ferociously than Piggy and Poxy, dressed like clowns with their pom-poms and flared skirts. And there was Dawn. Dawn, bouncing up and down, screeching out her encouragement from near the finishing tape.

Phew! Gawd. If I'd … if I'd planned it meself – phew – I couldn't 'ave done better.

Leaving Potter prostrate, and Williams bent double, spewing up, poor sod, Billy indulged in a few short back and forth warm-down jogs. Having established that it had all been easy-peasy, he made his way to the winner's desk and Sir Sidney Crompton.

'Well?' the Headmaster said. 'Was I right? Or was I wrong?'

'Er, right Headmaster. Thank you for giving me the chance, sir. Left it a bit late, though, as you probably saw.'

'Yes …' mused Sir Sidney. 'Indeed, you did. Benson was on the gate and said that you had it all under control. Only, for some inexplicable reason, to go to sleep. The same in Class, so I understand. Tell me, Hughes. Apart from the cleanliness of plastic ducks, is there anything on your mind, m'boy?'

He could not believe his luck, an open invitation, handed him on a plate. It was almost too, too good to be true. The old rogue! He knew. Stood there with that eyebrow of his raised - he bloody well knew!

'Hughes …?'

CHAPTER SIXTY

A cheer went up as he boarded the bus. Not joined in by everyone, he noted, but loud enough for it to be acknowledged with a loll of his tongue and wobble of the head. Job done, an unoccupied pair of seats afforded him sanctuary. He chose Tim's place, next to the window. Outside, the grey of the playground stretched morbidly away, empty and forlorn.

With the bus idling, waiting for the signal to go, a touch on the arm interrupted his brooding. He expected it to be Dawn. But it was not Dawn. It was Sally. Sally, on her last day of school. 'Here. You look as if you could do with it,' she said, and, making no further comment, left him with a Mars Bar.

'Sal?'

She paused and looked back. 'For Clem having roughed you up the other night. Enjoy. You never know. It might be your last.'

The driver put the bus into gear, the door slid shut, and with Poxy, Piggy and Dawn bustling down the aisle, they were off.

As he anticipated she would, Dawn flopped down beside him. 'Busy being photographed in their costumes, they were,' she said. 'Had to go and fetch them.'

'Mm. Yeah, whatever.'

'Misery,' she retorted, and fell silent, enabling him to finish his Mars Bar in peace.

Having done so and licked his fingers, he said, 'When's yer birthday?'

A cloud of uncertainty passed over her features. 'Soon,' she said. 'Why?'

'Er. So, I can send you a card,' he said, changing tack. 'You know. From yer "brother".'

'Brother …?'

'Yeah! Then we could sit in Barney's tin bath together.'

For a girl she made a reasonable attempt at a snort. 'Dream on,' She said. 'I'm not two and you're not four.'

'No. That's the point,' he said. 'I'm four-teen – what did you expect? Be reasonable. I mean! Me goin' out with an eleven-year old. Imagine the piss that'd be taken out of me by the gang,'

'What's left of it,' she said – and came back at him. 'But if it bothers you that much, wait until I'm twelve. If it were Carol it'd be different. I've heard you've been ogling her – so don't go saying you haven't!' she said, and, arms folded, thumped herself into the back of her seat.

As suddenly as she had gone into the sulk, she snapped out of it again. Eyeing the cardboard tube containing his winner's certificate, she said, 'You going to show it me or not?'

350

'What?'

'You know what. Don't be difficult.'

'D'yer know, you'm real pretty when you'm angry,' he said.

Without any visible sign of a reward, he sighed and pulled the tube up a couple of inches exposing its Sellotaped seal. 'An' the scroll's tied with a red ribbon put on by the Head's secretary. An' I don't want it bein' messed with. Anyway! Shouldn't you be getting off?'

'I'm staying at Carol's, helping with Tim,' she said.

'Oh – right,' he said, and, on impulse, pulled the whole tube up and out his kitbag. 'Then yer can give Tim this. You'll probably do a better job on it than me. It's his t' keep, tell 'im. An' yer never know, he might let yer have a butchers at it.'

It was the best thing he had ever done, he decided. If nothing else, it clearly had given Dawn pause for thought. Sat with the tube wedged between her thighs and held innocently erect, she said. 'Are you sure? I mean, why not do it together? Let's face it, as far as I know, you haven't been to see Tim, not since … you know.'

'No. No, I 'aven't. But I'll 'ave t' see me mum first an' grab a sandwich. Then there's trainin'. I-I dunno.'

'Yes, well, I do.' she said, caressing the tube. 'I'll come with you to your mum's. Show her this.

351

Eat your sandwich. Tell her what we plan to do. And then,' she said, giving him a victor's smile. 'Go and do it – simple!'

'Er – yeah. All right. Yer can come t' Barney's. But not as a couple. Just friends - okay?'

She gave a solitary nod. 'Okay. Friends, it is,' she agreed, adding, after a pause, 'until I'm twelve.'

Thirteen'd be better' he said, to which she gave a slow shake of her head.

'It's twelve or nothing. Take it. Or leave it. It's up to you.'

'Oh. Dawn! How lovely to see you!' his mother said, only for her expression to suddenly change. 'What's he done?'

Dawn put on one of her cheeky grins. 'Don't worry, Mrs Hughes. You're not about to become a grandmother,' she said, and raised the tube. 'He won the cross-country – over five miles, it is! The winner's certificate's inside!'

'But donated to Tim,' he emphasised. 'It's written on it all proper, like.'

'And tied with a red ribbon,' Dawn blurted. 'Even I haven't seen it yet.'

'Even you …' his mother said, causing Dawn to blush.

Clearly having picked up on the fact, his mother merely smiled, more to herself than anything.

In more serious mood, she stated that she was proud of him. 'It's a lovely gesture!' she added, only to spoil it by demanding a hug, and, if that wasn't enough, followed by a kiss.

The ordeal over, she ushered Dawn and himself through to Mr Barnes. 'A visitor for you, Barney!'

'Eh?' Mr Barnes said. 'Oh ah! Young Dawn, daughter of that there rapscallion plum thief. No wonder he turned out to be a copper. Takes one to catch one, as they say. Tell me, how is your father?'

'He's fine, thank you, Mr Barnes,' Dawn said, her voice begging to fade. 'Still misses mum, of course. We all do.'

Even Mr Barnes remained silent, the only sound coming from his precious clock and the occasional spit of his equally precious fire.

It got to him. 'I'll 'ave me sandwich later, mum,' he said. 'I'll just get me kit and walk Dawn up to Tim's an' see 'im fer a bit.'

'Yes,' his mother said. 'Yes – and be sure to give him my love.' 'And, Billy!' she shouted after him from the front door.

'What?'

'No … no, it's alright. Just – just watch how you go, that's all. Goodnight, Dawn. Night, love. Come again!'

353

Yeah. I remember it as if it were only yesterday. Me and Dawn, hand-in-hand, every inch a couple, but not a couple. Just friends.

CHAPTER SIXTY-ONE

Once again, it was Carol who came to the door. 'Hi!'
she said to Dawn. 'I began to think you weren't
coming. And Billy – two for the price of one. Tim'll
be really chuffed. Come on. Come on in!'

A sheepish Tim met them at the lounge door,
flushed and seemingly unsure of what to either say or
do.

Carol took charge, giving Tim a guiding push
back into the room. They followed, him with his
kitbag, Dawn with the tube and enclosed certificate.

The tube was the first thing that Mr Robinson
teasingly picked up on. 'Ah, Champagne!'

Given a nudge, Dawn stepped forward and
presented the tube to Tim with a pride that could not
have been bettered if it had been she who had won the
race.

Gingerly, after much picking, Tim unwound
the Sellotape and in his prissy neat way crumpled it
into a ball and handed it to his mother. Only then did
he lift the cap from the tube. He reached inside, and,
at long last, withdrew the scroll.

'Read it!' Dawn urged. 'Go on!'

'Yes, Tim,' Carol said. 'Don't be a ninny.
Get on with it!'

'Patience,' Mr Robinson said. 'Take your time, Son. You never know, it might be a bomb.'

Tim pulled on the ribbon revealing to one and all that it was no bomb, but a rolled sheet of thick paper. He opened it out and studied in silence. Presumably reading he, blinked, and stared at him. Finally finding his voice, he said, ''You've been working all year for this. I – I can't accept it.'

Carol took the certificate from him and read out loud, 'Donated to his friend Tim Robinson by the winner of the Hollersham Secondary Modern 1965 cross-country event, William Hughes.'

'That's the only way the Head could word it,' he admitted. 'Sorry.'

'Don't be daft! It's lovely!' Carol said, flung her arms around him, and with two soft pads pressed to his chest gave him a real smacker of a kiss.

Out the corner of his eye, he caught sight of Dawn shrunk into the background, eyes cast down as though staring into the pattern of the Robinson's carpet.

'Don't I get one from you as well?' he said, trying to make light of the matter; an invitation she declined.

'I'm too young,' she said, nose in the air. 'And, anyway, Daddy wouldn't like it.'

'No,' he mumbled. 'Probably come down on me like a ton of bricks.'

Breaking an awkward pause, Mrs Robinson said, 'Well I'm certainly going to give him a kiss, even if you're not!'

Thankfully, to a muted cheer, the kiss proved no more than a motherly peck.

'Well, he's not getting one from me either, Dawn,' Mr Robinson said. 'But what I will do, Tim, taking it you'll agree, is frame the certificate and put it behind glass – how's about that?'

'Yes – thanks, Dad. In fact, if Billy's got time, we could go up now and suss out the best place to hang it.'

Having no option but to follow, he scrambled up the stairs to his friend's bedroom. No sooner had he closed his door behind them than Tim admitted, 'It's not the real reason. It's to show you this!'

His mini breakdown clearly a thing of the past, Tim skimmed an envelope at him. It took little imagination to guess what it contained.

'Yeah, well, there we are,' he said, handing the letter back. 'Not half as bad as you first thought. And, let's face it, Trish is right in what she's put. You did provoke Kenny. And, well, are you?'

'What?'

'Going to shake hands? I mean, you could do it this evenin' if you got yer skates on. Come on, why don't yer? The truth is, we need yer. Ask Mr Collins, if yer don't believe me. I mean, Sam 'ad t' go in goal in our last seven-a-side. Great fun, they are. An'-an' – an' yer see plenty of the ball. An' there's a friendly comin' up. Now, yer wouldn't want t' miss that, would yer.'

For a few heart-stopping moments, it seemed he had jumped the gun. But it proved a false alarm. Tim's apparent aimless gazing about his bedroom had a purpose. More than one, as it turned out.

'I think it's best hung there,' he said, pointing to an area of blank wall situated next to the door. 'Subtle, see. Wouldn't hit you in the face the moment you walked in then. What d'you think?'

'What do I think, Tim Robinson? Me thinks you'm evading the question, pal,' he said, and grabbed his friend round the neck, struggling with him until they were both on the bed giggling like a couple of eight-year-olds.

'Well?' he said, when they had finished and sat up. 'Are you? Or aren't you?'

'I will tell you,' Tim began, cautiously, before finishing in a gabbling rush, 'But only after you've told me what's going on between you and Dawn.'

Of all the folk, both children and adults, Tim, he realised as never before, was the only one he felt safe in opening his heart to – certainly where potentially sticky problems such as Dawn were concerned. With Tim, it would go no further. And so, he told him, from the kiss all the way through to her ultimatum.

'Yeah,' Tim said. brows raised. 'Difficult. I mean. Nature tells us one thing, but society another. Let's face it, we all get the rands. But with a twelve-year old? And the thing is, I reckon she'd be up for it – gawd. I wouldn't want to be in your shoes if … you know.'

He shook his head. 'It's those love spiders again. Everybody fancying someone who fancies someone else. l mean! Just look at you and Jennifer Duggan.'

The hairs at the back of his neck bristled. 'What about Jennifer Duggan? I en't said nothin' about no Jennifer Duggan,' he said, and gave his pal a thump for good measure.

Tim kept his cool, however. 'You don't have to, Bully-boy. You've given it away a million times over – ever since Junior School. But, if you're hell bent on her, I'll tell you what to do.'

And, with that, the annoying little twit said no more. He just sat there, swinging his legs.

'Well!'

'Yes. Quite well thank you, Billy. In fact, I might stroll over with Carol and Dawn, if they'll come, and offer Kenny my hand.'

'Ha-h!' he said. 'Now finish what you started, or you won't get out of here alive. What's this masterplan, then, clever lickle Timmy-wimmy?'

Back came the leg swinging, this time accompanied by a click-click, clicking of the tongue.

359

It stopped. 'Okay. What you do. On the sixth, you post a really nice card off to Dawn. And, please! Not from her brother. Sign it "With Love from – guess who? Kiss, kiss, kiss. Then, when you see her, ask her out. Court her in front of Duggan and see if there's any reaction. If not, then you've still got that mischievous, pretty little minx who, I understand, has already been taken home to visit mummy. You can't lose – can you, sunshine?'

'Yeah,' he said, stroking his chin. 'I might do that. An' 'ave 'em both! Thanks, pal. Thanks, fer the benefit of your vast experience. And now. I must be off. See yer later. Er, with Carol. Yes?'

As it turned out, there was no Tim, no Carol, and no Dawn. Nor was there anyone else, for that matter. The rain saw to that.

CHAPTER SIXTY-TWO

The enemy came by minibus. Out they poured, a boisterous lot numbering only ten players plus a cumbersome figure wearing a pair of wraparound sunglasses and clutching a small suitcase to his side.

Mr Collins relieved him of it and held out his hand. 'Ben Wallace, I take it. It was Sam who rang you. I'm Albert, his partner in crime, acting as your referee. Unless, of course, you wish to take a half, whistle supplied F O C.'

The man gave a rueful smile and tapped a lens of his sunglasses with a fingernail. 'Well, thanks, but no thanks. Apart from not seeing too well, I'm not that hot on all the rules.

'Oh, right. Fair enough,' Mr Collins said. 'Played as a lad, though, I expect.'

Back came the smile, perceptibly more reflective than before and topped by an equally reflective 'Humph. Nobody would give me the ball. Useless, I was. Terrified of the thing.'

Mr Collins scratched behind his ear. 'Then how come you ended up managing this lot? And, more to the point, caching them.'

'Ah, well,' said the man, before adding conspiratorially, 'Psychology. Listen you lot, I said.

361

I've been a diabetic since the age of six. Type one. So, injections every day and a whole lot more. I was the one left to stare out my window while all the other boys kicked a ball about. Whereas you lot – blah-di-blah-di-blah… There's more to it than that, of course. But you get the gist. And, to their credit, they knuckled down. They might look a dodgy bunch. But they've hearts of gold.'

'I'm sure they have,' Mr Collins said, and gave him a friendly pat on the shoulder.

At that point, a blue-topped grey minivan pulled into the carpark and crunched its way towards the minibus.

'Ah, good!' the Hollersham Rovers Manager said. 'My two star players. Well, they can take care of themselves. This way, is it?'

Rather than making their own way, the players in question sat chatting for a good couple of minutes before climbing out of the van and locking it. Markedly different in both mannerisms and dress than the main group, they looked out of place. In fact, the driver reminded Billy of Kenny, athletic looking, and clearly not short of a penny or two while the other, a raw-boned six-footer, most probably their centre half or, heaven forbid, centre forward, gave him the screaming ab-dabs. For the first time in weeks he wished the muscle and height of Clem was playing in front of him.

As ordered by Sam they stepped out of the hall in an orderly fashion. Their appearance sparked a bout of spasmodic applause and cheers which, if nothing else, encouraged him to stick out his chest and keep his eyes fixed to the front. Only when he had reached the far goal did he feel free to stand and stare. Amongst a scattering of adults were Trish, Allan and Jenny, while a few yards further on stood Tim – good old Tim acting as sub. Flanking him were Carol and Dawn. The latter inclined her head towards the other two and, to his embarrassment, made her way upfield.

She positioned herself behind his net. 'Hi! Thanks for my card. A bit early, mind, but lovely. Especially the kisses. Have a good game – bye!'

He blew the air from his cheeks and watched her go. Like Tim, it struck him, a substitute; not quite the ticket, but tasty enough all the same.

'Oi, Hughesie! You going to get the ball out the net, or what?'

'Oh. Yeah, sorry, Oz. Weren't concentratin'.'

'No, we know. Too busy eyein' up yer eleven-year-old tart.'

He set his face to ugly, rolled up his sleeves, and strode purposefully towards his so-called friend.

From out the blue, Sam stepped between them and grabbed both by the hair. 'Save it for the opposition,' he said, and yanked both their heads back. 'You again! You're like your father – fist happy. As for you, Master Cutter, I heard what you said, and it's out of order. I'm relying on you two to keep the goals against down to below a dozen – savvy? So, you do what I've tried to drum into you, William. You give loud and clear instructions. And what you can't safely catch, you punch away, palm or whatever, anything that comes into the box. While you, Oswald, you obey and keep it simple – safety first, remember. No dithering, from either of you. Understood?'

'Yes, Sam,' Ozzie said.

'Yes, Sam,' he said.

And the two of them were made to shake hands.

To his relief, the raw-boned six-footer played as a centre half, while his mate, the Kenny look-alike, played a somewhat unorthodox roll in midfield, a schemer cum support striker who had arrived as though out of thin air to head home the first goal.

By half-time, they were four-nil down and flagging.

While Sam handed out the oranges, Mr Collins gave them a pep talk. They were not to let their heads drop, he said. 'Remember, they're a league side who play together regularly. Harry them more. Wingers, don't just wait for the ball to come to you, find space and demand it. William, you're doing fine. Ozzie, considering you're not a centre-half, the same. Just keep on going as you are. As I said. Keep it under a dozen, and you'll have done yourselves proud. So, when you're ready, gentlemen. Up and at 'em. But don't expect any favours from the referee. Although, I've heard he's given to accepting back-handers,' he said, as he made to go, waggling his fingers behind his back inviting them all to stuff his palm full of orange peel.

Their spirits fully restored, they lined up for the second half. It progressed much the same as the first. Despite all his efforts, four-nil soon became six-nil – and, to his frustration, almost immediately, he was left to deal with yet another avoidable corner kick.

Over it came. 'Mine!' he shouted, eyes focused on the flight of the ball, fist at the ready. And he made good solid contact, but not with the ball. Rather than fist upon leather, it was bone upon fist, and the Kenny look-alike bit the turf.

Mr Collins took immediate action. 'Alright-alright!' he said, and waded into the resultant melee, whistle blowing.

'It were an accident!' he said to the raw-boned centre-half, 'It were 'onest. I 'ad me eye on the ball, committed like, I were, an'-an'-'

'Don't worry,' Lanky assured him. 'He's had worse – just as long as he hasn't broken his back.'

'His back?'

'Yes. Well, he did hit the deck a bit hard. A cut eyebrow's nothing. Just a lot of blood, that's all.'

A belated Rovers' manager arrived with his suitcase.

However, once opened, Mr Collins more than pulled a face. 'You can't use any of that, man! It's unhygienic. Give him blood poisoning more likely as not. Trisha!'

Even before she got to him, he had the hall keys dangling for her to take. 'You know where everything is. Any problems, just give Sam a shout.'

With help, the player struggled to his feet, and Trish was left to it. Off they went at a steady pace, talking, even laughing together.

Kenny's scowl said it all. Although, not entirely all, as he later discovered from Tim.

CHAPTER SIXTY-THREE

Dawn, Tim and Carol were waiting for him outside. Carol took it upon herself to do all the talking. 'Dawn heard what Ozzie called her and how it probably embarrassed you. She appreciates what you were stopped from doing on her behalf, but now sees that you were right. Clowns like Ozzie and Clem would only get at you because of her, and she doesn't want that. It's not fair on you, or her, come to that. So, she'll do what you want and wait until she's thirteen. Which doesn't mean – and this comes from me and not her – which doesn't mean she wouldn't welcome whenever possible, like at our house for instance, a nice little kiss and cuddle now and again. Okay?'

'Mm, I'll think about it,' he said …and laughed.

There was no holding Dawn back, however. Regardless of who might be watching, she stepped forward and wrapped her arms about him in the most expressive of hugs.

His duty done, including the obligatory kiss, Carol led her away, leaving him with Tim.

'Phew!' he said. 'Didn't come t' me rescue, did yer?'

'No,' Tim said. 'She's a lovely kid, still not over losing her mum like that. So, do us all a favour and treat her right. In other words, forget all about Jennifer Duggan.'

'Like you've forgotten about Trish, I suppose?' he retorted.

This Tim, this new Tim, who only recently had been on the verge of a breakdown, clearly knew something. He could not hide the fact. It was written in his confident manner, in his smugness and the shine reflected in his eyes. Above all, he was nearly wetting his pants in anticipation of being asked. Before he could, however, as he had fully intended, the pigeon landed.

But Tim knew him as well as he knew Tim and was not fooled by his tight-lipped silence.

'You know, you rotter!' his pal said – and rushed out what he could not have guessed: that the old Mill House was a cash sale and that the Chambers' new property was in North Lincolnshire. 'Miles away! In fact, what's more, with Clem having been chucked out and no Kenny, I might even get a game!'

'Mm, yeah,' he said, his thoughts already having drifted elsewhere, to a blue-topped grey Minivan still parked on the premises. 'Yeah, I'll see yer tomorra. A bit late now, en't it? An', well, I've got t' see Sam about this,' he said, holding up his finger. 'Giving me real gip, it is.'

The hall seemed crowded, what with the injured Rovers player and his raw-boned mate, amusingly known as Lanky Lowe, Trish, Sam, Mr Collins and Kenny.

Unfortunately, he put his foot in it straight away. 'Come to see how the Kenny look-alike is,' he said – and immediately attempted to back-track. 'An'- an' get me shoes. An' see what Sam makes of this.'

Sam shook his head and sighed. 'I don't know. A right pair you two are! Could just be dislocated, I suppose. But, then again, it might well be broken. Whichever, make an appointment to see Dr Murdoch, and if he thinks it needs X-raying give me a shout and I'll run you in.'

He thanked Sam and went to retrieve his shoes. Even knowing roughly where they were, he took his time over it, more interest in what was being said by Mr Collins.

'Of course, it's too late to join the league this season. For one thing we're nowhere near ready. And, to cap it all,' he said, ruffling Kenny's hair, 'we're about to lose our star player. So, as we also need a replacement centre-half, you two guys would be more than welcome. Unfortunately, for now, it's only two training sessions a week, seven-a-sides, and as many friendlies as we can arrange.'

'No problem,' Lanky said. 'It'll give us chance to get to know the lads. And, let's face it,

Jamie's already met your goalkeeper – haven't you, Jamie?'

It was then that he decided to re-join the group. 'Yeah, I'm sorry about that, but I did 'ave t' go fer the ball.'

'I know. So did I,' Jamie said. 'In fact, you did me a favour.'

'Oh?

'Indeedee-deedee,' he said, slipping his arm round Trisha's waste and giving it a squeeze. 'If it hadn't been for you, I wouldn't have met this delightful young lady.'

Mr Collins coughed. 'I'd be careful, if I were you. I'm her father. And this fellow here,' he said, resting his hand on Kenny' s shoulder, 'is her boyfriend.'

'Yes, well,' Jamie said, completely unfazed 'the two of you should be proud of her. A right professional job, she's done on me,' he said, touching Trisha's bandaging with his little finger. 'Right professional. And taught by a Mrs Dodds, I hear. Right here in the village.'

Kenny made a move. 'Yeah, hooray for Mrs Dodds. Come on, Trish. Time to go.'

Mr Collins gave Trish a nod as if to say, 'better had'. They all watched her hand over the keys before being ushered away by Kenny, the banging of the outside door marking their departure.

Billy yawned, made an excuse, and followed.

370

The playing field lay silent and eerie, as would the car park if not for the streetlamp near its entrance. It picked out Jamie's Minivan … as it would him, he realised, if he tried to hear all that was being said between the not-so-happy "lovers", as Tim would scathingly have it.

The school railings that bordered the playing field brought him practically within earshot, especially of Trisha's voice, higher pitched than Kenny's, and increasingly agitated.

'Nothing happened, I tell you! Yes, I was right up close to him, I needed to be. But he was as good as gold, not a single grope. Honest! As for him putting his arm round me and – and squeezing, it was a gesture, that's all. A thank you gesture. Really! I know you're upset, moving away and all, but if you can't trust me, we may as well finish right now.'

Kenny's reply proved almost impossible to understand, rather like the picture in one of Barney's incomplete jigsaw puzzles.

Trisha's reply helped to fill in the gaps, however.

'I'm going in,' she said, firmly, and by all accounts did just that, earning for herself a prolonged blast of a car horn.

CHAPTER SIXTY-FOUR

When the nights drew in and training was switched to a Sunday morning, the seven-a-side matches dominated the sessions.

After one full ninety-minute match, Mr Collins and Sam took him to one side. 'I understand you're something of an athlete,' Mr Collins said, to which Sam added. 'Yes, a damn good one, by all accounts. Inter-school marathon champion, no less!'

'Yeah …'he said, smelling a rat. 'Why?'

Sam laughed. 'Ah, no flies on this one, is there, Albert.'

'I never imagined there would be,' Mr Collins said, put an arm round him, and spoke in conspiratorial tones. 'As you know, William, all these seven-a-sides are to give us an idea of where our strengths and weaknesses lie. In other words, to enable us to put out the best possible formation for when we join the league. You with me?'

'Yeah! You want t' put Phillip in goal instead of me!'

Mr Collins gave his shoulders a squeeze. 'No, no, no. Listen. Tell him, Sam. If anything, it's a promotion.'

'That's right,' Sam said. 'An opportunity to play a star roll as part of a dynamic midfield duo. Jamie the creator stroke support striker. And you –'

'You,' Mr Collins butted in. 'You're to mop up when things go wrong. In other words, go use your pace and energy to harry, tackle and generally close things down, allowing Jamie to get back into position.'

'It's up to you,' Sam said, in a manner that effectively ended the double act. 'Entirely up to you.'

As established members of Abbotts Lovell FC, it came as no surprise to anyone when Mr Collins gave Lanky Lowe and Jamie Horten an open invitation to attend the annual village Christmas dinner and dance.

'Mind you,' Sam added. 'It'll cost you twelve quid. But well worth it. And we can always find you a barn to sleep it off.'

Billy took great pleasure in informing the pair that, as an under-sixteen, he could get in for six quid but, unfortunately Mr Collins overheard.

'Correct, William. So, it's soft drinks only.'

Tim came over at that point and pulled him to one side. 'Guess what.'

'Er … Christmas 'as bin cancelled.'

'Don't be daft. Jasmine Cottage! Have you seen?'

He put his finger to his lips. 'There's more to it than a For Sale sign,' he said. 'Big stuff I've known fer ages but couldn't say. An' still can't. Be better'n Bonfire Night when it all kicks off, though, I can tell yer. ….'

An' I weren't far wrong were I, Ma? Sent 'im packin' yer did with a rocket shoved up 'is arse an' a banger rammed down 'is throat. As good as, anyway – the bastard.

But, as Barney said after that little episode, "Drink drives a man on regardless of the odds stacked agin' him".

As the first snow began to fall, Daddy Dearest was 'ammerin' on our door again, pissed as a newt.

It's like it were only yesterday, Ma. Fer you as well, I should imagine.

Only yesterday …

"Maureen! Maureen, you come out 'ere. Come on, come 'ere before I … Oh, gawd! Maureen, d'yer hear 'oman? My lovely love, you are."

Yeah him down there in the snow an' you with yer head stuck out me winder. "Oh, it's you, Charlie. And you are, aren't you? A right Charlie in every sense of the word. Charlie by name, and a right Charlie in everything you touch. Get yourself indoors, man, before you catch your death. Go on! Be off with you!"

374

But still the blighter kept on, clearer this time, 'as t'
be said. Probably the freezin' air 'ad summat t' do
with it – I dunno. But I has t' hand it to yer, Mummy,
dear. Give it 'im straight, yer did. "There's nothing
more to discuss", you said, all cool and calm, like.
"You've got all the information you need. If you can't
make head nor tail of it, then get Hilda to read – Oh!
I forgot. She kicked you out, didn't she? Which is
what I'm doing, Charlie. It's called an eviction order.
You see, I need you out so that I can get my property
fumigated and redecorated. Like me, Charlie. Rid
myself of the stink of you and start afresh. In other
words, divorce, Charlie – divorce!".
But the old man weren't done even then. Ha! Talk
about tryin' t' assert his authority – the prat.

"Don't you get funny with me, 'oman! Evict me?
Who –yesh – who d'yer think you are?".
"Me? I'm Maureen Basset, Charlie. Took legal
advice and changed back to my maiden name – the
same name as you'll find on the deeds. Daddy knew
what he was doing, right enough. More's the pity I
didn't listen to his advice and dump you when I had
the chance. Well, I'm taking it now. If you want to
contest it, we can let the courts decide. Sound good,
won't it, Charlie? All the cruelty, both mental and
physical you inflicted on me and your son. And, if
you're wondering, it's all recorded with Doctor
Murdoch and scores of others. Yes, Charlie.

Witnesses. Like to the prolonged stabbing of Billy. In public! And there's not only Dr Murdoch's records but also a policeman's. A sergeant, n'less. Be fun, won't it, Charlie? Seeing you squirm. Contest it, and risk ending up with Sweet Fanny Adams. Which is what you deserve – Sweet Fanny Adams! So, night-night, Charlie. Thank you for calling".

CHAPTER SIXTY-FIVE

The layout was predictable, cloth-covered trestle tables positioned towards the back of the hall near to what they laughably called a kitchen. While at the other end, set in a corner next to the exit corridor, and overlooked at first, stood a makeshift bar manned by the solitary figure of none other than his father, clean-shaven and disturbingly jovial.

'Ah! There you are, Son! Come t' 'ave a drink on yer old dad 'as we? Well, what's it t' be?'

'Er, an orange juice, please, Dad.'

'Tut-tut,' his father said, and put a finger to his lips. 'Just a touch,' he said, adding something from an optic to a colourless liquid already in a tumbler. 'There! Put hairs on yer chest, that.'

It tasted vile and made him cough.

'Sip it, son. Sip it,' his father said, and turned to serve Major Craig and his wife.

Having done so, he returned to him. 'Yer ma and the old man she's shacked up with not with you, then? Pity. I were rather hopin' she'd see what an effort I'd made on 'er behalf. I mean, she don't really want t' split us up, does 'er now. Had good times, me and yer ma, picnickin' by the river'n that. Wanted t' do that not so long ago, 'er did. As a family, she said.

377

You, me, and 'er. Well, I'm up fer it, come the spring, yer can tell 'er – an' how smart an' sober I am. Patch things up between us, it will,' his father said, and nodded in apparent agreement with himself. Then, smacking his lips together, he eyed him, evidently deep in thought, 'Who's she with?'

'The police,' he said, and paused, before adding. 'Just the one. His daughter's at the Thirteen an' Under's party at the vicarage. I went last year, remember?' You know, when mum helped out with the grub an' –'

'Yeah, yeah. Well, that's as maybe. An' yer can tell 'er she don't frighten me with that board 'er 'ad put up. Chucked it in the back field, I did. Now get off with yer. I've work t' do.'

The sort of work, he noted as he made his escape, that entailed filling a small glass from a different optic and swallowing whatever it contained in one. An act clearly not gone unnoticed by an eagle-eyed Mrs Dodds.

Feeling mightily pleased with himself, he clapped the newly arrived Jamie Horten on the shoulder. 'Here we are, then! The dynamic duo reunited.'

'You don't say,' Jamie said, and forcibly removed his hand.

Unperturbed, he pointed to the table where Jamie and his pal Lanky had been placed. Yer names are on the cards. Me an' me mate Tim are with yer.

Tim's great. But the other two – phew! Sal's okay. But, don't ask 'er fer a dance or anythin' while Clem's around, know what I mean?'

'Very informative, Billy,' Lanky said. 'Pity, though. About the dance, I mean. Just the right height, she is. And bored out of her brain by the look of it.'

'Yeah, well. Probably is,' he said. 'Only went with 'im t' get 'erself a job in their farm shop.'

Appearing suitably impressed, Lanky cocked his head to one side and gave a slow, somewhat drawn out nod. 'I see … And did she? Get a job, I mean.'

'Oh yeah – six months ago! Assistant Manageress.'

Jamie nudged his friend and muttered something into his ear, after which, each raised a hand and touched palms.

Introductions made, the meal eaten, Lanky showed great interest in Clem's work on the farm and his family's history, providing him with a platform from which to take centre stage.

Occasionally, he addressed Tim or himself and, even less, poor Sal, obviously bored to the back teeth with the whole affair, Nevertheless, slowly she began to thaw, warming to the attention increasingly being paid her by Jamie.

Lanky sighed and sat back in his chair. 'Drink, Clem?' he said, cutting across Jamie. 'What's your tipple, pal? You know. Before you and Sally go shakin' them things on that there dance floor, man!'

'Actually,' Sally said, curtly. 'I'm not a man – or hadn't you noticed?'

Much to Clem's amusement, Lanky looked mortified and apologised most profusely. 'Always did put my foot in it, I did. Let me make amends and get you all a drink – what's yours, m'lady?'

The order was taken, Clem choosing a pint of rough cider, Sally a gin and tonic, himself and Tim lemonade, and Jamie half a lager.

Accompanied by Clem, Lanky wended his way to the bar.

All too contrived, he felt, recalling the whispered words and touch of palms. A double act if ever there was one. With no Clem around it paved the way for Jamie to reach across the table and touch Sally on the back of her wrist.

A double act, yes. But not in the way he had expected it to pan out.

Having gained Sally's attention, Jamie said, 'Believe it or not, but Lanky's an expert ballroom dancer who'd really – and I mean really – like you to dance with him.'

Sally's cheeks changed colour. 'Oh… she mumbled. 'So, all that –'

Jamie replied with nothing more than an expressive "You've got it" face.

'Then why didn't he just ask?' she said, to which Jamie nodded at him, the blighter.

'I were only tryin' t' keep the peace! Look what he tried t' do t' me over nothin'.'

Sal acknowledged the fact with a raised brow and sighed. 'Yes,' she said, on the back of it. 'Yes, Billy was probably right to say something. Treading on eggshells gets a bit wearing at times I can tell you. And the fact is, I'd love to have a dance. Unfortunately, I'm no ballroom dancer.'

Jamie waved the comment aside. 'No problem. Lanky'll guide you round. The two of you'll have a laugh. And, anyway, I expect they'll put on some modern stuff now and then, won't they?'

Clem turned his chair round, supped his cider, and watched Lanky's tuition of Sally in silence.

'She's getting it!' Tim said, in all innocence.

'Er,' Jamie said. 'Not a ballroom dancer, then, Clem? Like me.'

Clem twisted round, eyebrows lowered and muttered something about not wanting to make a prat of himself.

Jamie moved quickly on. 'And what about you two?' he asked Tim and himself.

381

'When the music changes,' he said, and pointed to Jenny, stood sipping her drink on the side lines. 'She's my bird, the one with Trish.'

'And I've already caused enough trouble,' Tim said, but didn't elaborate.

Thankfully, the music did change; from the likes of Glen Miller and waltzie-type stuff to Chubby Checker and The Beatles.

'Come on, then, Billy-boy,' Jamie said. 'If I can manage a Twist, then so can you.'

'Yeah – I'm comin'. Hang on'!' he said, 'I'm comin'. But don't say nothin' about me an' Jen. It's a secret 'til we'm older, like. Probably when I got a job.'

'Very sensible,' Jamie said, grabbed him by the elbow, and pulled him in the direction of Piggy and her mate Christine.

'What yer doin'?' he said, panicking. 'Not them two! I thought –'

'Shsh!' Jamie demanded, tugging him to one side. 'Look. You have to box clever. Circulate. Have a couple of dances with anyone but the one you really want to be with. Soon, she'll be asking, "Why them? What's wrong with me?". Then, you thank the first couple, and move on. Strategy, see. Get it?'

'Yeah. Make 'er jealous, like.'

'No, not jealous. Just less of a target. Less inclined, shall we say, to turn you down. Because we're – what?'

382

'Er, devious?'

Jamie appeared not to see the funny side, however. 'No, Billy. We're doing the gentlemanly thing by circulating. So, here we go. I'm the tallest so I'll take the one in blue, okay?'

'Yeah. An' leave me with Piggy, I suppose!'

'I'm sure she's very nice,' Jamie said, and moved on, leaving him to make a decision, one he flapped and dithered over, but got there in the end.

CHAPTER SIXTY- SIX

Of late, whenever he called on Tim it always seemed to be Carol who opened the door to him. 'Don't tell me. I heard all about it last night,' she said, sounding more like Mrs Duggan every day. 'Hurry up! Don't just stand there letting in the cold.'

Once in, she led him to the lounge where his visit had obviously interrupted a game of chess.

Hardly daring to breathe such was the apparent depth of Tim's concentration, he kept his voice down to little more than a whisper. 'Who's winnin'?'

'You and that slime ball, Horten, from where I was sitting.'

'Tim …' Carol warned, in response to which Tim confronted her across the table, his cheeks, normally pink at best, threatening to burst into flames.

'Yeah. Well!' he blurted. 'You weren't there, were you? It was all a set-up. And you!' he added, elbowing him in the ribs. 'You played right into the pretty boy's hands. "My bird" – ha! You wanted to hear yourself.'

'Tim, that's enough, Carol said. 'It was a dance, what did you expect? I don't know, I'd hoped we'd got over all this sort of thing – I really had!'

'It's alright. Really,' he said. 'Tim's right. It were a fix. I picked up on it early doors but guessed wrong on how it were goin' t' end up. An', let's face it, who was there around our age t' dance with? Two lots of two, an' Sal. An' with Clem around I weren't goin' t' risk it with her, were I? So, me an' Jamie circ – circu – you know. An', anyway! Why shouldn't I dance with Jenny? An' if you'd 'ad any balls you could've got out there yerself – couldn't yer!'

Like a clown puppet fitted with a sprung neck Tim sat repeatedly nodding. 'I know. I know, I know…

'Right!' he said. 'If yer know. Then next year I'll drag you out there an' me an' you can circum – whatever it is. But only on one condition.'

Tim knitted his brows and uttered a sulky 'What?'

'That it's your turn to dance with Piggy.'

To his relief, the puppet accepted what he said with yet another nod, and, more importantly, just when the moment seemed to have passed, there crept in the faintest glimmer of a smile.

Later that evening, with the chess set put aside and Carol having prompted Tim to take his pills and retire for the night, she escorted him to the front door.

Once there, she sank back spray-legged against the porch wall, closed her eyes, and allowed the air to seep from between her lips.

'Carol?'

In slow motion, making use of the wall, she rolled her head to the side, and eyed him. 'I can't take much more,' she said. 'He tries, I know he does. But the slightest… Flaming dance! I mean, there were us thinking it would aid his recovery. The same with the football. You know, get him involved in the community again. But – oh, I don't know. He's my brother and I love him dearly. But I'm too young to be his minder, substitute girlfriend and mother all rolled into one. I'm thirteen, for pity's sake, not thirty. And I'm telling you now. Never mind Tim. One more setback, no matter how trivial, and we'll both end up in the nuthouse.'

'No you won't,' he said. 'Fer a start, where's yer mum and dad in all of this?'

'At gran's,' she said. 'She … she's had a fall and being awkward about it – don't ask.'

He did not ask. He said nothing, contributing to a silence that grew increasingly surreal, not helped by the on-off flickering of a Christmas decoration in the hall.

A less intrusive light came from the Collins's coach lamp. Situated over the garage doors, the light it cast reached, but barely penetrated, the porthole window next to Carol's head. What it did pick out, however, was a certain blue-topped Minivan parked in the Collins's driveway.

'Does – you know?'

'No,' she said. 'And I'd like it to stay that way, if you don't mind, or he'll be imaging all sorts.'

'I en't stupid,' he said. 'What d'yer take me for?'

Catching him off-guard, rather than bite back she slid her forearms over his shoulders, bent forward, and kissed the tip of his nose. 'I take you for the village bad boy who's come good,' she said, and kissed him again, properly this time, the effect more to his liking than anything Dawn had, or probably ever could have, achieved.

And it did not stop there. 'That was for what you did for Tim earlier, backing him up over this silly dance business. Did him more good than any of my chess playing, feeding, or general mollycoddling, I assure you. Thank you,' she said, toying with the hair at the back of his neck. 'And now this one's for me,' she said, slowly and deliberately bringing her lips forward, inviting him to do the same. They kissed, and kissed, and as they kissed, she clung to him with all the fervour of a desperate child, drawing him in, until there was not so much as a hair's breadth between them.

CHAPTER SIXTY-SEVEN

In spite of the dark, aided by his father's boasting, the For-Sale sign readily came to hand. Standing it upright proved no problem, shouldered and balanced, a different matter. In the end, to drag it round to the front of Jasmine Cottage seemed the easy option.

The sign taken without mishap to the area of the original hole, its exact position necessitated a hands and knees job. Once located and the hole emptied of displaced soil, all seemed set. A spell of cumbersome manoeuvring, a heeling in – and Geronimo! Almost as good as having rubbed off Carol Robinson.

Job done, the lure of his bed and the seeping warmth of Barney's inglenook fire drove him on towards the back door of Old Forge Cottage.

It was locked – bloody locked!

Suddenly, light flooded out from the kitchen. With his eyes cupped and his nostrils pressed to the window he peered in. His mother failed to notice him at first. Then, she reached for the cold-water tap, and let out an inhuman shriek.

In the circumstances, to say nothing and leave her free to drag him indoors and indulge in an uninterrupted rant seemed the wisest course of action.

And, so it proved. Only when she had run out of steam did she begin to make sense. '.. and just look at your trousers! Your school trousers, Billy. You'll be needing those come Thursday. Get them off – go on! And what were you doing out there, anyway?'

'Puttin' the sign back up.'

'The-? At this time of the morning? Why, it's pitch black!'

'I thought you'd be pleased,' he said, and hung his head, an old trick that invariably worked. First, the bluster, and then the backtracking.

'Yes, well, as it so happens … but don't ever do anything like that again! Nearly gave me a heart attack, you did. Now get some breakfast down you. Then get changed. We've work to do – chop-chop!'

Thankfully, his father's bicycle had gone from beneath the widow, the For-Sale sign stood unmolested and erect, and yet his mother showed no sign of moving. Gazing wistfully about her, she appeared to be taking in, not just Jasmine Cottage, but practically the whole village. Eventually, as though to herself, she said, 'It's not how I remember it. People moving out. New folk moving in. And where have all the post war babies gone? All gone a'courtin', as Daddy would have said … all gone a'courtin'.'

389

'Mum? Mum, I thought we'd got work t' do? Come on, now. Open up an' I'll make us a hot drink, yeah?'

At first, it was as though she had not heard. But she had. She eyed him, eyed him and twitched him the briefest of smiles. 'And you'll be next, no doubt,' she said. 'I sense it, I can feel it in my bones.'

'Yeah, an you weren't far wrong, were yer, Ma? But yer shouldn't've said it.
Yer really, really, shouldn't ...

CHAPTER SIXTY-EIGHT

As anticipated, Carol opened the door to him. 'I thought I'd come and give you a hand with Tim,' he said. But, strangely, rather than stand aside and let him in, she stepped outside and closed the door to behind her. 'Yesterday,' she said. 'It never happened – right?'

'Eh?'

'I mean it, Billy. If I hear so much as a single word of it – one! – then I'll never speak to you again for as long as I live.'

His mouth opened and closed. 'Hang on,' he finally managed to say. 'Hang on. Fer a start, I en't said nothin' t' nobody. An' who were it who started it – not me!'

Her eyelids flickered, and she nodded. 'Yes. I know,' she said – and faced him, full on. 'But you know what boys are like, boasting to their mates and being coarse about it. I mean! If mum or dad ever got wind of it, I'd do away with myself, I really would!'

'Don't be stupid,' he said. 'You know you wouldn't. An' I promise, I en't said a dickybird to anyone. Or won't. But I won't say I'm sorry, because I en't. It came out the blue, somethin' made extra special 'cause it were with you. I lied earlier when I said I'd come t' help with Tim. Truth is, I'd come a'courtin' as me granddad would've said. I think yer lovely.'

She looked at him with what seemed a fresh eye, 'Well, what can I say? I'm flattered. But it's not on, so forget it. For a start, I wouldn't do it across Dawn. Who's still got your Get Well and Birthday Cards up, by the way. And August might seem a long way off, but it's not, not really. Then there's your "bird", I'm reliably told, the one that nobody's supposed to know about, but everybody does. Or seems to. I mean! How many of us do you want, Billy?'

'You,' he said. 'Nobody else. Just you. I want you.'

She heaved a great sigh and composed herself. 'Let me explain,' she said. 'What with one thing and another, I'd come to the end of my tether. It was either you or scream and pull my hair out. In short, I needed to be taken out of myself, and you, my love, did that for me. I felt it go. Boy, did I feel it. Nearly ripped me apart, it did. But oh, the calm afterwards. But as far as any boy and girl relationship goes, forget it.'

He sniffed and shrugged his shoulders. 'Please yerself,' he said, his thoughts already drawn elsewhere, something that she picked up on with a sixth sense formerly only attributed to his mother.

392

'He left around half seven this morning,' she said.

'Oh, right. Does …

'Not that I'm aware, of,' she said. 'So, let's keep it that – oh lord! Here's mum now.'

'No sweat,' he said. 'I'm just here to help with Tim, en't I? Hi, Mrs Robinson. Good timin'!'

She dumped a bin liner full of what he guessed was clothing and locked her car.

On impulse, he rushed to take hold of the bin liner and followed her indoors.

'Thank you, William. I think that deserves a cup of tea. Would you see to it, Carol? There's a love. I'm whacked.'

All throughout the supping of tea and clink of cups being settled on saucers, his mind dwelt on which of the two was more meaningful, "my love" or "there's a love".

Carol interrupted his pondering. 'Billy! Billy, mum was asking what you'd been up to.'

'Oh, sorry. Helpin' mum clean up Jasmine Cottage, mainly. Collected up all the dirty crocks, I did, then swept an' damp mopped the kitchen floor. We 'ad a viewin', see, which the agent is hopeful on. But mum sez not to count our chickens. Oh, an' she left some details for me dad on a residential caravan up at Middle Morton.'

Mrs Robinson made a face which seemed to suggest she was more than impressed. What about, he was not sure, although she continued to show interest in him.

'And what do you intend doing when you leave school, William? I mean, you're not academic in any way. So, farm work of some description would it be?'

'No way!' he said. 'I mean, I know I'm no egg-head like Tim – when he goes t' school, that is. But I en't stupid. I'm goin' knockin on a few doors on the factory estate tomorra t' see if I can get a Saturday job. An'-an', an if nothin' comes of that, as soon as I'm sixteen I'm joinin' the army.'

That made Carol look. And he could picture it. Himself, in uniform – with medals pinned to 'is chest. Even Jenny would be impressed with that.

Tim, on the other hand, only sneered. 'You? With a gun in your hand? Don't make me laugh!'

He felt his hackles rise but said nothing. Bugger the lot of 'em, he thought. That settles it – he ruddy well would join the army.

CHAPTER SIXTY-NINE

It came as no surprise to see Tim chaperoned at the stop by Carol. If nothing else, at least his pal had turned up, even though clearly not wishing to join him.

'Mornin',' he said to no-one in particular, dumping down his school kit-bag. 'Comin' trainin' with us now I en't got Benson, is we, Piggy? Got t' stay fit, yer have. Never know when it might come in handy, job wise, like – eh, Oz?'

'Yeah. Like for chicken shit shovellin',' Ozzie said, setting off the titterers amongst the group.

Bolstered by his army plan, he chose to ignore them and leave it to others to speak on his behalf. But nobody did. Apart from Piggy, that was, and for what it was worth she needn't have bothered.

In the end, it fell to Trish to add something more meaningful. Queueing behind her and Jenny in readiness to board their usual ex-army crate of a bus, she turned to him and said, 'Daddy was sorry he couldn't offer you any Saturday work, but he'll ask around. So, keep on as you are. You're doing fine.'

Seats were occupied as though by rights, the familiar pattern of singles and pairings disrupted only by the addition of another member of the Granger clan with her mop of ginger hair, and the fact that Tim now chose to sit with Carol rather than him.

Well, sod him, he thought. Sod 'em all. Every one of 'em.

Field after field after field, the monotony broken only by the occasional skeletal oak or isolated roadside cottage.

A touch on his arm startled him. 'You all right?' a disconnected voice said, and the figure of Dawn slid in beside him.

'I er, I didn't realise we were here,' he admitted.

'Obviously not,' she said, and gave him a peck on the cheek.

He raised his arm, inviting her to snuggle in. 'Now give us a proper kiss,' he said. 'An' not so wet as the last one yer give me.'

'Takes two,' she murmured, took aim, and delivered something more sensuous and far less demanding than anything Carol had attacked him with.

'Wow,' he said. 'And that from the one-time youngest girl in the school. And, before you know it, the Main Block.'

'Yes. 'Well, don't worry. I'm older than my years,' she said. 'Had to be.'

'Yes …' he said, tightening his hold on her. 'Yeah, I know,' he added for good measure, and planted a kiss in her crown of Jenny-type curls.

Hand in hand, they walked through the school gates together. Together, that was, until Carol and Tim rudely brushed past them.

'Charming,' Dawn said. 'You wait until I get hold of Carol.'

'Er, no,' he said. 'No, I shouldn't if I were you. It's um – it's Tim's first day back, remember. An' knowing him, the babbie's probably about t' shit his pants. Just ignore 'em. Same as they did me at the stop this mornin'.'

'What! After all the help and support you've given them? They've no right!'

'B-but that's just it, en't it? I know too much, see. An'- an' I've bin sworn not t' say nothin'. B-b-by Carol – yeah. An' Mrs Robinson, who'd had t' come home from seein' to Tim's gran who'd had a bad fall. But, well, there you are! I've already said too much, I 'ave. Best give 'em plenty of space, I reckon.'

They walked on in silence. Then, when it came to going their separate ways, Dawn said, 'D'you know. You've grown up of late. I'm proud of you. But I think you're wrong about me not saying something to Carol. She's my best friend, always has been. And we tell each other everything.'

'Leave it fer her t' say summat, then! That'd be best. Mind you, I don't know if any of it'd make any sense, if her did. Didn't know where she were when I went round t' see Tim. End of her tether, her said. Wanted to scream an' pull her hair out, her said. A right job I 'ad with 'er. Luckily, that's when her mum come home. I just carried a load of washin' in for her. An'-an', an' we all had a cup o' tea. What with that an' Mrs Robinson yackin' away I don't know if Carol, well, if she even noticed I were there.'

'Mmm,' Dawn went, searching his eyes. And that seemed to be it. Whatever she thought, she kept to herself.

At the milk break he made sure to stand behind their usual table, in full view of the door through which New Block pupils usually entered. Although it repeatedly opened and closed, as the minutes ticked by it became increasingly clear that she had stood him up. Well fuck 'er, he thought, and snatched up a third bottle from its crate, tore off and cast aside its silver top, downed the milk in one – and belched. However, as though the two were connected in some way, while wiping the back of his sleeve across his mouth, she appeared, the swing door clanging to behind her.

She came bustling towards him, 'Only got a minute,' she said. 'Just to say you were right. Tim was in a state and made it clear before they'd left the house that he didn't want to talk to anyone. And Carol apologises for the two of them nearly colliding with us at the school gates. The thing was, Tim had an appointment with the Head. Apparently, he's granted Tim one-to-one tuition until Easter.

He conjured up a sniff and shrugged. 'So, you've sin Carol. Big deal.'

'Yes. That's right. I've seen Carol,' she said, looking him fully in the face. 'And you and I need to have a little talk don't you think? But school's not the place. Nor the bus. It'll have to wait until Sunday.'

'Sunday?'

'That's right. Even if we have to have it in Barney's flippin' greenhouse!' she said, and flounced off, much to the amusement of a dinner lady.

'Hormones, Pet. Up one minute. Down the next. But don't worry. It can only get worse.

CHAPTER SEVENTY

With his mother in a flap over something or other that had not risen, he took the opportunity to slip away and join Mr Barnes in the lounge.

'Don't know why she had t' invite 'em in the first place,' he lamented to the fire- poking old man, who paused mid-poke, and aimed a raised eyebrow at him.

'You bain't gone and follered in your father's footsteps and heaped shame on that young lass of Stewart's, has you by any chance, mister? That bain't what this visit is all about, I take it. Because from where I'm sitting, it strikes me you be full o' the jitters.'

He closed his eyes on his anger, took a deep breathe, and said, 'Well, fer a start, you en't sittin'. An' what's more, unless someone's got there before me, she en't what you'm thinkin'. So, stop yer pokin' an' put some wood on. It's freezin' in 'ere!'

It was as though the old codger had not heard. Humming to himself, he poked on, saying that it let in the air and helped it draw. Then, finished poking, he inserted three windfall branches into the smouldering slack,

The job presumably done, he staggered to his feet, arched his back, and studied him. 'Good,' he said. 'Because she takes after her mother, God rest her soul. A finer woman as one could ever wish to meet. You've chosen well, lad. Don't go and cock it up – d'you hear? Because it won't only be Stewart you'll be answerable to. It'll be me!'

By the time Sergeant Adams and Dawn arrived, the table was laid, his hands washed and, although he was loathed to admit it, the room comfortably warm.

Coats were discarded and talk turned to the inevitable subject of the weather. 'At least it's nice and warm in here,' Mr Adams said, inadvertently playing into the hands of a smugly satisfied Mr Barnes.

'Cheer up, William,' Mr Adams said. 'We've got the World Cup to look forward to. Named in the squad are we – first choice goalie?'

Dawn jumped in full of childish exasperation. 'No, Dad! I told you. He plays in midfield now, together with that older boy I pointed out to you yesterday, in Hollersham Market.'

'Yeah,' Billy said, on the back of a sigh 'Should've bin trainin' with him this mornin', but … you know.'

Mr Adams screwed up his face and peered through the window. 'Mm, yes. Well, it appears to have blown over now, though. In fact, there's that very same young man out there now. Him, and a lad in an invalid chair, together with, not one, but two young ladies. Lucky chap.'

His mother made as though to leave the table, paused, and said that the day's scraps were by the back door. 'Perhaps you and Dawn could take them out to them for me and say hello.'

'What!' he said, wide-eyed and open-mouthed. 'And leave you three adults alone together? Oow, we don't know about that. Do we, Dawn?'

Clever me, he thought, the occasion brought to life, fuelled by laughter, a playful flick of a cloth aimed at him by his mother followed by a not-so-playful cuff on the back of his head by Dawn's dad.

'Go on, Dawn love,' Mr Barnes chipped in with. 'Take 'im away afore the metal cuffs are slapped on 'im.'

'Yes,' his mother said. 'Go on if you're going, Billy. Ten minutes, mind. No longer.'

'And while you'm out there,' Mr Barnes called after them. 'Tell 'em – at my expense, mind! — tell 'em I'll have one of them there fancy pedal bins put out so folks who has a mind to can tip their bread scraps into it.'

'Will do, Barney!' he shouted back, and shook his head in disbelief. 'Silly old goat. It'll be nicked within a week.'

'Well I for one don't agree,' Dawn said. 'And I think it's lovely of Mr Barnes. Look. See that?'

'What?' he said, although having witnessed Allan thrill to the sight of two ducks race one another to a titbit thrown by the poor sod.

'Yeah, s'pose,' he said. 'But it'd have t' be padlocked. Anyway, this is Sunday, what were it you were so keen t' tackle me about? I en't done nothin'.'

'You must think me stupid,' Dawn said. 'For a start. This is hardly the time or place, is it? As. You. Well. Know!' she emphasised – and elbowed him in the ribs.

'Ow! That hurt.'

'Then stop ogling Jenny,' she muttered.

'Hi!' she then said to the gathering, radiating nothing but the most enthusiastic of smiles.

CHAPTER SEVENTY-ONE

Mr Adams flustered his mother by lifting a bottle of wine out from under his chair. 'Not champagne, I'm afraid, folks. But should complement your Sunday masterpiece, Mrs Hughes! And, let me say, so well presented. Reminds me of how my Normanton aunt used to serve it up. You from Yorkshire stock by any chance, Mo?'

Blushing from ear to ear, his mother shook her head. 'N-n – no! No, Abbots Lovell born and bred, me. And, er, and you're aunt?' I mean. Is she still …?'

Mr Adams arched his brows and sighed. 'One of many incidents of food poisoning, I'm sorry to say.'

Mr Barnes brought the handle of his knife down on the table with a bang. 'That bain't funny, young Stewart. It's about time you dropped that sort of humour and grew up!'

'Yes, Barney. Sorry, Barney. And, just for the record, Mo. She's eighty-seven and still going strong. In fact, I'll run you up there to meet her if and when you've a mind to.'

'Well, thank you, kind Sir,' his mother said. 'Only, well, how can I put it? You see, Billy's the runner in the family. Whereas, I'd prefer to go by car, coach or train. But, yes. Given at least three days' notice, I'd love to go. Thank you, Stewart. Thank you, very much. And for the wine. That was thoughtful of you.'

With the last of the dinner plates scraped clean and stacked together with the others, his mother did one of her drop-jawed staring acts. 'The wine! I'm so sorry. I left it to chill and forgot about it. I'll just whisk this lot away and sort out some glasses.'

Dawn immediately rose from the table and rushed to open the kitchen door, 'Can you manage, Mrs Hughes? I mean can I help in any way?'

'Yes, Luvvie. I rather think you'd better,' his mother said, adding loud enough before the door closed on the pair, 'The truth is, I've suddenly come over all unnecessary.'

Within minutes, Dawn emerged from the kitchen carrying a jug of his and Mr Barnes' favourite treat, thick, creamy, custard. Next came his mother with Mr Adams's bottle of wine together with three glasses and two of their poshest cups.

'Huh! Guess who the cups are for,' he said.

'Now!' his mother said, totally ignoring him. 'Who's for jam roly-poly? And who's for apple crumble?'

The choices made and the puddings served, the wine was uncorked – "plop"!

Adults could be just like little kids, he thought, and drained his cup of the stingiest amount of wine in the world.

'Yuk!' Dawn said and poured the contents of her cup into his. From then on, she made do with tap water, saying next to nothing, while all about her the chatter focused on the imminent sale of Jasmine Cottage and the plans for the modernisation and extension of Old Forge cottage.

'So, Dawn' his mother said, resting her hand on his girlfriend's forearm. 'If ever you want or need to stop over for any reason, we'll be able to fit you in!'

Not until his mother began stacking the empty pudding dishes did Dawn come back to life. A flick of a condemning look in his direction, and she was up and away, insisting, in spite of his mother's protestations, on helping. 'No,' Please, Mrs Hughes,' she said. 'The truth is, I need to ask a favour.'

A minute or two later, his mother reappeared. 'Don't concern yourself, Stewart. There's nothing for you to worry about. Dawn needs to have a private, word with my son. So, upstairs with you, Billy, please. You'll find her waiting for you in my room. Go on – chop-chop!'

'What for? What's it about?'

'I've no idea,' she said. 'But judging by the look on your face, I'm pretty sure you have.'

CHAPTER SEVENTY-TWO

He tapped and entered to find Dawn sat legs dangling over the side of his mother's bed. 'Oh?' he said. 'I thought you'd be in it, waiting for me in the nuddy.'

'Ha-ha. Well, dream on. You're not joking your way out of this one.'

'What one? I dunno what yer on about.'

'Hmph!' was all she came out with, and waited, chin up, eyes set.

What?'

'She made no reply.

Damn Carol, he thought. Damn, damn, damn her – and mentally mimicked Dawn's "We tell each other everything".

'Well?' Dawn said.

He shook his head and did his best to look confused. 'No, you'll have t' give us a clue.'

Clearly taking the piss, she widened her eyes and huffed. 'A clue? Hmm, well. Let's see. You've been round to give your support to Tim and Carol. Nothing unusual in that. In fact, you even watched them play a game of chess. And, yes! You did come across Carol at the end of her tether, feeling like screaming and pulling her hair out. Little wonder! And what else? Oh yes. You did carry a load of dirty washing in for Mrs Robinson. And yes, you did all have a nice cup of tea together. Does any of that help jog your memory? In other words, what else was there? Anything you've, sort of, you know, forgotten, or, more likely as not, decided not to tell me.'

He felt his chest tighten. 'I don't feel well,' he said, rubbing his hand in a circular motion over his discomfort.

'Very convenient,' Dawn said.

'It en't my fault I can't remember! There wuz loads goin' on, weren't the? Have a heart, won't yer?'

'Yes, Thank you. I will,' she said pleasantly enough, only to then harden her look and, with it, her voice. 'Because someone's gone and broken mine. And you know who.'

'Over what, for fuck sake! I've had enough of this – d'yer hear? Enough!'

With her eyes brimming with unshed tears, Dawn shuffled her behind nearer the edge of the bed. But he was having none of it, 'Oh no you don't' he said, and blocked her off.

'Don't use that word, then,' she said. 'It's vulgar. And I don't like it.'

'What word?'

'The F word, as if you didn't know. And if you have to use it, then – then save it for your army pals!'

'Ha!' he said, a wave of relief both hot and cold getting trapped in his throat. 'You - you tellin' me, that's what all this is about?'

'All!' she said, as the tears began to flow and give her a snotty nose. 'It's alright for you. But where does that leave me? Where!'

He pulled a corner of a sheet out from under his mother's eiderdown, and, together, they dried her eyes.

'There!' he said. 'Now listen, you silly girl. I only said it t' shut Lady la-de-da Robinson up. Mekin' out all I were good fer were farm work. Of course, 'er useless son's gonna be Prime Minister, en't he? You know — this brain box who went t' pieces over the girl from next door getting' a boyfriend.'

Dawn pulled up a pillow, stood it upright and, resting back into it, stared into the distance. 'So, you're not going into the army after all.'

'Only if there wuz, nothin' else – but I'm tryin'. I really, really am. An'-an' Mr Collins is lookin' out fer summat for me. A real good bloke, he is. In fact, him an' your dad are the nearest I've ever 'ad to havin' a proper dad. Could never please me own, I couldn't. An' I can tell yer now. It weren't no fun hearin' an' seein' him knock me mum about – the bastard!' he said, to which Dawn stared brows puckered into the pattern of his mother's eiderdown.

'You as well,' she said, bringing her eyes slowly back up to meet his.

Strange girl that she was she then gave him the gentlest of smiles and re-laid her pillow. 'Slow-coach,' she said. 'Kick off your shoes and come and have a bit of Dawn.'

The knock when it came gave both of them a start.

'Dawn! Your dad's ready to go now, Luvvie – chop-chop!'

Downstairs, his mother spoke openly about them. 'Snoring their little heads off, they were.'

With what he considered justifiable indignation, he voiced his objection. But she was having none of it. 'As I believe I've pointed out before,' she said. 'What goes on under my roof is my business and my responsibility. So put that in your pipe and smoke it, young man – understood?'

In the background, Sergeant Adams nodded his approval. That given, all that remained, it seemed, was for them to make their way outside as a group and say their goodbyes.

Dawn, somewhat embarrassingly, proved extra attentive. Twiddling with the hair at the back of his neck, she asked what he was planning on doing next.

'Probably go fer a run,' he said, a plan forming even as he spoke. 'You know. While it's still light.'

411

'You do that,' she said, and gave him a particularly meaningful hug.'

CHAPTER SEVENTY-THREE

Once into his rhythm his enthusiasm for the job in hand strengthened with every stride. Vault the meadow gate, take the stile on the run and the old quarry awaited him.

Once there, he paused, a nagging intrigue having got the better of him.

But no – no, it had not been a trick of the light or a figment of his imagination. With the benefit of higher ground could be made out glimpses of the striking blue of Jamie Horton's Minivan roof. Tucked away at the end of Quarry Lane could mean only one of two things; either it was there for privacy and a touch of the naughties, or merely parked to walk from there up to Cooper's Farm or The Common. Whichever it was, it amounted to the same. A flippin' wasted journey, let alone time. Even so, he pressed on, a run being a run if nothing else.

He pressed the doorbell and stood back.

'Oh,' he said, when the door opened. 'Oh, it's you.'

'Well, I do live here,' Trish said. 'But if it's Jamie you want, I'm afraid you've missed him. 'Mother', she mouthed. 'Sunday training proving a bit of a problem of late, it seems. But, never mind. Are you coming in or not? I mean, forgive me for saying, but you do look somewhat mithered. Stressed, even. Is everything all right?'

'Er, no. Not really. It's like they say, en't it, everythin' comes in twos. First up, though is t' do with Dawn, an' I thought you might give us some advice.'

'If I can,' she said, and nodded down at his running shoes.

Having kicked them off, he followed her through into the hall mumbling anything that came to mind for having shown surprise at finding her at home.

'You worry too much,' she said, opening the lounge door. 'It's only Billy, folks. He's been a run by the looks of him and has popped in for some advice.'

Encouraged to enter by Mrs Collins, he ventured as far as Mr Collins's much prized Turkish carpet. 'One thousand five hundred stitches to the square inch,' he said, pointing to it.

'Precisely!' Mr Collins said. 'Well remembered. And a run, to boot. That's the spirit. No training. Go for a run! Now. How can we be of help?'

His tale of woe told, the room lapsed into silence, Mr Collins holding court by repeatedly nodding to himself. 'The army, you say. Mm …

414

'Mm, indeed!' Mrs Collins added. 'No wonder the poor girl was taken aback. But, never say die, William. Rest assured that Albert is keeping his eyes and ears open for you. The thing is, dear, what's the priority? A job? Or appeasing this young lady of yours?'

'Both,' he said, thinking the question a stupid one.

'Daddy,' Trish said. 'Billy came here because he needed advice on something, and he hasn't had the chance to say on what yet. Not really. Have you, Billy?'

'Er. No. Not really. You see, it's about a ring or summat. I've got a bit of money with Miss Pringle. But, well, that's really fer savin'. What I thought was, if I went car washin' I could get enough dosh to, you know. The thing is, I don't know nothin' about jewellery. Or-or, or if there was summat better than a ring. And where would I go t' get it even if there was?'

Mrs Collins drew breath 'A ring,' she said, spreading her fingers to best display her own collection. 'Rings are usually meant to signify something. An engagement. A wedding. Or the birth of a first child,' she emphasised and broke off to give what amounted to a hollow laugh. 'I mean. Don't get me wrong. But I trust that none of these apply in your case, William.'

415

'Gerroff,' he said, at which point Trish intervened.

'It's simple,' she said. 'Go and see your old neighbour Mrs Perkins. She runs a catalogue and there's a jewellery section in there, I believe. Choose something more like a gold cross and chain, for example. Something feminine and tasteful that can be tucked out of sight on P.E and Games days. And, what's more, you only pay in instalments.

'Mrs Perkins?' he said. 'But that means Piggy would spoil it by blabbin'. She would, I know she would. She wouldn't be able to stop herself.'

'Not if I did it all for you,' Trish said.

And to set you on your way,' Mr Collins added, 'there's two cars in the garage that could do with a weekly wash. What shall we say? Half a crown a car? Fair deal?'

'Fair deal!' he said, and the two of them smacked palms.

CHAPTER SEVENTY-FOUR

He dumped his kitbag down as per usual and bid the gathering a muted 'Mornin'.'

Ignoring Jenny, he said to Trish in not much more than a conspiratorial whisper, 'Around seven this evenin' for you know what, tell yer dad.'

She nodded and mimicked him. 'And before the end of the week with any luck for you know what.'

It earned her a thumbs up, perhaps not the prettiest of girls, but neat and tidy with everything in the right place and proportion. Horton was a fool. A right towny bastard who needed his lights kicking in.

Not until the Morton crew were clambering aboard did the penny drop. Of course! Coopers farm shop complete with Miss self-confessed, up for it, good at it, like mother like daughter Sally Hicks. And where did the farm track lead – from the farm and down to the end of Quarry Lane. Yes! Of the three contenders, Hicksie, Jenny, and Piggy – ha! It didn't bear thinking about. His money, every last penny of it, was on Hicksie. Even so, the lack of proof, the gnawing sense of not actually knowing, not for sure, got to him. It clawed at his innards and left his mouth dry, Sunday suddenly seeming a long, long way off.

Tim bounced down beside him. 'Guess what?'

'Hmm . Yer mummy's bin sittin' you an' Carol in the bath together again?'

'Funny, ha-ha, I don't think. I wish I'd never told you about that now – no! The thing is. Apart from going with dad to his gym twice a week which has done me the world of good, he's also gone and ordered a new telly in time for the World Cup. You'll come round and watch it with us. won't you? Say you will. I mean. I know I haven't exactly been myself these past few weeks. But I'm over the worst of it now. And, well, Carol was asking about you only the other day. Couldn't't've got through it all without you, she reckons.'

'Oh ar? Well, in that case. you try keeping me away, Tim Robinson. Engerland! Engerland!'

'Great!' Tim said. 'Just as long as it is Engerland and not Car-rol! Cos remember, I've got muscles now. So, watch it. Ta-ta!'

Not until Friday morning at the stop did Trish draw him to one side and slip him a small paper bag. 'I think you'll be pleased. It's housed in its own natty little box that I've taken the liberty of wrapping in gold coloured paper. Oh, and there's a gift tag attached for you to sign.'

418

'You're a brick,' he said, and risked giving her forearm an affectionate rub.

Never before had the colour risen in Dawn's cheeks like it did on her opening the box. 'For me?' she said, knowing full well that it obviously was.

Delicate and classy and above all made of real gold, the cross and chain drew attention from those seated nearby: a sniff from Ozzie, a comment from Carol on how it was highlighted by the black of Dawn's hair, while Piggy was Piggy and largely ignored.

With everyone back in their seats Dawn examined the gift tag for what seemed the umpteenth time. 'For upsetting you,' she read. 'From Billy Windmill kiss,' And, as soppy as girls were, had to sniff away a runny nose.

'It's beautiful,' she managed to get out. 'But –
'

'No buts,' he said. 'I run a car washin' business now. Already got three customers, I 'as. An'- an' an' should get more! Mum's put a card in Miss Pringle's. So, with this an' that an' the early mornin' strawberry pickin' when it starts, I'll be quids in!'

'And school?' Piggy said.

419

'Easy-peasy, Catch this old crate at the crossroads with the Morton lot. Then wash me hands when I gets t' school-'

'Ha!' Ozzie went from the seat in front. 'And that ugly mush of yourn while you'm at it, Hughsie. Probably leave more round yer gob yer than what yer tek t' the weigh-in. And yer know it!'

'Yeah, well. Which is more'n you'll ever know, Cutter. Goin' places, me. It's only the start an' things is already on the up.'

'Yeah,' Ozzie sneered. 'Up yer arse wiv the rest of yer bullshit.'

He chose to ignore the jibe and put on a superior air, held until reaching the school gates. There, the instant the bus came to a halt, he rolled up his sleeves and loosened his tie.

'No you don't,' Dawn said. 'Please. Don't spoil it. He's just a crude nobody who'll never amount to anything. And, what's more, probably jealous.

'What? Of you, havin' me,' he said, and when the way was clear shuffled out into the aisle after her. No sooner was he upright she flung her arms about him and kissed him more passionately and demanding than ever before.

'Oy! When you two lovebirds have finished, I've a schedule to keep to. So, get orff my bus!'

CHAPTER SEVENTY-FIVE

Laughing together, they passed through the gates and into the school. Not until they were due to go their separate ways did Dawn break what had developed on her part into a thoughtful silence.

'It's lovely what you've done for me. Giving up a possible army career by sorting out a job for yourself. As for buying me this gorgeous cross and chain, well – what can I say? And, what's more, you having the guts to put into words that you were sorry. It makes me feel, oh, I don't know. I just wish I was older, that's all,' she said, and gave him what he took to be a parting peck on the cheek.

It was not.

'That's for now,' she said. 'For you to hang on to until I am old enough to demonstrate how I really feel. I love you, Billy Hughes and don't want to lose you.'

The second bell sounded; an intrusion that he chose to ignore and bade her do the same. 'Look, Dawn. Listen. For a start, I ent goin' nowhere. An' I thought we said that your age wernt a problem. I know you'm only twelve, but older than yer years you said. Had to be because of what happened to yer mum

421

'n that. And you are! More sensible an' growd up than me by a long Old Grumpy's chalk.'

'Mentally, perhaps,' she said. 'But not physically.'

'Ah! I get it now. Gawd I'm slow. You think, because I got you that cross and chain, you wouldn't be able t' say no t' some nookie'

'No! It doesn't come into it,' she said, her pained expression immediately humbling him.

'Sorry–sorry, sorry, I got it all wrong. Sorry. But summat's brought this on. So, you'm twelve. So what? You'll be thirteen before you know it. A teenager. And that always sounds better, don't it?'

'Yes, I suppose. Alright,' she said. 'Forget it. We've got to go.'

But he was having none of it. 'Oh no! Not until it's right between us. Lessons can wait. We missed the bus, yeah?'

She went into thought mode, and eventually nodded.

'Yes. Okay. But, thanks to my sister, you'll have to be patient with me.'

He raised both palms and made a suitable face. 'As always. But not out here. The bike sheds. If we get caught, we can say we had to cycle in. Got it?'

Once having adopted temporary ownership of a bicycle each, Dawn composed herself, licked her lip, and began.

'The thing is, having an older sister acting as a mother has its advantages. She's been there, done it, got pregnant at fifteen and gave birth at sixteen – just. Not wishing me to go the same way and, let's face it, even younger, she sat me down and we had a good old one to one, as equals, sister to sister. And she didn't hold back. Very explicit and graphic, she was. Not just about the don'ts but also how to enjoy it without running the risk of pregnancy. In short, no going all the way until I'm at least fifteen or, legally, sixteen. And if and when we do, make sure it's with the use of a condom. Even then, she said, you can't always rely on a boy having one, or, using it, even if he has. According to her, that's how she got caught. You know, heat of the moment and all that stuff. And I can't let that happen to me – or Daddy, come to that. Not a second time… What bothers me, though – and it's pretty obvious – even if we say fourteen you won't be able to hold out for that long.'

'Oh? Who sez?'

She looked him fully in the face, almost to the point of defiance, and said, 'I do. Unlike girls, boys can't hide it when they're excited. Like now,' she said, and ran her finger down the length of his erection. 'Touch. Like you were doing to me in your mother's bedroom. All I can say is it's a good job Barney's stairs creak.'

'Yeah,' he said, and laughed, adding in a mocking whisper, 'Fast asleep they were. Dead to the world; the pair of them.'

Frowning, she said, 'You may well laugh. The point is, I liked what you were doing. Amongst other things, it took me back to when I was little and couldn't get to sleep or had a pain of some sort. Walk me up and down the room Daddy would, rubbing his hand over the back of my thighs and up over my bum just like you did, until I fell asleep with my head on his shoulder.

'Oh! I see. So, if Mum hadn't disturbed us, you'd have gone to sleep on me. Thanks. I'll remember that.'

She repeated her earlier peck of a kiss. 'No, my love, quite the opposite as you well know. Especially when you started digging your claws into the cheeks of my bum. Told me of your lust for me, Billy Windmill. A right turn on, it was. And that's the point my sister was making. Loving touch is the answer just as long as it doesn't go too far. I mean! Let's face it. We could oh so easily have got carried away and not heard that creak. Then where would we have been – up the creek without a paddle!' she said and, when he didn't get it, giggled like the child that, in part, she still was. And she was away, pausing only to look back and treat him to a finger wave.

CHAPTER SEVENTY-SIX

'A run?' Barney said. 'And so soon after yer evening meal? Serves you right if you'm as sick as a pig!'

'Yeah, well. I ent goin' far. An' I'll probably call in on Mr Wilks. See yer!'

'Tommy Wilks? What would a lad like you be wantin' with the likes of that old rogue? Call hisself a window cleaner – ha! Puts more grime on than ever he takes off he does!'

'Yeah, well. Mr Collins arranged it, so I got t' go – bye!'

Yes, Barny, you old bugger. Yer won't be sneerin' when I'm Carwash an' Winder Cleaner Limited. But first things first, Mr shit-face Horton.

First things first …

The problem lay, not in the soil, as Mr Barnes would say, but where to hide while still being able to keep an eye on both the farm track and Quarry Lane at the same time. Peering out from the rim of the quarry wasn't the answer. Nor, even though given serious consideration, was climbing a tree. No, the only answer was to lie in a three to four-foot strip of uncut grass backing the Quarry Lane hedge; by chance, a particularly unkempt strip near where Horton parked his van. Eavesdrop. Go purely by sound alone, Billy-boy, the prospect making his bones tingle. Even more so when he heard the scrunch of tyres on road grit, then a pause, followed by the reversing whine of an engine.

The thought struck him that if by any chance it turned out to be Jenny Horton he was meeting, then he would surely have picked her up on the way. But to his relief no sound of any description came from the van. All remained deathly silent.

Caught unprepared, his heart thumped at the sound of footsteps, some hurried, others slowed.

'Sorry I'm late,' came the breathless, unmistakeable voice of Jennifer Duggan. Here. Come on! Take this ruddy bowl. Damn thing's soddin' heavy,'

And, with that, the van door was heard to close. No sooner had it than the apparent desperation of the pair was not only relayed by the rear springs of the van but also a general buffeting of its interior.

Shaken, seeking within himself a sense of denial, he stumbled away.

With the night drawing in, Sally Hicks's old hiding and ambush spot barely accommodated him. But it did, just, at a pinch.

Yeah Sal – much maligned Sal. But human, and he wished she were with him. Just to talk, that's all. Just … talk.

An opening squeak and closing clang of the Quarry Lane gate brought him to his senses. On she came, walking with a crock bowl wedged under her armpit, her head angled towards the ground as though deep in thought.

He stepped out.

'Jesus! What the hell? You nearly gave me a heart attack!'

'Good, yer slut-faced slag. A bit cramped were it? In the back of Horton's van – eh? I mean! How could yer? An' on yer own cous- '

'Well if she can't give him what he needs then someone else has to don't they? In fact, you could say I'm was doing her a favour. Now get out my way, you great oaf!' she said, and rammed the rim of her bowl into his midriff. She tried to run. But he snatched her skirt. Jerked to a halt, she staggered back and despite her efforts to keep her balance landed on her behind, 'Rape! Help me somebody! Rape!'

He grabbed her by the arm and dragged her up onto her feet. 'An' yer can cut that out. Yer evil! D'yer know that – evil! First Wiggy, then yer dad. An' now Trisha's boyfriend. Oh! An' of course, there's poor-'

427

He stopped and listened, having picked up on what she must have heard a minute or two before–and froze.

'Rape!' she shouted, making out she was pulling up her knickers as she ran. 'Rape!'.

'Come on, Lass! This way!' sounded the voice of Walter Cooper 'Cyril – the gate. Charlie – you see to that son of yourn, the varmint. Ought to be strung up, he had – strung up!'

Numbed, panic stricken, he finally gathered his wits about him and ran towards the main gate.

Cyril was already there, leaning his forearms on its top rail, and grinning.

'Keep Dad away from me,' he screamed. 'Please, just keep him away.'

EPILOGUE - 1970

I came to, woken as it were by the sound of my own voice echoing through my head and over the village rooftops, the light now not coming from a streetlamp but the sun. What was more, as I gazed downward, in an otherwise deserted village, I saw the one person, ponytail and all, who provided me with some form of hope, a way out of my despair.

It was not as strange as I might have imagined, seeing her with a child. And it was hers, no doubt about that. None too steady on her feet and wearing nothing but a sun hat, the toddler took in every move that Trish made. Head cocked, she watched the pick of a runner bean, followed its flight, and attempted a clap when it landed on a cloth.

The flitting of a Cabbage White distracted her – and she spotted me, her eyes as round and blue as her mother's.

Elbows held as though to form wings, she made her ungainly way to Trish, patted her on the arm, and pointed, 'Man.'

Trish rose, quickly at first, then more gracefully and gathered up her daughter. 'Billy?'

'That's me, Billy the baby eater – what's yours taste like?'

'That's not funny, Billy. You could've been anybody stood there watching.'

'Yeah – yes, I'm sorry. B-but, the thing is, I'm starvin.' Really, really starvin'.

'And in trouble. I mean, when aren't you? You're all over the local news and now you want to involve me!'

'Please, Trish. You know I didn't do it! There's only you and Tim…'

Ignoring me, she allowed her child to slide down her body to stand once more on the ground, took her by the hand and walked her towards the house.

She paused, paused and looked back. 'Give me ten minutes to settle Sophie down, then you can come in. But only on the understanding that it's hands and face, eat, and then away.'

The water felt good, even better when cupped and slapped over and over my face. Better still, when it was just held there.

Finished dousing, fatigued, unable to move, eyelids lowered I rested my forehead on the rim of the sink.

'No, you don't,' Trish said, thrusting a towel into my hands. 'I'm sorry, but you haven't got time for that. Come on! Come and sit down before you fall down.'

I obeyed, guided like an old age pensioner to the kitchen table.

Before me stood a mug of water into which Trish heaped spoonfuls of sugar. 'Drink it,' she ordered. 'Then there's cereals.'

A toaster popped up two slices of bread. She went to them while urging me to gulp down the much-needed water.

Revived, I focused on my saviour, watching, as Sophie had, her every move; her stretch and reach into a high cupboard, her squat and lift of a bottle of milk from the fridge, everything about her neat and easy on the eye.

Clutching the bottle of milk, she pulled open a drawer and selected a spoon. 'Toast will be with you in a sec,' she said, setting down the milk and spoon.

I clamped my hand over hers trapping both it and the spoon. 'Marry me.'

She drew back her head and blinked. 'Marry? Who me? The girl whose father made her out of matchsticks? Although, I do recall at one point being promoted to ladder rungs.'

'Yeah, well. We were just kids, weren't we? I mean, it weren't as if I didn't like yer – I did! More'n like but didn't realise it. An' even if I had, I wouldn't've known what to say. I were never any good with words, you know I weren't.'

'Except when you were in trouble,' she said. 'Now, eat your toast while I go and put something more decent on. Too much bare flesh isn't fair on you, Billy. I'm sorry.'

'I saw a lot more of yer in the garden,' I said. 'And all I thought were how perfect you were. You – and Sophie! Made me want to cry, it did.

'Brought on by a bout of home-sickness, no doubt,' she said, and eyeing me, added, 'Don't worry, it's only natural. Now, if you'll excuse me.'

'No! Don't go. Please, Trish. I'd be the bestest ever dad for Sophie in the world – promise I would! She's lovely. And you're lovely. In every possible way you'm truly, truly lovely. An'- an' I en't no good without yer. You know I en't.

'Shush, Billy. Shush!' she said, and slid in opposite me, taking my hand into both of hers. 'Billy, I can't marry you even if I wanted to. You see, I'm already spoken for.'

'Not Horton!'

'No, don't worry. Not Jamie. Not that I blame him for what's happened. Not entirely.'

She shook her head. 'I've got the most wonderfully supportive parents anyone could wish for and I've let them down. Not for the first time.'

She had gone to a private party in Hollersham with Sally, she said – at which point I saw red. 'Huh! I might've guessed she'd be–'

But she was having none of it.

432

'No, Billy. I'll not have that. If anything, Sal tried to dissuade me from doing what I did,' she said, and paused, chin down, before admitting that Horton had also been at the party. 'I kept my distance of course, pretending to be having a great time, even joining in a game of oranges and lemons. To cut a long story short, I got caught with – with my not-so-bad-looking partner for a third time. Well, the rules were… and I was determined to milk it for all it was worth. Rub Jamie's nose in it. Get my own back. Need I go on?'

I shook my head. 'No. I just wish it'd bin me.'

She gave me a twitch of a smile. 'Well, I'll take that as a compliment, but if you'd ever asked or tried it on, the answer would have been the same as it was to Jamie. No.'

'Well then! You made it easy fer Jenny then – didn't yer?'

'Yes,' she said. 'Yes. Putting it like that I suppose I did. Who knows? An arm twisted off my favourite doll. My trio of Beswick horses found lying on their sides with legs snapped off. It follows a pattern, you see. Patterns I ignored. Kenny probably next had he not escaped by going to East Anglia. But then along came Jamie, the one I thought I would go forward with. All in all, quite a list, wouldn't you say. I hate her as much as you must do. But an incomplete list, as you well know, Mr Absconder.'

'Eh? Don't know what yer on about.'

'Oh, but I think you do, Billy. Don't protect her after what she did to you. As long as I live, I shall never get over how my Wiggy must have suffered. He wasn't a doll or a china horse or a boyfriend, but a –. I want to know the truth, Billy. It's the only –'

I instinctively reached across the table for her, but she shrank from me, leaving me with no option, but to close my fingers and sit back.

Red-eyed, sniffing back the tears, she said in fits and starts that the only thing that would help in some way was to know the truth rather than have to imagine it. 'So if – if you have fee-feelings for me as you say you do then you'd tell me, no matter what,' she said, and faced me, full on. 'Stay put,' she ordered. 'I've a present for you.'

She returned wearing a skirt and blouse and raised what I took to be my 'present'.

'Me arra!

'That's right, Billy. Your Dutch Arrow. Perhaps it will help jog your memory. At the time we could see where you'd trampled the brambles down. Unfortunately, you were at least eight foot out. Daddy found it when clearing the ivy from out the back hedge years later. But that's neither here nor there, is it, Billy? You may not have found your arrow but what you did get was a perfect view of Wiggy's hutch.

'Yeah-yeah. Game over, cleverdick. Yeah, I had a clear view from the brambles. The truth is,

Jenny had already used the chopper on … you know, Wiggy. Made a right cock up of it, she 'ad and tried to blame the gippoes. I mean! What else was I supposed t' do? I named him Wiggy and there he were, lookin' up at me, sort of pleadin'.'

She gave a slow, considered nod and said, 'I'm glad you were there. Was it, you know…?'

'One blow,' I said, at which she rose and straightened her skirt.

'And now, I'm sorry, but you've got to go. Goodness knows what you'll tell them, but hopefully they'll go easy on you, whatever you come up with. Here's some biscuits to see you on your way. And here's your bus fare to Hollersham Halt. It's full daylight now, you're bound to be spotted, plus even you can't run the whole way back. Catch it from the new brick-built shelter opposite Daddy's place. It'll raise less suspicion from there. And if you sit kerb side and towards the back, I'll have a little surprise waiting for you. Good luck, Billy. And thank you. Having said that, I haven't seen you, Nor you me. Understood?'

Brick-built and deserted with built-in slits enabling me to see the bus's approach, the shelter could not have been bettered.

The driver took my money without comment and we were off. No sooner had I followed Trisha's instructions than the reason for them became obvious.

For there, at the old school pick-up spot, was not only Trish, but also an ear to ear grinning Tim. What was more, sat in the crook of his arm, sucking on her thumb, lay Sophie.

Returning the grin, I raised both of mine and stayed at the back window until they were out of sight.

With the bus changing down the gears preparing to stop, I froze. I could see them in my mind's eye: Mrs Dodds and, even worse, Mrs Craig, waiting to board. But, as it turned out, it was neither of those two but someone I could not help but recognise, and she me.

I gave my head a short sharp shake and put a finger to my lips. It did the trick. Having paid her fare, Dawn gathered up her belongings and made her way down the aisle to take up a seat directly in front of me. But she didn't speak. That, she left until we had left the bus at her stop, together but as strangers.

'Well?' she said the second the bus had pulled away. 'And don't lie to me. You were on the local news. And, what's more, Carol said that a police car had been parked outside your mum's yesterday evening.'

'Probably your dad, the dirty old sod,' I said – and laughed.

She did not laugh – or come anywhere near it for that matter.

I cleared my throat and composed myself 'Cheer up,' I said. 'After all, I 'ave made the effort to come and see yer.'

'Rot!' she said. 'You were with an outside work gang clearing a towpath. Went to fill a container with water from a standpipe and took the opportunity to run off so I heard'

'Yeah, well. Summat like that.'

'Yes! 'Summat' that will probably earn you a longer sentence. I mean! How stupid can you get?'

'Yeah, well. On me way back now, en't I? Get me skates on, retrieve the Jerry can, an' act the goat. Sorry I'm late, lads. Fell down this hole, I did. Weren't arf deep, it were!'

'And met a rabbit, no doubt.' she said.

'Eh?'

'Forget it,' she said, and sighed. 'I'll be two minutes.'

'But I gotta go or I wunt make it!

'But she was already on her way, leaving me with her baggage to part walk, part scurry towards what at one time had been the station master's house.

True to her word, allowing the house door to slam behind her, she came scurrying back. Having gulped in and blown out a lungful of air, she confronted me. 'If there's one thing you're good at – one! – it's putting the kybosh on everything. The prospect of your mum and my dad getting together for a start. Not to mention us. Well I'm sorry, but I've

437

no option but to return this,' she said, and slapped an easily recognised black box into my palm.

'Dawn? Please, Dawn. I want you to keep it. It's yours. Dawn. All yours.'

But she was already walking away.

'Dawn, you know this weren't down to me. That lying bitch!

'I loved you, Dawn!' I managed to get out, then in a fit of rage drew back my arm and threw the box and all it contained as hard and high as I could towards a distant copse of scrub and manky yews.

'Now that's stupid.' I heard her say before the door slammed shut – and it all came out in a rush.

'Stupid? Yeah, well that's me 'aint it. Always 'ave bin an' always will be. This 'aint over Dawn. I'll show yer. I'll show 'em all, you'll see!'

ABOUT THE AUTHOR AND
ACKNOWLEDGEMENTS

Due to failing eyesight in his thirties David gave up his day job as an industrial buyer which enabled him to concentrate full time on his passion for writing. David had already had several short story publications, an award for his use of dialogue, an agent and the freedom to follow Dickens's advice: "Once having set out my characters to play out the play, then it is their job to do it, as it were, and not mine". All helped to guide him before embarking on the production of two novels. The first one drafted and laid to grow cold the other is the one you have just read. From these early successes he came to the notice of WG Stanton, a renowned BBC dramatist who provided much guidance and ongoing support in the early years to get Billy Windmill where it is today. This book is indeed dedicated to his memory.

David also ran a writing group for over twenty years, providing a platform for budding writers of all ages and backgrounds, to great success.

Billy Windmill had already been dubbed a prize-winning novel by his Agent who unfortunately went bankrupt on him by the time it was finished. After taking considerable time producing two other first drafts novels, at the agent's bequest, he decided to get

Billy Windmill, the first in the trilogy, out there and self-published.

****

An abundance of assistance and support from family and friends was given to help get this book from concept to publication. Eternal thanks to his good friend Pam Pattison who proof-read all the chapters throughout its creation into this final edition. Thanks and gratitude also to his daughter Tracey Pengilly, second proof-reader and self-publishing assistant, making this publication technically possible. Further sincere thanks to the talented Bridget Ramsey who designed the front cover and Kim Chapman, a very successful editor, who gave the book its final read through.   Your   comments   and   support   were invaluable.

****

If you enjoyed this book, please do take the time to write an honest review as your feedback is very important to the author. If you spot any errors kindly report these to tracey@pengilly.co

David's books were 'out' in
July 2019 and he died content
and peacefully on 15th October
2019.

Printed in Great Britain
by Amazon